In Love With You

Faye Darling

Copyright © 2023 by Faye Darling

Beach Cottage Publishing LLC

All rights reserved. The characters and events portrayed in this book are fictitious. Any similarity to real persons, living or dead, is coincidental and not intended by the author.

No part of this book may be reproduced, or stored in a retrieval system, or transmitted in any form or by any means, electronic, mechanical, photocopying, recording, or otherwise, without express written permission of the publisher.

ISBN Paperback: 978-1-960626-04-2

ISBN Ebook: 978-1-960626-05-9

For everyone who prefers to live in the fantasies they create
in their head rather than the real world

Author's Note

Be Advised: This book is a spicy, **open-door** romance, which means the characters' sexual encounters are depicted **on-page**. Because of this, IN LOVE WITH YOU is intended for a mature audience only.

Trigger Warnings: My personal story often plays a large role in my writing, but this time it played a larger role than usual. I share this so my readers understand that what is depicted in the novel comes from a place of catharsis and nothing else. With that said, please be advised there are **on-page** depictions of a **parent suffering from cancer, mentions of the death of a parent,** and **episodes of grief.** While this is catharsis for me, it may not be for everyone else, so please be kind to yourself and make sure you are in a steady mental/emotional place before you read the book. Other trigger warnings include: **off-page domestic abuse, on-page violence,** and **allusion to suicide.**

One

Ryder

WELL, HELLO THERE.

Aren't you a mysterious little thing? Appearing in my life as if from nowhere.

Maybe you opened this book expecting to pass invisibly through its pages the way you're used to doing. Perhaps reading has always felt like an adventure to you. An escape. A heart-tilting journey through the eyes of someone else. And you take in chapter after chapter until that final sentence, when you are forced to hold your breath for one second, two, then let go of everything and everyone you've come to know over the course of all those pages. And those people? Those characters? They never even knew you existed.

But you're not invisible this time. You're not just passing through, unnoticed. Not if I have anything to say about it. Not on my watch. Not with this story. *My* story.

Do you want to know a secret?

FAYE DARLING

I can feel you here.

Phantom tickles on my sea-roughed skin. Your warmth, your curiosity twisting through me, breathing me back to life.

And I like it. I like it a lot.

A little too much, probably.

And I know—I've got this feeling curling up in the center of my chest—I'm going to like you, too. Whoever you are. Wherever you are. Because you've taken the time to join me. Here. Right here, where I currently bob on my surfboard in the lineup, dawn summoning pinks and peaches and violets to life, mixing all those soft, sensual colors into the dark stew of my beloved Pacific. Evergreen-slathered hills rising at my back above the white sand beach. Sheer cliffs extending out into the sea like protective arms on either side of this one-mile-stretch of coastline. Sheltered. Safe. Culling the silkiest waves from the cold, wild ocean in the beating heart of Oregon's North Coast.

I close my eyes, the whisper of a smile on my lips at the thought of the sea. At the thought of you. This is my church, my sanctuary. This is where I find my peace. I want to know, though, where it is you find yours? Maybe you could write it in the margins of this book for me, or in a letter. Maybe, somehow, it'll reach me. Maybe, somehow, I'll just know your answer.

"Outside," Mark, my best friend since grade school, bellows, a mischievous cackle breaking on the tail-end of the word.

There's only a handful of us here today. Wednesday morning. Late October sucking in its dying breath. The tourists are all but gone, the Portland contingent trapped in their little valley, in their urban wilderness I've never had an urge to explore. So, it's just us locals left to surf the waves, a few unfamiliar faces keeping to the fringes.

I'm the closest one to the peak of the approaching wave Mark points out.

As it shivers up and up, I lay my long body flat against my board and paddle, driving my wide palms through the icy chill of the water. Salt in my nose. Anticipation on my tongue. When I'm exactly where I need to be to catch the wave, I sit up, swivel my legs, grab the nose of my board, and drive hard toward shore.

Hammer down, son. I hear my dad's voice echo in my head the way I always do when I'm trying to catch a wave. My old man taught me to surf when I was a kid. Somedays, when I roll out of bed well before the sunrise, pack myself into the cold, damp passenger seat of Mark's truck, and rumble up the twisty highway to this little cove, I tell myself I do it just for me. For the ocean to kiss my soul in greeting one more time. But really, I think most days I do it for Dad. To keep his memory alive. To keep myself close to him, a man who believed he had been borne from the saltwater, a man who was robbed of his life, his ocean, and his family well before his time.

Hammer down, son, I hear again, and I take in a deep, deep breath.

There's a moment when I'm surfing—a moment of pure bliss—when the sea recognizes me, scoops me up in its arms, and everything melts away. I feel weightless. Board and body, mind and spirit. Nothing else matters in that moment when the ocean allows me to become a part of her.

I hold my breath as that moment descends. I paddle once, twice, then pop to my feet, a sly grin branded on my cheeks. A need writhes deep inside me to impress you.

FAYE DARLING

You, who I've only just met even though it feels like we've known one another for a lifetime.

A shadow hooks in my peripheral vision farther down the wave as I bend my knees a little more, twist ever so slightly at the hips. At first, I think maybe it's just you, revealing yourself in a way you haven't yet. A way I didn't know you'd be capable of.

But then I see it. See *her*.

Some chick wearing a shorty wetsuit, even though the season for such attire is gone. She wobbles, like a foal trying to stand for the first time, on a board that's way too short for her apparent skill level. My eyes go wide the moment I realize she's headed straight toward me.

I barely have the chance to bark, "Hey," before our boards collide, then our bodies. A tiny *oof* from her as we plummet into the cresting wave.

The cold is electric shock therapy, and the fury of the underside of this wave threatens to scramble more than just my brain.

Small hands that can only belong to this woman slap at my shoulders and chest as the wave tugs us along, holds us down, and threatens to rip us apart.

Underwater, I open my eyes and blink through the rising foam and churning colors of the sea. I find an ink spill of black hair floating all around me. I follow the strands back to the woman who wears a look of panic on her face I don't need to see clearly to recognize. That need to protect, to shelter, rises up in me. I reach through the water and find the curve of her waist with my palm. I guide and kick us toward the surface.

As soon as we reach the air, she gasps for it. Sputters and coughs and tries to push all that hair plastered to her face away. Without thinking about it, I reach out and help, knuckles grazing her cheek as I slip a few soaked strands behind the seashell curve of her ear.

I jerk my hand back when I remember we're in this situation because of her. My mouth opens, the words to tell her off forming behind my teeth, but I never get a chance. Another wave is about to break over the top of us.

Again, that protective beast within me roars, and I instinctively reach out for her, this time my arm belting around her middle.

She begins to protest. "What are you—"

"Hold your breath," I say as the wave thunders into a foaming mess all around us.

We both suck in another batch of oxygen before I tug us under the chaos, the boards still attached to the leashes at our ankles towing us toward shore.

I feel her hands grip the forearm I have wrapped around her, and I suddenly wish those were your hands, that her body was your body, that when the wave passes and we resurface, I'd be able to look at you. *Actually* look at you. And I'd ask if you were okay. Laugh with you if that's what you wanted. Maybe cup your cheek in my hand if you were too shaken up. Thumb stroking your jaw. If I'm being honest, my eyes would probably drop down to glance at your lips, because just thinking about you has that warmth curling through my chest again, our connection strengthening with every passing sentence.

The wave passes. I kick two bodies to the surface. And when I look down into the face of the woman I grabbed instinctively, I know in an instant she isn't you. Because that warmth is zapped out of me, replaced by a frigid, off-kilter sensation. My blood heats. Anger rips through me in an instant. I know it probably has more to do with the fact that she isn't you than the harrowing ordeal she's just put us through in the surf, but my rage is present, nevertheless, and it needs to go somewhere.

"What the hell were you thinking?" I shout at her.

"Let me go, asshole.".

She squirms hard in my arms, her heel connecting with my upper thigh. I release her before she can plant a blow any higher. I yank the end of my leash. Get a hand on my board before another wave comes. I'm still fuming. "You can't drop in on someone like that. Don't you know how dangerous that is?"

If I don't say something and she does it again, the next surfer won't be as kind. Yes, this is me being kind. I've watched other guys get into fist fights over this kind of shit. Watched tires get slashed, boards get broken.

"I didn't see you." She's already tugged her surfboard back to her and is climbing on top of it. It tilts hard to the left then harder to the right as she tries to find her balance.

I smirk at her as she grips the rails of her board tight. Then, I swing a leg over my own board smoothly, still watching her try and steady herself. A bit of my anger diffuses as it's replaced by amusement. "Clearly."

She rolls her eyes. "What?"

"You're new at this, aren't you?"

"If you're about to be *that guy* right now, I'll happily knee you in the groin."

"What guy?" I throw a glance over my shoulder to make sure a wave isn't about to break over the top of us again. Nothing but the soft nudge of the ocean swell, the colors shifting to cool shades of blue and green and gray as the sun climbs higher.

"The guy who finds his masculine identity in teaching women how to do things."

The sea rises beneath us, sending me upward on my board and her jolting to one side. I press a flat palm to her arm, the chill of her exposed skin like a block of ice. The kind that burns. Goosebumps, thick and plump, have cropped up on her flesh where it is exposed beneath the short sleeve of her wetsuit.

"I'm not trying to teach you anything," I say. Her amber eyes flash a shade darker as they catch my hand on her. I jerk away. "Except maybe a little bit of etiquette."

"I know the etiquette," she huffs. Her gaze softens, and the bite all but disappears from her voice. "I just didn't see you."

The way she looks at me now makes the hairs on my neck stand erect. Like she's tracing every part of me. My shoulder length blonde hair twisted into a knot at the nape of my sturdy neck. Broad shoulders planted atop a solid chest and torso—all muscle. The stubble on my jaw I didn't have time to clear away this morning before Mark bleated his horn in front of the cottage. The deep, ocean blue of my eyes. And I wonder if she's asking herself how she could have missed me earlier. Six-four. Big and trim. Would you have missed me? Would you have been able to take your eyes off of me? I don't know what you look like. Tall, short, thin, curvy, dark, pale, striking, subtle. But whatever reflection you find every time you glance in the mirror—I'm sure *I* wouldn't be able to look away.

"Hm," I hum at the thought of you.

"What?" this woman asks, thinking she was the one who conjured the sound in me. Her eyes darken again. Narrow again, too.

"Ryder!" Mark cuts off whatever I'm about to say to her, paddling into my line of sight, his bright red hair almost blinding as the sun catches on the water droplets clinging to its strands. "Gotta go. Can't be late again."

"Yeah," I say to Mark while looking at her. "Me neither."

I can already hear my sister, voice working around a mouth full of impatience, as she chastises me for being late to take over Mom duty, making her late for her shift at the hospital in turn and blah, blah, blah.

But I don't move right away. I don't stop staring down at the woman wobbling on her surfboard a few feet away from me.

She is a question poised on the tip of the tongue afraid to be asked. An aggravating riddle you want nothing to do with and, at the same time, can't help but try and figure out.

Before I can even find out her name—a way to draw a line underneath our less-than-pleasant encounter—she's paddling away with the tide, back to the lineup, where my buddy Nick is about to catch a decent-looking wave. The wound-tight quality he always has is gone in this brief moment of time.

"Ry," Mark snaps over the crash of the breakers. He waves to me from shore, then cups his hand around the side of his mouth to lift his voice. It carries past me, to Nick. "Nicholas, we're gonna leave your sorry ass."

Nick growls as Mark derails his focus. He loses his balance and topples head-first into the face of the wave. Nick is the nicest guy I know, if not a little too nice at times, but even that won't stop him from releasing a string of expletive-shaped bubbles underwater.

I chuckle under my breath. Start to paddle again. Sun on my freckled cheeks. An easy, off-shore breeze in my damp hair. A warmth blooming out from the middle of my ribcage. I can feel you here still. More so when it's just the two of us. You're like the echo of a song. The kind of melody that cannot be scrubbed from the mind with soap and water alone.

But I don't want to scrub you away. I think I'd rather have you in my head, stuck on repeat, than anywhere else.

Stick with me, will you? Together we can see where this thing goes.

Two

Ryder

Oof, YOUR TOUCH RIGHT now as you turned the page gave me a little thrill. Heart plummeting. Goosebumps rising on my arms. Shivers crawling over my scalp. Do you realize what you're doing to me?

I'm grinning like a goon now as I ride shotgun in Mark's truck on the drive back into town. I have my forehead pressed against the window, watching the trees pass above us in a blur on this windy stretch of highway.

Mark snaps his fingers an inch from my ear. "Hey."

I shove his hand away and sit up. "What the fuck, man?"

Nick's deep laugh in the back seat has me glaring at him in the reflection of the rearview mirror. He's changed out of his wetsuit. We all have. But Mark and I are in thick flannels and dark wash jeans while Nick is sporting an old-school three piece tweed suit, curved collar of his dress shirt buttoned over the hollow of his neck, a sleek-looking red necktie peeking out from the V of his suit vest. It's a look that would have *Peaky Blinders'* Tommy Shelby envious of. It's a look that's gotten Nick into more fist fights over the years than I can count and me swooping in from the wings to back him up, of course.

"Laughing aside, I'm with Mark." Nick threads a cuff link through the hole at the end of his shirt sleeve, the black tattoos that cover the backs of his hands a sharp contrast to the light color of his shirt.

"You're with Mark on what?"

"Fuck," Mark breathes. "Did you even hear what I said?"

"We're worried about you," Nick adds, trying to clarify, I think.

I quirk a brow, still not following.

"It's like you're here, but you're also somewhere else," Mark says. "You doing okay? You know...with your mom and all."

"M'fine," I grumble, twisting to look out the window again.

"You sure?" Nick's hand falls on my shoulder. His concerned look falls on my face.

I shrug him off. "Wasn't even thinking about Mom."

"Lady trouble, is it?" Mark asks, the snicker that follows sounding almost sinister. "Again?"

"What do you mean *again*?" I watch the flash of tree trunks straight-on, glimpsing bits of blue sea shimmering in the gaps. I lick my lips, tasting the salt the ocean has left behind. Like a lover's mark. A simmering little afterthought. Faint, but present. Much like yourself.

"Who was the child you dated last summer?" Mark asked. "What was her name?"

"Ella," Nick offers a little too quickly.

"She was twenty," I say. "Hardly a child."

"Nine years difference, bro," Mark says. "Then there was the spring fling from hell. What was her name?"

"Never learned it," Nick says, then sighs. "Gone too soon."

"Daisy Denis. Julia Piper. Madison Bridger. Vanessa Waterman."

"Mallory McManus," Nick adds. "Kelly Flynn."

"Enough," I say, peeling my eyes away from the trees again. "Like you two don't have your own lists of failed relationships."

Mark clears his throat pointedly. Tosses me a knowing glance before looking back at the road just as it curves around the base of Neahkahnie Mountain. We're up so high and the cliffs here are so severe that miles and miles of coastline to the south is visible—a thread-like spool of sand beating back a froth of foamy breakers pushed ashore by the wide breadth of the Pacific. It doesn't matter how many times I see this view, it always takes my breath away, if only for half a second. The rain, the sea, the deep green of the fir trees. I love this part of the country, this little pocket I call home, even if my friends are giving me shit. Distracting me from the view, from sharing it with you.

"Gina's name over and over is still a list, Mark," I say. He's been in an on-again-off-again relationship with the fourth member of our friendship quartet since I can remember. Maybe since the first day of kindergarten when Mark walked right up to Gina Dubicki on the playground, a shoot of Queen Anne's Lace gripped tightly in his pudgy fist, and asked her to be his soulmate. Because, when you're five, you think that's how love works. You just ask.

Maybe it does.

IN LOVE WITH YOU

Maybe that's why, after decades of breaking up and getting back together, Mark and Gina are getting married in a little over a month. I'm the best man.

"Seriously, Ryder," Nick says, still frittering with that damn suit in the back seat. He teaches high school history. He doesn't schmooze high-class clients for a top financial institution. Why does the way he looks matter? "What's going on with you today? Anything you'd like to share with the class?"

"Yes, Mr. Forrester," I say, trying to sound as nasal as possible. My best imitation of one of his students. I clear my throat, my voice returning to its normal timbre. "I sort of met someone."

Mark backhands me. "I knew it was a lady thing."

"When'd you meet her?" Nick asks. "Last night?"

"Hard to tell you when they arrived in my life," I say, eyeballing the side streets that bisect the highway outside of the small town of Manzanita. "It's like they were nothing to me, then suddenly they were right there, listening to everything I had to say like they couldn't get enough."

"Is that what they call it these days? *Listening*?" Mark laughs like he's just made the funniest joke in the world.

He doesn't realize that his dig is like a hand clenched around my gut.

I wish I could do more than just talk to you. If you were here, in person, right beside me, I'd take your face between my wide, wide palms and stare into your eyes, memorizing every whorl, every fleck, every depth of color in them. I'd drag my knuckles down the swell of your cheek and the cut of your jaw. I'd lean close. Breathe in the smell of you. Salt and citrus? Rosewater and musk? Maybe you'd be so intoxicating I wouldn't be able to resist leaning even closer. Brushing my lips across your neck. Leaving a lingering kiss on the soft place just behind your ear.

Shit.

I hope that didn't freak you out. I hope it doesn't feel like we're moving too fast. It's like they say—when you know, you know.

"It's not that dipshit who snaked your wave this morning is it?" Mark asks, snapping me back to reality.

I smooth my hair back with my fingers and let out a long sigh, blinking several times just to get a grip on things again. That soft warmth in my chest suddenly feels like ember sparks cackling up from a fire, ready to wreak havoc on my heart.

"She didn't snake my wave," I say. "But no, it's not her."

"She had a nice rack," Mark says.

My comeback is quick. Well-deserved after the last fifteen minutes of shit-on-Ryder time. "How's that fiancée of yours?"

But Mark takes me seriously. "Do you know how many kinds of roses there are?"

"Over three hundred species," Nick says. Mark and I both twist toward him, and he shrugs, not even looking at us. "My grandma was really into roses."

"Whatever you say, Rain Man." I snicker and turn around.

Mark is already looking at the road again, guiding us into another sleepy little town pushed back from the coast. We cross the river that topples into Nehalem Bay and push on just as a light mist begins to fall in this small wetland.

"I thought there were only like ten," Mark says. "So, when Gina asked what kind of roses, all I could say was red sounded nice. But then she was like, *no, what kind of roses*. While all you motherfuckers were jerking off, drinking beer, and watching TV last night, I had to listen to Gina talk about the wide variety of roses for hours."

Nick laughs. "Which ones did you decide on?"

"Hydrangeas," Mark deadpans.

"I'm not an expert, but I don't think that's a rose," I say.

"It's not." Mark holds his breath. Wrings his hands around the steering wheel. He exhales all at once, warm air fogging up the windshield briefly before it clears. "Gina's mom called after two hours of that bullshit and said she heard hydrangeas and dahlias are in vogue this year for autumn weddings."

"Wow," I say.

"Tell me about it."

"No, I meant wow about you using the phrase in vogue."

Mark lets out another heavy breath. "Can we move my bachelor's weekend up? Before I drown in flowers and fluffy phrases like in vogue and très chic? I need fishing, camping, and booze. Lots and lots of booze."

"Two and a half weeks," I say. "Then you can get punch drunk in the middle of the woods, a fish on the line and a campfire waiting for you in the evening."

"Remember, no strippers," Mark warns.

"Why would you even think—"

"Gina would kill me," he says. And she would. She put the crazy in crazy ex-girlfriend during their year-long separation in their early twenties. She'd follow any chick Mark ever talked to in public and scare her out of pursuing him. He liked it, though. I know he did.

"Better call Mercedes and tell her to find another gig, then," Nick says.

"Ha-ha." But nothing about Mark's tone is ha-ha right now.

FAYE DARLING

"Nah, man," I say, squeezing his shoulder and giving him a good-for-nothing shake. "It's gonna be a good ole boys weekend. You, me, and Nicholas,—real back country shit."

"As long as back country isn't code for strip club..." Mark shoots me a grin that has a shimmer of fear behind it. If I were marrying Gina, there'd be more than just a shimmer. I love that woman like a sister, but, just like my own sister, she scares the living shit out of me most of the time.

"Chill, bro. There won't be a woman in sight."

"And to think Gina's brother throwing a bitch fit over not being my best man nearly made me cave," Mark says with a snort.

"Now, Blake would've taken you straight to a strip club," I say.

"Probably just to break up the wedding."

"Little shit," I grumble.

"Don't forget he's coming," Mark says.

My fist clenches, knuckles cracking, threatening to break. I grit out, "How could I forget?"

"You left him off the list," Mark says.

"I left him off on purpose."

Blake Dubicki dated my sister, Steph, in high school. He was her first boyfriend, first love, first heartbreak. A lot of people credit the fact that our dad died when we were so young for Steph's inclination toward men who treat her like shit. No father figure in her life and all that. I know a few people lump me in there, too. Four years older. The only male role model she had, really. I should've done a better job at showing her what it was like to feel safe and secure in the presence of a man. Instead, I was a fucked up little shit who only knew how to stir up trouble and hit things with my fists. People mostly.

IN LOVE WITH YOU

People who stomped on my little sister's heart. People like Blake Dubicki.

I take a deep breath, mostly for your sake. I don't want to scare you off before you've gotten a chance to really know me. I've changed a lot in the last few years. I was forced to.

While I can learn to control my temper, the need to protect what I love is something I don't think I'll ever be able to control. It's something I never want to control, honestly.

And Gina's little brother Blake tests every ounce of control in my big body.

"Just don't kill him before the wedding," Mark says. "That's all I ask."

"No promises," I say. Another fist curling. Another crack of knuckles.

I look out the window as the road curves around the last bend of the bay, the thick tracts of evergreens returning, the pull of the tide an invisible finger beckoning me from their shadows. The rain sets in. Heavy drops trailing across the windowpane. I watch them catch on the glass before they begin to run and are eventually flung carelessly onto the dark roll of asphalt, forever disappearing behind us.

Three

Luna

You again.

I should have known no amount of distance I traveled would keep you away.

Do all writers talk to their readers the way that I do? As if they are present in every aspect of their life, not just the stories they write?

Perhaps I'm the only one who finds comfort in you, if not a little bit of added pressure. Okay, a lot a bit of pressure. Because you've found me. Again. When I was trying my best to hide from you and everyone else who needs Luna, romance writer extraordinaire, instead of Luna, burnt out, creatively blocked thirty-three-year-old woman.

And in case you didn't understand what I meant by that last part, no I don't have any new material for you to devour. Not yet. Maybe not ever if inspiration doesn't strike. And fast.

IN LOVE WITH YOU

After the success of my last series, I made the decision to take a year off from all things writing. To regroup. To recharge. But twelve months turned into eighteen. Now, I'm expected to emerge better than ever. Explode back onto the literary scene with my best book yet.

But every time I even think about writing, I feel a hand clench around my heart. I feel a ball and chain tied around my ankles, holding me in place, threatening to drag me through the floor. To make matters worse, every day for the past three weeks my agent has emailed, called, and even threatened to get on a plane and fly to Oklahoma to track me down if I don't have something she can pitch to my publisher.

Her threat to track me down in my hometown is part of the reason I left the Sooner State in the first place. Just a part.

Blocked. Hopeless. Uninspired. Tired. Bored. Those are other parts.

Truly, the list of reasons for my departure is endless and doesn't really matter. The fact is I flew into Portland three days ago and was greeted immediately by my favorite cousin, D.J. He whisked me through the smug little city, then the green and gold hills outside of it, which were practically foaming at the mouth with mist and mystery, and welcomed me into the cramped two-bedroom situated above the bar he inherited from our grandfather in the crook of the North Oregon Coast. D.J. gave me a ring full of keys right after we arrived. One to the apartment, another to the front door of The Tavern, and one to our grandfather's old pickup truck.

I used to spend six weeks every summer here. The ocean, the trees, the family business that was so different to what I knew back home—I loved every minute of it. Not to mention this is the place where my love for storytelling was born.

FAYE DARLING

There's something magical about the heavy, cool air here. I know if I'm going to get my legs back under me after my hiatus, this will be the place.

Now, I'm doing what I always do when I travel for research. Trying out new things, visiting new places, hoping I'll find a story hidden in the pines. Wrapped around the curl of a wave. Twisting through the weathered faces of the locals.

How's it going, you ask?

Not sure, dear reader. Not. Yet. Sure.

I found a wetsuit and a surfboard in the storage shed behind The Tavern yesterday afternoon. Decided to take them for a test drive when I learned the weather would be nice right around sunrise. I haven't surfed since I lived in Ecuador for a few months when I was nineteen, fresh out of high school, still wanting to be a travel writer.

That was a lifetime ago.

To say I am rusty on a surfboard is an understatement. I ran smack into a local on the first wave I caught. Then nearly drowned in misogyny and heavy-lidded glares once we both breached the surface.

Still. There was something about that man.

A mystery stitched into his bones that felt a lot like the beginning of a story.

Even now as I steer my grandfather's pickup truck down the twisty back road that leads to The Tavern, I can't stop thinking about that man. Eyes so dark blue they were nearly indigo—like storm clouds, like ominous curiosity. Electricity popped between us when he touched me. Arm wrapping around my waist to keep me close when a wave crashed over the top of us, palm pressing into the bare skin of my arm later on. He was handsome in all the ways a woman can appreciate. Equally as frustrating with his digs and tip-toe-around-it jokes.

I shake his pretty image from my head.

There's no way that man is going to be the fresh hit of oxygen I need to breathe a new story to life. Don't go getting attached, do you hear me, reader? I sure as hell won't be.

The Tavern appears out of nowhere, like a damn jack in the box. A hefty building made of dark and warping wood. I jump on the brakes. Practically roll into the dusty parking lot on two wheels. The surfboard in the bed clunks against the side of the pickup before I hear nothing but the rattle of tires on gravel, every bit of the undercarriage of this old thing threatening to shake loose.

D.J.'s jacked-up black truck is missing from its usual spot in the back corner of the parking lot beside the dumpsters. Inside, a note written in impressive cursive informing me about a morning run into Portland clings to a magnet from the poetry set I sent him several Christmases ago. I'm not the only writer in the family, but I think my six-foot-seven wall of a cousin would rather take a bullet in the arm than admit he dabbles in poetry or art of any kind, really.

Thankfully, D.J. *does* admit to dabbling in good food and excellent coffee.

Fried eggs. Crisp bacon. Sourdough with homemade raspberry jam. I settle into the little table in the corner of the long and narrow kitchen. The windows set into the wood paneling hold a view of the lush green forest rising up in the hills behind The Tavern. Fog curling through the trees like campfire smoke. Chitter of birdsong. The low, distant hum of ocean waves breaking miles away.

FAYE DARLING

I'm midbite into a slice of toast when my phone vibrates. A text message from my agent.

Vera: Forget about the pitch. Just send proof of life. Worried about you.

I chew as I open up the camera app on my cell. Swallow down the toast. Pick up the massive mug in front of me. I snap a picture of my face, the bottom half buried in a steaming cup of dark roast, and send it to her.

My phone buzzes almost as soon as I put it down.

Vera: Great. Now, let's talk pitch.

I grumble around another bite of toast and make the screen go black. I slam the phone upside down onto the table, hiding it behind the ceramic fir tree napkin holder that I make a mental note to give D.J. crap about later. It's too cute. Hand-painted. The trees might as well be holding hands and have googly eyes glued to their tops. My phone vibrates once, twice. I ignore it. Eat my bacon and stare out the window as the dark evergreens ripple in the wind.

What I can't ignore is the guilt, like a knife in the gut being plunged in and out, in and out with every buzz of the phone.

I've never had trouble hunting down inspiration for my stories before. Some literary critics have called my process fearless. I'm sure you know this. I'm sure you're the kind of reader who knows everything about me and my process. Or you don't. Perhaps you only know me through my books, the author bio at the back. How much you know about me doesn't really matter, though. You're here, that's what matters. So, then be here. Help me—*god.* I sound fucking crazy. Asking a reader for help...a reader who exists only inside my head.

Whatever, let's go with it. Work with what you got and all that bullshit, am I right?

IN LOVE WITH YOU

Let's brainstorm together. Find a way through this prickly thicket, you and me. Sound good? Great.

Now.

Where was I?

Ah, yes. Inspiration. Thank you for reminding me.

I've never had troubling hunting it down. Until now. And I don't have time to wait for it to strike the way it does for some writers. My bank account is dwindling, my readership—looking at you, sweet cheeks—is getting impatient, etc., etc. So, perhaps, and I'm just thinking out loud here, it's time for a good kick up the ass. Maybe, instead of waiting for inspiration to find me the way I've been doing for the past few months, because I've seemingly forgotten how to do this, I need to seek it out with a bit more oomph. Like I used to.

My phone buzzes again, and I sink low in my chair.

Later, I tell myself, drawn suddenly back down to Earth. *I'll seek inspiration out later.*

First, coffee.

Four

Ryder

MARK DROPS NICK OFF at the high school on our way into town.

West Cove is so small if you sneeze at the wrong time you'd miss it. Three blocks along Highway 101. Shops dedicated mostly to the tourists. Tchotchkes and antiques and homespun beach-themed crafts. A couple of restaurants, too. The bakery my sister and mom go to every Sunday. Or, I should say, used to go every Sunday. Before Mom got too sick. Then there's the little grocery store, overpriced and understocked. After that, it's nothing but houses, glimpses of the seven-mile stretch of West Cove's beach, then nothing but trees and rugged coastline until you bumble into the next town and the next after that.

Maybe none of this is new to you. It could be you've driven through my neck of the woods plenty of times, both of us oblivious to the other's existence. That thought warms me. The idea of passing you on the sidewalk or the beach, smiling at you in a kind, friendly way, not knowing that fate would bring us together in this way. You, looking in. Me, beginning to pine.

Possibly.

Maybe I'm beginning to pine.

If that freaks you out, forget I said anything. I've never had anyone in my head like this before, and I don't know how to turn off those kinds of thoughts.

Mark pulls up to my family's cottage, parking behind the old Camaro my dad and I started restoring when I was eleven, just a few months before his accident. I finished it on my own, though, with a little help from Mark and his stepdad.

My best friend idles in front of my house just long enough for me to hop out and snag my board and wetsuit from the truck bed. Then, he peels out into a slick U-turn he's been making ever since he got his license and takes off with a friendly lift of his fingers.

I've lived in the same two bedroom cottage with my family since I was a baby. This place is etched into my bones. Cedar shake siding. Rhododendron bushes out front that bloom bright purple every spring. Covered porch with Adirondack chairs. Twin Valhalla ladders, made of pieces of driftwood we collected from the beach, hanging from the ceiling on either side of the porch steps. Welcome mat in front of the door Mom found at a garage sale—*Bless This Mess.* Smell of woodsmoke. Scatter of sand on the porch. My sister appearing from behind the door, wearing her scrubs and a grimace that could crush skulls.

"You're late," Steph says, shouldering her purse and draping her purple puffer jacket over the crook of her elbow.

"You ever think you're always early?"

"Don't start with that bullshit. Not today." Steph puffs up her cheeks the way she does when she's annoyed. Then, it's straight to business. "Mom's had her meds and a sponge bath. She's alert today and in a decent mood, so don't fucking ruin it."

"Oh ye of little faith."

She shoots me a pointed look. "I mean it, Ryder."

"I won't."

"You working tonight?" she asks, sliding into her jacket and swiping her ponytail out from under the collar.

"It's Wednesday, isn't it?"

Three nights a week, I tend bar at my buddy's tavern a few miles out of town. It's a bar his grandfather, Derek Howard, a founding member of the legendary Timber Razers Motorcycle Club started when he laid his bike down on the road and fucked his hip up too badly to get back on again. He purposefully bought an old homestead off the main thoroughfare so that the majority of the tourists couldn't find it and his club would have a home base. Now, his grandson, Derek Jr., or D.J., runs it, and even though D.J. has never had an interest in becoming a Timber Razer, the club members still treat him like one of their own, their loyalty to the late Derek Howard tied to everyone who shares his blood.

I met D.J. surfing three years ago. He overheard me telling Mark and Nick I needed to find a job by the end of the week and, after taking one look at me and asking a few questions about my history, he offered me the position. The Tavern's customers aren't exactly stuffed unicorns. More like stuffed grizzly bears, but instead of cotton, they're filled with razor blades and brass knuckles, stitched up with barbed wire instead of silky thread.

IN LOVE WITH YOU

"Yes, smart ass," Steph says. "It's Wednesday."

"Then, yeah," I say with a big-shouldered shrug. "I'm working."

"I'll be back before you have to leave." Steph steps onto the porch and into a shaft of sunlight pushing through a break in the clouds.

That's when I see it.

Beneath a thick sweep of concealer is the tell-tale sign of a fresh bruise on the top of her left cheek, just beneath her eye.

I take her chin in my fingers and ease her face upward so I can get a better look at it. Fire sparks in my veins at the thought of anyone laying a finger on my little sis. That protective beast again, roaring.

She bats my hand away. "Don't worry about it."

"I'll kill the bastard," I say through clenched teeth.

"Do you even know who the bastard is?"

"You seeing Blake again?"

She makes an aggravated noise at the back of her throat. "God, no."

"Trent Bailey's little brother, then?"

Steph shakes her head. "You don't know him."

"I can get to know him." I grip my surfboard so tightly I feel it give beneath the pressure. Just a little. "I can get to know him real quick."

"He's...history."

"Yeah," I grit out. "I've heard you say that before."

Steph looks me in the eye. Bores holes through my own. If I had blinked I might not have caught the flash of fear that preceded the look of pure apathy in her expression right now. She does that. When she's hiding something. She shoves her worries into some deep dark place in that small body of hers for later. I hate to think what it will do to her someday. I am the sibling most likely to explode, but Steph is the one most likely to implode. And I think imploding is far more destructive than exploding ever could be. Coming from me, that's saying something.

"I'm serious this time," she says.

"If you'd just let me take care of—"

"Don't," she says.

"Don't take care of it?"

"Don't even finish that sentence or that thought in your big, stupid head." I watch a tear spring up in the corner of her eye. I reach out to wipe it as it begins to fall, but she beats me to it, erasing it from existence. I take a breath and hold it at the back of my throat. My sister is one of the smartest, strongest, most independent women I know, but when it comes to guys, she can be so, so stupid. Her voice softens. She breaks eye contact. Stares at the keys wound around her fingers. "You can't."

Two words. Two simple words. And yet, they hold so much meaning. Leave so many gaps to be filled in. I exhale and let myself slip into those gaps for a second. Allow myself to understand the reality of it all.

Would you think less of me if you knew my past? Knew why I couldn't get into another fight? It's not that I don't trust you. I think I've told you more about myself in two hours than I've told anyone before. No, trust isn't the issue. It's that once you know you can't *un*know. All I will say now is that I would be risking more than just split knuckles or a bruised face if I got into another fight. If the cops were called. If I took it too far.

And I can't take that chance. Not with Mom in the condition she's in. Not with Steph poised to be left all alone. Not with you in my head, expecting certain things from me.

IN LOVE WITH YOU

"Just stay away from that prick," I tell Steph, swallowing hard. "In fact, stay away from all pricks. Stay away from all people with penises in general for a while. Just to be safe."

"Fucking hell," Steph groans. "How about I just become a nun?"

"Perfect." I say.

Steph is grasshopper-fast, hugging me tightly for half a second before jumping off the porch. She takes off across the front lawn, the auburn tint to her brown hair catching fire in a beam of sunlight. She climbs into her car that sounds the way I imagine a washing machine on four wheels would sound like and speeds off. Steph lives across town in a duplex she can afford all by herself, but she's here more than she is there and at the hospital the rest of the time. I keep telling her to move back into the cottage, but she likes her freedom too much. Or the idea of freedom at the very least.

I watch the faded blue paint of her car blaze down the street until it's nothing but a blur, then nothing at all.

Five

Ryder

I WANT YOU TO meet someone.

I know, I know. I've introduced you to Mark and Nick and Steph and even hinted at D.J. But this is different. This someone is my favorite someone in the entire world. And the moment I walk into the cottage, she's calling for me.

Are you ready?

"Mom?" I say as I step through her bedroom door at the back of the house.

The curtains are open, letting in as much natural light as is possible in the southwest corner of the little house. This room used to be my favorite. It smelled like pumpkin spice all year round, because Mom loved fall before it was trendy. There was always music playing softly in the background, a pile of clean clothes on the velvet chair in the corner, soft-glowing lamps turning everything gold, Mom's makeup strewn over her vanity, Dad's surfboard leaned against the far wall, black and white pictures of the coast hanging everywhere. Now, it smells clinical, a bit like bodily fluids. A hospital bed has replaced my parents' comfy queen. Beside Dad's surfboard, Mom's wheelchair.

Mom is sitting up in the bed, her long blonde hair brushed and braided over one shoulder the way she likes. She looks thinner than when I left her a few hours ago. Like the tumor in her brain has eaten her away in my absence. She smiles at me, or tries to, with only one side of her face. She's lost control over the entire right side of her body, and I'm scared her left side is getting weaker by the day.

But Steph was right. There's a spark in her blue eyes I haven't seen in weeks. She makes a garbled noise that sounds like my name.

I go to her bedside and kiss her on the cheek. She giggles as I pull back.

"What do you want to do today?" I ask.

Her eyes flash to the wheelchair. "Beach," she mumbles. It sounds more like *beet*, but I understand, and that's all that matters.

I layer Mom like her once-famous twelve-layer chocolate cake. Stretchy thermal underwear over the soft leggings Steph dressed her in this morning. Sweatpants over that. Wool socks over thin ankle socks. Fleece vest zipped over her t-shirt. One of Dad's old flannels buttoned to her collarbone. A crew neck sweatshirt with a handstitched outline of an ocean wave below the left shoulder. One of my old high school hoodies overtop. Gloves. Scarf. Beanie. Boots.

"Hot," she mumbles, then sticks out her tongue and exaggerates a pant. "Too hot."

FAYE DARLING

I look up at her from where I crouch in front of her wheelchair, adjusting the foot rests. Her cheeks are feathered with pink splotches and a trail of sweat is slipping down her temple.

"Maybe I overdid it," I say, and she gives me a look that says, *ya think?*

I shed a few of her layers. Leave my hoodie slung over the foot of the bed along with the sweatpants, scarf, and thin socks. Then, I drape a knit blanket over her lap and tuck it under her skinny thighs. She grunts. Makes that panting sound again.

"It's cold outside," I say. "Colder on the beach."

Are you like this with the people you love? With the person you love the most? Are you as protective as I am? I'd like to think you are. Maybe not *this* protective. Steph says I'm overprotective. She says it like it's a bad thing. Told me my problem was that I'd gladly step in front of a speeding bullet for someone and, more times than not, they'd never even think of doing the same thing for me. It's probably why my past relationships haven't worked out. Remember that list my friends rattled off in the truck? I'm protective, jealous, territorial. Maybe I smother people. Maybe I just haven't found anyone who will smother me back.

Would you?

"Hot, Ry-*er*," Mom snaps, interrupting my conversation with you.

"You can stand to lose the crewneck," I say, bunching it up around Mom's torso and easing it over her head, her arms. I fold it neatly and set it in her lap. "But it's coming with us. Just in case."

"'kay," she says, then thrusts a shaking, gnarled hand toward the door. *Forward*, it tells me. *To the beach*, it says.

IN LOVE WITH YOU

I chuckle, pop the brakes, and wheel her toward the front door.

The walk to the beach is just shy of ten minutes. I set off down the long, smooth street we live on. There's a slight decline to the road, so I give Mom a good push, jump on the back of her wheelchair, and let physics do the rest.

Mom squeals as we begin to gain speed. Wind ruffling the wisps of blonde hair sticking out of her braid. Fresh air on her cheeks, washing away the staleness of the house that's seeped into her bones like a different kind of sickness—cabin fever.

I kick off from the ground, pushing us faster. Another squeal. A muffled giggle. Mom's an adrenaline junkie at heart. She moved from landlocked Idaho when she was eighteen to get away from her up-tight parents, the ones I've never met. Mom met my dad rock climbing outside of Bend when he was a cocky little shit. Her words, not mine. Still, she used to say she let him give her everything she ever loved: climbing tips, surf lessons, a glimpse into the wilder pockets of the PNW, my sister, me, and his whole heart. Every ventricle, every chamber—beating, just for her. And fuck if I don't want that kind of love someday.

Shit.

I've never said that before. Not even to myself. But especially not to an audience.

I can still feel you. Turning these pages. Hanging on every word.

Would you just pre—no, that's a crazy idea. Forget I said anything at all.

I slow Mom's chair down to a crawl as we approach the highway. Look left, right, left again, just to be sure. When it's clear no cars are close, I amble across, guiding the chair at an

33

angle so it misses a massive pothole just on the other side of the 101. Mom's humming some tune. Sounds a little like *Led Zeppelin*. Maybe *Cream.*

Okay, I'll just say it. What I stopped myself from saying to you before.

Would you just pretend you are here with me? Or, at least, let me pretend you're here? If you were, I'd put you on my back, your legs wrapping around the solid muscle of my abdomen. Maybe the heels of your feet dig into me a little. Maybe I like it more than I should. We'd both jump onto the back of Mom's wheelchair, the way I'm doing now after kicking off from the ground. Your squeal would be the echo of Mom's, yours small and tight, right in my ear. I'd feel your breath. Warm, intoxicating. I'd adjust my head and angle it toward you. The outer curve of my ear would be a butterfly's wing against your lips. Maybe you'd gasp a little. Maybe you'd take my ear between your teeth and softly nip at its edges, teasing. Then, because this is my fantasy, Mom would start to sing clearly, her words understandable, and you'd know every single one. You'd belt out her song—a duet—as I step off of the back of the wheelchair the way I am now. And you'd keep singing until I pushed us up the last bit of incline, past the little motel on the left, parking the wheelchair in the dune grass.

I close my eyes as I stop walking, the wheels of Mom's chair halted right at the edge of the sandy path that winds through the dunes to the beach. I need one second, one more second in that space with you.

But you've slipped from my back. Your breath is nothing but chilled wind on my neck. I can only feel you at a distance. Heart beating miles and miles away.

Mom shakes the left arm of the chair. "Ry?"

"Sorry," I mutter, the word breathy, just as far away as you are.

I put the brakes down and gently pick Mom up, trying to keep the blanket tucked around her the best I can.

I'm not exactly a small dude. I can easily bench press twice my body weight. Lifting Mom should be easy, but fuck. It should not be *this* easy. Like she's nothing but a skeleton. More bones than meat and flesh. Closer to death than she is to life.

That last thought is a maul, splitting me, splintering me. My breath hitches and a hard lump lodges itself in my throat. I try not to let it show though, because Mom's looking right at me—that twinkle in her eye—and I know she's thinking something happy. Trapped in an old memory that involves the two of us, or sending up silent gratitude to the universe for a son like me.

But I can tell you, can't I?

Tell you that I'm scared.

Really fucking scared.

Somedays I feel like I'm standing in an old attic. Between the rafters. Waiting for my feet to drop through the flimsy ceiling beneath me.

The doctors who told us Mom's brain tumor was inoperable estimated she had eight to ten months to live, but it's been three months since then and everything's progressed so quickly I'm really not so sure how much time she's got left.

If I could trade places with her, I would.

If I could give her my tumorless brain and take hers instead, I'd tell the doc to reach for his scalpel and start gutting today.

I shuffle over the sand and try to put all the coulds and shoulds and if onlys out of my mind and focus on this moment. The one happening right here on this beach, where a soft breeze is blowing up from the southwest. Cool still, but warmer than if it were coming from the other direction. Not overpowering, either, which is good. It means Mom might be able to last here a little longer than usual.

"Mm," she hums, eyes on the ocean now. *Her* ocean.

The thin clouds have turned the color of the waves from a blueish-teal to a rich jade-gray. They topple over one another like a litter of excited puppies set loose on the slick surface of a frozen pond.

I set Mom down in the sand and ease her back against a giant log that's been smoothed by wind and rain and tide over the last year or so. It cradles her spine perfectly. I tuck the blanket around her lower half and plop down beside her. Draping an arm over her shoulders, I draw her to me, locking her against my side. Her fingers try their best to knot around the hem of my flannel—always needing to hold something, someone—and then she sighs, sinking into comfort that is rare these days. I imagine you are here with us. Not just on the other side of this book, if that's what this really is, but nestled against my other side. Your cheek on my chest. Our fingers threaded together.

Mom mutters something. *Ohree. Rory. Ss-ory.*

"Story?" I ask.

"Sss," she hisses. Her way of saying *yes*.

I don't know what I'm going to say until I open my mouth. Even then, it's like the words sprout legs and dance out of me to their own secret rhythm.

"Dad used to bring us here," I say. "Every Sunday afternoon." Mom sighs again before she burrows deeper into my side, her bony shoulder connecting with my ribs, her fingers winding tighter around my shirt. I keep talking, keep remembering for the both of us. "It didn't matter if it was raining and forty-three-degrees or if it was sunny and pushing eighty, we just had to come to the beach. You'd pack a picnic—whatever leftovers were in the fridge—and we'd gobble it all up after hours of playing in the surf or digging in the sand or lying on our backs, watching the clouds shift across the sky."

Mom tries to say something, but this time it's nothing but garbled noise. She uses her good arm to lift her useless one and drags her hand slowly through the air. Her hands drop and she says that word again, clearer now. "Ite."

"Kite?" I ask.

"Sss." She pats my knee.

"Sometimes, we'd fly kites," I say, recalling the memory she's nudged me toward. "You had one that looked like a jelly fish, those peach-colored spindles twirling in the wind, making the thing look like the sky had become the Deep Blue and we were in some magical place where we could breathe underwater."

Mom pats my knee again. "Sss."

"Do we still have that kite?"

"Mm."

"Is it in the house?"

She shakes her head in response.

"The shed?"

"Sss."

"Maybe we can fly it tomorrow," I say, but the hope in my words is already dying. "If the weather is good."

And if she has the energy for it.

If I'd remembered, I would have looked for the kite earlier. Brought it with us.

FAYE DARLING

Maybe it's better that I didn't. Maybe it will be good for her to have something to look forward to.

We sit quietly for some time, listening to the stories the beach has to tell us instead of the ones I have to recall. Two seagulls fighting over the remaining husk of a crab another bird must have plucked from the salt. The undertow shouldering through the breaking waves, the water jumping high before dropping low. A leaf tumbleweeding across the hard, damp sand. The cry of one of the bald eagles that nest in a tall tree just to the south. The soft press of a dark raincloud inching toward land. And wave after wave after wave cackling, hissing, crashing onto shore.

"Looks like rain," I say when the cloud is close enough to see the haze of wet trailing underneath its belly. Mom is silent, her eyes on the water. I wait a few seconds. Keep my eye on the cloud. I clear my throat. "We should go."

Mom mumbles a couple of words I don't understand. Then, she holds up her left index finger. That message I hear loud and clear. One more minute. One more minute on the sand. One more minute to watch her beloved Pacific live and breathe the way it has for millions of years, the way it will keep on living and breathing long after she has stopped.

I settle back onto the log, Mom pressed to my side, and watch.

One more minute.

Six

Luna

I'M SITTING ON THE forest floor behind the bar, surrounded by sword ferns and bird song, wearing nothing but my lacy underwear and matching bralette. The rain pelts my scantily clad skin, and I welcome it with a wicked grin. I've made myself uncomfortable in the hopes inspiration will find me in this altered state. It usually works. Of course, I think I've really just been waiting for you to wander into my head again, reader. Give me a little silent direction on what I should do about this whole book debacle. A little push toward a new project.

"Luna?" I hear my cousin calling my name in the distance.

One of my eyes opens, and I gaze through the trees to find D.J. wandering in a mix of plaid, leather, and denim through the empty parking lot. The faint plume of smoke coming from the end of his cigarette curls skyward like the cragged hand of the undead shooting up from a grave. Slowly. Ominously. I don't think the undead would smell like earthy, Turkish tobacco, though. Although, if I ever decide to write a book about zombies, I might just have to add that little detail for shits and gigs.

"Luna?"

I grunt as D.J. calls my name again, because I can feel you now. Finally. Where the hell were you, reader? Lost in some daydream with a sexy, flawed, utterly delicious man, perhaps? It's okay if you were. I'm not chastising you. I'm only jealous. You think you could somehow send a message to me describing him in full detail? I could use one of those types for a novel right about now. Thanks.

Pulling on my t-shirt and slipping into my cut-off jean shorts, I pop to my bare feet. Crash through the underbrush. Scuttle across the parking lot.

"Lulu," D.J. says, grinning as he twists toward me.

"Don't call me that, *Derek.*"

A mangled, borderline-tortured sound crawls out of his mouth at the sound of his given name. "Don't call me *that.*"

D.J. Derek Junior. Named after his father and our notorious biker grandfather. It's not that they were rotten namesakes, it's just that D.J. has never been the type to find comfort living in someone else's shadow. Sometimes when I look at the sheer size of him I wonder if he willed himself to grow that tall just so his shadow would engulf everyone else's.

"You got a lady friend I should know about?" I ask, stopping a few feet in front of him.

"No." He takes a deep, cheek-caving drag on his cigarette. My tongue tingles, longing for just a taste. But I haven't smoked since I lived in Cairo a few years ago. And I'm not going to start up again for nostalgia's sake. It won't taste the same anyway. Won't even come close. D.J.'s fuzzy brows get even fuzzier as they furrow, his gaze landing on my shirt. "You got a boyfriend I should know about?"

"What?" I ask as he flicks a finger against the tag sticking out on the front of my t-shirt. Inside out. Backwards. "Oh. No. This is the byproduct of overthinking."

"Mm-hmm," he hums.

"If there's no lady, then why were you up in Portland all morning?" I ask.

"Meetings."

"Sure," I say sarcastically. "Meetings."

"What?"

I squint-smile up at him. "You so have a secret girlfriend in the city."

"You know I'm too busy for girlfriends." He takes another puff. Offers the cigarette to me. I wave a hand at it. He gives me a questioning look. D.J. is only a year and a half older than me, and seeing as both of us were only children, we are each other's surrogate siblings. The wild, slightly-nagging little sister wanting to prove how badass a preacher's daughter could be in front of the cool-headed, free-thinking older brother. Our childhood was dirt bikes and rooftop parachute jumps and invented games that always somehow involved fire. Our teen years were D.J. pushing me through air ducts to steal beer and cigarettes from Grandpa's office and me playing wing woman at beach bonfire parties when D.J.'s socially awkwardness was more noticeable. Before the muscles, the tattoos, the jacked-up pickup truck, and the whole owning a bar thing. So, when I wave my hand at the cigarette, like it's beneath me now, D.J. gives me a look, then snorts. "You go straight-edge on me, Lulu?"

"No," I grit out. That damn nickname. "I just have taste now."

"Ah, so you went pretentious on me."

"That a problem?"

"Seeing as your shirt is on inside out and backwards," he says with a gruff laugh, "I don't think so."

"I'm glad we can still be friends, then."

D.J. flicks the ash off the end of his cigarette. Kicks a leg out and starts slowly toward the front door of The Tavern. I follow, scuffing along in my bare feet, the gravel pressing into the soles I've toughened up over the years. *Country feet*, I can hear my mama say.

God, I haven't heard her voice in my head in a long time. It gives me the chills. The good and the bad kind all at once. I miss her. Damn, I miss her like crazy.

"Did your overthinking do you any good?" D.J. asks.

"You mean did I get struck by lightning and now have my next bestseller tearing through me like electricity, dying to get out and zap the world?"

"Yeah."

"Nope."

"Give it time," he says, opening the door for me to walk through first.

I grumble something incoherent. Time. Exactly what I don't have.

"When does the bar open?" I ask.

"Couple of hours," he says. "But the crowd doesn't shuffle in until about seven or eight. Why?"

"Thought I'd hang out down here tonight," I say. "Try and see if anyone strikes me as interesting."

"Please don't decide you're going to write your next novel about a biker gang."

"Why not?"

"One, it's been done again and again."

"Every story has been done again and again," I say. "It's my perspective that will make it unique."

"Two," D.J. says, as if I hadn't said anything at all. "I know what your research process is like. It's up-close and personal. Following people around. Tangling yourself up in their lives. Timber Razers are...well...necessary evils in my mind and not the kind of men I'd feel comfortable you trailing just for a story."

"Motorcycles, danger." I shrug. "Could be fun."

"Could be a heap of trouble."

D.J. slips behind the bar, the wood's finish peeled off in places, carved up in others. Cigarette burn marks. The permanent marker chicken scratch where grandpa wrote down The Tavern's very first order—Scotch, neat, and two shots of tequila—close to the taps. He misspelled tequila though. Two Ls, not one. I sit down on a stool right in front of those markings. Rub my thumb over the double Ls for good luck. He's been gone about as long as my mom. Seventeen years next summer.

"What do you suggest I do, then, Mr. Secret Trips to Portland?" I sigh. Let my cheek sink onto my hand, propped up by my elbow. "Writing books is like any other job, essentially. How do you push through when you feel like there's no way around a problem?"

"Easy." D.J. stubs out his cigarette on an ash tray nearby. I don't think any establishments are still allowed to let anyone smoke inside, but try telling a gang of angry bikers and roughed-up fishermen they have to take their cigarettes outdoors. "I look at what's right in front of me, find the simplest way through, and dive in."

I lift a brow. "You *dive in?*"

"Yep," D.J. says, reaching for a rocks glass and pouring a finger of whiskey in the bottom. He sets it in front of me. "All in."

"That's great in theory." I knock the drink back in one go. "But I don't know what's right in front of me."

D.J. clears his throat, sweeps a hand to the rain-splattered window. A view to the parking lot. To the tall evergreens that shroud the twisting road that winds back through the hills, back through the little beach town called West Cove, back to the spray of the sea and the salt-rough men who surf its waters. I groan. Extend my empty glass toward my cousin. Give it a shake.

"There it is." He takes my glass. Fills it up.

"There's what?" I make a face at the soda water he's replaced my whiskey with.

"There's you, realizing what's right in front of you."

Seven

Ryder

IT'S THE FIRST TIME since I felt you push into my world this morning that I'm glad you aren't *physically* here, because, even though it's a week night, The Tavern is packed. Crack of pool balls breaking. Deep-bellied laughs. George Jones on the juke box. An argument in the corner, another at the end of the bar. Bikers at almost every table, sea-hardened locals filling in the gaps. I'd probably have to smash a glass over multiple people's heads to keep them from looking at you, from touching you.

My heart is puttering a little faster at only the thought. I take a deep breath as I pour a beer for a fisherman who is in here as much as the Timber Razers and try and remind myself you aren't physically here. That you are safe. You are safe, you are safe, you are safe.

"Cheers," the fisherman husks, dropping a crumpled five on the bar top. "Keep the change."

FAYE DARLING

As I smooth out the bill and turn toward the cash drawer on the wall at my back, I stiffen. On nights The Tavern is this crowded, I'm hyper-aware of everything. So, I don't miss the moment something is out of place. *Someone* I should say.

A lone woman weaves through the room. Long, dark hair cascading over bare shoulders. The tight, velvet suit vest she wears as a top reveals more cleavage than every woman in this bar combined. A sliver of skin bared just above a pair of cut-off jeans shorts. Cowboy boots on her feet, mud clinging to the soles. She roves toward the bar from the back of the room, and when she's only a few feet away I stiffen again. Freckles sprayed over high cheekbones. Eyes like shards of amber. A riddle I can't work out, can't leave alone. She's the woman who dropped in on me out in the surf early this morning.

A middle-aged Timber Razer with a wiry beard hanging down to his chest drags a hand over her ass as she passes his table. He licks his chapped lips. Waits for retribution, reciprocation. She just keeps walking. Like he hadn't touch her at all. Like he doesn't exist to her.

Maybe she seems unfazed by the sleaze machine sitting a little too comfortably in his chair, but it sure has my heart hammering even more, my blood rising from a simmer to a boil. I clench my fist around a bar mop. Grind my molars around until I feel them start to give in my gums. I suddenly want to grab a fistful of that asshole's beard. Use it like a whip to slam him into one of the wooden posts nearby. Drive his face through the glass top of the juke box.

Like I said, I wouldn't let you step foot in this place on a night like tonight. If I'm getting this worked up over some chick I barely know, imagine what would happen if I caught him with his hands on you? This isn't the type of place where the cops get called, but with my history, I can't risk even the slightest possibility of the police. Not after what happened years ago at the dive bar in West Cove.

So, I turn away and put the woman out of view as she passes a high-top table full of men, eyes stitched to her chest, the curve of her ass, the swing of her hips.

A low whistle from the table has me twisting the bar mop in my hand. Tight, tighter. Then, a stool scrapes against the hardwood floor. The sigh of a body dropping onto it.

"D.J. around?" the woman asks.

I exhale before I spin on the heels of my boots and face her. Her lips, painted in a dark mauve lipstick, part as recognition ripples across her face. In this brief moment she's wide open. Riddle solved. Question answered. It's as if I can see straight through to her center. Something soft there, softer than she lets on. A lot of hurt, too. But her eyes narrow, as if she knows I'm seeing in, and that softness disappears. Walls going back up. Shutting me out to her true self.

She opens her mouth to speak, but I beat her to it. No sense trying to play dumb. Like I don't know who she is. Like I didn't recognize her the second she stepped into my line of sight.

I grip the edge of the bar, my arms spread wide, my muscles shifting beneath the worn fabric of my favorite green flannel. "You make it a point to ignore the weather?"

Her eyes are still narrowed, a scowl prominent on her face, but there's a flicker of humor in her expression. Just a flicker. Then, all serious again as she scoffs. Leans back a little, like she doesn't want to be any closer to me than she has to.

"That your best pick up line or somethin'?" she asks.

I can hear it now. The slight twang in her accent. It's subtle. As if she's worked hard to erase it over the years.

FAYE DARLING

Do *you* have an accent, I wonder? A twang, a lilt, a drawl? Is your voice low-pitched or high? Silky smooth or as rough as gravel in a blender? Smoky, maybe? Like a jazz singer trapped in the hazy Shangri-La of an old speakeasy.

I nod to this woman's bare arms, nothing but gooseflesh. "A shorty wetsuit in October? Sleeveless vest in the high-forties? Jean shorts to boot. Most women would be complaining of frost bite by now."

"Well," she grits out. "I'm not most women."

"Noted."

An older Timber Razer called Snakeback stalks up to the bar. Stops right in front of me. All he does is make eye contact and nod gruffly at me. I pour him one of the wheatier beers on tap and take the fistful of ones he slides me to cover it. D.J. doesn't do tabs here. Got too tired of hunting down all the Timber Razers who owed him hundreds of dollars and trying to get them to pay up. There was a bit of backlash. At first. But D.J. just reminded them who he was and where they were drinking. Hasn't been a problem since.

"So...D.J.?" The woman pulls out a little red notebook from her back pocket, a golf pencil with no eraser jammed through the spiral binding. She drops both onto the bar top. Looks up at me through long, long lashes. "You seen him?"

"Depends," I say, shrugging as I move down the bar to refill another customer's beer.

"On what?" she asks, lifting the volume of her voice as I breeze past her.

"What are you?" I look at her notebook as I pull on the tap's knob. "A journalist?"

"Novelist, actually."

IN LOVE WITH YOU

I whistle as I level the glass out, a thin layer of foam forming a nice head on top. I walk it down the bar. Take the cash from the crusty, time-worn townie. Then, I follow a flash of leather as a Timber Razer steps up a few feet away, summoning me with a nod, the tattoo on his neck stretching.

"What do you want with D.J.?" I ask the novelist as I pass her again, tilting my chin to the Timber Razer as I approach him.

"Double Maker's, straight," he growls.

The novelist talks as I pour the man's drink. I try not to look at her. I can't study her without worrying you might get jealous. Now, if that was you standing over there across the bar, I wouldn't be able to take my eyes off of you.

"He said to meet him here around this time," she tells me.

I raise one eyebrow at her as I concentrate on the honey helix of bourbon falling into the bottom of the glass. "He told *you* to meet him *here*?"

In the three years I've known D.J. he's never once asked a woman to meet him at The Tavern. Come to think of it, I've never seen him with a woman period. Unless him helping the silver-haired grannies from the shopfronts to their cars in the middle of West Cove counts, which I don't think it does. He has been making his trips up to Portland more and more frequent lately, but I assumed that was tavern related. Maybe not. Maybe he's met someone. Is trying to keep it a secret.

Still, that wouldn't explain why this pretty little thing is sitting here, in the middle of this crowd, asking after him like she knows him well.

"Stop looking at me like that," she says with a huff.

"Like what?"

I slide the Timber Razer his drink. He hands me a credit card, and I run it as fast as I can, because his gaze tightens the longer I take. I don't offer to print him a receipt in the hopes he'll leave a tip, either. There's a reason D.J. pays his bartender's more than most places. These guys aren't big tippers. Their form of gratuity is not beating the shit out of The Tavern's employees just for the hell of it.

"Looking at me like I've got three heads," the novelist says. "Now, D.J.?"

"I don't know." I gesture to the packed bar with a sweeping arm. "I've been a little preoccupied tonight if you hadn't noticed."

"Yes, pouring drinks is so damn difficult," she says. "It might just make you miss the *fucking giant* moving from one part of the room to the next."

"He's not the biggest guy in the joint tonight." I flick my nose to the pool table, where a Timber Razer is standing up after pocketing the eight ball. "Steel is half an inch taller than D.J."

How do I know this, you ask? Good question. About a year ago, one of the young club members made an off-hand comment that Steel was little compared to D.J.. Steel didn't hesitate to tell D.J. to bring his ass out from behind the bar, then snapped at me to find a measuring tape. One of the young Timber Razers held the end of the tape while I climbed onto a stool to pull it taught. Later, D.J. asked me if I fudged the results just to avoid the fallout of an atomic bomb. I told him Steel honestly had half an inch on him, and he laughed. Said that was probably a good thing. Illusion of power.

"Ah, good." D.J.'s voice booms from halfway across the room as he shoulders his way toward the bar. He claps me on the shoulder, then drops that hand firmly on the woman's. "You two are getting acquainted. Luna, this is who I wanted you to meet."

IN LOVE WITH YOU

Luna. So, that's her name.

"This is why you wanted me to meet you down here?" Luna asks D.J. as her eyes turn to slits again, her gaze aimed at me. "This is the saltwater-hardened, bleeds-flannel, reeks-of-the-PNW research subject you had in mind when I asked what your take of 'right in front of me' was? Come on, Deej. He's..."

"Someone care to fill me in?" I ask. Because every word that came out of her mouth just now is confusing the hell out of me. Is it you? Probably not. You're probably way smarter than me. Don't worry, I don't mind. I like the idea of that, actually.

"Ryder is North Coast through and through," D.J. says to Luna. "You can't get more local than him. He *is* the inspiration right in front of you, whether you like it or not."

Luna growls. "I need a shot of Jack."

I don't make a move to fill her order. "Inspiration? What inspiration?"

"For her new book," D.J. says. "We think you'd make a perfect research subject."

"*Derek*," Luna warns, her voice low and gruff.

"*Lulu*," he chides.

"You're a bartender, right?" Luna asks me, ignoring the confused look on my face. "Been serving drinks all night, yeah?"

"Yeah," I say slowly.

She slaps her hand against the bar top. "Shot of Jack then."

I look at D.J.. Furry brows dropped low over his dark brown eyes. Ruddy cheeks that drag with the slight downturn of his lips. He nods once, and I reach for a shot glass under the counter. Pivot back for the bottle of Jack. Start to pour.

"Luna is my cousin," D.J. offers.

FAYE DARLING

"Ah," I say as if that explanation covers everything. It doesn't. Doesn't even begin to. All it does is tell me why Luna is here in the first place. Maybe she's staying upstairs.

The surface of the liquor begins to ripple as it nears the brim. I've barely stopped pouring when Luna's hand darts forward. She knocks the shot back. Slams the glass on the bar top a second later. Snaps her fingers for another.

This chick should be irritating the hell out of me right now. Snapping her fingers. Talking about me as if I'm the last person on earth she wants to spend time with for whatever her book research entails. But, somehow, she isn't aggravating me. She's making me curious. About her project. About her.

I watch the column of her neck move as she swallows back the second shot. Study the purple stamp she leaves behind on the glass—a perfect replica of her full bottom lip.

"I've got business to take care of," D.J. says with a step and a turn away from the bar. "I'll leave you two to get more acquainted."

D.J. is the type of guy whose presence lingers long after he's left a space. It takes a few seconds, even after he's wended through the masses and disappeared into the store room, for me to truly register his absence. When it does, I feel it like an itch in my throat. One I can't reach no matter how hard I try. Awkwardness. Irritation. That's how it feels. Between Luna and me.

"What's your book about?" I ask, leaning toward her. Getting close enough to smell the top notes of her musky perfume.

I stop myself from laughing out loud. Because as soon as I leaned closer I felt another shift in the air. Is that you, I feel, baby? Are you starting to get jealous? Or is that just excitement? Should I lean closer to Luna? Like this. Resting the full weight of my broad upper body on my forearms, pushing into her space. I can almost taste the alcohol on her breath. Can almost feel the heat kicking off of her skin. My eyes drop briefly to her chest, lingering for a few seconds before lifting my gaze back to her face.

What would you do if I reached out and brushed a strand of her hair back? Tucked it behind her ear. Let my fingers rest on the hinge of her jaw. Would you close this book and throw it across the room? Would your heart beat a little faster? Would you burn with envy or longing? With rage or desire?

Don't worry, baby. I'll keep my hands to myself. I just think it's cute. How invested you seem to be in this whole scenario.

"People, things." Luna answers my question dully, her eyes flicking up and down the length of the bar, moseying from one face to the next, slowly. Taking them in perhaps? Making notes in her head for later? Or is she just trying to look anywhere but at me?

I clear my throat. "And you want to...use me in it? Research?"

Still not looking at me, she says, "I can find someone else since it doesn't seem like you're interested."

"Who said I wasn't?"

"I did." She sits up straight and looks right at me. "I need a kind of comfortability with the people I choose to study."

"And you don't have that with me?"

"No." Plain. Simple. It hurts. Just a bit.

"How come?"

She smirks. "First off, you're really fucking intense. Holy shit, are you always that rigid? I mean, look at the way you hold yourself. Like you're gonna jump across the bar any second and bite someone's head off."

A flash of a memory. White-hot, blazing through my brain. Me, slamming a man's face through a whiskey glass right after he backhanded my sister.

I blink. Try to shake the memory away.

"For another," she says, continuing, "I see straight through you. That good ole boy act might work on most people—"

"Good ole boy act?"

"You know," she says. "Flash that singular dimple, bat them pretty long eyelashes. Get your way. Really, I think you're just arrogant, which pisses me off, and when I'm pissed off, I'm closed off. Can't be closed off when I'm doing research. So, no matter what D.J. thinks, no matter what I need to get this book written, we will not be working together."

A half smile hitches on one side of my face, no doubt flashing my *singular* dimple at her. That's right, baby. There's just one. You'd love it. Probably want to dig a fingertip into it or your press your lips against it. No need to feel embarrassed about it, because I'd let you. Luna on the other hand, will never have that opportunity.

"Do you always do this, *Lulu*?" I ask, remembering how much she seemed to hate D.J. calling her that. A tiny crumb of retribution.

Her jaw clenches. "Do what?"

"Make split-second judgements about the people around you?"

"Not always." She levels me with a tense stare. "Only with people who annoy me."

I laugh drily at the back of my throat. Shift even farther forward. So close that, if I wanted to, I could grab a fistful of her vest and tug her mouth against mine. *If* I wanted to. "You know what I see when I look at you?"

"What?" she asks, voice even, if not a little too rough. Like she's trying to contain something warring within her.

If calling her Lulu was a measly crumb of retribution, then what I'm about to say is a whole slice of the damn cake. "I see a scared little girl hiding behind false bravado and sharp words, and the sad part is I don't even think you know what it is you're afraid of. It's like you've shut your eyes and are waiting for the fear to pass you by before you even have a chance to recognize it, to deal with it like a fucking adult."

Her eyes narrow again, hold my gaze for one second, two, her breath beating against the contours of my face like a wave against a cliffside. Then, she jerks back, widening the space between us exponentially.

I expect a crisp, cold retort, another crash judgement intended to make me feel small. Every muscle and bone in my body turns to stone in preparation.

But she just sits there. Glaring at me. Crushing her bottom lip beneath her teeth until a tiny prick of blood appears—crimson dancing through dark mauve.

I swallow, my throat bobbing violently. Do you hate what I've said as much as I do? Are you wishing I could take it back the same way I am? Because the longer she sits and stares at me in silence, the louder my words play back to me in my head. *Deal with it like a fucking adult.* Shit. That was harsh.

My mouth opens, a bumble-fuck of an apology about to spill out of me, but before I can utter a word, she snags her little red notebook, slips off the stool, and retreats toward the back of The Tavern. I watch her unlock the door that leads to D.J.'s apartment and wait for her to glance back at me, glare at me, at least, but she doesn't so much as blink in my direction. I suck in a noisy breath as she ducks into the stairwell, the door swinging closed behind her.

"Fuck," I mutter.

I know, I know. That was an asshole thing to say. I'm not entirely sure it was the truth. The words just sort of stumbled out of me. But what did she expect? Telling people exactly how she feels about them without even trying to get to know them first.

I'm more than just the tense, arrogant asshole she says I am. I hope you understand that. I hope you've seen that much already.

A Timber Razer raps his knuckles on the wood at the other end of the bar top to get my attention. I flip the bar mop in my hands over my left shoulder and head that way, trying to forget this last encounter. Trying not to stew in Luna's words. Because, even though I'm more than that person she said I was, she was also right. I am all of those things, too. I'm just not *only* those things.

Eight

Ryder

It's almost three in the morning. Tucked beneath several thick quilts in my bed upstairs in the cottage's loft, I lay awake. I'm thinking of you. Wondering how you've been, what you've been up to these past few days. It's been a while since I've felt you close.

Thursday, Friday, and Saturday came and went—nothing. Not even the whisper of your presence. I thought maybe I offended you somehow Wednesday night. Or that I scared you off. I was beginning to think you wanted nothing to do with me. That you closed the book on me and left me to stumble around on my own.

But here we are. Middle of the night. And I can feel you again.

Something that was once clenched tight in me lets go, and I feel my whole being unravel, the old bed springs groaning as I do. The creak of the bed mixes with the wind as it screams against the side of the cottage, drowning out Mom's sound machine from her room at the foot of the stairs that lead down from the loft I've used as a bedroom since Steph was born.

What are you thinking right now?

Would it be selfish to hope you're thinking of me? Wondering what kind of clothes I'm wearing—nothing but my plaid boxers, baby. Wondering what state my hair is in—blonde waves pulled into a loose knot on the crown of my head, strands beginning to unravel as I toss and turn in bed. Wondering if I want you here beside me?

The answer is yes.

Over and over again, yes.

I want you to find a way to slip into the book you're reading. Step onto the page, then through it and into my world. I want you here with me in the flesh, where I can see you, taste you, touch you. Wrap you up in my strong arms, crush your body against mine until our chests are flush, our hips are locked together, and the air I breathe is yours, the air you breathe is mine.

This heady desire is making me dizzy. It's making me feel things inside that heart of mine, beating in my rib cage, that I don't think I've ever felt with anyone else before. This intensity. This—this—passion that feels a little bit like—

No, I can't say that. Not yet. It's too soon. We both know it.

So, I'll just lay here, pretending I'm holding you, pretending you exist completely in my world for a little while longer.

A distant crack sounds outside as the wind turns fierce. It's probably a tree branch dropping into a neighbor's yard, splintering on impact, driving its wood deep into the muddy lawn. I perk my ears back and listen to the storm that's brewing. The beach right now is undoubtedly a battlefield of chaos. Hungry waves taking bites out of the dunes high up on the shore. Wind churning up the water as it's carried back into the belly of the sea. Driftwood tossed around, featherlight in the violent fists of the ocean that clutches it.

My digital clock flickers, along with the light from the streetlamp outside casting a golden beam through the window at the other end of the loft. The North Coast loses power regularly this time of year. Sometimes the outages are quick ten minute bouts, other times they last for days. This storm draws the saying to the front of my mind, not *if* but *when*.

I exhale fully as I wriggle down into the cushion of my old mattress. Distract me, will you? Until I fall asleep?

If you were here with me, you'd be temptation in the sheets. Heat flashing off of you, making my pulse quicken and my stomach swoop low. I might be able to lay here, unmoving, for a few seconds, but then one of my hands would slide up the notches of your spine to cup the base of your skull. I'd angle your head until it was in perfect alignment with my own, so that when I lean forward, our noses brush just before our lips. Maybe you gasp at the rabbit-soft touch. Maybe I groan because I've been imagining doing this to you for what feels like forever and I just can't believe it's finally happening.

At this point, I might get a little carried away. A soft kiss becomes a little rough, our mouths straining against one another's as we try and find a rhythm that is perfect for us. Once we do, I'd wrap you tighter in my arms, my hands stealing down your back, fingers grazing the smooth bare skin beneath your shirt. Peach fuzz and soft, supple planes. My hands would drift a little higher, my thumbs wrapping around your sides, caressing more of you.

FAYE DARLING

Your leg would slide up and over mine, our hips grinding a little into one another's, and you'd feel just how much I want to be here with you. But I'd pull away, our lips suddenly quivering, aching for each other's touch again.

"I want to go slow with you," I'd whisper, staring at your eyes glistening back at me in the dark. "Take my time."

Maybe you'd nod. Maybe you'd whisper something back, agreeing, contradicting. But I'd shift away from you slightly, then move toward you again so that only our lips touch, mine parting yours, my tongue exploring. Your hands on my bare chest. My fingers twisting through your hair. Heat builds between us, our lips a conduit for our passion, moving freely.

I won't want to, but I will. I'll slow us down. Soften our kisses until they're nothing but sweet pecks. My forehead will fall against yours when I've finally pulled away, my hand resting against the side of your face.

My eyes close, this fantasy of us becoming too much. The ache in my heart, in that sweet space between my thighs where I've grown hard—all of it, too much.

I drag my pillow up and over my face and groan into it. All this imagining has only made me want you more. Has only made me realize you're still so far away from me. Close—so, fucking close I swear I can smell your scent sometimes—but far.

There's a loud mechanical whir outside, followed by a distant electrical pop. I push the pillow away from my face and am greeted by a total black out.

Pulling back my sweat-soaked blankets, I climb out of bed. I'm still hard from all that imagined fooling around with you, so I take a steadying breath at the top of the stairs and try and prepare myself.

IN LOVE WITH YOU

I descend the steps. Just the thought that I'm about to check on my dying mother has everything returning to normal down there.

The door to her room is cracked open. Open more than I remember. I hear whispers inside. The hair on the back of my neck launches itself upright. My fists clench. Fire sparks to life in my veins.

Squealing hinges. A fist cocking back. I'm about to drive my knuckles through the skull of the silhouette standing over my mother's sick bed when a familiar voice hisses at me.

"Fuck, Ry, it's me."

Steph. It's only Steph.

I unclench my fist, but I wound myself so tight so fast, I'm still a coiled spring waiting to be set off.

"The hell are you doing here?" I whisper.

"Checking on Mom," she says. "Power went out."

"No dip, Sherlock. But you couldn't have gotten across town *that* fast."

"I slept in the front room."

"When'd you come in?"

"Just before midnight," she says. "You were asleep."

"Why?"

"Because the body needs sleep, Ryder."

"Not why was I asleep, smartass. Why did you decide to sleep over?"

Steph is quiet. Nothing more than a shadow checking Mom over. Should it concern us that, even though we can hear her breathing, Mom hasn't even so much as tried to open her eyes? She used to be the lightest of sleepers, starting at every little creak of the house in the night. After all of Steph's and my sharp whispering, Mom should be fully awake. Don't you think?

While Steph pulls the blankets up around Mom's chin and strokes her hair back from her forehead, I just stand there, staring at her dark form. Heart in my throat. Gut ripped out of its cavity. Floor creaking, like I'm standing on a trap door about to give out beneath my feet.

I swallow loudly right before Steph touches my arm, and we slip out of Mom's room and into the kitchen.

"Why did you sleep over?" I ask her again.

"It's my house, too," she says. "Do I need a reason?"

"No, but you'd put your big brother at ease if you gave him one."

"Do you have a girl upstairs?" Steph asks instead.

"What?" It's a good thing the power has gone out, otherwise Steph would see the blaze of red in my cheeks. "Why would you ask that?"

"I heard some...sounds," she says, taking on a sly, mocking tone.

Now I know there's no way she could have heard whatever sounds I imagined you making, but perhaps I didn't dream up my own little noises. Not all of them, at least. But if Steph thinks I was up there all alone, groaning and sighing, she'll either tell me I'm disgusting or will mock me relentlessly for the rest of my life. I don't even want to know what she'd say if I told her about you. How I can feel you even though I can't see you. How we've had this deep, soulful connection right from the get-go. Steph wouldn't understand. I mean, would people believe you if you told them the man you're reading about is falling in love with you?

Shit.

IN LOVE WITH YOU

I was going to wait to say it, because I didn't want to freak you out. But it's out now. I can't take it back, can I?

Love.

It's a big word. It can scare people, especially this early in, but how else do you explain the flutter I get in my chest every time I recognize your presence? How do explain the fact that I think about you almost every second of the day? And fantasy or not, I've never kissed anyone the way I imagined I would kiss you. It's always been sloppy and detached, a preamble to fucking. But with you? I don't know. It was different. Good. Right. Could you feel it, too?

So, yeah. I think I might be—sentence by sentence, page by page—falling in love with you. Is that crazy? It doesn't feel crazy. It makes my chest swell with warmth, like a hot air balloon taking flight.

"Why are you smiling?" Steph asks.

"I'm not smiling." But I am. My cheeks hurt I'm grinning so hard.

Steph scoffs. Crosses her arms sharply over her chest. "God, Ryder. Please don't tell me you're fucking women upstairs while our mother is dying down here. That would just be—"

"I'm not *fucking* women up there."

"Sure," she says, unconvinced. She backs herself into the archway that separates the kitchen from the living room. Stops. Like she's waiting for me to ask her a question. The same question I did before she changed the subject. Like she's ready to answer this time. Or thinks she is, at least. Steph is like a cat. You have to let her come to you.

"Why are you here tonight?" I ask, keeping all accusation out of my voice. "Really?"

FAYE DARLING

She bristles, but I know it's an act, because she sighs right afterward. Presses her spine into the three inches of sheetrock that make up the archway. Her chin tucks into her neck, her gaze on the floor at her feet.

Silence unspools between us, and we are adrift at sea, being pulled in opposite directions by a rip current. Just when I think we will be separated by too vast a distance, Steph produces an invisible rope. Casts it out in my direction. I grab hold of the end and let her drag me back toward her.

Steph's voice is small. It cracks as she whispers, "I just needed to be home tonight."

"Because of Mom?" I ask gently.

She shakes her head.

"Why, then?"

She shrugs.

"You can tell me," I say.

I barely hear her this time. "I needed to feel safe."

"Who is he?" I ask, trying not to completely shred the words on their way out of my mouth.

She sucks hard on her nose. "No."

"You don't have to protect him."

Steph pushes off from the archway and closes the distance between us, falling against me with a hollow *thump*. I can feel the dampness of her tears where her face presses against the top of my abdomen.

"It's not him I'm trying to protect," she says. "I can't lose you again. Not now."

My hand reaches up to pat her back, but she's already stepped away from me. I watch as she folds herself into the darkness of the house, making her way to her bedroom. The door clicks closed a second later, making it clear that's all the information I'm going to get out of her tonight.

I hover in the kitchen, listening to the sound of my own breathing roll in and out of me like the tide. My body is a mix of emotions. Happy, sad. Angry, elated. Confused, exhilarated.

My eyes grow heavy the longer I stand here. Sleep gnaws at my edges. I wait a few more seconds before I climb the stairs. Crawl back into bed. I fall asleep before I even have a chance to realize it's happening.

Nine

Luna

YOU SURE HAVE STAYED away, huh, reader?

Three days since I felt your nagging presence urging me to write you another book. We've had longer separations, though, haven't we? I think you just know when I need some space to think. To work. To create.

Or maybe you just don't like experiencing every mundane episode that is my life. Maybe you like to skip ahead to the critical points in my story. The way you're used to doing in books.

Whatever. I don't make the rules here. Do as you please, reader.

In case you're curious, it's Sunday afternoon. D.J. and I are crunched into a small booth in the back corner of a burger joint called Bun on the Run. It's quaint. 1950's vibes with a modern sheen. Turquoise and pearl-white checkered floors. Silver glitter specks in the red vinyl booths. *I Love Lucy* posters adorning light gray walls. Mini jukeboxes at every table. Waitresses in poodle skirts and roller skates. Busboys with paper soda jerk hats. A line trailing out the door, the sun beating down on heavy jackets and knit beanies. The sky is eggshell-blue, not a cloud in sight. It's hard to tell there was a storm last night that robbed the power for several hours.

"Don't give me that look," I say when I can't stand my cousin's face any longer.

"What look?" D.J. asks around a mouthful of fries.

I bite into my cheeseburger. "Like you're trying to read my thoughts."

"Well?"

"Well, what?"

"Look, I'm not going to tell you what you should do," he says. "But ever since you rejected my idea of using Ryder for book research, I can see you regretting it more every day."

I take a noisy swig of my Dr Pepper. "I don't regret it."

It's a lie, though. I haven't been able to get the idea of writing a novel about a quintessential North Coast man out of my head. Haven't been able to get Ryder out of my head. He's an asshole, sure. But that body. All hard muscle and tension packed into a plaid flannel that looks like it's been washed one too many times by the sea. And that face. Sharp edges and bright eyes, a softness lurking just beneath the rough surface of his features. Just the thought of him makes me shiver. There's a story coursing through that man's veins. I can feel it. I know it's there, within my grasp. But I can't bring myself to reach out and take hold of it.

Not after what I said to him.

Not after what he said to me.

FAYE DARLING

No one's been able to read me so clearly, to cut through that barbed façade I put on. But he did it. Did it without even trying, it seemed. And that scares me. Scares me more than calling my agent and telling her I don't have any pages to give her, not even a pitch.

I'll just have to find something else to write about. *Someone* else to write about. Maybe I'll have better luck packing up and heading back home. Find some boring old farmer in the dust and wheat of northwest Oklahoma and turn out a quick, easy romance the market will love.

But I can feel you shifting in your seat. Can feel you fidgeting as I think it. You don't want an easy romance. Not from me. You want a story you can get lost in. One that makes you forget you're reading about these characters. Makes you believe you're right there with them, tangled up in their sheets, in their lives.

I grumble around my straw as I chew it flat. It's paper, not plastic, so it collapses quickly, falls to pieces on my tongue. I end up swallowing a small chunk before I pull back. Glare at D.J.

"Even if I decided I wanted to use Ryder, I don't think he'd agree," I say.

A stupid half grin. A tilt of his head. Like D.J. knows something I don't. "I think he'd surprise you."

My gaze swoops toward the window, where a glimpse of the bay winks out across the highway at me. It's all blue glass black dots as fishermen troll the calm waters in their skiffs. I can still feel D.J. staring at me. He's relentless. I know him. He won't let this go. Maybe I need to put my big girl britches on and get on with it.

IN LOVE WITH YOU

Even if it means spending time with that truth-telling jerk of a man.

Oh, you like that idea, don't you, reader? Fine. Have it your way, then.

"When's his next shift?" I ask.

"I can get him there tonight," D.J. says, sounding a little too eager.

"Fine," I say dully.

Are you happy? I'm only doing this for you.

Fine, I'm doing this partially for you. Partially for D.J. And, okay, yeah. Since you've twisted my arm. I'm doing this partially because a question was asked the moment I ran into that man out in the surf and I fear if I don't find it's answer I will spend my whole life ruminating on it. Wondering. Waiting for it to appear in other ways. And who has time for that, really? Do you?

Yeah. Didn't think so.

Ten

Ryder

I'M TRAPPED WHERE I usually am on a Sunday afternoon: between Mom and Steph on the couch. Mom's legs are stretched across mine, her feet being rubbed by Steph, who is welded against my side. *Gilmore Girls* is on the TV. One of the early episodes we've all seen enough to be able to quote it verbatim.

Yes, I watch *Gilmore Girls*. With my closest family being my mom and sister, there was no way I could escape it. But I like it more than I care to admit. It's soothing. For the most part.

"Fucking kidding me," I mumble, eyes on the screen. Luke and Lorelai are in a fight. Both of them being idiots. Scared and screaming. "Just kiss her and shut up already."

"Don't like it when Mommy and Daddy are fighting, do we?" Steph teases. Mom's been in and out of sleep for two episodes now, otherwise she'd laugh. Nudge my shoulder with her knuckles. Be secretly pleased I'm so invested in her favorite show.

"No," I say harshly. "I don't."

Steph elbows me in the ribs. "It's just a show, Ry."

"I know."

"Mm-hmm," she says. "Sure."

My phone vibrates in my pocket. Steph jerks upright. Mom's eyes flash open for a quick, waking moment before flipping closed again. I answer without getting up. How could I? Steph's already burrowing back in like I'm the giant stuffed teddy bear she used to sleep with when she was a kid and Mom is belting me to the couch with her bony legs.

"Hello?"

"Hey, man," D.J. says on the other end of the phone.

"What's up?"

"Shh," Steph hisses.

"You shush," I whisper back.

"I know Sunday is your day off," D.J. says, "but Phil called in sick and everyone else is tied up. I'm desperate, here."

I pivot my cell so I can whisper to Steph without D.J. thinking I'm talking to him. "Will you be okay if I take a shift at the bar tonight?"

"Why wouldn't I be?" she says, not looking away from the television screen.

Our conversation from last night replays in my head. Her saying she was staying over because she wanted to be somewhere safe. Her telling me she couldn't lose me. I search her face for any sign of worry. Anything that will tell me to stay here on this couch, my mom and my sister right beside me where I can protect them.

FAYE DARLING

But Steph laughs at a joke Lorelai has made. Something about Danishes and coffee. Steph continues to rub Mom's feet.

I readjust the phone. Clear my throat. "I can cover Phil's shift, no problem."

"Thanks, man," D.J. says. "See you tonight."

"See you."

I'M WEDGING LIMES AT The Tavern a few hours after leaving Mom and Steph on the couch to finish another Sunday *Gilmore Girls* binge when I feel the energy of the room shift. I glance up just as Luna waltzes up to the bar. She's wearing a baggy mechanic's jumpsuit that somehow still manages to show off every one of her curves. The name *Jim* is stitched onto the left breast pocket with cherry red thread. Her hair is plaited into two boxer braids that roll back over her head like the roller coaster she is.

I try not to look at her full-on. For your sake, for my sake. I slice my lime wedges. Try to keep my shoulders loose, not rigid. Try to keep the arrogance off my face, although I'm not entirely sure how to do that. This is my face. It does whatever the hell it wants.

If only you could talk to me. Distract me. Do more than make my pulse race as you press closer, way too curious about this situation. That's not helping, baby.

Should I apologize to this woman? Tell her I didn't mean anything I said the other night? Not that it wasn't the truth. Not that it wasn't exactly what I thought about her. Should I apologize for being so harsh with the truth, then? Nah, that's a douche move, isn't it? A sorry not sorry kind of thing. Arrogant, even.

My knife plunks against the cutting board, the sharp scent of citrus released into the air. I imagine this is the way Florida would smell. Lime-soaked, sun-drenched. Heat and humidity, bikinis and body shots. I've always wanted to visit. Experience a warm beach instead of a cold one. Have you been there? Is it nice?

Why am I thinking about Florida all of the sudden?

My palms begin to sweat.

"I want to be clear." Luna hops onto a stool directly across from where I stand. She doesn't seem to care that the Timber Razer covered in tats and leather two stools down is currently devouring her with his eyes. My fingers instinctively tighten on the knife in my hand. "I do not have a crush on you."

"I uh—" I swallow. "I didn't think that you did."

I need to do something else. Something other than hold a sharp instrument. I set the knife down and reach for a clean shot glass, the open bottle of Jack.

"And I'm not flirting with you," she adds.

Tell me something, would you? Is she being confusing or is it just me?

I'm silent as I pour Luna a shot of Jack with my back turned. I am aware of my shoulders beginning to stiffen beneath my flannel. I will them to relax a bit.

Maybe she's *trying* to confuse me. People do that, don't they? Yeah, that must be it.

But why?

I spin slowly on the heel of my boot and ease the shot down onto the bar top next to her thumb, which is absently rubbing the drink order someone jotted down in permanent marker ages ago.

"I don't think you're flirting," I say. I don't know what she's doing, but whatever it is, it's the farthest thing from flirting I've ever witnessed.

"It's just book research." Luna throws back to the shot. Slams the glass down. "Nothing more."

"Oh-kay?" I say, closing my fist around the shot glass. I make no move to refill it. I don't make a move, period. I just stand there, eyebrows raised, gaze trailing over her face, searching for anything I might be missing from her words alone. But there's so much going on there, I can't figure it out before she speaks again.

"Okay," she says, like we've just spat into our hands and shook on an agreement. An agreement I'm still unsure about. Did she saunter over here just to make it clear she doesn't like me? Because I think she's made that pretty obvious. She nods her head, those braids swinging up and over her shoulders. "Glad we cleared that up. Now, tomorrow—"

"Hold on a minute."

"Why?"

"Why?" I repeat back. "You tell *me* why."

"Why what?"

"Why the hell are you talking about tomorrow? What's going on then?"

A set of knuckles raps on the bar two stools down. The biker who was trying to eye-fuck Luna wanting another Jack and Coke. I don't acknowledge him. He can wait a minute.

"I thought I made it clear?" she says. "Book research."

"Thought I was too arrogant for you?"

IN LOVE WITH YOU

I pick up the knife again. Turn the halved lime I abandoned into a pile of wedges. Funnel them into a plastic container with the rest.

"Just arrogant enough, I've decided," she says. "So, tomorrow—"

"No," I say.

"No, what?"

"Make me understand this a bit better," I say, reaching for another whole lime. "Why the change? You said some not-so-nice things about me, I said some not-so-nice things about you. Then you walked away. We haven't spoken in a week."

"Four days."

"Half a week then, smartass."

"Fine, where is this headed?"

"Half a week of silence and the first words out of your mouth are *I don't have a crush on you*?" The knife drops cleanly through the lime, spritzing the backs of my hands in juice. "What are we, thirteen? Check yes or no?"

"Check yes or no?"

"You know," I say. "When you were in middle school and you wanted to know if the person you liked had a crush on you, so you'd write them a note, asking, and they'd check the yes box if they did, the no box if they didn't."

"Check no," she says quickly, gruffly. She draws her legs up underneath her, sits up on her knees, and leans over the bar top. "Stop getting hung up on the minutiae of this whole proposition. The point is, I changed my mind. People can do that, you know. I've decided I want to do this."

"Do what exactly?"

FAYE DARLING

"Follow you around, take notes on the humdrum routine you call life, figure out what kind of story is lurking in the shadows of your world."

"You sound like a stalker," I say.

"Or a writer."

"If that's what you want to call it, sure."

"Hey," the Timber Razer I've tried to ignore barks. "Some of us are thirsty for more than pussy around here. Stop trying to feel her up with your words and get me another fucking drink."

There's something I've kept you in the dark on, baby. Something I feared would send you running the moment you found out. I don't know, maybe you've guessed. Listened to what my sister has said, watched my memories betray me in front of you. Maybe you've already drawn your own conclusions. But I gotta come clean. Tell it straight. Right now.

About five years ago, the man my sister was seeing started getting rough with her in the local dive bar in West Cove. I was there with my friend Nick, keeping an eye on Steph from across the room the way I always used to. I glanced at them once and they were both laughing, but when I glanced again, they were on their feet, faces constructed of nothing but rage. Then she pushed him back when he tried to pin her against the wall, spit spewing from his lips. I was already on my feet, Nick trying to hold me back, get me to calm down, when Steph's boyfriend clenched his fist around her throat. Backhanded her in front of everyone.

Nick let go of me real quick after that, and everyone in the bar parted around me like they were river water and I was a big, motherfucking rock in the middle of the stream.

IN LOVE WITH YOU

I don't remember much about what happened next. But I do remember taking a fistful of that asshole's hair and using it to drive his pretty face into a low ball glass on a nearby table. I blacked out completely after that. Came to with shards of glass in my knuckles, blood sprayed across the t-shirt I had on under my flannel, cops cuffing me.

Don't worry, baby. I didn't kill the guy. He survived. Barely. But he pressed charges.

I spent a little over eighteen months in prison. I got out earlier than I should have for good behavior and because I gave my word that I wouldn't lay a hand on anyone else again...unless I wanted to land back behind bars.

So, there you have it.

My big, dark secret laid bare.

Are you terrified of me now? Ashamed? Is your stomach churning like the sea in a violent storm, bringing every bit of filth and murk to the surface?

I won't blame you if you close this book right now. If you lay it down and forget about me. Forget about what we've had these past few days. It's not what I want you to do, not at all. But I would understand, I think. With time. I would understand with time.

I can feel that you're still here, though. Still hanging with me. I'd smile right now if that Timber Razer demanding his drink hadn't stolen every ounce of joy I have inside me. I'm grateful to D.J. for hiring me when no one else would, don't get me wrong, but to say I'm not constantly pushed to the limits by his bar full of hardened bikers is an understatement.

My fist is welded around the knife in my hand, my eyes trained on the split-open lime on the cutting board beside the blade.

FAYE DARLING

"You fucking slow, boy?" The Timber Razer asks, flicking his glass across the bar. It slips over the edge, and I reach out to catch it before it can break over a caddy full of clean pint glasses. "Pour the damn whiskey."

I glower at the man, my eyes daring his to meet mine. But his lids are heavy with drink, his gaze loose and all over the place.

"Think you've had enough," I say, slow and in control. I've still got the knife gripped in my hand, too afraid to let it go. Too afraid to use it, either.

I can only see Luna from the corner of my vision—a blurry form—but I feel her watching me intently the same as you. Interest piqued. Breath bated, awaiting the fallout. With you, though, I know you're at a safe distance, off the page, literally and figuratively. With Luna, however, I am very much aware of where she is in relation to me. To the potential swing of my fist. If this thing goes south, if it comes to it, I don't want her to be a casualty of my temper.

"Just pour," the Timber Razer says, putting a hand to the pocket of his leather vest. Maybe it's an act. But maybe he's got a weapon stashed there. Switchblade, pistol. Hard to tell beneath the heft of his sausage fingers.

Now, I can predict where the sweep of my rage might extend, but there's no telling where this drunken asshole's might. Plastered or not, the fight's not worth it.

But I'm not a pushover, either. Not some biker's bitch.

"Make you a deal," I say. "I'll pour you another, on the house, then you find a place to sit that is as far away from this bar top as you can manage."

"Make it a double then," he says.

"Gladly."

IN LOVE WITH YOU

I finally let go of the knife, filling the man's glass from the well and handing it back with a tense look. He takes the drink, gets to his feet, and clocks Luna up and down. He scoffs. "Doesn't seem like she'd be the type to put out anyway."

A growl manifests low in my chest, and my eyes narrow to the thinnest slits they can manage. I wait until he's a few wobbling steps away before I turn and look at Luna.

I don't know what I expect from her. A blush to be painted across the tops of her cheeks. An angry twist to be stamped on her features. A forced, husky laugh escaping her lips, maybe.

Whatever I expected it's not this.

She's bent over that small red notebook I saw four nights ago, scribbling. Her tongue peeks out of her full lips, eyes alight and distant. Like what that asshole said didn't seem to faze her. Like she didn't hear him at all.

"Doesn't that bother you?" I ask, because fuck me, I'm a little bit more than curious. I react if someone breathes too close to me and she doesn't even seem to care when a man makes an obscene comment directly to her.

"Just a sec," she says, pencil flying across the page.

I watch her cheeks fall into a deep scowl, a line bisecting the middle of her forehead. I have the urge to reach out and trace that puckered line of skin with my fingertip. But the line is gone in an instant, expression placid once more before her mouth moves around near-silent words. Her eyes narrow as drastically as mine had a minute ago.

"Are you...recreating my conversation with that asshole?" I ask.

"What was it he said at the end?" she asks. "Doesn't look like she'd be much fun?"

"Doesn't look like she'd put out," I say, then shake my head. What am I doing? "Does that kind of shit not bother you?"

"What shit?" she asks, scribbling for a few more seconds before she closes the notebook, slides the pencil back through the spiral at the top, and tucks it in the back pocket of her jumpsuit.

"What he said to you," I say. "Doesn't that bother you? And the way guys look at you."

"The way guys look at me?" She tilts her head to the side, one braid falling over the slender column of her neck.

"You know what I mean."

"I do?"

"Stop that."

"Stop what?"

"Repeating everything back to me in question form," I say. "Be serious for a second. That guy on Wednesday night who copped a feel—didn't that bother you? Just a little bit?"

She smirks, leans back and traces me with her eyes. From the upper curve of my topknot to the scruff on my chin to the tattoo on the inside of my wrist. The infinity symbol that matches Mom's and Steph's. I turn my arm slightly so she is forced to look elsewhere. "You care a lot about what people think about you, huh?"

"What?" I ask, too dumbfounded at first to answer her. "No. Couldn't care less."

"Really, though," she says.

I shrug. "I don't know."

Honestly? I've never thought about it before. Growing up, I was never the popular kind of guy. Instead of captaining the football team, I smoked pot under the bleachers on Friday nights with Mark. Instead of trying to fit in, I tried to stand out. Ditched school to surf. Chased the girls who had reputations instead of prospects. Punched first asked questions later. I cared about my friends and my family—the people who actually mattered—and to hell with the rest of the world. I always thought I was the kind of guy who didn't give two fucks about anything, especially being liked.

But maybe acting like I don't care is a way to hide the fact that I do care. That I care a lot. Do you think that's what she's trying to get me to admit? I've never thought of it that way before, but...I don't know. This chick is messing with my head again. Looking through me in a way that makes me want to bolt. Run straight out the door. Jump in my Camaro and drive until I forget what she's said.

I take up the knife again. Finish wedging the lime. "Say I care a lot about what other people think?"

"Say you do."

"What's it to you?"

She lifts one shoulder. "Just trying to figure you out."

"For book research?"

"Yeah," she says, pausing briefly to swallow. "For book research."

I scoop the lime wedges up with the blade of the knife and shuffle them into the container with the rest. I wave the knife through the air once before reaching for the last whole lime. "I'm not saying I'll do it, but if I did, what would it entail?"

"Book research?"

"Yeah," I say. "Apart from you stalking me."

"I need to make this clear." She steeples her fingers and lays her arms down on the bar. "I write romance novels, but during book research I do not partake in romantic notions. I do not like you. I will not like you. This is a professional, business transaction."

"Transaction?" I ask, swallowing down the multitude of questions clawing their way to the surface about why she doesn't seem to flinch when a stranger gropes her ass but she has to tell me repeatedly how much she does not and will not like me. I'd be offended if the idea of you wasn't the undercurrent of my every thought. Where you are right now in space and time. What dreams you have for your life. What sounds you would make if I kissed a path down your neck, the slope of your chest. What it would feel like to touch your bare skin.

"I'll compensate you for your time," Luna says, dragging me out of my daydream of you.

"How so?"

"Two-fifty a day, full access."

"Two-hundred-and-fifty dollars?"

"No, llamas," she says with a huff. "Yes, Ryder. Dollars, greenback, cash-a-mola."

The knife in my hand slips and the lime sails off the counter. Rolls into that dark, sticky place beneath the shelving under the bar top. I gawp at Luna. Open mouth. Eyes pried wide. What kind of writer pays their research subjects that much per day? I'm not going to lie, my family needs the money. Mom hasn't been able to work since before her diagnosis and, with my record and daily caregiving, I can't find anything steadier than this. Steph has been picking up the slack, but she's got her own bills to take care of. I do some fast math. Just a week being the subject of Luna's book research would set us straight for the next month.

IN LOVE WITH YOU

Luna rolls her eyes dramatically. "This is the part where you pick your jaw up off of the floor and ask me what full access entails."

I blink away the brain fog. "Right."

"Fuck me," Luna mutters under her breath before she clears her throat. "Ideally, I'd like to shadow you for a few days. Real fly-on-the wall shit. You go about your daily routines and I...watch. Once I get a feel for who you are and what you do, I'll probably ask a million questions, have you teach me a few things if I need the mechanical understanding of, say, tasks you perform that I'm unfamiliar with."

"What kinds of tasks?" I ask.

"I don't know," she says, annoyed suddenly. "The last time I did this was with an olive farmer in Greece who drove a moped around his island. I had him teach me how to drive the thing, change the oil, fill up the gas tank. Shit you think is stupid and mundane I might find essential to the character I'm creating."

"So, like, bartending?"

"I know how to mix drinks." Luna waves a hand through the air like I've just said the most idiotic thing on the planet. "D.J. says you backpack a lot."

"Yeah."

"You know how to light a camp stove?"

"Of course."

"I don't," she says. "Do you understand the rules of the game now?"

"Last week, out in the surf, you said the last thing you wanted was a surf lesson from me," I say. "Now, you want me to teach you how to light camp stoves and, what, split wood?"

FAYE DARLING

"I know *how* to surf, I'm just not good at it yet," she says. "And splitting wood is exactly what I want to know how to do. But not just the mechanics. How you learned to do it. What goes through your head. How you obtain the wood. What type of wood is best for the kind of fire you want. How *you* start your fires. What do you do if that all goes to shit."

"That sounds—" I stop talking, swallowing down the last of my sentence. If this chick is willing to pay me enough money to take care of my family for a little while, then I don't want to piss her off the way I did on Wednesday and have her find someone else. Even though I'm sure she's already tried to find someone and failed if she's circled back to me.

"What?" she asks, a challenge in her voice.

"Nothing."

"Say it."

"Nah."

"Look, I don't want to do this with someone who's going to hide what they're thinking from me," Luna says. "If I'm going to invest in you, all I ask is that you're honest with me, even if you think it'll make me mad or make you look like an ass."

I sigh. "It just sounds so boring, is all."

She stares at me, her expression blank and unreadable. Her amber eyes are a shade darker tonight, like the shards of stone have been placed in a lightless cupboard, just a sliver of candle flame saturating them. I hold her gaze for a moment. Maybe a moment too long for your liking, but I cannot deny that Luna is a mesmerizing creature. You can see that, can't you?

It's Luna who breaks our eye contact first. She looks to the empty shot glass she slammed onto the bar top earlier. She picks it up. Moves it toward me. A silent request.

I reach for the bottle of Jack, obliging.

"Did D.J. tell you anything about me? My writing specifically?"

"He said a few things on Friday when I was working," I say, trying to recall his words as I slide the full shot glass to her. "You're good at what you do. Better than you'd ever admit."

She tips the glass slowly, letting the smooth liquor run all the way down her tongue, feeling the burn until the whiskey runs dry. She sets the empty glass back down on the bar, and there are those eyes again.

"Flannery O'Connor said anyone who survived childhood has enough material to write for the rest of their lives," she says. I nod, even though I don't know who she's talking about. Do you? "But I say writers have to continue to seek out new material. They first must live in order to write characters and stories that feel like they're also alive.

"A lot of people would disagree with me," she continues. "But, then again, those people haven't written the kind of books that I have. I've traveled the world, folded myself into culture after culture while they've sat at home, watching television or reading other books for inspiration. I've hunted down my inspiration while they've waited idly for theirs.

"So, yeah, Ryder, asking you a million questions about a seemingly mundane task might seem boring to you, but it's a part of my process. It's a layer that gives my stories and my characters depth. Stories don't simply exist as words on the page, they exist in the spaces between those words as well. Like a ghost lingering, unseen, in the corner of a house. It's essentially invisible, but it still changes the way people perceive that house, don't you think?"

FAYE DARLING

I reach out and take her empty shot glass. Fill it to the brim. Knock it back for myself. The burn punches the back of my throat and I hiss as I swallow it down.

Luna laughs. Just once. I think it's the first time I've heard her laugh, and the sound lands sweetly on my ears. She slips off of the stool, tapping the bar top between us.

"You surfing tomorrow morning?" she asks.

"Dawn patrol, yeah," I say.

"We'll start then," she says, and before I can agree or set my own conditions, she's slinking back toward the stairs that lead to D.J.'s apartment, leaving me to wonder what the hell I've just gotten myself into.

Eleven

Luna

OKAY, READER. YOU WIN.

The book you've been waiting for is officially in the works.

Sure, you won't read it for another year or two at least, but I know you can feel it building—that kinetic spark in the air, lightning yawning to life in the middle of a thunderstorm—and it sends a zip of excitement up your spine. Doesn't it?

Right now, the book is just a mood. No plot, no characters. Pure, raw feeling.

Hopefully, a few days with Ryder will change that. After a week, two at most, I plan to hop on a plane, get back to the little hunting shack I live in back in Oklahoma, and write as quickly as my fingers will type. I'll please my agent, my publisher, you, and maybe even myself.

The longboard I found in my cousin's shed belonged to my uncle. Before he traded the haphazard wilds of the Oregon Coast for the urban jungle of Manhattan, where D.J.'

s mom was from, that is. They left almost as soon as D.J. graduated high school. Never wanted The Tavern when it was offered to them. Haven't returned since. I stare at the board, leaning against a massive fir tree growing between a few weather-washed picnic tables above the sand and surf. I can't imagine leaving home and never returning. Even though I hated Oklahoma growing up, I still find my way back there eventually, no matter how long I spend away. Home is nothing but the end of a tether. You can't escape it, no matter how hard you try. I wonder when Uncle Deke's tether will be tugged and he will come crashing back into The Tavern.

"Local spot, babe," some guy shouts, bringing me out of my head.

Does it not bother you? The question Ryder posed last night hangs in the calm, early-morning air. It settles into the chill, and that chill settles around the bare skin of my arms poking through the short sleeves of my wetsuit. There are things in this world that bother me more than assholes being assholes. Pick your battles and all that.

But sometimes. Sometimes, I just can't help myself.

"I had no idea," I say, an air of bullshit to it all. I keep my eyes on my surfboard, following the thick blue lines that run from stem to stern.

"Of course you didn't," the guy says. "None of you day-trippers ever have a clue how things work around here."

"No, I meant I had no idea I was so intimidating."

My head swings toward the asshole. Short, stocky, jittering at the edges. Like he's just drunk too much coffee. He's not alone. Standing a head above him, a smirk stamped on his stubbled cheeks, is Ryder. Ocean eyes and a leathery personality. Who would miss him? I recognize the asshole now as his buddy. The one who kept shouting that they had to leave last week. Another man—just as handsome as Ryder, but much more clean-cut—lingers a few feet away, hidden in the morning shadows of the forest. Both Ryder and Mr. Clean-Cut look like they're trying not to grin.

"What?" the jittery guy says, brows smashing into one another just above the bridge of his chunky nose. The perfect mix of angered and bewildered.

"Tell me." I stand up. Pivot so my body is squared to his.

"Tell you what?" he spits.

I cock my head to the side. "How small are your balls?"

"What?" More angered than bewildered this time.

"If a woman like me intimidates a guy like you, then how small are your balls?" I drop my gaze pointedly. Look right at his crotch. His wetsuit reveals the truth—well-endowed—but I can't help myself. I pull my lips into a tight bundle and push them to one side. "We talking grapes or peanuts here?"

His ears are the first thing to turn red, then the rest of him. From anger or embarrassment it's hard to tell. Either way, it makes Ryder laugh. Hard. I lift my gaze from his friend and find, for a brief flash, that rough exterior of Ryder's is momentarily smoothed over. There's a glint in his eyes. A soft, easy-going quality to his big frame. My stomach does a backflip. My heart is a hammer in my chest. I bite down on my lower lip to hide a smile and refocus on his friend.

"They're bigger than grapes," he says, shifting his surfboard in front of his waist.

"You got proof?" I ask, and his nostrils flare wide, like I've flipped a lever on his internal switchboard and he's .02 seconds away from spontaneously combusting.

Ryder seems to sense this, and that easy-going demeanor is zapped out. Replaced by ridges and tension and a sliver of angst. His friend barely flinches forward and Ryder steps around him. Presses his knuckles lightly to the top of his friend's right peck. "Chill out, Mark. This is D.J.'s cousin, Luna. She's just busting your balls a bit."

"Literally," Mr. Clean-Cut says as he smiles at me. A behemoth hand, smattered in tattoos, snakes through the gaps between Ryder and Mark as he reaches out to shake. I slip my palm into his, noting the warm, smooth quality of his light brown skin. I feel instantly at ease in his presence. "Nick Forester."

"Luna," I say, then turn toward Mark as he levels me with a glare. "I'm not trying to infiltrate the inner circle or whatever. Ryder is just helping me out with a project."

"Is he?" Mark asks drily.

"I am," Ryder says. "She's a writer."

"She's not a journalist, is she?" Mark asks, narrowing his eyes.

I scoff. "*Not* a journalist."

"Mark doesn't trust the media," Nick says.

"And she's D.J.'s cousin?" Mark asks, ignoring Nick completely.

"The one and only," I say.

"All right." Mark nods once. Strums his fingers over his surfboard. He tilts his head and looks up at me beneath his thick lashes. "Just don't drop in on me and we'll be cool."

Before I can say anything, he's jogging toward the water, his warning lingering in the air.

"He's not always an asshole," Nick says, shaking his head at Mark's retreating figure.

"Assholes make the world more interesting," I say.

"Fodder for your stories?"

"Exactly."

We pick our way down to the sand, clambering over a series of large, flat stones built up from the beach to the overlook that act as a staircase. At the edge of the water, Nick straps the leash of his board to his ankle and heads into the surf, leaving Ryder and me alone.

Ryder looks past me to the north shoulder of trees that keeps the cove protected, then to the mare tail clouds dyed the color of raw salmon that hang overhead. It gives me the opportunity to take him in at close proximity in the daylight. The bridge of his nose is thin and crooked. A stripe of silver skin cuts his right eyebrow in half. Both of those details could be explained by a number of things, but I'd bet they're byproducts of a fistfight. He has a tiny constellation of freckles beneath both eyes, though they're faint. You really have to be looking for them. His stubble isn't a sandy blonde like his long hair, which is free and waving in the breeze. His facial hair has a slight red tinge to it. Strawberries in lemonade.

"So," Ryder drawls as his eyes land on mine.

Heat seeps into my cheeks, though I don't know why. I've done this countless times—study men up-close for book research—and have never once felt like this. It reminds me too much of high school. Staring painfully across the biology lab. Will Jacobs all cute-faced and hunched over his lab notes, shiny black hair falling into his obsidian eyes. My body, a mess of out-of-whack hormones and too much daydreaming. And if he'd ever so much as glance my way? A blush, spreading from the tops of my ears to the tops of my breasts, would bloom on my skin. Sweaty palms, unsyncopated heartbeat.

"So," I repeat back to Ryder as I dip down to strap on my leash.

Ryder laughs once behind closed lips, then squats down at my feet. His fingers brush against the back of my hand as he takes hold of the leash, undoing it. My heart is a hammer again. It pounds a series of nails up my throat, making it painful to breathe.

"What?" I ask when he doesn't explain why he's moving the leash to my other ankle.

"I think you ride goofy."

"You ride goofy," I snap.

That laugh again, this time less amused, breathier. He squints up at me from his crouched position. A breeze blows a few strands of his hair against my fingertips. I have the urge to rake my hand through it.

"When you have your left foot back on the board, not the right, it's called riding goofy," he says. "I've been watching you and, I think you've been trying to ride regular when you should be goofy."

I've been watching you.

I mean, you heard him say that, right? It wasn't just a fabrication of my own mind? That's usually my job. To watch people. And if someone is watching me, I tend to notice, because, oh, yeah, that's right, I'm watching them already.

I've been watching you.

Do you think he meant it? Do you think Ryder has slipped into a blind spot I was unaware I had?

"How can you be so sure I ride goofy?" I ask.

Ryder stands—a tidal wave building high above my head—and shoves my shoulders just hard enough to make me wobble backward. Instinctively, I put a foot back. My left foot.

"See?" he says.

I stare down at my legs, scissored above the sand.

"Huh," I say. Even though I'm still standing on the shore, I already feel more stable in this new position. I wonder what other positions Ryder could put me in to illicit this same stability in me? Dirty images flash through my mind. The two of us on just one surfboard, naked. The two of us backed against a tree, naked. The two of us rolling around in the sand...naked.

"Do you need me to do anything else before we...before?" Ryder asks. "For your research?"

"No," I say, then clear my throat. Collect myself. *Remember* myself. "Just...get in the water."

"That easy?"

"Yep," I say. "It's that easy."

And it is.

He surfs the way I imagine he always does, joking with the guys out in the water the same as if I wasn't here.

Except I am.

Even though I keep my distance, watching the scene as if through a wide-angled lens, every time Ryder catches a glimpse of me, there's a ripple of realization that rolls through him. Like a shock to his system. His entire body constricts. The fine features of his face—lips, nose, eyes—pull taut. Concentrating too hard. Aware of himself too much. In those moments, I lose sight of him and whatever ember-spark of inspiration I had been gleaning from him. Then, he catches another wave, body loose, a pepper-dash of a smile on his face, and he relaxes again. Forgets about me bobbing in the swell a few yards away. For a little while, at least. Then, his head twitches in my direction. Brick and mortar. Harsh lines and distance.

Now, don't start thinking this type of ebb and flow isn't working for me. Every research subject I've followed has come with some complication. That's why I choose this kind of process. I love the writing, don't get me wrong. You must sense that I do each time you crack the spine on one of my books, right? But I love the research just as much. Not everyone should write a book, in my opinion, but I believe every single person on the planet has a story worthy of being told. I have an inkling, a feeling swirling in the underbelly of my soul, that Ryder's story is very much worthy of being told.

Twelve

Ryder

I'M STARTING TO THINK this was a bad idea.

And I'm not just talking about me driving Luna's truck home from the surf break while she takes notes in the passenger seat. Because it definitely is. This old pickup feels like it could fall apart any minute. The whole thing shakes any time the highway pitches uphill and the clutch sticks every time I change gear. But, no, that's not the only bad idea.

I'm nervous.

Can you feel my stuttering pulse through these pages? Like a fucking speedway on race day.

Here's the thing. Luna joining a surf sesh? No biggie. Watching me tend bar at The Tavern? Whatever. But as we climb the steps to the front porch of my family's cottage, I come to the full realization that I haven't thought this through. Not at all. With Mom being sick and Steph having turned into a walking mystery over the past week, it's all such…a bad idea.

FAYE DARLING

Don't you agree? But Luna is breathing at my back, smelling like salt and a bit like the neoprene wetsuit she shed in the parking lot before we climbed in the truck, and I can't stop thinking that she's here in the flesh. And unlike you, she makes me pretty damn uncomfortable ninety-five-percent of the time.

My hand hovers over the doorknob. "I have to warn you—"

"You don't have a creepy porcelain doll collection waiting on the other side of this door, do you?" Luna asks.

"What? No."

"Good, because I researched this family in Connecticut once who were obsessed with dolls," she says. "I swear those dolls were possessed. Somehow, their eyes were always looking right at me. Or they'd be in one room, then suddenly appear in another. Once, an entire shelf of them flung themselves onto the ground, like they were trying to commit group suicide or something, and who would blame them? I mean—"

"Shut up a minute, would you?" I say.

Luna draws her lips in. Seems to hold back a laugh, amused by my gruff interruption, which only makes me more nervous. If she'd gotten pissed instead, I might have been able to escape this. Now she's quiet. Quiet and staring up at me with those amber eyes like she's waiting for me to say something.

What should I do? Tell her to leave? Tell her I'll meet her at The Tavern later? Tell her that full-access actually ends on this side of the door?

Or should I tell her the truth?

Ugh.

You're not being helpful, baby. All I can feel is you wondering. Wondering what the hell is going to happen next, like this is my story. Like I'm meant to decide. Not you.

I inhale through my nose. Hold my breath. I remind myself of the money and how badly we need it.

"My mom is sick," I say quickly, not sure where to begin. "Cancer. My sister and I—we take care of her. I probably should have said something before, but—"

The door swings open and Steph appears on the other side. One arm in her purple coat. Eyes as sharp as a boning knife, carving right into me. She's got her mouth open, about to chastise me for being late again, but then she sees Luna, and in a fraction of a second my sister's entire demeanor changes. Her knife eyes go dull. Her other arm finds its way gracefully into her coat. She smiles. She actually fucking smiles. I don't know the last time I saw Steph do that. Maybe never.

"Steph, this is—"

Steph cuts me off. "You're Luna Preston."

"Normally I'd deny it, but seeing as you're...Ryder's sister?" Luna says, taking a stab at Steph's connection to me. When Steph nods, Luna continues. "I'll admit that I am in fact Luna Preston. Well, not actually Preston. My dad would kill me if I wrote steamy romance novels under my real last name. Old Baptist preacher, tight moral compass. Would probably rather see me taken before my time than fess up to the fact that his only daughter writes books with the word fuck in them, forget the graphic sex scenes altogether."

Steph chortles, then snorts like she's a second grader and someone just made a fart joke. I can't help but feel like I'm missing something.

"Are you dating my brother or something?" Steph asks.

"God no," Luna says. A little too quickly. A little too loudly. Her admission sits heavy on my shoulders. I don't know why.

It shouldn't. Especially when I can feel you curled up in the shadows, melting into my world as you escape your own.

"I've read all of your books, like, a thousand times," Steph says, her chortle turning into fangirl giggles.

Maybe I should have looked Luna up online. Or raided Steph's bookshelf, apparently.

"Aren't you late for work?" I ask Steph.

She holds her index finger up, hushing me. She leans into the doorframe, looking as chill as Steph could ever manage, before asking Luna, "What are you doing here, then? At our house? In this itty bitty hiccup of a town?"

"Ooh, I like that," Luna says. "Hiccup of a town. Do you write?"

"I've always wanted to."

"You have?" I question.

Steph kicks me in the shin, and I try to disguise my wince.

"I'm a nurse," Steph says. "Just like Annabeth in *Kingdom Fire.*"

I assume that's the title of a book. One of Luna's books, perhaps? Kind of a cheesy name, if you ask me, but no one has, so I keep quiet. Do you think they would notice if you and I slipped away? Did some imagined canoodling in the bushes out back?

"My grandmother was a nurse," Luna says. "A noble profession, I've always said."

"A noble profession you're late for," I tell Steph.

"I'm not *that* late," Steph says. But she stands up from her position against the doorway and steps past Luna and me. "You never said why you were here."

"Book research," Luna says.

IN LOVE WITH YOU

Steph jabs at the air between us with the tip of her nose. "*He* is worthy of book research?"

Luna looks me over, from the mess of damp waves I call hair to my borderline-purple toes poking through my beach slides. She shrugs back at my sister. "We'll see."

We'll see. Like she has anyone else in mind.

"Bye, Steph," I say.

She rolls her eyes. "Later loser."

Luna and I watch Steph putter away in her little beater.

"Is she older or younger than you?" Luna asks.

"Younger," I say. "Two years and change."

"You guys close?"

I shrug one shoulder.

Luna purses her lips and mimics my movement. "What's that mean?"

"We've been through a lot together," I say. "So, yeah, we're close. I'd take a bullet for her, kill for her, go to jail for her."

"So, you're protective of Steph."

"I'm protective of a lot of people."

"That much I've gathered."

"What else have you gathered?" I smirk down at her. The longer we stand on the porch, the longer I can put off Luna coming face-to-face with my reality. Will she pity me? Will seeing Mom make her uncomfortable to the point she suddenly has to leave? I don't know which one is worse.

"No," she says.

"No, what? No you won't tell me or no you haven't learned anything else about me?"

"The first," she says, then clears her throat. "You said your mom was sick?"

FAYE DARLING

It takes me a few beats to follow the sharp turn in conversation. I blink at her. Start nodding and nodding, like a stupid bobblehead on a truck driver's dash. "Yeah. I'm sorry. I should have told you bef—"

"Don't apologize." Her small hand cups my elbow. Her touch is so light I can barely feel it through my weighty flannel. It still manages to coax chills to the surface of my skin. They fan out from our point of contact, spreading throughout my entire body like overgrown ivy. *Is that your heart beating faster or mine?*

She takes a half step toward the door, fingertips resting on the wind-blown wood. The hinges groan as she pushes the door open another inch. A view to the red brick hearth surrounding the woodburning stove. Black spots on the carpet where embers have, on occasion, jumped the grate. The hinges groan again as she pushes the door wider, glimpsing the leather loveseat beside a lamp that glows orange—the only source of light in the living room.

I remain frozen on the porch, unsure.

Why is it so hard to invite her inside? Why are we still standing out here, staring into the cottage instead of stepping into its warmth? It was so easy to let you in—as easy as taking in air—but why is letting Luna in seeming to be so difficult?

Mom calls out from her bedroom. Just a faint squeak, but I catch it. Something's wrong.

"Excuse me," I whisper, pushing past Luna. I leave her there in the doorway, deciding she can let herself in. She will eventually, I assume. She's paid for full-access, right?

A pot of freshly brewed coffee catches in my nose as I troll through the kitchen, but the smell is snuffed out the moment I push Mom's door open. She's crying. Or trying to at least.

IN LOVE WITH YOU

Her once-soft features are twisted into harsh lines and bulges. She mumbles something that sounds like sorry, but I can't be sure. The stench is ripe. Urine. I pull back the covers to find a growing wet stain, a dark ochre color, seeping out in all directions from under Mom's nightgown. She mumbles that word again, and she can't look at me.

"It's okay," I tell her, kissing the top of her forehead. "You're okay."

A floorboard creaks in the kitchen. I catch a flash of Luna, amber eyes staring at me, at Mom. She blinks several times, but doesn't have the decency to turn away. I stride to the door, not breaking eye contact, and give it a harsh shove. The latch catches with a loud *click*.

I stand there with a palm pressed to the face of the door, breathing and trying to decide if I want to tell Luna to get the fuck out of the house or ask her to step inside the room with me just so I don't have to be alone right now.

But I'm not alone, am I? I feel you here with me.

Thank you.

I inhale as deeply as I can manage in the wake of the odor building in this place and feel your presence twist closer, wrapping around me so gently.

Thank you.

Thirteen

Ryder

I GET MOM INTO a warm bath straightaway, then toss her soiled clothes and bedding into the washer as she soaks. Afterward, I settle Mom onto the couch, build a roaring fire, and turn on *Gilmore Girls*.

"Hey," I snap as soon as the next episode in the queue appears on screen. "You and Steph watched a full season without me?"

Not that I don't know every episode backwards and forwards.

Okay, I guess I must be comfortable if I'm saying that to you. Very, very comfortable. And not at all worried about losing my man card.

I look at Mom questioningly. She grumbles something that sounds like *I don't know* and avoids eye contact. I narrow my gaze. I have half a mind to back the show up. Mom probably was in and out of sleep when she and Steph binged it yesterday. But they stopped at the beginning of one of my favorite episodes. The one where the town hosts the twenty-four-hour dance marathon and Lorelai coerces Rory into being her partner.

"I'll let it slide this time." I set the remote down on the coffee table and turn toward the couch, about to nestle in under Mom's skinny legs.

That's when I see her.

Luna.

What the hell is she doing out there?

Through the sheer curtains covering the front windows, I catch her small curvy form circling my Camaro like a vulture. Bending to look at the tarnished chrome wheels. Standing high on her tiptoes to gawp at the roof. It's not until Mom grumbles that I realize I've been leaning over her on the couch and blocking her view of the TV.

"Sorry." I take a step back.

I had shut the bedroom door quick enough earlier that Mom didn't notice Luna, and she was gone when I carried Mom into the bathroom. This was another thing I was nervous about. Introducing Luna to Mom. When Mom was first diagnosed it felt like our house was a revolving door, friends and neighbors streaming in and out constantly. Quick chats. Long cries. Hot meals. Small favors. Slowly, the visitors began to dwindle. It's rare if anyone stops by these days, and if they do it's usually Mom's closest friends. Those people understand that Mom wasn't always like this. Skin and bone, garbled speech and depreciated energy. They remember how hard she could laugh, even if it was only at herself. They remember how she could pull the truth out of a person with a certain tilt of her head, a look in her glassy eyes. They remember her smile and her hugs and her stories and her wise philosophies. They remember, and so she doesn't have to be embarrassed about who she has become. But Luna is new. She doesn't know who Mom was, and I don't know how Mom will handle that—only being seen as this fragmented version of herself.

Honestly, I don't know how I will handle it.

What if Luna acts strange around Mom? What if she is noticeably uncomfortable or treats her like a child? What if she looks at Mom and laughs?

"What's it?" Mom says slowly, trying hard to push the right words out. Her eyes tick toward the window, where mine have been trained throughout the entirety of the *Gilmore Girls* theme song.

"I'm helping out a friend," I say, even though I'm not sure Luna and I are friends. Not sure we ever will be. "She's D.J.'s cousin, actually. A big time writer. She wants to follow me around for some kind of book research." Mom quirks a brow. "She's paying me a lot of money." Mom nods, understanding. "She's outside right now."

With her good hand, Mom slaps my shoulder. It's a strong slap, too. The kind that stings. I half-laugh, half-wince. She nods to the window.

"G-er," she mumbles. *Get her.* Mom plays at shivering. "Co. Brr."

"Are you sure?"

Mom fakes like she's going to slap me again, and I flinch. She laughs. A kind of howl that turns into a cough. I reach for the cup and straw Steph brought home last month from the hospital and help her take a sip of water. A string of spit stretches between her lips and the straw as she pulls away.

"Ry-er," Mom says, eyes swinging toward the window again.

IN LOVE WITH YOU

"Fine," I say. "I'll go and get her."

The door hinges open, and I step out onto the porch. I don't have to see Mom to know she is bending her ears to try and hear us out here.

"Hey," I say, stepping off the porch when Luna doesn't even look up from where she's squatting. She just scowls at the back bumper of the Camaro, studying the scratch marks from a drunken encounter I had with a parked car about a thousand years ago that still look fresh. She scribbles something into her little red notebook. I'm two feet away from her and she still hasn't looked up. "My mom is worried you're getting cold out here."

Luna stands, brushing invisible dirt off of her knees. I don't even think she had been kneeling. She just needed something to do.

"I shouldn't—" she begins, then stops. She clamps the notebook shut with one hand, threads the pencil behind her ear in a way I didn't know could be sexy. I lift my gaze to the tops of the hemlock trees that grow at the edge of our next-door neighbor's property. Sorry. I didn't mean to say that in front of you, that something about her was sexy. It just popped into my head. Luna sighs. "That seemed too private, you and your mom. I shouldn't have been so curious. I should've—I should've just waited. I think you wanted me to wait."

I shrug. "Not a big deal."

Except, I think it might be. Not gargantuan. Not mammoth. Just a medium-sized deal. She probably should've waited. I probably should have asked her to.

"Is she all right now?" Luna asks.

"Mom? Yeah." I scratch at my hairline with a thumbnail. Rock back and forth on my heels as I fill my lungs with sea-dappled oxygen. I let that big batch of air out in one huff. "She doesn't know you were in the house. Earlier, I mean."

"Good." Her face goes from sphincter-tight to jelly-loose just like that.

"So?"

"So..."

"You coming in?"

Luna tucks her notebook into the back pocket of her jeans. Starts off across the thick, damp lawn I probably should get around to mowing one last time before winter. I follow alongside her.

A twinge of guilt in my chest. A pang of longing in my gut. I wish I was walking you to my front door. I wish I was introducing you to my mom, not Luna. You, with your faint breathing and mesmerizing mystique. Mom would love you. Mom would reach out for you the way she's reaching out for Luna right now.

Luna doesn't hesitate to smile—no pity, no humor—as Mom weaves her fingers through Luna's and swings their arms side to side.

"Pre," Mom says.

"Thank you," Luna says, as if she doesn't need me to interpret and tell her Mom said she was pretty.

It feels like I've swallowed a clamshell and it's gotten stuck halfway down my throat.

This is wrong. It's all wrong. There's a good chance this is the last person Mom will ever be introduced to for the first time again. And it's not the person I think about as soon as I wake up in the morning. Or the person I think about right before I fall asleep at night. It's not the person I can talk to about anything and everything—the person I can spill all of my secrets to and know they won't disappear on me. It's not you.

That realization breaks me a little bit.

And I hate it.

I hate that it can't be you.

Fourteen

Luna

OKAY, READER, SINCE YOU have no problem shouldering into the private lives of strangers, tell me something—is it wrong that I'm up here?

In his room. Without his permission. Snooping through his world.

I know, on some level, this isn't right. But a man who can be as silent as the dead, cold even, for three whole hours and then scoop his sick mom up and carry her so lovingly back to her bedroom is a man who intrigues the hell out of me. I have to know more. More than what he's allowed me to glimpse thus far.

The loft is open, no door. Its ceiling is low and slants down on both sides until it's just a couple of feet off the floor, meaning Ryder most likely has to move along the centerline of the room or duck. The top of the stairs bisects the space. To the left, an unmade bed, dresser, and a clothes rail fashioned

IN LOVE WITH YOU

to the wall that's filled with flannel shirts. To the right, a few cardboard storage boxes, a workout bench, and enough weights to sink a small boat. I sit on the end of the workout bench and take stock of every minor detail I can collect. Smell of sweat mixed with salt and pine. A cool whip of ocean breeze floating through the cracked-open window above the bed. Ryder's name carved into the baseboard beside the stairs. The only real decorations in the room are the bright film poster for the *Endless Summer* documentary and an ornate piece of driftwood hanging by a length of rough twine.

I draw in a breath and hold it, trying to listen to the goings on downstairs. Muffled voices. The scratch of a record player. Ryder's mom's shrill but intoxicating laugh.

On my feet now. Padding across the room. I'm about to plunge a hand into the middle of his flannel collection when something catches my eye on his nightstand. A photograph, edges warped, a wrinkle down the middle that has been smoothed over. In the photo, a man who looks a little older than Ryder does now, but with a full beard, short curly hair, and a clear-headed look in his light gray eyes. The man has both arms draped over the shoulders of a young boy with a wild, open-mouthed smile strung from ear to ear. Hair, bleach-blonde and shaggy, sticking out in every direction. They're both wearing wetsuits, the ocean at their backs, the sun pouring over the top of them. I flip the photograph over to find an inscription in tight, looping print. *So you don't forget who you are in there*.

In there? In where? That's an odd thing to write on the back of a photograph, isn't it?

A floorboard creaking underfoot is the only indicator I am no longer alone. I gasp quietly and turn my head to look over my shoulder. Ryder stands casually at the top of the stairs. What's not so casual is his vise grip on the banister.

I put the picture back onto the nightstand and briskly walk to the center of the room, stopping a few steps away from Ryder. That scent of salt and pine is even stronger, spooling off of him. It makes me feel a little unsteady and also like I want to lean in. Press my nose to the curve of his shoulder. Breathe in so deeply that I am filled by nothing but his aroma.

"That picture is of me and my dad," he says, not looking at me. His voice is even, if not a little calculated. I watch that hand. Grip tightening. Knuckles whitening. "It was taken a few days before he died."

Guilt is a fist that likes to squeeze my bowels from time to time. The cramp is low, borderline debilitating. If I thought I was unsteady a second ago, I didn't know what unsteady actually felt like. I grab the ends of my sweatshirt sleeves and clench the soft fabric as if it's the only thing tethering me to the earth.

"I shouldn't have come up here," I whisper, my voice trembling slightly. When he doesn't say anything, doesn't even nod in agreement, I keep talking, needing to push past this tension somehow. "My mom died when I was sixteen, and if I found someone snooping around, looking at pictures of her and me without my permission, I wouldn't like it."

Ryder's grip eases on the banister, bit by bit, until he lets it go. Shoves that same hand in the front pocket of his jeans.

"Your mom died?" he asks.

"Yeah."

"How?"

I swallow down whatever bile is rising in my throat. "Breast cancer."

IN LOVE WITH YOU

He doesn't speak. He just takes his hand out of his pocket and cups my elbow, thumb curling around the crook of the joint, fingers spanning the entire breadth of my upper arm. It's the mirror image of my earlier gesture at the door before I even set foot in this cottage. When I was trying to comfort Ryder in a small, yet meaningful way. I read somewhere once that we touch people the way we like to be touched, and I don't know if Ryder knows about this or not, but it's such a kind, uncontrived act that a tear pushes its way to the corner of my eye. I wipe it away with the sleeve of my sweatshirt before he can see.

"You want to order a pizza for lunch?" he asks, squeezing my arm so lightly I barely feel it, then letting his hand fall away.

I try and clear my throat of the thick emotion coating it, but I still only manage a breathy whisper. "Absolutely."

Fifteen

Ryder

THURSDAY MORNING, I WAKE up to a text from Mark saying he's not paddling out. Wedding planning crisis. Nick already bailed last night, claiming he was behind on grading student essays.

I sigh. If Mark and Nick are both out, that means Luna and I are surfing alone. I can hear the rain on the windowpane above my bed, can feel the wind shake against the house. The weather is not ideal as it is, but with her barely able to stand up on her board and only my eyes on her, I'll feel more like I'm babysitting than anything.

Once I text her that no one is paddling out and to meet me at the house around ten, I crash back onto my pillow, content to sleep right up until Steph heads to the hospital for her shift.

Then I get an idea.

There's some place I want to take you. Call it our first official date, if you'd like.

IN LOVE WITH YOU

I'm sorry I won't be able to show up on your doorstep with a bouquet of your favorite flowers and watch your front door swing open to reveal you on the other side. And I'm sure you'd look like a mouthful of something sweet I'd want to devour in an instant.

But I'd like to think flowers and looks aren't all that matter to you. That it's simply enough to spend some quality time with the people who adore you.

Dressed in head-to-toe rain gear for the absolute slaughter coming down from the sky, I cut through a neighbor's back yard, slink through the thick patches of Oregon Grape beyond, and arrive on the next street. I untwist the cap of the thermos of coffee I made before I left the house, and guzzle down the hot liquid. I follow it up with a few bites of a protein bar.

The light from sunrise pounds hard against the gray clouds, trying to get through. But it doesn't do much except lift the shadows from the neighborhood adjacent to mine just enough to highlight the spires of fog slipping out of the trees.

I track the shoddy line of asphalt road due east for about a quarter of a mile before I duck down a side street, heading north again.

Another sip of coffee. Final remnants of the protein bar. I stuff the wrapper in my pocket. Cap the thermos.

The houses thin out as the road nears the small, forested area that separates the north end of town from the south. A strong gust of wind picks up the branches of the evergreens that grow on the fringes of this area, blowing dead limbs and old needles onto the sparse tufts of grass on the ground below. They cover the muddy footpath that leads into the forest. If

FAYE DARLING

I hadn't walked the trail a thousand times before, there's no way I would even know it existed.

Today, you feel more real than you have before. Like you're not just a feeling pressing in on me from some far off place, but as if you are here. Right here. I can almost see you from the corner of my eye. I catch sight of you in certain slants of the rain. You walk beside me. You see what I see, smell what I smell, hear what I hear. Baby, you're a part of me, the same way I'm sure I'm a part of you by this point.

I imagine weaving my long, thick fingers through yours. Holding on to you in an easy way, as if our hands were made for each other. Pieces of a puzzle snapping satisfyingly into place.

Can you feel the warmth of my touch? The beat of my heart as it drums through every single vein in my body?

I might be compelled to stop and kiss you right here right now. Beneath the cover of the trees. Between the twist of bramble bushes in the undergrowth. Rain sifting down. Electricity building between us with every passing second.

But I would restrain myself.

I would wait to press my lips to yours until the right moment, the right place.

Don't worry, baby. We're almost there.

Just a few more steps.

The trail bends and bows a few times before it crosses a stream, where flat stones dropped in the water make it passable. One last curve and I see it. *We* see it.

An old-growth cedar tree twenty times larger than any of the others that sprout up around us sits in the middle of a ring of decking meant to keep people from stepping on its roots, loosening it from the earth.

IN LOVE WITH YOU

I settle us in on the far side of the ring, perching on top of the railing that blocks off the rest of the forest. The rain hammers down, cold and wet. Imagine with me, will you? Imagine you're here.

Without hesitating, I put my arm around you to keep you from shivering. I draw you close. Press my lips to your ear, reveling in the way you squirm just a little at the feel of my stubble, my sultry breath. I'd whisper something—something suggestive or something funny, you decide—and you'd laugh this sweet little laugh. Then, you'd sigh and melt into my side. Your shoulder would dig into my ribs in a way that makes me know you're real.

We'd stare at the colossus trunk of the cedar. Follow the natural patterns etched into the bark up to the canopy, wide and arching. We'd blink through the rain. Maybe catch a single drop in our gaze to follow back down, where it would crash onto your lower lip.

This is when I would kiss you.

My arm would glide from your shoulders to your waist, touching every bit of you along the way. You'd look up at me, as if trying to anticipate what's to come, because you feel it too. Like the wind changing directions suddenly, the entire landscape drawing in a breath.

Softly, my nose would brush yours as my lips hover over your mouth. At first, I think I want to drag out this moment. But the longer I do, the wilder my heart beats in my chest, the harder it is to hold back.

Maybe you surprise me by leaning into my touch, eliminating the last of space between us and pressing your mouth to mine so gently it feels like the brush of a bird's wings. Delicate, vulnerable, adrenalizing.

Except now that I've tasted you—sweet and salty, all at once—I'm greedy. Ravaged by a hunger for you and you alone.

Nothing that happens next is delicate.

My free hand cradles the base of your skull, and I angle your head so that I can get closer. I part your lips with my own, my tongue curling into the warmth of your mouth. Sizzle-pops of sensation shoot through me, and they must shoot through you, too, because I imagine you make this low moaning sound I can feel all the way down at the juncture of my thighs.

I pull back slightly, but only so I can nibble and suck on your bottom lip. You gasp. Take the collar of my jacket in your hands, holding on tight. As if you need an anchor. As if you're one second away from slipping right off of this railing. So I strengthen my grip on your waist, bolting you to my side, showing you how safe you will always be when I'm next to you. Don't ever forget that, baby, because I mean it.

My tongue is exploring again, tipping us over the edge of a hot, wet slide as the rain soaks us. I don't think we feel it though. And when the wind shakes through the trees, we don't even notice. We're tangled up in one another—tongues and limbs and souls—and nothing else can even nip at the fringe of our awareness.

As I imagine wrapping you up in my arms, bending you back so I can kiss the exposed arch of your neck, a shock of realization zips through me. I'm no longer just falling. I've fallen—past tense. Gravity has returned. I feel sure-footed in the way I feel about you. And I could try not to think these words out loud, could try and hold them in a little bit longer, but what good will it do? So, here it is.

I love you.

IN LOVE WITH YOU

I've never even set eyes on your face and yet I know this to be true.

And I know how that must sound to you. Oh, god, I can feel the way you're absorbing my words—like you're unsure if you trust them or not. Like you're wondering if I would say this to you if you were actually here. Believe me, I've never wanted you to be here in the flesh more than I do right now. But I'd like to think I'd still feel the exact same way. I'd like to think I would love you just as intensely, just as deeply.

My next intake of air is shaky, because I've never said those three words to anyone who didn't have the ability to say them back. My head is suddenly foggy with want and longing and confusion. I rub my hands over my face and force myself to focus on the present moment.

The rain zinging through the gaps in the forest's canopy. The incredible berth of the cedar in front of me. Smell of the dirt, sharp and iron-tinged. Sound of the wind catching in the high branches of the trees. Distant hum of the ocean waves cracking against themselves.

I breathe it all in. Close my eyes. Tilt my head back.

Water droplets catch on my forehead. They're cold. So cold that, after a time, they make me shiver. I unscrew the cap of my thermos and warm myself with the last dregs of black coffee. Then, I slide back onto the decking, back onto the trail, and head toward home, where I know Luna will be waiting for me.

Sixteen

Luna

FRIDAY AFTERNOON, RYDER AND I sit on the back deck of the cottage, eating the cheeseburgers I drove across town to pick up for us for lunch. It's been four and a half days of research and, I'd like to say I've gathered droves of information, that I'm ready to call my agent and tell her I'm finally ready to write something new, but Ryder is making it difficult.

It's not that he's deliberately trying to make this process slow, but he's still seventy-five-percent closed off. Seventy-five-percent mystery.

In order to write characters that feel like they're living, breathing beings, I have to know the innerworkings of my research subjects well. Usually, I can gather the majority of what I need to know about a person by observing alone. Not with Ryder. He seems hyper-aware of me most of the time. It's as if he spends just as much time as I do watching the people around him, keeping his guard up as he does so. And just when

I catch a glimpse of his true nature—a shared laugh with his mom or an old rock song whistled while he stokes the fire in the woodburning stove—his eyes tick toward mine, and a hardness builds behind them. He pushes against me, keeping me out.

It's starting to feel like every step forward I make is followed by two steps back, and I'm sick of it, reader. Absolutely sick. This strange tension needs to be broken.

How, you ask? I have my ways. A good shock to the system oughtta do it. Catch him off-guard...if that's even possible. Do you mind sending up a prayer to whatever higher power you believe in that what I'm about to do does the trick? Thanks. I appreciate you.

I chew and swallow the bite of burger I've just taken and twist slightly in the deck chair so I can look at Ryder from a better angle. Fuck me, he's handsome. That scruff-covered jaw. Those deeply-saturated eyes you could just lose yourself in, drown in. Gladly. I'd drown in them gladly. Don't even think about reaching for a lifebuoy.

What am I doing? I'm not supposed to be ogling the man. I'm supposed to be shocking him. I clear my throat and ask the most surprising question I can think of on the spot. "So, how many women have you slept with?"

He chokes on a bite of burger. Starts to cough. He takes a long sip of the Dr Pepper I brought back from Bun on the Run for him even though he asked for a Coke—who the hell drinks Coke?

"What kind of question is that?" he asks when his airway is clear.

FAYE DARLING

"One I ask when my research subjects need to be jarred out of their hidey-hole." I laugh. A bit more like an evil-genius than I intended, but whatever.

"You think I'm hiding?" he asks, his words smothered in a self-conscious glaze.

I take another bite of my burger. Let the shrill squeal of the seagulls roaming the neighborhood take over the soundwaves in the lull. Then, I look at him again. Make eye contact. Or try to. Problem is he's staring at the moss-covered fence across the yard, his blank expression telling me he's lost in his head. Like he's having a conversation with himself.

A shiver travels the length of my spine at the thought, and I wonder...no it's too crazy of an idea. Okay, maybe not. I mean, I talk to you in my head after all, right? Hold these semi-one-sided conversations all the damn time and I'm not crazy.

Now, I feel you getting confused, so I'll just say what I was going to say in the first place and hope you can swallow it all without laughing. I wonder if Ryder has somehow figured out a way to talk to you, too, and is telling you everything he is holding back from me.

But that's a wild notion, isn't it? I mean, what would he even say to you? Would he know you were there? Would he sense you the same way I do? Hm...

He's gone too quiet over there. Has been in his head too long. That's when I realize I never answered his question. I suck down some of my own Dr Pepper before I speak. Try and be as honest as I can. "I think you're extremely self-aware when I'm around."

"Sorry."

"Don't apologize."

IN LOVE WITH YOU

"I just...don't like feeling watched like this," he says, blinking twice, as if he's telling you goodbye and returning here to the present moment with me. He stabs a fry into Bun on the Run's signature sauce, which tastes like spicy barbeque in mayonnaise. Smoky, creamy, delicious. You gotta try it sometime if fries are your thing.

"What did you think this was going to be, then?" I ask.

He pops the fry in his mouth and shrugs that one-shouldered-shrug I've gotten used to over the past couple of days. Every time he does it, my stomach does this little crinkle thing and I can't feel my toes for a full minute and a half. I'm saying it's sexy, reader. You know, in case I needed to spell that out for you.

"I don't mind when you ask me questions?" He says *that* like it's a question.

"You just don't like it when I stare at you from across the room and study the mechanics of your every move?" I monotone.

"Yeah." He palms the back of his neck. "I kind of hate that, actually."

"All right."

"Sorry."

"Don't," I say with a tight sigh, "apologize."

"I feel like I should." He slides down in his chair, his knees falling farther apart. His legs are so long one of those knees settles against one of mine. My skin flecks with goosebumps at the feel of rough denim against my bare legs, visible from the frayed hem of my shorts to the tops of my white sneakers. I can blame it on the cold if he brings it up, even though I'm rarely cold.

FAYE DARLING

"Why do you feel like you should apologize?" I shove a few fries in my mouth to try and focus on something other than Ryder's closer than close proximity to me. The heat spooling from his leg onto mine. The smell of him—so manly—trying to consume the fresh, ocean-drenched air around us.

"You're paying me a lot of money for your research." His mouth twists up in pain. Like guilt is there, doing her dark magic thing. "And, clearly, it hasn't been worth it."

"It has," I say. Why do I suddenly need to reassure him? Five days ago I would have called him a pussy, told him to make it worth it, and stormed off. But what little I've gotten to know him in the quiet spaces he allows me to slip through is that he's more sensitive than he lets on. Behind that stone-wall of stoicism is a big, squishy heart. I suddenly feel the need to protect that heart. "I'm just on a deadline, is all."

"Ask me anything, then," he says, my words somehow sparking a bit of life back into his body. My blood pumps hard through my veins, like I'm thrilled I might've caused that reaction, that spark. "Anything at all."

"Where do you go?" I ask, because now I'm too fucking curious about this.

"What do you mean?"

"Sometimes, you're plain old closed off and other times," I say, "you just seem far away, lost in your head."

"You notice that?" A deep blush crawls up his neck, duck-dives beneath the thick stubble on his jaw, and pops up like a firework in the night on his cheeks. My toes tingle.

"Yeah," I say. "And whatever it is, it's got you blushing."

"Shit," he mumbles.

"Ryder?"

"Can you ask the sex question again?" he asks quickly.

IN LOVE WITH YOU

"No." I finish off the last greasy bite of my burger. "This is a far more interesting topic."

Wouldn't you agree, reader? Trying to figure out what makes a man blush is so much more intriguing than learning some simple facts about his sex history. And it's not like you're going to be able to tell me if you two have been talking. As far as I know, this form of communication only works one way.

"You'd think I was a lunatic if I told you," he says.

"Now I've gotta know."

"You've gotta know?"

"Yes."

He chuckles.

"What?" I ask.

"Sounding a little desperate there, my friend."

"Well..." I say. "You intrigue me. Naturally, where you disappear to in your head intrigues me just as much. So?"

The tip of his tongue darts out to wet his lips. "So?"

I lean toward him. Press the pad of my index finger to the middle of his forehead. "Where do you go in that head of yours?"

"In that intriguing head of mine?" he asks, and his blush deepens. I can't tell if that's because I've touched him or because he's thinking about that hidden place in his mysterious noggin.

"Yes," I say, sounding breathless.

"Is this a part of your research?" he asks, his voice sultry and smooth. A smirk drags across his face. "Or just because you're a curious little monster?"

My heart kicks hard in my chest. My skin goes numb, like I've been lifted out of my own body for a moment. I know it's been a while since I've taken a breath because I've been holding it for as long as Ryder has been looking me, waiting for an answer I don't know if I want to share. An ache spreads over my lungs, and I finally suck in some air. But it's shallow, more of a wheeze than anything. Ryder's head cocks to the side at that sound, those ocean eyes calm and playful and curious. That blush still stains his cheeks. I have an overwhelming desire to run my fingertips up his neck. Press a palm to the expanse of his face. See how hot his skin has been made by his blush. See what he might do next.

"Luna?"

He says my name in a way no one ever has before. Delicately, slowly, like he's opening an immaculately wrapped present, afraid to damage the ribbon or rip apart the paper. I hear my name in his voice echo over and over in my head. *Luna? Luna?* Dipping low on the 'lu' and climbing high on the 'na'. *Lu-na. Luna.*

"Talk about disappearing into your own head," he mutters, and I realize just how far I've gotten lost in my thoughts. Lost in him.

I fake a cough and twist my upper body away from him, so I can only see him in my peripheral vision. That should be safe, right?

"Maybe the sex question *would* be better," I say, forcing a laugh. He scowls at me, blush all but gone, eyes narrow. There's still a bit of playfulness in them, though. "Or, maybe not. Maybe we should go back to silence. Complete and utter silence."

A heavy exhale studders out of me as soon as Ryder flashes a smile. He packs his mouth full of fries and nods, agreeing on the silence. Then his knee knocks against my leg again as he settles back in his chair, and I feel it everywhere.

IN LOVE WITH YOU

And I keep on feeling that touch long after he's pulled away, long after we've gone inside. I even feel it later on, as I drive back to D.J.'s place alone, guiding my grandfather's old pickup around the deep bends in the road. The sun has dipped low, brandishing the evergreen hills that roll westward in a golden sheen. I imagine the heat of the sun is just as hot as the place on my leg where Ryder's knee had rested.

Ryder is like a new car you decide to buy. You've never seen the model before you make the purchase, but as soon as you drive off the lot, you can't stop seeing it everywhere. You can't stop wondering how you ever missed it in the first place.

Seventeen

Ryder

"Did someone teach you how to surf or did you pop out of the womb with the know-how?"

"How old were you when you had your first kiss?"

"Are the plaid flannels a personal fashion statement or do they require you to take a course on Pacific Northwest clichés to be eligible?"

Luna has been peppering me with questions during my busy Saturday shift at The Tavern. Really, she's been peppering me with questions ever since she showed up at the cottage this morning in a bone-dry wetsuit wondering why the hell I hadn't been on the beach. Answering her never-ending cycle of questions seemed like a good enough apology for forgetting to text her about the too-rough surf. Plus, after our conversation over burgers yesterday, I'm trying to be helpful and not closed-off. Even though it's hard for me to let people in—you, my darling, have been a surprising exception—I don't want it to seem like I'm trying to weasel more money out of her by dragging out this process, either. Some people might take advantage of her generous compensation, but I am not that kind of guy. My mom raised me to be an honest man, and honest I will be. In more ways than one.

Of course, I'd rather be thinking of you in my free time instead of answering her questions. But maybe you want to know my answers, too. Maybe you want to get to know more about me, just like Luna. I like that idea. I like it a lot.

I place three beers on the bar in front of a Timber Razer and deposit the cash he gives me into the register before leaning onto my elbows in front of Luna's stool.

"Care to share how all those questions you just asked connect in that curious mind of yours?" I ask.

"Will it help you answer them?"

"No," I say. "Probably not."

"Then, answers first, please," she says. Her pencil is poised over her open notebook, her eyes darting from the half-filled page to my face and back again. Why do I get the feeling as soon as I start speaking that pencil is going to take off across the paper like a race horse set loose on the track?

I tick my eyes up and to the left as I try and remember every question she just asked. "My dad taught me, I was thirteen, and yes."

Luna jams the eraser end of her pencil against the corner of her mouth and squints at me. "Is that your answer to the very first question I asked or all of them?"

"All of them," I say. "I did not pop out of the womb with the ability to surf—my dad taught me when I was a kid. My first kiss was at the ripe old age of thirteen in Kayla Cunningham's basement two seconds before the power blew out for a week and a half. I was convinced for over a year that if I kissed a girl, the electricity would go out, so I avoided lips like the plague for a time. And yes, there is a course every man who lives here must take before he is worthy of the plaid flannel."

"Really?" Luna asks.

I chuckle. "No, there's no course."

"No, I meant, did you really think if you kissed a girl the power would go out?"

I shrug. "I was thirteen, what do you think?"

"I think that's a long time to avoid kissing," she says, taking the pencil into her mouth and biting the end as she smirks up at me. "Especially after getting a taste for it with your very first smooch."

"Smooch?"

"Yeah, smooch."

"What are you, an eighty-year-old woman?" I ask. "Who still uses the word smooch?"

"Me." Luna taps the pencil against her collarbone, fully bared thanks to the deep-v of her Black Sabbath t-shirt. "The writer."

"Ah." I lean back from the bar, but keep a grip on the edge countertop, the veins of my forearms carving clear paths up to my elbows, where the rolled sleeves of my flannel sit. "So, your readers are eighty-year-old women, then?"

"So what if they are?" She sticks me with a cold glare. Eyes narrowing. Lips pursing.

"Down girl," I say, nodding to a regular customer who shakes an empty glass at me a few stools away. "I think it's cute, is all."

I keep an eye on Luna as I refill the customer's drink. Maybe I'm seeing things. Maybe it's the fact that The Tavern is extra busy tonight. All those bodies milling around. All that heat. But

IN LOVE WITH YOU

I swear Luna's cheeks are now adorned with pink splotches that hadn't been there before. Her jaw clenches briefly as she swallows hard, then she starts scribbling furiously in her notebook.

"What's cute is that you thought if you kissed a girl the electricity would wig out," she says loudly, so I can hear her over the noise. I'm no expert, but would you say she's deflecting? Pinning it all back on me?

"I can be superstitious when I need to be," I say, trying to shake away the memory of the blush I may or may not have seen on Luna's face. I don't really want to think about her blushing. Not while you're here, not in general.

"No one ever *needs* to be superstitious," she says, the playful quality her voice had slowly taken on all but gone. Serious Luna again. Introspective Luna.

"You know what I mean."

She chews on the side of her cheek and stares long and hard at her notebook. I can sense it—can you? That feeling that she wants to say something, but is holding back. Why?

"Spit it out," I say as I return to her end of the bar.

"Spit what out?"

"Whatever it is you're going to say."

"I don't have anything to say." She won't look me in the eye, but just glancing at her face tells me everything I need to know. She's lying. The mask she's wearing right now is one I've grown accustomed to seeing over the week we've spent in close proximity. I saw it when she talked about her mom dying the time I caught her snooping in the loft. I saw it whenever my mom coughed a little too hard or whenever she noticed me looking at her in the rare moments she wasn't fixated on me. It's the kind of mask that conceals every single emotion that exists within her, turning her into some kind of hard, expressionless vessel. Almost like her consciousness, her heart, her soul—everything that gives her character and life—has been vacuumed out of her skeleton. It's off-putting, to say the least.

And she thinks I'm the one hiding behind my walls.

"Come on." I knock my knuckles against her shoulder lightly. "We're friends by now, wouldn't you say?"

"I guess," she says flatly. Still not looking at me.

"All right," I say. "And friends tell each other what's on their mind, right?"

"You'll think I'm being judgmental and get all pissy."

"You sure about that?"

Her eyes make a slow, exaggerated rotation in their sockets, before landing on me. "The last time I made a harsh judgement about you, you nearly bit my head off."

"We didn't know each other then," I say, bristling at the memory of our first conversation in this bar. "It's different now."

"Okay," she says, sucking air in through her teeth. "When my mom died, I felt like my life was so out of my own control that any chance I got to take charge of something, I would. If that meant dyeing my hair bright purple or running around outside in the winter without a coat or hooking up with anyone and everyone, I'd do it just to feel like I had dominion over *something*. So, call it a superstition or whatever you'd like, but if I had to guess I'd say the real reason you didn't kiss anyone for a long time after the power went out had more to do with fighting to keep control of something in your life, just like me. Power outages are prime examples of things you cannot control. But, if you allow yourself to live in some kind of illusion of control, like, say, thinking that withholding your kisses would keep the electricity running smoothly, then the list of things out of your control become fewer. They become tolerable. And, if I really had to guess, I'd say most of what you do—most of what you've ever done—comes back to grappling for control."

It's like Luna has taken two ends of a snipped wire and twisted them together. I don't know how, I don't know why, but everything she just said makes total sense to me. She's taken every stupid, reckless action I've ever done and given it meaning. Given it a reason for happening other than because I was an idiot or because I was young or because I was pissed off. In a way, she's looked straight through my bullshit and dredged up the truth. And she doesn't even know the half of it. I haven't even told her about the months I spent locked up.

My chin drops against my chest, and I stare at the patterns in the wood grains skittering over the bar top. "Fuck."

"Told you it'd be better if I didn't say anything," Luna mumbles.

"No, it's not that."

"Okay?" She raises a single eyebrow in question.

I blow out a warm batch of air through tight lips. "You're right. You're one-hundred-percent right."

"Excuse me? Did you just say I'm right?" Luna lets out a breathy, borderline-relieved chuckle.

"Don't let it go to your head," I say, looking up at her. She's biting her lower lip to keep from grinning like a total loser.

"No, never."

But I don't want to flesh everything out with her. I don't know *how* to do that sort of thing. Not in a way that would make any damn sense. Maybe if it was you sitting across the bar from me, helping me understand myself, things would be different. I think I'd be able to talk to you. Tell you every detail of my life without worrying you'd hate me for it.

"You want another Jack and Coke?" I ask, wrapping my hand around her empty glass.

She's too busy scribbling in her notebook to do much more than nod, and I am perfectly okay with that.

When I set her refreshed drink down in front of her a minute later, she clears her throat and rapid fires another set of questions, moving our conversation right along.

Eighteen

Ryder

THE RUMBLE OF A truck engine outside the cottage shocks me awake a little past three in the morning. I fell asleep less than an hour ago after my long shift at The Tavern. I should be dead to the world. And yet...

My ears tick back. Goosebumps crawl to life on the surface of my skin.

Up in the loft, I'm blind to the street since the only windows are posted on the ends of the house. I don't hang around waiting to see if anyone drives past the place. I'm downstairs and on the front porch in exactly three breaths, glaring down the long bed pickup truck idling in the middle of the street directly in front of our yard.

I'm a nano second away from letting out a deep-bellied *hey* when Steph's tiny form comes into focus. She doesn't have shoes on, so she shifts from foot to foot to keep out the chill of the asphalt while her small hands hang onto the edge of the open truck window. Even through the padding of her thick purple coat I can see that every muscle in her body is tense. She's been sleeping in her old room every single night since the power went out and although she still hasn't told me the reason, I'd bet money it's because of the asshole in that truck.

Steph's whispering something to the driver, talking so low and fast I can't make out what she's saying. The noise of the pickup's engine doesn't help.

My protective instincts tell me to march over to the truck and kill whatever's inside. But the logical side of my brain holds me back. Tells me this guy is not worth jailtime...yet. As soon as he raises his voice, as soon as he so much as flinches toward my baby sister, it'll become worth it. So, I linger on the dark porch.

The asshole drives a nice truck, I'll give him that. Old, but kept up well. I can hear the care he puts into the engine from here. But I don't recognize the vehicle. And a truck like that one? I would have definitely taken notice of. He's an out-of-towner, no doubt. A blow-in.

"Like hell," he says at a normal volume. But since he and Steph had been whispering up 'til now, it sounds like he's shouting at her.

Okay, what should I do, baby? Stand here and wait for shit to get worse? Or head over there and nip this bullshit in the bud?

Fuck it.

My bare feet slap against the concrete walkway. I march halfway to the street and stop just as Steph rears back and slams the heel of her hand into the door of the guy's truck. She whispers something after that. I hear the word *obligation*—I think—but that's it.

IN LOVE WITH YOU

This guy's laugh has me moving again. Low and sinister. You know the type. The one that sounds more like a snake hissing to ward off a threat than a genuine show of humor. It makes my jaw clench.

"*Stephanie*," I say, my low voice vibrating in my chest.

Steph grips the windowsill of the driver's door and stares at the ground—eyes closed, probably—for a few seconds before she swings her head to look at me.

"I'm fine, Ryder," she says, but I can hear the waver in her voice.

"It's late," I say. "You should come back inside."

"Listen to your brother," the driver says sharply, as if he knows me. "You and I, Steph? We're done here."

I take another step toward the truck, and the asshole punches the gas. Steph barely has time to jump back before he takes off. I stalk toward her as I watch the taillights fade into the fog settling over the street. I flip him the bird, even though I know he won't see it. Good. Fucking. Riddance.

"Who was that?" I growl.

Steph checks my arm as she pushes past me, already wiping her eyes free of the tears that have quietly been falling. I catch her elbow. Whip her toward me.

"Let go of me," she shrieks, ripping out of my grip. She keeps walking toward the cottage, huffing and muttering obscenities under her breath.

Like I'm the asshole.

Like I'm the one she's angry with.

"I can't help you if you won't let me," I say.

She twists around just before she reaches the front door. She pounds back down the steps and the walkway, stopping just inches away from me. She glares up at me, the whites of her eyes the only thing truly visible.

"I never asked for your help, Ryder," she says. "I *never* ask for your help. You just swoop in every time I'm in any kind of trouble and decimate the problem before it can even be solved. You don't see the truth. You see what you want. Then you use whatever delusion you've cooked up as an excuse for your misplaced actions."

Steph's smarter than me, I'm not afraid to admit that. I don't fully understand what she's trying to tell me. I got lost after she said I swoop in without being asked. But I try not to let on.

"That guy gave you a black eye."

"Because I gave him worse."

My face twists in confusion, and I cock my head to the side. Steph has a firecracker temper, sure, but physically she's a matchstick. Unless she took an iron skillet to the douche bag's head, I doubt she gave him worse. "It doesn't matter. You're not—"

"I'm a woman, so I couldn't possibly do any damage, right?" She scoffs. Snaps three times in front of my face. "Wake the fuck up, Ryder. Women can be just as abusive as men."

"You're not abusive," I say. Steph has a short fuse, yes, but she's got a big heart in that tiny body of hers, no matter how far away it seems at times.

"No," she says, the tension in her voice easing. She takes a step back. Shoves her hands deep in the pockets of her coat. "But I can still inflict my own kind of damage."

"What does that mean?" I ask, hoping the sincerity in my voice overrides the gruffness that's there too.

She bites her lower lip. Shakes her head.

IN LOVE WITH YOU

I step forward and squeeze her upper arm. "You can tell me, Steph."

"No," she says, her voice cracking. "I can't."

I open my mouth to say something, but she's walking away again, turning toward the dark house. She taps up the steps and slips inside before the words I want to say even arrive on my tongue. I hear the front bedroom door shut. The click of the lock.

Steph has shut me out before, but not like this. Hell, she was so pissed at me for the first few months I was in prison she could hardly look at me. But she still came to visit.

Now, I just don't know. She's always walked around like she's got a piece of driftwood shoved up her ass, even when she was a baby she was a grumpy little smush, but this isn't the same. It's like her anger is guarding something that terrifies her. Whether it's connected to that asshole who just drove away or not, I'm not sure.

She called me delusional, right? That word is pinging around in my head now, her words finally catching up to me. Maybe I am delusional. But you can still trust a delusional person with your secrets. Your burdens. Right?

Unless she can't. Unless she feels like she can't trust me. Not anymore.

Why not?

My head is a swirl of confusion as I lock the front door and climb the steps to the loft. I want to find an escape from this mess. I've got a bottle of whiskey stashed under my bed, but sometimes alcohol only makes things worse for me. I have another idea, if you're up for it? We could escape together.

I'd say we both need a lift after that drama, don't you think?

FAYE DARLING

Taking a deep, steadying breath I sink onto the edge my mattress, imagining you are already here waiting for me. In my mind, you sit up on your knees and press your chest to the taut muscles of my back. You plant a hot kiss on my bare shoulder and tell me not to worry about my sister right now, to just focus on you and you alone.

I can do that.

You slide your arms around my middle, locking me tight against you, your heartbeat a sturdy *thump, thump, thump* between my shoulder blades. I swivel in your arms and catch your lips in mine, tasting sweet temptation on my tongue as desire carves its way from my mouth to the place between of my legs.

Do you understand how badly I want you? All of you?

It's why I take your hand in my fantasy and guide it down along the ridges of my abs until you reach the hard outline of my erection.

But I quickly let go of you. Even if this is just a fantasy—my fantasy—you are so, so real to me, baby, and I don't want to force you to do anything you don't want to. All I want is for you to realize how badly I ache for you. But I also don't know how I can be sure this is all okay with you. I want you—fuck, baby—I want you so much.

So, let's do it this way. If you're okay with me touching you—if you *want* me to touch you, my imagined version of you that is—then keep reading. But if you're not into that for whatever reason, then skip ahead to the next chapter, but know this: Whatever you decide, it doesn't change the fact that I still love you. That I still want you here with me in this story, moving through my somewhat boring life alongside me. Imagine me leaning through these pages right now, pressing a kiss to your actual temple, and telling you how amazing I think you are. Because you are. Truly amazing.

I'll close my eyes for a second while you make up your mind about what we do next.

I take in a lung-filling batch of air. Hold it. Let it go.

Will it freak you out too much if I tell you how fucking happy I am that I can still feel you close? That you're wanting to continue this little fantasy?

Now...where were we?

Right. My bed. You curled around me from behind, your hand hovering over my erection.

Your breath is a stone tumbling down a hillside. Sporadic. Out of control. You massage me gently, and my head arches back, landing on the top of your shoulder. A moan studders out of me, and you make a pleased little laugh before you stroke me again through my boxer shorts, pinpricks of pleasure popping up all over my skin.

Those pinpricks are replaced very quickly with an insatiable desire, an agonizing ache.

I growl. Twist completely around. Knee in the mattress. Bending you back. I hold myself above you, both of my hands pressed into the bed on either side of your head. Your hips rock up so that you can wrap your legs around my waist, the heat between us colliding in a sweet, sweet melody.

"What do you want, baby?" I whisper in your ear.

I can feel your pulse racing, can almost feel that desire slipping through the pages of this book, reaching me in a way that has never felt so palpable. Are you panting? Are you on the edge of something sinfully delicious?

Fuck, I have never wanted you to materialize more than I do in this very moment.

In our fantasy, though, my lips are still pressed to your ear, the question I asked still dangling between us.

"You," I imagine you say. "All I want is you, Ryder."

My grin splays across the side of your neck, and you giggle at the scratch of my stubble. I drag my teeth down to the collar of one of my old t-shirts, because, yes, in our fantasy you pulled one of my shirts out of my dresser to put on while I was outside. You wear just the shirt and your underwear. I bury a kiss in the hollow of your throat as one of my hands snakes beneath the hem of that shirt, fingers walking up sheafs of bare skin, hot and sticky with lust.

When my fingers reach the back of your neck, I sit up on my knees, snapping you upright so that you're sitting on my lap. A tiny yelp of surprise leaves your lips at the action.

I free you of the shirt, our naked chests pressed flush to one another and heaving with every humid, weighty breath we take.

If you have long hair, I brush it back over your shoulders. If your hair is short, I rub a thumb along your cheek. Then, I lean back slightly, taking you in. Savoring every bit of you.

Well, aren't you just a marvelous beauty?

I kiss your sternum as your hips shift, rolling yourself over the top of my firm cock. The world tilts to one side, and I groan into your chest before spreading my fingers over the lower stretch of your abdomen. I slide my hand down, grazing over that sweet place at the base of your pelvis.

When I stroke your sex with deft fingers, you arch back, leaving your neck exposed. I latch onto it with my lips, sucking and licking and nipping, all while working you over with my fingers below. Fast, slow. Soft pressure, hard. I follow your lead, the sound and tempo of your breathing, your gasps, your moans acting as my guide.

I lock eyes with you, wanting to watch the exact moment you come completely undone. And then, suddenly, you're shaking against me, chasing your climax, letting me into a sacred piece of your world. That private space where you're nothing but pleasure and release, nothing but freedom and beauty.

You collapse forward, tucking your head into the curve of my neck. Your panting slows with every passing second. When you shift a little on my lap, you must feel how hard I am, how turned on I am by you finding your ecstasy.

"Now," I imagine you say, "What do *you* need?"

"I want to feel you," I whisper in the dark. It's the truth, one that extends beyond the context of this scenario. I want to hold you for real. Touch you for real. Be in this bed, coming undone with you for real.

But in this imagined scenario, you grin at me deviously, hook your fingers around either side of my boxers, and tug. My rock-solid cock bobs into view, ready to worship you more than my fingers ever could.

You slide off of my lap and turn away from me, falling onto the bed and catching yourself on your forearms. You look over your shoulder at me. That grin again. It makes me ache. Almost makes me come right here right now.

Lifting your ass in the air, shimmying your underwear down to your knees, you offer yourself to me.

I stand up on my knees and move closer to you. I ease your legs a smidge wider, palming your ass. Then, I take my hard length and rest the tip against your warm entrance.

You take a quick breath, but there's no need. I take my time, sliding into you slowly, filling you up like a smooth shot of whiskey until I am buried to the hilt, that shot glass almost overflowing.

I pause there, reveling in the feel of you. I never knew anyone else could feel so good, so right. Like we were fucking made for each other.

Then, I start to move. Slow at first, finding a foothold in your landscape, and then faster once I slide into that sweet spot that has both of us huffing out sharp breaths. I grip your waist with both hands, driving you back into me the same time my hips thrust into you.

Out of this fantasy, back in reality, you've got me so hot and bothered I can't stop myself from shedding my boxers and wrapping a hand around my hard length. I close my eyes and shuttle my hand up and down in time with our imagined scenario.

In that scenario, you let my name fall from your lips in a hushed whisper just before you tilt your head back over your shoulder, a raw and ravenous look in your eyes.

Fuck, baby. You might just be the death of me.

A warmth blooms low in my gut, spreading slowly, then quickly, until I feel like a fucking jet engine about to take off, everything building and building until—

"Fuuuck," I husk as my soul lifts out of my body for two brief seconds, right before the sharp shoots of pleasure pulsing along my shaft drag it back down again, making me aware of everything, all at once. The sticky sweetness of a full release. The mental clarity that rocks through me. I swear I can hear a leaf fall just outside the window. I swear I can smell your scent through the pages of this book.

IN LOVE WITH YOU

Still in our fantasy, I imagine my chest collapses over your back, my hands pressing into the mattress to keep most of my weight off of you. My lips ghost down your neck until I can kiss a single notch along your spine.

I pull out of you the same moment you glance over your shoulder at me again. But for a lightning-flash-moment, you're not you. Your face is too familiar. Whatever features I've been imagining for you are gone, replaced by high cheekbones, alabaster skin, and striking amber eyes. I blink, and it's Luna's face staring back at me, her curvy body bent over in front of me.

I blink again and she's gone. You return to me. Guide me down onto the mattress. Tangle yourself around my body.

All I want is to live in this moment with you for a little longer.

But seeing her has jarred me out of our fantasy.

I open my eyes to the dark of the loft. My hand is still wrapped around my emptied cock, my stomach wet and sticky. I let go of myself. Feel my heartbeat pounding in my chest. I suck in a shallow breath, a thousand emotions carving their own separate paths through me, making me a delta of guilt and joy and anger and shame and happiness and guilt again.

"I'm sorry," I whisper aloud to you, because just thinking it the words doesn't seem good enough.

There isn't an explanation powerful enough to try and justify what my brain did back there. Imagining her instead of you. Not being immediately put off by the idea.

Fuck.

I feel like an absolute idiot, a fool. I won't tell you how much I love you right now, or how much you mean to me, how much all of what we just did together meant to me, because I fear those words will only sound hollow in your ears. So, all I will say is that I'm sorry.

I'm so, so sorry.

Nineteen

Luna

Whoa.

Hey, there.

You seem a little apprehensive about stepping into my world right now. Maybe I'm wrong, but that's how it feels on this end of things. Everything okay, reader? All good?

I can sense you wanting to move this along, for me to stop asking questions, so let's get to it.

The ocean was too dangerous to surf again so far this week. But this morning—Wednesday—Ryder texted me early telling me to meet him and his friends at the bakery in West Cove instead. I was a little relieved, if I'm being honest. Ryder is more open around his friends than when he's around his mom and sister, probably because he isn't trying to protect the guys. I will say, I feel like after our chat over burgers, he's been better about letting me in, whether I'm asking him questions or not.

FAYE DARLING

We've been at the bakery long enough for me to consume a massive cinnamon roll with cream cheese frosting and half a lavender latte, prepared by a real grumpy+sunshine couple, Allen and Sally. Wondering if I've got a bit of back story on them? You know I do. Allen and Sally have known Ryder's family ever since they moved to West Cove twenty years ago to open the bakery. I'd be lying if I said it wasn't cute when Sally reached over the display case and pinched Ryder's cheeks when I asked what he was like when he was a kid.

"Just the cutest," she'd said, and he blushed. He actually blushed.

"The cutest little brat you'll ever meet," Allen grumbled from the kitchen.

Now, with the morning rush filing through the bakery doors, our only focus is on Mark and the numerous woes of his soon-to-be nuptials. Ryder and Nick give their opinions candidly, and I sit next to the window beside Ryder, listening intently. Hell, reader. I'm listening *con*tently. What I wouldn't give to be a fly on the wall for every conversation going on around the world. The stories I'd hear. Ah...makes me wistful just dreaming about it.

"How do you feel about bow ties?" Mark asks, his bottom lip resting against the edge of his coffee mug. He takes a sip, his eyes darting from Ryder to Nick to Ryder again.

"Are we forming a barber shop quartet?" Ryder asks, snorting out a laugh.

"Thank you," Mark says loudly. "That's what I told Gina."

"I like bow ties," Nick says, adjusting his cufflinks with his tattoo-covered hands, as if to prove his superior taste.

"Of course you do," Mark says, gesturing to Nick's entire ensemble. Starch-white dress shirt with a charcoal tweed suit vest buttoned overtop. The chain from his pocket watch swoops down from a pocket on his vest to one of the lower buttons. Nick's attention to detail is impressive.

Ryder snickers around a bite of a bear claw donut. He's sprawled out over his side of the booth. Long legs spread wide enough that our knees touch. One arm draped over the back of the bench behind me. Every time I shift, I feel his fingers catch in my hair or brush against my shoulder blade. I've come to learn that his mom and sister are what my mother would have called touchy-feely people. A hand on your knee, fingers in your hair, an arm fitted flush against your own. I tell myself Ryder's touches don't mean anything. That he's just used to having some point of contact with another person. But it's hard not to read into it.

All right, well, you chew on that bit of somewhat juicy info, if you'd like, but I'm missing out on conversation gold while I've been over-analyzing the actions of another human who is *literally being paid to spend time with me*.

Yep, that's shocked my head right out of my ass.

I slide an inch toward the window so my knee and Ryder's are no longer touching.

"And, get this," Mark says, pausing for dramatic effect. "Gina wants her mom's dog to be the ring bearer."

"Gina wants or Gina's mom wants?" Nick asks.

"Exactly," Mark says.

"What is this sudden obsession with dogs, anyway?" Nick sits up a little straighter, a hand swinging through the air. "You go to the beach nowadays and the dog to human ratio is insane."

FAYE DARLING

Ryder leans close to me, the stubble on his upper lip grazing my earlobe. He drops his voice to a whisper so only I can hear. "Ten bucks says Nick's about to rant."

A girlish giggle bubbles out of me. Where the fuck did that come from? I don't think I've ever made that sound before in my life. It wasn't even funny, what he said. I think it was the stubble graze that coaxed it out of my lungs more than the words he whispered.

Ryder leans away from me just enough for me to see the questioning look on his face. I clamp my lips down in an attempt to set my face in a serious line. *You're thirty-fucking-three, Luna*, I tell myself. *Pull your shit together.*

"What did you just tell her?" Nick asks.

"Nothing, man," Ryder says, hiding a smile with his coffee. Dark roast. Black as coal. Hot as hell. That's how the man takes his coffee. No nonsense. A person's coffee preference can tell you more about their personality than just about any test on the market. In my opinion, at least.

"You don't like dogs, Nick?" I ask, trying to deflect from any conversation that might make me admit why I giggled. And because watching tight-buttoned, kind-as-hell Nick rant sounds like my idea of a good time.

Nick smiles warmly at me. Usually my bullshit detector goes off at that sort of thing, but no alarm bells blast inside my head. I think he meant that smile, straight down to his core. Like I said, kind as hell.

"I like dogs," Nick begins. "It's just—does everyone and their mother have to have one? They dig and drool and shit *everywhere*. Most of them are untrained, too. Example. I was on a run the other day and this couple had six dogs—*six motherfucking dogs*—and not a single one of them was on a leash. They were running rampant. Two of the bigger breeds in the group came charging toward me. I nearly tripped. And did the owners say a word? Did they apologize? Of course not. I swear, if I hear someone shout, 'they're friendly' to me one more time..."

Mark leans diagonally across the table to talk directly to me. "Nick is the kindest human being you will ever meet unless he's on a rant."

"And unless you're a dog or a dog owner, apparently," Ryder says.

"That settles it." Mark sits back. Finishes off the last of his coffee. "Our ringbearer will be a dog. Just to piss Nick off."

"Get him to crack during the ceremony," Ryder says, a mischievous gleam in his eye.

"Show everyone he has a dark side," Mark adds.

"If that's what will make you happy," Nick says, sending me a *save me* look. "I'm here for it."

"Fuck it," Mark says, throwing up his hands. "It's Gina's world, right? We're all just living in it."

"Chin-chin," Ryder says boisterously, holding up his coffee mug to cheers.

"But this weekend, it's Mark's world we're all just living in," Nick says.

"This weekend?" I ask, my curiosity piqued.

"We're gonna get fucking hammered," Mark says, then wolf-howls. Allen pokes his head through the kitchen window and glares at Mark, who doesn't even seem to notice.

"This weekend is Mark's bachelor's getaway," Nick says. "A weekend in the woods, fishing, drinking around the campfire, and sending our bachelor off in style."

I twist in my seat, a spark of electricity popping in my chest. "I want to come."

"Boys only, girlie," Mark says.

"Oh, please," I say. "I'm not trying to steal your man cards. I just think it would be the perfect way to collect ample research for my novel."

"It's not a good idea," Ryder says.

"Why not?"

"Just think about it for a minute."

I wait a beat to answer even though I've done absolutely zero thinking. All I know is that if the bachelor's weekend is anything like this morning I'll have more than enough research to start my novel finally. "I did, and I still think I should join y'all."

"Come on, Ry, if she thinks it'll be good for her research," Nick says, fighting my side.

"Gina wouldn't like it," Ryder says, his brow furrowing. But I get a sense it's not just Gina who wouldn't like it.

"She did say if there were strippers, she'd murder me," Mark says.

"I'm not a stripper," I say. Should I be offended by that comment? "I'm just going to sit in the corner and watch. And yes, I realize that sounded borderline dirty, but it's the truth. I want some authentic, Pacific Northwest camping/fishing experiences. Don't make me beg."

Ryder pats my upper arm. "How about I tell you all about it next Monday?"

I shirk away from his condescending touch. "Second-hand experience doesn't hold a candle to first-hand."

"No," Ryder says, with a finality that slaps me in the face.

"I'll pay you double," I say, trying not to sound desperate. But the way I see it, the faster I collect research, the faster I can return home to Oklahoma to write this book. If I don't turn something in fast, my publisher will drop me even faster. Like a dying woman watching her life flash before her eyes, I see every book I've published in the past decade float past me, as if someone's thrown them in a giant toilet. A hand from above is poised to flush at any moment. My heart beats quick. My palms sweat.

"She's paying you for this?" Mark asks. "Damn girl, if you wanna use me for research, my wallet is open and my schedule is yours. Just pick a day."

"How about this weekend?" I say quickly.

"You're relentless," Ryder grumbles. "I said no."

"Fuck," I snap, making everyone at the table jump. I look right at Ryder, trying to keep the panic out of my eyes. But I can almost see it as it reaches out and gnaws at his insides a little. "Ryder, please."

"You really want to spend a weekend in a secluded forest alone with four guys?"

"Yes." And I know how axe-murdery the entire situation sounds, but I trust Ryder, and I trust Nick, and I think Mark is virtually harmless. Am I crazy, reader? Actually, don't answer that.

Ryder sighs, but it quickly turns into a growl. He looks at Mark, who just shrugs, then back to me, not even bothering to check in with Nick. "Fine."

"Thank you," I shriek, throwing my arms around Ryder's big, burly shoulders before I've even had a chance to second-guess myself. One of his hands presses into my back, fingers spreading wide. But he pulls back right away, like he's thought better of reciprocating my touch for some reason. I try not to let the twist of disappointment in my chest get to me. Try not to roll my eyes at how stupid it is for me to even be disappointed at all. I got my wish. A weekend in the woods. For the first time since I arrived, I think this project might actually be heading somewhere.

Twenty

Ryder

MOM'S EYES ARE BRIGHT as they track the jellyfish kite through the blue sky Thursday afternoon.

Forty-eight hours of torrential downpour, waves thrashing all the way to the dunes, and now—a beautiful calm. Not a single white tuft overhead. Even the waves have mellowed. Small and smooth. Peaceful. That's the coast in the autumn for you, though. Unforgiving and then overtly generous. Like the best makeup sex you can imagine.

"It almost has a life of its own, wouldn't you say?" Luna hums.

She is sprawled out on the hand-woven blanket I packed in Mom's beach tote before the three of us left the cottage. Mom leans against a log beside her, running her fingers through Luna's long, dark hair. Idly. Automatically. Both of their eyes are rapt by the kite flying high above us, tethered to the ground by a heavy piece of driftwood. I sit on the other side of

Mom, watching the two of them watch the kite. There's only so much entertainment to be had from gawping at a piece of nylon waving in the breeze, wouldn't you say?

"Sss," Mom says, answering Luna. *Yes.* "Like a-nance."

"Like it's dancing?" I ask Mom, trying to clarify.

"Sss."

"Or like it's trying to float free," Luna says, her voice distant. It's a hollow tone with soft edges I've come to know as her philosophical voice. Though, I'm certain if I told her that's how I saw it she'd punch me in the arm or whip out a remark that stings more than the comment would be worth. She takes a deep breath in. "An exotic creature, trapped. Beautiful, but desperately sorrowing. A life in a box—stowed away—until it's allowed to be on display, but only to a certain point. Only until the entertainment ceases. Then, the tether is tugged. The idea of freedom quashed. Yet still, it never stops trying to break away. To fly free."

"Luna?" I say in a joking tone. "Do you want me to cut the kite away from its string?"

Mom giggles, but Luna is silent, her eyes running over every inch of that fabricated jellyfish bobbing in the sea breeze. Like she's considering it. Like she's silently asking the kite what she should do.

"Another time, perhaps," she says, reaching back to rub Mom's knee. She's barely spent a couple of weeks with us, but she's already caught on to the fact that Mom's main method of communication is through touch. Always has been. "For now, let's just enjoy it's dance."

"Sss," Mom says loudly, her fingers tangling in Luna's hair as she pulls down the length of the long strands. If this hurts Luna or bothers her in any way, she doesn't let Mom know.

IN LOVE WITH YOU

I lean back on my elbows and continue to watch the pair of them. The slight upturn of Mom's mouth as she tries to smile. The freckled tip of Luna's nose gleaming in the sun. Their breathing is easy, slow, relaxed. There's a calmness that fans off the pair of them. I can feel it, all the way from where I lounge. And I want to dive into that feeling. Curl up. Live in it.

Ever since Luna started coming around, Mom's health has been on the uprise. A bit more energy each day. Longer windows between needing to sleep. She actually sat up at the dinner table last night with Steph and me. She even let Steph help her spoon tomato soup into her mouth.

For the first time in months, I've been hopeful. She could really turn around. Kick this tumor in the ass. I don't want to say it, because I don't want to jinx it, but I know I can trust you with this. She might be able to live.

"Wha?" Mom asks, the word still garbled, but understandable, at least. She's looking right at me.

"What?" I ask back.

"Fay," she says. *Face.*

Luna lifts her head up and glances back at me. "Seriously, what's with your face?"

"What's wrong with my face?"

"You're...smiling," Luna says, her brow furrowing. "But in a really creepy way."

I can feel the tops of my cheeks aching when she mentions it. I am smiling. I hadn't noticed I was at first. It's not some tiny smile, either. It's big. Teethy. I let it fall, but it appears again naturally.

"I can't help it." I look up at the kite, hoping my grin will drop naturally, but it doesn't. I shrug. "I guess I'm just happy."

"Kendra, I love you," Luna says to Mom, "but you raised a real weirdo for a son."

Mom laughs at this. Hard. Finally, the smile falls off my face as I glower at Luna. She smirks back at me, holding my gaze for several beats—long enough for me to flash back to my fantasy, where her face appeared over your shoulder—before she lowers her head back down onto the blanket. Mom mumbles something that sounds a lot like *weirdo*.

"I have half a mind to leave you both here," I grumble, only half joking.

"Ff-ooh," Mom says. *Fuck you*.

Luna and I both fold up, laughter building from deep in our guts. Mom bobbles her head, pleased with herself, and settles back on the log she's leaned against.

See what I mean about hope? Even Mom's sense of humor is returning.

My laugh turns into a sigh, and I lean back again. Ocean waves buzzing in my ear. Luna's ongoing laughter threading through the air. Nothing but blue sky in my vision. Blue sky and a glimmer of the jellyfish kite, bobbing and bobbing in the wind. Caged or free, it doesn't matter. Right now, it looks beautiful to me. The only thing that could make it more beautiful is if you were here, fingers laced through mine, laughing with Mom and Luna.

Twenty-One

Ryder

I PULL UP IN front of Mark and Gina's monster two-story that sits one street back from the northernmost stretch of beach in West Cove a little after two on Friday afternoon. Gina's dad owns one of the most popular restaurant franchises on the Oregon Coast. He bought Gina the house as soon as she finished her business degree. It was a partial graduation gift, partial welcome to the family business gift. Mark, who never had two pennies to rub together growing up, resisted moving in with her a few years ago. Resisted hard.

But Gina has always managed to get her way.

Mark kept his job in construction, though, even after Gina's dad offered him an administrative position with the company. I think it was more the expectation to wear a suit every day than the fact a job was being handed to him just because of who he was dating that put him off more than anything.

I honk twice and wait for Mark to come running.

FAYE DARLING

Everyone is getting off of work early so we can trek into our campsite along one of the rivers bubbling out of the coastal mountains before dark and wake up in the morning fully ready to commune with nature.

You wanna know something? More than I'm craving you, I'm craving being outside for more than an hour at a time.

Okay, maybe I'm not craving the outdoors more than you, but it's close, baby. You okay with a little competition?

I didn't mean it like that.

Fuck, I'm an idiot.

I've tried not to say much about what happened early Sunday morning, because...well, I'm embarrassed about it. And still sorry. But let me say this one thing and then I'll never bring it up again, because if it's painful for me, then I know it's gotta be a little bit painful for you, too.

Just put yourself in my shoes. Can you do that?

Better yet, just think of every other book you've read. You've most likely fallen in love with one of the main characters before. Just a smidge. Maybe you've fallen in love with hundreds of them. Maybe that happens with every single book you read. And, chances are, not a single one has ever loved you back, let alone noticed you in their world at all.

I'm not saying what I did was okay, picturing Luna in bed with me instead of you, I'm just saying that this is new for me. Being in love with someone I've never actually met, someone I can only ever feel. And, because it's new, I don't know what the hell I'm doing. *Clearly.*

So, do you think you can forgive me?

A set of knuckles raps on my window. I crank the glass low, only to be immediately attacked by Gina. She latches onto me. Hugs my neck. Breathes into my hair.

IN LOVE WITH YOU

"Hey," I say.

"I'm sorry I haven't been a better friend to you lately, Ry," she says. "I've been wanting to stop by, see how your mama is doing, but—"

"You've been busy," I say, rubbing her arm. "I get it."

"I want to ask how she is, but I'm afraid to hear your answer," she says, voice still muffled by my hair. "But tell me anyway. How's Mer-mom?"

That's what Gina's always called Mom. *Mer-mom*. Gina's mom is deathly afraid of the ocean—really must be hard living on the coast—and Gina has always been enamored by my mother, who would take me and my group of friends surfing or boogie boarding or to her super-secret spots along the coast. Mom could spend hours out in the water in her wetsuit. She'd swim and surf and float. Gina was convinced she was a mermaid. Started calling her Mer-mom in middle school.

"You want it straight?" I ask, catching a piece of Gina's dyed-blonde hair in my mouth. I hook a finger around the strand and pull it out.

"No," she says, her voice a crackling squeak. "Yes."

"She's been doing better lately," I say, trying to keep my hope in check. "But still not good."

"Fuck," Gina whispers, a sob racking through her. I pull her closer, dragging her halfway through the window. Gina is a second sister to me. One that didn't need as much looking after as my own. Probably because her dad immigrated from Poland in the late '80s and her mom comes from one of the oldest Italian-American families in the state. Genetics at play or not, Gina is tough as nails, fiercely direct, and has a big fucking heart. She sniffles. Curses again. "I'm not the one supposed to be falling apart, here. I'm supposed to be comforting you."

"That's okay," I say. It just feels nice to be hugged by someone that isn't Steph or Mom. If Gina is good at anything, it's doling out hugs.

"You coming with us, babe?" Mark asks, opening the passenger door.

Gina sniffs again and pulls herself out of the cab of my Camaro. She runs her hands down my arms in the process and grips my fingers in her fists. Her makeup is smudged where she's been crying.

"Don't get my man killed this weekend," she tells me, her features nothing but stern.

"Babe, relax," Mark says, and Gina shoots him an icy glare. He stuffs his backpack behind the passenger seat and holds up his hands in surrender. "I know, I know. No strippers."

"Damn straight no strippers," Gina squeezes my fingers sharply. "And no trying to swim in the river at night when you're blasted, either. No jumping over the fire. No sparring with those big bowie knives again. No—"

"Fun," Mark says. "No fun. Got it."

"Hey," I give her hands a shake. "He's safe with me."

"I want to believe that," she says.

"Babe," Mark says, climbing over the gearshift in the center of the car. He grips the steering wheel with one hand and sticks his puckered face close to the open window. "Kiss."

Gina drops my hands and leans in, kissing Mark mere inches from my face. I look past them. Study the hydrangea bush that still has dusty purple flowers clinging on for dear life. When I catch a flash of Gina's tongue dive into Mark's mouth, I decide to clear my throat. They press their lips together one last time before pulling apart with a loud *smack*.

They make me sick.

They make me envious.

I want to kiss you like that in front of my best friends.

I want to kiss you. Period.

"Should I be worried about this woman named Luna who's joining you this weekend?" Gina asks me, a pair of shark eyes boring holes through my skeletal system.

"Wh-what do you mean?" I ask.

Gina punches me hard in the shoulder, her knuckle finding that especially sensitive place between muscle and bone. "You think I'm stupid or something?"

"Never said that."

"Babe, you're the smartest person in this driveway," Mark says. *Suck up*.

"I'd like to think that was a compliment, but," Gina quirks her mouth and slides her eyes from Mark to me and back again. "There's not exactly a crowd out here."

"Ouch," I say, placing a hand over my heart.

Gina pinches the skin of my forearm and twists until it burns. "Mark told me everything about this writer woman. So? Should I be worried about her?"

"Nah," I say. "She's cool. I don't think she'd try anything with your hubby-to-be if that's what you're concerned about."

"It's not." Gina's eyes collapse to slits. Her head cocks to one side like she's trying to read my mind. "She's not dicking you around is she?"

"What? Why would you say that?"

"Mark said he saw something at the bakery the other day," Gina explains, and my eyes cut to Mark, who is sliding down in the passenger seat, already nursing a flask. "Said you two looked pretty cozy on your side of the booth."

"So what if we did?" I challenge. But, honestly, I don't know what Mark thought he saw. Two friends comfortable in one another's presence? There's no way Luna thinks of me in any other way. I'm more of a necessary evil, a means to an end. That end? Her novel. The thing that will nudge her career forward. Of course, I'm not going to say those things to Gina and let her try to tell me otherwise.

Gina folds her arms over her chest. "Just be careful."

"Thanks, Mom."

"Fuck you, asshole," Gina says, punching me again. Seriously, how does she hit that pain point every single time? It's like a superpower or something. Or the byproduct of growing up with a little brother as wild and devious as Blake Dubicki. Survival of the fittest and all that may imply. "If she puts your heart on a string and plays it like a yo-yo like that last woman you dated, I'll kick her ass and grin while I do it."

"Okay, babe," Mark says, resting his elbow on my thigh as he leans over to wave at Gina with the hand he has clutched around his flask. "Bye, bye."

"I love you," she tells him with a sugar-dusted smile that turns bitter a second later. "And put that damn flask away until you get to the woods. Ryder can't get into any more trouble."

"I'll take care of it," Mark says, untwisting the cap and chugging until the thing is empty. He sighs. Wipes a dribble of alcohol from his lips. Smiles up at Gina. "All gone. Open container? Open container of what, officer? Wait. Dude. There's more booze in the trunk, right?"

"I thought you were taking care of it." I lie just to watch him squirm a little.

IN LOVE WITH YOU

"Shit, I forgot," he says. He snaps his fingers, like a plan has just materialized in his head. "We'll swing by the market on the way out of town. Buy a few cases of Bud. You got cash? Gina, babe, you got cash? They're cash only at the market."

"Fifteen years ago they were," I say, stifling a laugh.

"Fuck," Mark says. "Really?"

"Yeah."

"How'd I forget that—fuck! You think I got that thing old people get sometimes?" he asks. "You know when their brains get all out of whack and they can't remember shit?"

"Alzheimer's?"

"That's it. You think I got that or something?"

"Nah, I just think you're drunk."

"Probably right," he says, then exhales a hot batch of air straight into my face. Yep. Definitely drunk. "How are we gonna get booze then? Steal it? Ha—steal it. I forgot about credit cards. You okay to drive man?"

"I'm completely sober."

"Just wondering if your world was spinning, too," Mark says, closing his eyes. "Now. Back to our booze problem."

"Don't worry about it," I say, slapping him on the chest a few times and pushing him back toward his side of the car. "I was only messing with you. I've got you covered."

"Fuck, man." He laughs, turning red. It's like I've just said the funniest thing he's ever heard. He slaps his knee. "You really had me going there for a second."

"Watch him," Gina tells me as I put the Camaro in reverse.

"Watch who?" I play dumb.

"She means me, man," Mark says, then drops his voice to a whisper. At least, *he* thinks it's a whisper. "She has eyes everywhere."

163

FAYE DARLING

"I heard that," she says as I back onto the street.

"Love you, babe," Mark yells, big and loud and with a cheesy ass wave.

"You'd better," she shouts.

And we're off. Tires churning on a smooth stretch of asphalt. The Camaro nothing but a blur of yellow whizzing through a landscape of green.

Twenty-Two

Ryder

We head toward The Tavern, where we've planned to meet everyone.

Mark has the music cranked up so loud—some hair band from the '80s—that I can hardly even hear myself think. Do you like this kind of music? Heavy guitar, screeching voices. It's fine if you do, but I'm partial to the sound of bands like Creedence Clearwater Revival and The Rolling Stones and Lynyrd Skynyrd. The kind of rock that just flows out of the musicians. Not sounding forced. Not trying too hard to be something the people want. It just is. It just exists. And I like the idea of that—just existing. Experiencing everything moment to moment, the good and the bad.

That was a thought I had a lot in prison. When I would ask myself what I was going to do with my life when I got out. I decided I just wanted the freedom to go wherever, do whatever. Of course, life had other plans for me, but still.

FAYE DARLING

It's a fascinating idea, don't you think? Who knows, maybe someday me going wherever, doing whatever, will lead me to you. The you that exists in the real world, not just as a thought at the back of my mind.

"Don't roll the window down," I tell Mark as we scream down the winding road.

But he's already got it cranked open, his head sticking out of it, mouth hanging open like he's some kind of dog. He tries to push himself further out the window, but I grab him by the belt of his cargo pants and tug him back down in his seat.

"Fuck happened?" he asks, blinking quickly.

"You tried to fly," I say.

"Hells yeah." He claps his hands. Whoops. "I'm fucking flying."

"Yeah you are," I say as we pull into the parking lot.

Nick is already waiting for us, leaning against his Subaru that looks like it's had a fresh wash. He knows where we're going, though. Has been there countless times before. The road that leads to the trailhead is nothing but mud from frequent washouts. Why he decided to wash his car right before this little adventure is a mystery. But Nick's like that, I guess. Clean. Cares about appearances. I blame his upbringing. Even though he moved out of his parents' house and to West Cove with his chill-to-the-max Irish grandma in high school, he still hasn't unlearned everything his up-tight Dad and appearances-is-everything stepmom had taught him.

My eyes narrow on Nick as I steer us closer to him. Luna stands beside the back hatch of his car, looking up at him as he leans close, talking to her, making her smile. It makes me nauseous for some reason. Some reason I can't explain, or don't want to explain. Not to you. Not right now.

What I wouldn't give to be back at home, curled up on the couch with Mom and Steph watching *Gilmore Girls*. Maybe you'd be there, too. Maybe we're not on the couch. Maybe you and I are upstairs alone, tangled in the sheets. The thought sends a thrill through me.

"Nick wanted the cider," I say, scrubbing my hands over my face. I feel Luna's eyes on me. Will she write this entire scene down in her notebook later? Will this part make it into her book?

"Nicholas," Drunk Mark says, clucking his tongue. "Shame, shame."

"Cider is underrated," Nick says. He scratches his thick, dark beard. "It has a superior refreshing quality when compared to beer and, quite frankly, can give you just as much of a buzz."

"Yeah, if you're a lightweight," Luna mutters.

Nick blushes. He actually fucking blushes.

My hand fists at my side, but as soon as I notice, I unfurl my fingers.

"Where the hell is Blake?" I growl, pacing the space between Nick's car and mine.

Thankfully, none of my friends tell me to chill. Mark and Luna are too busy picking their poison out of the cooler and Nick knows better than to say those words to me.

"Hey, how's Stephanie?" Nick asks, trying to distract me instead.

I watch Mark and Luna walk a few feet away from the back of my car and shove keys through the sides of their beer cans. They press their lips to the punctures, nod at one another, and crack the tabs at the same time. Luna's throat ripples as she chugs.

Twenty-Four

Ryder

"*THAT'S* YOUR TENT?" I eye Luna's tent as I snap the rainfly into place over my own.

"Yes," she says defensively. "Is that *your* tent?"

"How old is that thing anyway?" I squint at the tiny thing, which is nothing more than a small stretch of canvas held up by two short poles in the middle, leaving both ends exposed.

"I think it belonged to my grandfather at one point."

"Try your great-grandfather." I can't help but laugh, just a little. Things have felt so tense ever since I kissed her that it feels good to laugh. Even if Luna is glaring at me as I do so. Actually, her glaring while I'm laughing helps ease the tension even more. Makes our dynamics seem normal again. "If it were the middle of July and you were at some nice campground where the chances of predatory animals wandering through were low, your tent might work. *Might*."

"What?" Her face crumples in the beam of my headlamp, then her features turns to stone. She mutters, "That bastard."

"What bastard?"

"My former favorite cousin and oldest friend," she says, tossing down the last tent stake she had in her hands. "D.J.'s dead to me now. Dead."

"You know how I get over things?" Drunk Mark slurs from his spot by the fire. Yes, somehow, even Drunk Mark can start a fire. Of course, Nick had to jump on him when he wanted to pour the entire bottle of lighter fluid on it. I don't think Gina would appreciate a groom with no eyebrows.

"Murder?" Luna asks.

"Yerp," Drunk Mark says around a burp. "I *murder* the fuck out of a beer."

Luna chuckles, then sighs. She folds in on herself just a little. Head bowing. Elbows tucking into her stomach. Is this how she looks when she feels...defeated? Because I have to say, it's kind of cute. Not that I think she's cute. Don't hear me saying that. You're cute. You're totally cute. Cuter than Luna.

But I'd like to think Luna and I have become friends over the past couple of weeks. I've only ever seen her confident and ready for battle. Never like this. Not even when she told me about her mom's passing. She still seemed in control. The master of her world.

"You can't sleep in that thing," I tell her.

Really, she can't. I'll be up all night worrying that every minor creak of a tree in the night is a cougar pouncing, a coyote sniffing around, or Blake finding an easy entrance into her personal space. I don't think kissing her would be an option at that point. Fists. That would be my option. Blake's nose crunching under my knuckles. His blood sprayed over the forest floor.

"You can share my tent, babe," Blake says, snickering as he takes a sip of beer beside Mark. The flames of the fire dancing in the pit paint waves of light and dark on his smug little face. I growl at the back of my throat, staring him down.

"There's plenty of room with Mark and me," Nick offers.

"Yeah and then my sister can murder her Sunday afternoon," Blake says, and he has a point. Gina might be okay with Luna tagging along, but I don't think she'd be very forgiving to find out her betrothed had slept beside another woman in a small tent. Blake empties the rest of his beer and throws the bottle onto the fire, glass shattering. "The solution is simple, *roomie*."

"The solution *is* simple," I say in a low, gravelly tone that strikes the air with authority. Take a breath, baby, because you might not like what I'm about to say. "She's here because of me, so she'll sleep with me."

Not like that. That's not what I meant. Sleep beside me. Just beside me. In a separate sleeping bag. Clothes on. No kissing. Friends helping out friends. That's okay, right?

Ooh. Okay. Is that a pinprick of jealousy I feel coming from you?

Is it wrong that I kind of like it?

Because it means maybe my feelings aren't one-sided. It means you might feel the same way I feel about you?

My skin is hot at the thought. I very much wish it was you about to share a cramped tent with me tonight instead of Luna. There'd probably be absolutely no sleeping, but that wouldn't matter, right? Who needs sleep when you have love sustaining you?

"Steph's..." I don't know what to tell Nick. That I'm worried about my sister? That she's hiding something from me? That she's just as scared and as worn out as I am about everything going on with Mom? "All right. She's all right."

"Good," Nick says, scratching his beard again. "Well, tell her I say hello."

"Sure, sure," I say, only half-interested in my reply, because my focus has been drawn to the BMW that's just zipped into the lot.

Blake Dubicki, asshole supreme.

With a thunder of gravel beneath his tires he blazes across the lot, driving straight for Mark and Luna. Mark stumbles out of the way, but Luna stands her ground. Even as Blake slams on the brakes, his car coming to a halt just inches from her, she doesn't so much as flinch.

I do, though. Hands clenched, chest puffed. Blake used to do that kind of shit with Steph as a joke. A joke I've never found funny. I take one step toward Blake's door when a meaty hand pushes against my chest.

"Not worth it, Ry," Nick mutters as Blake steps out of his car.

He's wearing a pair of expensive sunglasses even though the clouds are so dark it's practically nighttime. *Moron.* He slides the glasses down his nose just enough to gawp at Luna. Eyes traveling over her every curve. Teeth raking over his bottom lip.

"Who brought the snack?" Blake asks, smirking.

I grunt, and Nick gives me an easy shove toward his car. He uses his teacher voice to round up the group. "Come on, everyone. Let's get going before we lose the light."

Drunk Mark wobbles toward the Subaru, but I barely notice him. My eyes are fixed elsewhere. Luna follows Mark, but Blake grabs her wrist and yanks her back. His mouth is practically swallowing her ear as he says something to her I can't hear. Then, he slides his hand around the curve of her ass, sticking his hand in the back pocket of her waterproof hiking pants.

I shouldn't worry about her. I don't *want* to worry about her.

But this is Blake. He thinks he can get away with acting like a sleaze bag just because of who his daddy is. Just because he's got enough money to pay his way out of any kind of trouble he makes. Just because he can turn on the charm in front of the right sort of folks and get away with anything.

All the things he did to my sister during their relationship, all the times he hurt her and somehow managed to talk her back into his arms, flood my memory as I eye his hand palming Luna's ass through her pocket.

My heart hammers in my chest, and my vision blurs around the edges. All at once, I feel woozy and fired up and sick to my stomach and like I could flip a car over by myself. I know this mix of feelings well. It's how I felt right before I put that guy who touched Steph in the hospital and myself in jail.

And I hate it.

I hate this feeling more than just about anything.

It makes everything seem so out of my control.

Luna was right when she said most of what I do is because of a need to be in control. I know I could punch Blake in the face right now and take back my control. But where has that gotten me in the past? Where will that put me in the future? I can't let this asshole have all the power over me, though. Not for an entire weekend. I need to find another way to take control. One that helps me stay in the driver's seat without crashing the whole motherfucking car.

And the answer is standing a few feet in front of me.

Look, baby, I apologize for what I'm about to do, but I'm afraid if I don't do this, I'm going to do something else. Something that could rob my freedom again.

It's nothing personal. It's just a survival tactic.

I start off across the parking lot just as Luna tries to remove Blake's hand from her pocket. He laughs and drags a finger down the length of her face. Boops her on the nose.

"Ryder?" Nick says at my back. "What are you doing?"

"Nipping this in the bud," I say.

"What the fuck's that mean?"

Luna takes a step away from Blake right before I spin her around by the waist so she's facing me square-on. That look on her face—almost like innocence—sends my heart pounding out a different kind of beat.

I grip her cheek in one of my hands, my palm nearly engulfing that side of her face. She's always seemed so solid in my eyes that I haven't realized just how small she actually is. How fragile. I tilt her face toward mine and slam my lips onto hers, the collision so harsh and unexpected, she reaches out and grips my thick flannel in both of her fists to steady herself.

Maybe it's because I've wanted to kiss you for so long now and that desire is spilling over into this moment, or because Luna's lips have always secretly been so tempting to me, but I moan against her. Pry her lips wide with my own and snake my tongue inside her mouth.

Okay. I hadn't meant to do *that*. All I wanted was to send a message to Blake that he needs to back off. In a way that shuts him down, not fires him up. I wasn't supposed to shove my tongue down this chick's throat. But fuck, it feels good. And she meets me stroke for stroke. Small firecracker pops of pleasure spark all over my skin.

My hand slides to the back of her skull, moving her to find a better angle. She tastes like beer and sin. She feels like fucking magic.

I find myself not wanting this to end, not wanting to rip myself away, but then I think of you and what this might be doing to you, what you might be thinking about me, and I step away from Luna, our lips smacking loudly as they pull apart.

That innocent look is still there when I look into her eyes. Shock, too. And something else, something I can't quite pin down.

My head cranks around when I remember why I kissed her in the first place, and I stick Blake with a glare so fierce, his Adam's apple jumps noticeably in the middle of his neck.

Message. Received.

I don't say anything to Luna. I don't know what to say, if I'm being honest. I only have two words on my mind as I drag her by the wrist across the parking lot toward Nick's car, and those words are for you.

I'm sorry.

Again.

Shit.

Twenty-Three

Luna

WHAT THE FUCK, READER? What the actual fuck just happened?

He kissed me.

Out of nowhere, a kiss. Unexpected, terrifying, exhilarating, vindicated.

I trail behind the pack as we hike into our camp site. My fingers swoop up to touch my lips every five seconds, because I can still feel Ryder's mouth on mine. Can still taste him on my tongue.

He was being a complete, closed-off ass around me while we were hanging around the parking lot, right? And then, *bam*, a kiss.

A kiss.

I feel sixteen again. Heart weightless, body sizzling with desire, head dizzy from trying to figure out what it might mean. I can't even concentrate on the beautiful scenery I'm so far lost in my own head.

IN LOVE WITH YOU

But I try.

I take a deep breath, loop my fingers through the straps of the backpack I borrowed from D.J., and try to focus on the landscape instead of Ryder's lips and tongue and—

Stop it, Luna, I tell myself. *Focus.*

The trees are giants surrounded by fallen needles, ferns, and ivy-covered underbrush. Recent rains have dredged up the deep, earthy smells of the forest. Cool evening air. Clouds like cotton tufts pressing down. It's hard not to relax out here. Unspool. Unwind. It's hard not to understand why Ryder and his friends choose to disappear out here for a weekend instead of heading to the city, hitting up bars and chasing the nightlife.

Feeling this calmness wind through me slowly tells me more about Ryder's character than spending countless days at his house ever could. He's pent-up and tense most of the time, but this is his escape. I don't even have to ask him if it's true. It's something I feel settling into my own bones.

My fingers itch for the pencil and notebook in my borrowed backpack. Short lines crop up in my head, begging to be written down and woven into whatever story I decide to tell after I'm finished here. After I leave this place.

A chill rocks through me, robbing a tiny bit of the peace I was starting to feel.

After I leave this place. It's always been a comfort, knowing I'd visit exotic places, lose myself in the people who live there, and then retreat to my tiny hunting cabin to do my favorite thing in the world—write.

So then why does the thought of flying back to Oklahoma make me feel a little sick this time?

"Home sweet home," Nick says as he pushes a Vine Maple aside a few feet off the path ahead, offering a glimpse of a small clearing, the remnants of a campfire ringed in rock, a couple of stumps and small logs dropped around it for makeshift seats.

"How often do y'all come here?" I ask the group.

Everyone's been quiet, cordial even, ever since we packed into Nick's Subaru back at The Tavern and headed inland, following old logging roads and pothole-laden streets to reach the trailhead. Maybe it was Ryder's and my kiss that subdued the group. Maybe it was just their way of meeting nature—in a still state of mind. But even Mark has been silent, save a few murmurs and giggles in his buzzed state. So, it's not shocking when no one answers me.

Blake and Mark slip through the gap in the saplings and Nick looks pointedly at Ryder, a knowing smile hitching up on one side of his face.

Ryder sighs through clenched teeth. Like he's annoyed with my question. Still, he answers it. "We've been coming here a few times a year since high school."

Nick snorts. Tightens his gaze as Ryder steps past him, then softens it as I step up. He lowers his voice so only I can hear. "Ryder spends more time out here on his own than the rest of us combined. He even lived out here for a whole month right after he got out."

"Got out?" I question. Out of where? A situation? A place?

Nick's face suddenly looks like someone has gripped the skin at all four corners and stretched it wide. His dark eyes are massive, regret writhing inside them. "He hasn't told you, has he?"

"Told me what?" I ask slowly.

"Forget I said anything," he mutters, pulling the Vine Maple further back, a clear signal for me to step through and join the others. "It's his story to tell."

IN LOVE WITH YOU

Intrigue. Mystery. A troubled back story to coax out of the shadows, perhaps? The writer in me is overjoyed, the rest of me is a burning building about to collapse—no matter what I do to distract myself, whenever I think about Ryder, I instantly feel the ghost of his lips on mine.

Reader, what do you think the repercussions would be if I walk up to the man right now as he's unrolling his tent from its stuff sack, climb him like a tree, and kiss the daylights out of him?

Shit.

That's a bad idea isn't it?

Yeah. Thought so.

A long time ago, I learned to never get involved romantically with my research subjects. It gets...messy. My head right now is a prime example of that. But I'm a big girl. I can keep things strictly business. This weekend I will be Luna Preston, the professional writer capable of keeping her feelings out of it, not Lunetta Malcolm, the thirty-three-year-old preacher's daughter who hasn't been with a man in almost two years.

I rest my backpack on the toes of the hiking boots that once belonged to my aunt and root around for my notebook and pencil. A headlamp, too, since the light is all but gone, and I'll need to see to take notes.

Or...I look around the campsite. Even though Mark is chugging a beer, the rest of the guys are focused on camping tasks. Ryder is assembling tent poles. Nick is laying out the fabric of another tent nearby. Even Blake is working on his own shelter, staking up a tent as far away from Ryder as he can manage.

Okay, then. Survival first, note-taking second.

I scribble down the single line I've been dying to get onto the page since we started hiking, then fish around in my pack for the tent. When D.J. handed it to me, he smiled like a goon and told me if I needed help setting it up one of the guys would know how. He laughed when I balked at him, even though I've never assembled a tent like this in my life.

I love men, don't get me wrong. Men are amazing. But I am fiercely independent, have been fending for myself since I was sixteen, and you can bet your left butt cheek I'm going to fail miserably a thousand times over before I ask someone else, especially a man, to help me.

My tent springs free, and I go about setting it up like I know exactly what I'm doing. Like I've been doing this sort of thing for decades.

FAYE DARLING

Okay, that was cheesy. You make me say cheesy things, apparently. Thanks for that.

"Are you sure?" Luna asks.

I blink stupidly at her for several, long seconds. I think I expected her to put up more of a fight. To suggest strapping pieces of a tarp to either side of her tent. To suggest roughing it in the old canvas scrap regardless of the dangers it poses.

"If he's not," Blake says, "I am."

"I'm sure," I say to Luna.

She looks me in the eye for a solid thirty seconds, searching for any unsurety, I presume. Then, her face hardens. Her lips purse. She nods. "Thanks."

Without another word, she starts to dismantle her tent.

Twenty-Five

Ryder

WE EAT. WE DRINK. We tell stories. We laugh. We sit in silence, letting the buzz of the river rolling nearby and the wind shivering through the trees settle around us. Then, well after midnight, we all slowly depart for bed. I'm the last one up. Partly because I want to make sure the fire is truly put out and no one has left any food out in the open for small or large critters to come hunting for in the night, but mostly I'm the last one up because it might be easier if Luna falls asleep before I come in. It might save some awkward fumbling.

I'd be lying to you if I said I hadn't caught glimpses of her around the fire tonight and thought about that kiss. It's been a while since I kissed anyone. Every woman I've dated since I got out of prison hasn't been able to get past the fact that I served time, so, a year and a half ago, I kind of just gave up trying.

FAYE DARLING

When the fire is nothing but cooling black coals and the rest of our dinner and snacks are packed into thick plastic bear canisters, I walk a few hundred feet away from camp and relieve myself.

I take my time strolling back to our tents.

A mist is beginning to fall, which will no doubt be followed by a heavy, heavy rain if the look of those dark clouds has anything to say about it. I love the way rain sounds as it beats on my tent. I love the way the wind rattles the nylon fabric, threatening to shake the whole thing down. Lying there, tucked in the warmth of my sleeping bag, listening to the natural world spin all around me—there's nothing else like it.

The zipper whines as I open the tent flap. I click off my headlamp after I drag the zipper closed again. It takes a few seconds, but my eyes adjust to the darkness inside. Hunched way over, I step out of my boots and tuck them into the corner near the foot of my sleeping bag.

Luna shifts in her sleeping bag as I slide into the top of mine beside her, my knee bumping what might be her hip, or maybe her ass, as I tuck myself in. My shoulder accidentally nudges her sideways.

"Sorry," I whisper quietly, in case she's awake.

The tent is small. A two-man tent I bought because it was basically the size of a one-man tent for a guy my size.

My leg knocks into her as I shimmy out of my cargo pants, stripping down to my boxers. My elbow digs into her frame when I tug off my top layers.

She grunts a little. "Right now, you're a loose dog running through any boutique my mother ever told me to keep my hands to myself in."

"Sorry," I say, biting my lip to keep from smiling at the thought of a young Luna being told to not be as curious as she wanted. "Almost done."

"Almost done doing what?" she hisses.

"Getting out of these clothes," I say.

There's a zip of awareness that passes palpably between us. I hear her gulp.

"All right."

"Sorry, it's a tight squeeze in here."

"Stop apologizing," she says.

"You really hate that, don't you?"

"If you can't control it, don't take the blame for it," she says. "You didn't make the tent."

"Yeah, but I did buy it."

"You didn't force me to sleep in here."

"I sure as hell wasn't going to let you bunk with Blake."

She scoffs. "Like that was going to happen."

"I'm sor—"

"I swear, if you finish that sentence, I'll..."

I wait for her to finish her own sentence, but her words just trail off into the dark. I toss my clothes at my feet and burrow into my sleeping bag, trying to find a comfortable position that also doesn't involve me crushing Luna.

"Why did you kiss me today?" she asks.

The question is a left hook in my blind spot. It nearly knocks me to the ground. Luckily, I'm already there, so I wouldn't have far to fall. I squeeze my lips together until I can feel the skin start to tear. "It was either kiss you or kill Blake."

"Why?"

"You're seriously asking that?"

"I know he had his hand in my back pocket and was basically telling me how delicious my ass was," she says, and I wish she hadn't told me that last part, because now I'm sweating and my fists are clenched and— "But I was going to take care of it."

"Blake and I have...history," I say.

"He used to date Steph, didn't he?"

"Who told you that?"

"Nick," she says. "I think he hates Blake as much as you do. He was telling me how much he was looking forward to this weekend, but with one exception."

"He said that?" I ask. I didn't know Nick hated anyone. Not even the nightmarish family he ran away from as a teenager.

"You could have just moved me behind you or led me back toward the car," she says, then inhales a sharp breath. When she speaks again her voice is a feathery whisper. "You didn't have to kiss me."

She's right. I could have done both of those things. I could have just turned my back on the whole thing. I could have left her to fend for herself.

"I wasn't thinking clearly," I say, trying to justify my actions.

"Is that the only reason you did it, though?" she asks. She gulps again. "Because you hate Blake and just wanted to mark your territory? Or..."

"Yes," I say. "That's the reason."

"But is it the only reason?"

"I'm too drunk for this," I say, rolling over onto my side so that I'm facing away from her.

"You barely had anything to drink."

Of course she would notice that. Of course she would be watching my every move. She's using me for her stories. Trying to give shape to whatever character she decides to make up about me. That's it.

"Maybe I thought you'd want to know what it was like," I say.

"What it was like?"

"Kissing me."

"What gave you the impression I wanted that?"

"I figured it'd be good for your research."

"Yeah." She sounds small. Distant. Like she's on the other side of the river, hundreds of yards away, and not two inches behind me. "Research."

"Since you write romance and all," I add, although I have no fucking clue why. I need to stop talking. I close my eyes and pray to the gods of sleep that they show mercy tonight. Strike quick. Knock me out cold.

"Maybe..."

"Maybe what?"

"Maybe you could do it again?" Her voice is a trembling whisper, like she's not so sure what she's asking or why.

I look over my shoulder at her. Nothing but a pair of big eyes poking out over the lip of her sleeping bag. "For your research?"

"Yeah," she says, but something in that affirmative sounds hollow. Not that she's unsure if she wants me to kiss her, but unsure if she wants to say it's for the sake of research.

Gina's words echo in my head. *Mark said you two looked pretty cozy.*

My heart is beating so fast she has to be able to feel it pulsing through the fabric of our touching sleeping bags, she has to be able to hear it pounding in this small space.

Silence. A full minute of heart-racing, breath-bated silence.

She stares at me. I stare at her.

FAYE DARLING

And then—

It's hard to say which one of us moves first, but one minute I'm rolled as far away from her as I can get and the next I'm lying halfway over the top of her, our sleeping bags swishing noisily as my lips vie for purchase on hers. Our noses glance off of each other, our teeth clash. There's a neediness, an urgency, to our kiss. A now or never sort of thing.

Her hands slide out of her sleeping bag and carve a path up the back of my neck, fingers tangling in my mist-dampened hair. She pulls me down on top of her, crushing me against her until there's nowhere left to go except straight through the tent floor and into the bowels of the earth, the fiery pits of hell, which is exactly where you'll most likely want to send me after this. I'm aware of your presence, but not as sharply attuned to every rise and fall of your emotions the way I usually am. It's hard to think about anything seriously with Luna slipping her tongue in my mouth.

She tugs sharply on my hair, a pain that raises every hair on my body. I groan against her lips, and she snickers. Wraps her fists around the roots of my hair and tugs again. This time, it's nothing but a sweet, dull ache that has other parts of me raising now.

I bring my arms out into the open, wrap them around her, and roll onto my back, bringing her to rest flat over the top of me. I suck on her lip before she rips herself away. She tries to straddle my hips—I think—but her sleeping bag works against her. She slips right off the other side, the tent trembling as she crashes into it. A surprised yelp and a giggle follow.

"Now who's a loose dog in a boutique?" I ask in a husky whisper.

"Making out in a tent is always more romantic in books and movies," she says. "In real life it's just bolts of slippery fabric and not enough space."

"Do you want to stop?" I ask.

"I never said that."

I emit a low hum that rattles my chest, surprisingly pleased by her answer. I don't know what to say. She's awoken something inside of me. Something that fell into a deep hibernation years ago. It's intoxicating.

Reaching for the zipper on her sleeping bag, I try and find her eyes. "May I?"

"Mm," she says, biting her bottom lip in a way that makes the world tip on its axis just a little. She still isn't looking at me as I drag the zip low. As I flap open her sleeping bag, exposing bare legs, a hint of black cotton panties, and a long sleeve t-shirt two sizes too big, a cartoon cowboy riding a bull screen-printed across her chest. I put a knuckle under her chin and tilt it up so she's forced to meet my eyes. When she does, the world stops tipping and everything snaps into place.

She sits up the best she can in the sliver of space between me and the wall of the tent. She slides a knee over my hip, trapping my torso between her thighs. She's high up on my hips, not even close to my slowly-hardening length, but I let out a pleased sigh anyway. Just the weight of her feels incredible.

"Can I touch you?" I whisper.

She bites her lip again. "Mm-hmm."

I glide my hands up her bare thighs. Her skin is warm, despite the obvious chill in the air. I dock the heels of my hands against the sharp bones jutting out of her hips, spread my fingers around the curve of her until they meet at a low knot in her spine.

Luna's eyes close. Long, dark lashes dropping over alabaster skin. Her head hangs back and she relaxes into a sigh, sinking farther into my body.

"I haven't done this in so long," she whispers. "Would you think I'm crazy if I told you it just feels nice to sit here with your hands on my body?"

I want to tell her it's not crazy at all. I want to tell her it's been a long time for me, too, and I wouldn't mind sitting like this for an eternity. Hands on her hips. Her body pressing into mine. My exhale bleeding into her inhale.

"God, you're beautiful," I whisper before I even think twice.

As soon as the words leave my lips, a chill settles over me, like the most honest truth in the world has sunk into every fiber of my being. I think I've wanted to tell her how beautiful I think she is since the day we ran into one another on that wave.

"You're beautiful, too," she says.

"Nah," I say.

"Really," she says. She bends at the waist and props herself up with one hand placed on the ground beside my right ear. With her other hand she guides a fingertip down the length of my nose so slowly it brings goosebumps to the surface of my flesh. "The wayward curve of your nose, beautiful. Like a bend in the river. It tells a story. And these eyebrows?" She smooths her thumb over one brow, then the next. "They catch the secrets your ocean eyes give away. Beautiful. But I believe it's your lips that hold the most—"

I lift my head slightly off the ground and kiss the words back into her mouth. She swallows them down, nearly taking my tongue with them.

No one's ever said anything like that about me before, and while I've never really cared about how I looked or what others thought about me, it's nice to hear those things. Nicer still to hear how specific those things are, to know how *deeply* Luna has been paying attention to me. This definitely doesn't feel like she's *just* using me for research.

Luna rests her forearms on my chest, curving her hands around my bare shoulders. She sucks on my bottom lip as I let my fingers trail from the outside of her hips to the lowest swoop of her stomach. One hand slides down between her legs and over the outside of her underwear. The fabric is soaked through, and as soon as I push up and against her, cupping her firmly, she pulls away, gasping. Her eyes look a little wider than they did a minute ago.

I freeze, my hand still attached to her base. Maybe I read the signals wrong. Maybe this *is* just research, and I've crossed some kind of invisible line she drew in the sand.

"We can stop," I whisper, even though it's the last thing I want. I have this image playing in my head of Luna calling out my name as I make her come that makes my chest tighten the way it used to when a new *Harry Potter* movie was coming out and I just couldn't wait to see it.

"No, it's not—" Luna swallows loudly. Buries her face in my shoulder. "I just—I haven't done this in a long time."

"Yeah, you said that."

"So, I'm just—"

"You're nervous?" I offer, trying to connect the dots she's offering.

FAYE DARLING

She nods, her long black hair falling down onto my neck, wrapping around me like a silk scarf I never want to take off.

"What do you want, then?" I whisper, trying to tell my hand, still pressed against her, to mind its manners and be patient.

"I want—" She heaves in a shaky breath, then looks right at me. She drags her fingers along the line of scruff covering my jaw. "I want you to touch me."

"You're sure?"

She sits all the way up. Swivels her hips and grinds down against my hand. She looks me right between the eyes. "I want you to make me come."

Fuck me. Sheepish to confident in less than two seconds. This woman is going to kill me.

But I don't move my hand. Don't flinch a single finger. I'm looking up into her face, but I'm thinking of you suddenly. I feel you so, so close. What are you thinking? You feel like a mixed bag of emotions. Jealous. Lust-filled. Thrilled. Overwhelmed. Do you like this, baby? Do you like...watching?

I can't tell you I've done all of this with Luna tonight because it might turn you on in some way, because it wouldn't be the truth. I love you, more than I could ever express, but a part of me is drawn to Luna, too. I don't think I realized how much until I kissed her today. I don't think I realized how much I've wanted her until she climbed on top of me.

And it pains me to say this, but Luna is real. She is smooth flesh and hot blood and solid limbs. She's gorgeous, alluring. She's here. She exists in this space with me.

I think if I don't pursue the possibility—wherever it might lead—I will regret it. So, if you're okay with that, then watch. Imagine you're Luna, if you'd like. Imagine you're here with

IN LOVE WITH YOU

I lift my head slightly off the ground and kiss the words back into her mouth. She swallows them down, nearly taking my tongue with them.

No one's ever said anything like that about me before, and while I've never really cared about how I looked or what others thought about me, it's nice to hear those things. Nicer still to hear how specific those things are, to know how *deeply* Luna has been paying attention to me. This definitely doesn't feel like she's *just* using me for research.

Luna rests her forearms on my chest, curving her hands around my bare shoulders. She sucks on my bottom lip as I let my fingers trail from the outside of her hips to the lowest swoop of her stomach. One hand slides down between her legs and over the outside of her underwear. The fabric is soaked through, and as soon as I push up and against her, cupping her firmly, she pulls away, gasping. Her eyes look a little wider than they did a minute ago.

I freeze, my hand still attached to her base. Maybe I read the signals wrong. Maybe this *is* just research, and I've crossed some kind of invisible line she drew in the sand.

"We can stop," I whisper, even though it's the last thing I want. I have this image playing in my head of Luna calling out my name as I make her come that makes my chest tighten the way it used to when a new *Harry Potter* movie was coming out and I just couldn't wait to see it.

"No, it's not—" Luna swallows loudly. Buries her face in my shoulder. "I just—I haven't done this in a long time."

"Yeah, you said that."

"So, I'm just—"

"You're nervous?" I offer, trying to connect the dots she's offering.

FAYE DARLING

She nods, her long black hair falling down onto my neck, wrapping around me like a silk scarf I never want to take off.

"What do you want, then?" I whisper, trying to tell my hand, still pressed against her, to mind its manners and be patient.

"I want—" She heaves in a shaky breath, then looks right at me. She drags her fingers along the line of scruff covering my jaw. "I want you to touch me."

"You're sure?"

She sits all the way up. Swivels her hips and grinds down against my hand. She looks me right between the eyes. "I want you to make me come."

Fuck me. Sheepish to confident in less than two seconds. This woman is going to kill me.

But I don't move my hand. Don't flinch a single finger. I'm looking up into her face, but I'm thinking of you suddenly. I feel you so, so close. What are you thinking? You feel like a mixed bag of emotions. Jealous. Lust-filled. Thrilled. Overwhelmed. Do you like this, baby? Do you like...watching?

I can't tell you I've done all of this with Luna tonight because it might turn you on in some way, because it wouldn't be the truth. I love you, more than I could ever express, but a part of me is drawn to Luna, too. I don't think I realized how much until I kissed her today. I don't think I realized how much I've wanted her until she climbed on top of me.

And it pains me to say this, but Luna is real. She is smooth flesh and hot blood and solid limbs. She's gorgeous, alluring. She's here. She exists in this space with me.

I think if I don't pursue the possibility—wherever it might lead—I will regret it. So, if you're okay with that, then watch. Imagine you're Luna, if you'd like. Imagine you're here with chuckle. Not a sharp *ha* or a breathless rib-buster. It's a sound that feels genuine. As if it's the laugh she saves for when she's completely comfortable, completely herself. It fills me with a sense of contentment that I caused that laugh.

I slide my hands around her back, scratching it gently. It has her nudging her forehead against my neck, reminding me a bit of a cat. The idea has me laughing.

She rolls onto her cheek and looks up at me. Two of her fingers walk up my chest.

"What do you need?" she whispers.

My fingers keep twirling invisible patterns over her back. "What do you mean?"

Her voice is a thin layer of fog lifting off the tops of the evergreens. "Can I touch you?"

I smile at the way she mirrors my question from earlier. She raises an unassuming eyebrow, and I nod.

"I want you to say it," she tells me.

"Yes, sweetheart," I say, lifting up to kiss the tip of her nose. "You can touch me."

Twenty-Six

Luna

I FEEL LIKE CANNED cranberry sauce resting on top of a porcelain plate in the middle of a Thanksgiving table after what Ryder just did to me.

It was a little forward of me to ask him to kiss me again. A little dubious of me to say it was all for book research when it absolutely was not. But my word, reader, I think that might've been the best orgasm I've ever had in my life. Uptight preacher's daughter, my ass.

"What do you need?" I ask Ryder for a second time as I unzip his sleeping bag. A cloud of his concentrated manly scent is released into the air as I pull back the flap to reveal his bare chest, and I promise you, if I breathe in too deeply, I will come again from the smell of his body alone.

Salt.

Sweat.

Musk.

IN LOVE WITH YOU

I can't help myself. I bend forward, wrap my lips around the center of his rock-solid peck, suck the taste of him off of his nipple, then lick a line up to his collarbone. He squirms underneath me, his hands attaching themselves to my hips once again and guiding me further down his body. And I thought his pecks were hard.

He still hasn't answered me.

I grind against him once, then lift my weight off of him. His eyes are almost frantic, all that salt-soaked blonde hair a wild mess.

"Don't tease," he ekes out, as if it's painful.

"What do you want?"

His breath is hot as it swirls out of his nose and spreads across my bare middle. I'm rarely cold—it's how I can dress so scarcely, even on the edge of winter—but even if I were, I think that breath would keep me warm the whole night long.

I ease back down, grinding down on him in slow, controlled circles. I thread my fingers through his hands, using his arms to steady myself as I rock against his throbbing erection. "Is this what you want?"

His answer is nothing but a strangled groan.

Okay, reader. What do you think? Should I force him to give me a verbalized response or should *I* decide what it is he wants?

I really hope that wasn't a strange question to ask you.

Hopefully, if you're a fan of my five-alarm-spice romance novels, you found it engaging instead of appalling. What would Ryder think if I told him I could feel you? That you're almost always present in my world? He'd think I was insane, right?

"I want," he begins, but his words crumble as I ease off of him again, waiting for him to express his desire. His eyes burn as they fixate on me. He wrenches his hands out of mine and grips the sides of my torso tightly. Thumbs digging into my ribs. Fingers spreading over the breadth of my back.

You, I think, trying to communicate with him telepathically. *You, you, you.*

He growls just before he rolls us over so I'm on my back. My legs instinctively cinch around his waist. He steals a kiss as he thrusts forward, the length of him rubbing over me in a way that has my heart dipping low for a beat.

"You," he says, still gripping my sides tightly. "I want you."

I wait for him to plunge his fingers down the waistband of my underwear and slide them off, but he doesn't, and when I hook a thumb into the tops of his boxers, he wraps his hand around my wrist and pins my arm over the top of my head. He rolls his hips and grinds into me again, the movement heavy and heated and clothed. Very much clothed.

That's fine, I tell myself.

Maybe we have two different definitions of what it means to want another person. Maybe he just doesn't want me getting the wrong idea about what this is. Perhaps he thinks sticking his dick in me will make me fall in love with him when this—this hot, sweaty romp in his too-small tent—is nothing more than book research. Because that's what I'd said it was earlier. But that was before, when we hadn't even kissed a second time.

A thought nearly strikes me down. Does he think he's just doing me a favor? Does he think he's just helping me out with my novel?

Before I can overthink this, before I can become offended by his actions, I'm swept up in the throes of raw pleasure.

He grinds against me in a hard and steady rhythm that has me tingling. His brow crinkles in this sexy, *je ne sais quoi* way I suddenly want to study closer. When he dips lower, dropping more of his weight onto me, I can't help but drag my lips over that wrinkle. The salt in the sweat he's working up lingers on my tongue when I pull away.

Abandoning the arm he's been pinning above my head, he slides a hand down the outside of my thigh, hooking the crook of my knee and lifting my leg higher. The new angle of our hips gives us more space to move. His thrusts become harder, faster, and—

"Oh, god," I groan, a heady warmth rippling through me, followed by a slow-moving tingling sensation that starts between my legs and moves outward, into my extremities.

"Are you close?" he asks, his voice as deep and as quiet as an ocean trench.

"Mm-hmm."

Those tingles feel more like embers on the verge of bursting into flame. One more rush of oxygen, one more hard, strong thrust and I will be an unstoppable blaze. Wild. Out of control. And one look at Ryder—eyes hanging low, bottom lip crushed in his teeth, breath sharp and ragged—tells me I'll take him down with me.

His hips swoop low, nailing me to the ground with their weight.

"Ryder," I cry out, and everything in me shakes free. Wave after wave of intense pleasure slams through my whole being, and I cling to Ryder just to stay afloat.

"F-f-fuck," he studders as his eyes clamp shut and he falls over the edge of his own orgasm.

His movements slow until they eventually stop. He remains poised above me, his hips still pinning me down. I reach up and sandwich his face between my palms, because I am mesmerized by him. I can't fully comprehend the look in his eyes. How clear they are. How unmottled. And all of that tension that's usually strung tight between his features hasn't just loosened, it's been cut free. There—in the soft curve of his cheekbones, in the lazy posture of his lips—is a man whose exterior reflects his interior. Right now, he is not a walking contradiction. He is not angry *and* kind. Not reserved *and* open. He is only kind, only open. Right now, that big, gooey heart I've only caught in glimpses when he wasn't paying attention, is all that I can see. And it takes my breath away. Drags up a warm, fuzzy feeling inside of me I only thought existed in books and movies.

But as I push his hair back, tucking a strand behind the curve of his ear to get a better look, he blinks, and a look of worry rattles through him. That tension has been tied together again somehow.

He clears his throat and removes his weight from me, sitting back on his heels.

The cool air finally gets to me, turning my sweat to icy droplets. I throw an arm over my bare breasts, another around the soft bulge of my midsection. For the first time tonight, I feel completely exposed.

I sit up, pawing around in the dark for my t-shirt. As soon as I feel the soft cotton of the fabric, I slide it on, not carrying if it's inside out, backward, or both.

Ryder grips my crumpled sleeping bag in his fist and offers it to me. I practically rip it out of his grip, the slick fabric cracking. I throw it into the open space beside Ryder's bag and slide over.

A tear steals down the side of my face. I shuck it away with the back of my hand. I only ever cry when I'm angry.

But why am I angry?

"Are you—" he asks.

I cut him off. "I'm fine."

My legs are chucked down in the sleeping bag, but my hands are fumbling for the zipper. I can't find it. No matter how much I twist or turn, it's never where I expect it to be. That could be a metaphor for my life right now. I feel like I'm playing a game and the rules keep changing, making it impossible to know what to do next. I sniff loudly and slap another tear away.

"Luna?"

Ryder has managed to clean himself off, burrow down into his sleeping bag, and relax without even struggling. I try not to look at him as I continue to flail. As I continue to cry.

"I don't need you to explain," I hiss. Another sob shakes loose and, with my mouth open, it's not so silent. I suck in a quick breath, trying to drag it back down, but I hiccup instead.

"What would I explain?" he asks in that dumb, blameless way he's so good at.

"You know."

"I don't, that's why I'm asking."

"That it was a mistake, a favor, a—"

"A favor?"

"You know, to help me with my research," I say. He's quiet. Too quiet. I roll a complete three-sixty in my half-zipped sleeping bag, but still come up empty. "Where's the fucking zipper on this thing?"

FAYE DARLING

"Hey." A hand reaches out and grips my arm. Not too tight, not too loose. A Goldilocks kind of perfection. "Come here."

"M'fine." I hiccup again, this one punching my rib cage. Hard.

Ryder tugs me toward him. He unzips the top of his sleeping bag, rolls onto his side, and pats the empty space beside him. All I can do is stare at that space. Blurry because of my tears. I hiccup twice in quick succession. He laughs.

"You say you're fine, but clearly, you're—"

"Careful," I warn.

"Struggling a little." His thumb rubs back and forth over my arm, but he doesn't try and pull me into his sleeping bag again. Just maintains his grip on me and keeps the flap open, letting me choose.

I hiccup again. Wipe at a tear that is not an angry one, but a defeated one. Yes, reader, I will confess, maybe even a sad one. I don't look at him when I talk. "You said you wanted me, but then you kept your clothes on."

"Is that it?" he asks. I nod. And he laughs. He actually fucking laughs.

"Forget it," I groan.

"I didn't have a condom to offer," he says, trying to explain. "I didn't want you to have to make any kind of hard and fast choices."

"Oh." That's actually really sweet.

"I can help you find your zipper," he says. "Or you can crawl in here with me, which is what I had hoped you would do before you started panicking."

"I didn't panic."

"You didn't see the look on your face like I did. Bug-eyed, embarrassed."

"Wasn't embarrassed," I grumble.

"You covered yourself."

"I was cold."

"You're never cold."

"I thought—your face—you looked so open and honest in those few moments afterward. Then it was like you realized who you were in the tent with and closed yourself off again."

"I didn't realize I did that," he says.

"You did."

He's quiet again. Has both lips drawn into his mouth. I shoot an eyebrow toward my hairline, questioning his silence. He shrugs. "You don't like it when I apologize to you."

What I really don't like is the fact that he pays attention to me just as much as I pay attention to him. That he's studied me in a way that helps him know when I'm panicking, or that I'm rarely cold even though I've never said a word about it, or that he's not only listened to the things that irk the hell out of me, but he's made it a point to avoid doing those things.

I'm freaking out a little here, reader. Can't you tell?

"Do you really want me to share a sleeping bag with you?" I ask. "Or is this just another favor?"

"Favor?"

"Kissing me."

"You thought I kissed you as a favor?"

"For my book research," I say. "I thought you agreed."

"Was what we just did book research for you?" he asks.

"No," I say, faster than I'd normally admit to something like that. Truth is, I'm tired. I'm emotionally wiped. I just want to get to the bottom of this and get some sleep.

"It wasn't for me, either," he says.

And that's all I need to hear.

FAYE DARLING

I slide my legs out of my sleeping bag just as I hiccup again, because, no, hiccups don't magically disappear just because the tension between two people has finally been broken. Unlike the novels you're used to reading, this is real life, reader. My life.

Ryder wraps my hair around his fist as I glide down beside him. He holds my long strands out of the way as he zips me in with him. Lets them drop, spooling where they desire, as soon as the zipper snaps into place.

It's cramped and hot and smells like sex and sweat, but I easily relax against Ryder's muscled frame. His arm slides under my shoulders and he turns us so he's flat on his back and I am draped over his chest, his hand flared across my back, securing me in place. I press my cheek to the top of his peck. Rest my hand on the ridges of his abs.

Outside, the wind and the rain beat down against the tent. I close my eyes, sleep already steeping strong and hot behind them, and allow myself to wonder—in a way I never have allowed myself to do with any other research subject—what my future might be like with Ryder in it. Nights like this. Camping in the rain. Days spent on the couch watch *Gilmore Girls* with his mom. Surf sessions and burger dates and knee-weakening kisses and sex so good you forget you still have your clothes on for a minute.

My body jolts, and my eyes snap open.

No.

I can't allow my imagination to run rampant. I do not have the luxury to think of such things. Because, at the end of the day, Ryder *is* my research subject. I'm paying him.

No matter how good his body feels beneath mine right now, no matter how much I seem to be craving another glimpse of that wide-open look on his face, he is not mine to have. Someday, a version of him will belong to you and every other book-crazed reader who picks up my novel. Someday, he will belong to someone else, and I will only be a distant memory.

His strong arms tighten around my body, his breath already running away with sleep.

And I nestle in close.

Because someday isn't today. Today, he can be mine.

Twenty-Seven

Ryder

THERE YOU ARE.

Once I felt you pull away last night after Luna asked if she could touch me I wondered if that would be the end of us. A full night of sleep, breakfast over the campfire, and a run back to Nick's Subaru for a few bits of forgotten gear have passed without you. I had started to think I'd royally fucked up.

But I guess since you're here now, you're not totally pissed off with me. At least, it doesn't feel that way.

I always thought love triangles were stupid. Steph was a huge *Twilight* fan when we were younger. She'd read portions of the book out loud to me whenever she thought a passage would interest me. Of course, it never did. Still, I went with her to watch the movies when they came out, and the whole time I sat there thinking about how fucking stupid love triangles were.

But now I think I get it.

IN LOVE WITH YOU

I get how your heart can be tugged in two different directions at once.

If not my heart, then my interest, at the very least.

Last night with Luna...it was like nothing I've ever experienced. I've never felt so connected to another person before. Even with our moment of miscommunication. In a way, that moment brought us closer together.

I still have strong feelings for you—I still love you—but I'd be lying if I didn't tell you I feel myself being drawn toward Luna more and more.

When I woke this morning with her in my arms, it didn't feel awkward or foreign. It felt right. It felt good. And, this is nothing against you, because I know you can't control this, but it felt nice knowing I wasn't having to imagine her there. Her hot little body pressed against my chest. Her sleepy little eyes smiling up at me, a sheepish flicker in them that made my heart warm. She was real.

I can still feel that warmth hours later as I stand in the shallows of the river. Strips of sunlight poke through the clouds, adorning the green-blue water with flecks of silver and bronze.

Fishing is next in line, just after surfing, when it comes to the most peace-giving activities for me. The solace. The oneness with the natural world. Just like the line on the reel as it's being cast out into the water, everything seems to unspool. Every worry and fear and complication—they disappear the moment I set foot in a river, rod in hand.

I feel Luna watching me the same way I feel you watching me right now, too.

FAYE DARLING

Both of your views are of me. Waders jacked up over my shoulders. Flannel poking out just enough to give the monochrome of green all around a pop of crimson.

I walk to the top of my section of the run, just below the hole at the end of a small set of rapids. The rest of the guys are spread out downstream. Nick, then Mark, then Blake, keeping his distance from me. *Smart man.*

This river is one of the best streams in the area for chum salmon. They are Mark's favorite fish to go after, because they're fighters. They make you work for your reward.

Exhaling, I cast straight out into the middle of the river, reel my line tight, and let the rod tip track my spoon lure as it lopes downstream. The vibrations the spoon makes as it flops back and forth let me know everything is a-okay.

"Why don't you reel the whole time?" Luna asks, keeping her voice soft.

"With spoon fishing," I say, "you want the water to do the work."

"Where does this type of fishing get its name?"

I shrug. "Shape of the lure, I guess."

"My uncle taught me to catch catfish with my bare hands when I was ten," Luna says. "I've always wondered why some fish can go for a human hand while others go for shiny little things, like spoon lures, instead."

I reel my line in all the way, the bronze, oval-shaped lure pinging in the sunlight that's sneaking through a gap in the large, puffy clouds. I glance over at Luna as I wade back upstream to the top of the run.

"You noodle?" I ask, biting the inside of my cheek to hold in a smile.

"Don't sound so surprised."

IN LOVE WITH YOU

"I'm not." *I am.*

Mark is obsessed with a father-daughter duo online who noodle for catfish down in Alabama. The daughter is in her early twenties, small and fairly lean. Mark's showed me videos where she gets rolled around under the water by these massive blues. How she hasn't had her arm pulled clean out of its socket yet is a mystery to me. Those suckers put up a fight. It's hard to imagine Luna fighting that same fight now, let alone at age ten.

Luna stands up from the downed tree branch she's been balanced on for the last hour and a half. She lays her notebook and pencil down in a crook between two limbs then walks over to me, stepping into the water for the first time.

She's wearing waders, but they're D.J.'s, so they're baggy on her, ballooning out away from her smaller frame. I try not to laugh.

She leers at me. "What?"

"You look like you've been dropped into those waders is all."

"Told y'all I had gear," she says. "Never said it fit right. Now shut up and teach me how to spoon fish."

"Okay," I say, not hesitating, even for a second. My warmed heart has dropped briefly into the bottom of my stomach. I feel it slowly inching its way back up. Bit by bit.

My fishing rod isn't the right size for her. Isn't the right kind for a beginner, either. If she manages to get a bite, there's a good chance she'll lose it straightaway. Maybe even get dragged down with all that extra fabric from D.J.'s waders tugging her along, too. So I agree for one reason and one reason alone. When Luna sets her mind to something, there's no talking her out of it, and I'd rather be the one to show her how than for any of the other guys here to do it instead.

FAYE DARLING

I nod to the top of the run. "Start there."

"Why?" she asks.

"It's where the water levels out after the hole in the rapid."

"Fish like that?"

I catch Nick standing several yards downstream smirking at us. He was his friendly self as we all ate oatmeal and sausages around the fire this morning, but I could tell from the side-eyed glances, the muted laughter, that he'd heard Luna and me last night. I shoot him a glare now the way I did earlier. He holds onto his smirk for another second before he casts his line into the river, his attention drifting immediately with the trail of his lure.

"Yes," I tell Luna. "The spoon likes a level surface, too."

Luna reaches out and catches the lure, careful not to get stung by the hook dangling from its end. "Reminds me of a pair of earrings my mom used to have. It's pretty."

"It's shiny," I correct. "You get it loping in just the right way, too, it looks like it's a smaller, dying fish."

"Easy target."

"Precisely."

Luna huffs. "Sad isn't it? The way the food chain works. The weak ones being picked off by the strong. Enter humanity and the tables turn. The strong are picked off thinking they're catching something weak, but really they're the weak ones for not knowing any better."

I chuckle. She's too damn philosophical sometimes. It's hot...and a little bit terrifying. "Chum are catch and release up here, if that helps."

"It does." Luna releases the lure and grips the rod just above the reel. "Now, talk me through this."

IN LOVE WITH YOU

"Want me to show you instead?" I ask, just wanting an excuse to position myself at her back, curve my arms around hers, brush the tips of my fingers over her hands.

"I've been watching you closely," she says. "Toss me in the deep end, Ryder. Let me figure out on my own how to sink or swim."

"All right," I say, stepping back to give her the space she'll need. "Cast out into the middle, ninety degrees, then let the tip of the rod follow the spoon as you reel it in tight."

Her cast is a little long, but graceful, like she grew up fishing, and she probably did. But she doesn't reel enough and the spoon sinks too deep too fast. I tell her to try again and she does. This time, the lure gets to spinning like a boat's propeller.

"Cast, anticipate bottom as the spoon falls, then swing it across to get the proper drift," I advise as she walks to the top of the run for a third time.

She doesn't say anything. Just keeps her lips sucked into her mouth, her eyes steady as she trains them on the bronze glint of the lure. A cloud shifts overhead just as she casts, bathing her in a beam of golden sunlight. Everything—the lure, her eyes, the top of her hair—is set aglow. She looks majestic, beautiful. I have the sudden urge to close the space between us, take her face between my hands, and kiss her until her knees buckle.

But I don't.

The tip of the fishing rod jerks a few seconds after she reels the line tight, and she gasps. Another jerk, this time harder, like whatever is on the other end is trying pretty fucking hard to detach itself from the hook. Adrenaline zips through me.

"Fish on," I shout.

Luna alternates between tugging on the rod and reeling in the line, but soon, she's just doing her best to hold the line steady, keep the reel in her hands, and anchor herself to the riverbed.

"Whoa," she says as the fish on the end of the line jumps out of the water, spinning onto its side, and flashing us a streak of green scales before diving back under.

"That's a chum, folks," Nick says.

"Fuck yeah," Mark trills from farther downstream. He abandons his post and starts ambling toward us on the bank.

The chum tugs hard on the end of the line and Luna is jerked forward, feet stumbling through the shallow water. A prick of my protective instincts jabs me. I'm suddenly behind her. Torso pressed to her spine. Arms bending around hers. I grip the rod tight, feel the fight on the opposite end. The quick pace of Luna's heartbeat pounds through her back and into my stomach.

"Give 'em hell," I tell her, tugging on the rod to take some pressure off of the line. She starts to reel again, and we drag the fish into the shallows together.

She shrieks when the thing is fighting at our feet. Then she laughs, pleased with herself.

But the fish writhes beneath us, trying to make one final break for freedom, and Luna loses her grip on the line. We catch the reel at the same time, my hands covering hers. We start to tow in the line again, both of us fighting hard.

Once the fish is back in the shallows, Mark steps in with a net, scooping the chum up out of the water. A grin the size of the Pacific sits squarely on his face.

"Damn girl," he says, beaming at Luna. "You caught a big fucker."

IN LOVE WITH YOU

Luna knocks her head back against my sternum and smiles up at me before she lets go of the rod and heads for the net. I follow on shaky legs. Not because the fish was a fighter and wore me out, but because Luna is making my fucking head spin.

I focus on the fish. Ease the hook out of the side of the beast's gnarled mouth.

"Who has a camera?" I ask.

"I do."

Nick is on his way to us with his phone out. I dare a glance downstream, wondering what Blake is making of all of this. He's nothing but a speck in the distance, turned into a bush, most likely taking a piss. Fine by me.

"Do I have to hold it?" Luna asks, sounding a little apprehensive.

"Says the woman who noodles for catfish."

"You noodle?" Mark asks in awe.

Luna looks up at me. "I never said I *like* noodling."

I lean my rod carefully against a bush nearby and lift the fish out of the net. The thing squirms once in my hands before going still. Mark was right. This is a big fucker. Biggest chum I've ever seen up-close. I turn toward Luna and ease it into her hands, waiting until she has a good grip on its slippery body before letting go.

"Don't get me in the shot," Mark says, ducking beneath Nick's phone as he hops onto the bank. "Gina might have found out Luna was coming, but I don't want her getting jealous that she wasn't allowed to join in the fun."

"Gina and Mark, ladies and gentlemen," Nick says. "Cute or dysfunctional. You decide."

"Wait," Luna says as I move to step away. "You have to be in the picture, Ryder. You helped."

"You really want my ugly mug fucking up your picture?"

"Yes," Luna says, looking me dead in the eye. "I do."

I roll my eyes, but the flutter in my chest cannot be denied. I wade back into the water. Snake an arm around Luna's shoulders.

"Ready?" Nick asks. "One, two—"

Right when he says the word *three* the fish drops from Luna's hands, hits the water with a resounding slap, and darts off into the riffles.

Instead of the classic trophy fish picture—broad smiles and a statue-still fish—ours is a bit livelier. Luna's lips are wide and forming a perfect 'oh' as she shouts. Her eyes are shot through with panic as she realizes the fish, nothing but a blur of green mid-jump, is getting away. And then there's me. Laughing hard. Hugging Luna tightly to my side. Eyes tuned-in, not to the fish, but to her.

"Luna, your face," Nick says, laughing as he flashes us the photo.

"Yeah," she says, her voice taking on a breathy quality as she squints at the screen, studying it longer than anyone expects her to. She cuts a quick glance back at me. "*My* face."

Twenty-Eight

Ryder

THE FIRE IS DWINDLING down to embers as our conversation at camp gets its second wind, all of us sharing our favorite 'Mark Moments'. Blake has taken over the storytelling, and even though my jaw was tight the moment he opened his mouth, I eventually cave. Join in the laughter just as Blake finishes telling us about the first time Mark met Gina's grandparents from Poland. Mark had looked up on the internet how to say nice to meet you in Polish, but apparently didn't have the correct translation and ended up offending the grandparents to the point that they nearly turned around and flew home.

"What had he said?" Luna asks.

Blake rattles it off in Polish, then switches back to English. "It's the equivalent of saying fuck you very much."

"My good looks and charming personality turned the situation around though," Mark says, sloshing back another sip of whiskey Luna stole from The Tavern. "I won them over in the end."

"After my dad and sister spent over two hours telling them you didn't know what you'd said." Blake snorts. "I've never laughed so hard in my life. You're such a moron."

I grunt. The humor in the story is suddenly gone. Instead of glaring at Blake and trying not to throttle him, I bend down and throw another log on the fire, stoking the flames. I steal a glance at Luna and catch her looking at me. She quickly looks away the way she's been doing all night. Like she's suddenly embarrassed she's watching me. Like she hasn't been following me around for two weeks to do just that.

"So, Marky Mark," Nick says, clapping Mark on the back and steering the conversation in another direction. Leave it to Nick to be the one to turn things around. "How does it feel, after all these years, to finally be marrying the beautiful Gina?"

"You know what," Mark says, tilting the whiskey bottle back to take a big sip. "I think once all the chaos of planning the wedding is over, I'll be happy about it. Really happy."

"Yeah, man," Blake says. "How does it feel to know you're only going to fuck one woman again for the rest of your life?"

Mark laughs for a few seconds until the weight of Blake's words sink in. Then, he loses all color in his face and presses a fist to his closed mouth to keep from puking.

Blake snickers. Shoves Mark so hard he nearly falls off the stump he's sitting on. "Shit, man. Wait until I tell my sister how you reacted to *that*."

"Fuck off, Blake," I say. "You're not telling her shit."

"I have a Mark memory," Nick says, trying to corral the fight rising up in us. "It's no Polish mishap, but it *is* relevant. You and Gina had just broken up for, well, I can't remember which time it was, but we were still in high school. We'd ditched school that day because the swell was supposed to be sick, but it was flatter than it had ever been, so we spent most of the time just floating on our boards, talking. I remember asking if you and Gina were done for good and you looked at me with fierce conviction in those baby blues and told me it didn't matter if you got back together tomorrow and split the next day, because you were sure, in the end, you'd get married. And I'd laughed so hard my ribs ached for the rest of the day, because when you're a teenage boy you just don't hear one of your best friends say shit like that. But here we are. Still friends after all these years. About to send you off to get hitched to the love of your life. A toast, gentlemen...and lady." Nick lifts a can of cider into the air and the rest of us hold up whatever drinks we have on hand. "To Mark and Gina."

"Mark and Gina," we all echo.

Mark sniffs after we all drink, his eyes glistening in the firelight. He looks at Nick. "Fuck you, Nick. You were supposed to tell a story about me being a dumbass."

"Oh, I still could," Nick says. "I have an entire card catalog in my head of those."

"Maybe you should make the best man speech," I tell him, half-joking, half-serious.

"Nah," Nick says, then winks at me, letting me know I'll be just fine in two weeks when I have to stand up in front of all of those people and say something meaningful. I can be meaningful. In my head. On paper, even. But I always manage to fuck shit like that up in-person. One way or another. I take a drink of my whiskey and push those thoughts aside for a moment. I can worry about my best man speech later.

FAYE DARLING

The fire dies down again and the conversation soon follows. Mark stumbles off toward his tent first, followed by Nick. Blake doesn't budge. He just stares at Luna as she scribbles in her notebook.

I sit on the farthest end of the obtuse triangle the three of us make. There's no way in hell I'm going to bed before Luna. Not with Blake out here. Drunk and looking at her like that. No. Fucking. Way.

The stars are out, the clouds that brought a midday shower not long after Luna caught that fish all but gone. Every prick of silver light buzzes just beyond the dark branches of the fir trees. I can make out half of the big dipper, the handle of that spoon trapped behind the forest's canopy. My breath fogs in the cold air, rising with the smoke from the fire.

"So, you're a writer?" Blake asks Luna. I don't lower my head to look at him full-on, because if I do I'm afraid I'll drive a fist straight into his nose. I keep him in the corner of my vision, though. Catch his form as it inches toward Luna. The hairs on the back of my neck rise.

"I prefer storyteller," Luna says, not looking up from her notebook.

"What kinds of stories do you tell?"

"Good ones."

I laugh once, low in my chest. D.J. was the one to tell me she was an award winning author, and my sister was the one to show me just how wild people can go for Luna's stories, because she was too humble to tell me herself. But she doesn't even try to sound humble in front of Blake. Is her lack of humility with him a good thing or a bad thing, though? Does it mean she trusts him or wants to scare him off?

IN LOVE WITH YOU

You're leaning in, too, aren't you? Wondering how this is all going to play out. Come closer if you're that curious. Don't be shy. I haven't forgotten about you, either, baby. Like I said earlier, I've just been pulled in two different directions.

"I bet," Blake says, his voice a deep whisper I think he believes sounds sexy, but really just sounds like he's trying too hard. "I bet you tell a real good story."

"Hm," Luna hums. She closes her notebook. Shoves the pencil through the binding. Looks across the fire at Blake with her head cocked, her face hard to read.

"What?" Blake asks, taking over the stump Nick had once occupied. The one right beside her. My fingers flex around the cup in my hand.

"Just wondering something," she says.

"Oh yeah?" He's leaning so close that the wisps of her hair coming out of her braids are shivering in the wake of his breath. My grip tightens on my cup when she turns her head slowly toward him, her nose almost brushing the tip of his. If this is a game, I don't think I like it much.

"Yeah, I was wondering if you'd excuse me," Luna says, standing up and walking around the fire. She stands at my back, her heat almost as singeing as the actual flames. "Ryder promised he'd show me what the stars looked like reflecting off the river."

"I did?" I say, because my mind was a train barreling toward a completely different station than the one Luna has taken us to and I'm having a hard time pumping the brakes.

Her hands squeeze both of my shoulders before they glide down the front of my chest, her braids flopping over me as she bends down and drags her lips up my jawline to my ear. "Don't you remember?"

FAYE DARLING

I'm so caught up in the electric feel of her touch that I almost forget where I am. Almost forget that I'm meant to be playing along, getting us both far away from Blake.

"Of course," I say.

I shiver as her teeth nip at my earlobe. I stand up, letting one of my hands drop easily into Luna's before I lead her through camp.

"Good night, then," Blake mutters after we've already walked several paces into the forest.

Keeping hold of my hand, Luna pulls her phone out of her back pocket and turns on the flashlight, lighting up our path through the ferns and brambles and trunks of massive fir trees. A few more steps. A few more moments of silence. Then, Luna knocks into my side as a laugh nearly bowls her over.

"I bet you tell a really good story," she says in a twisted, low voice clearly meant to mimic Blake. She laughs again. "Where was he going with that line, anyway?"

"A complicated creature Blake is not," I say. "I think his one and only move to seduce a woman is flashing a wad of cash in her face and asking if she wants to ride in his Beemer."

"Ooh," Luna says, wriggling her shoulders. "I'm wet just thinking about it."

I don't know what comes over me—relief, lust, both—but I drop Luna's hand, cup her cheek with my palm, and tilt her face up so that my kiss can land smoothly on her lips. The gesture is returned in an instant, her tongue grazing mine as I back her into the wide trunk of a tree. My hand reaches down to rub against the front of her fleece sweats, and she twists her lips out of my grip.

IN LOVE WITH YOU

"Fuck," she says, moaning as I make the motion again. "This is not what I meant by Ryder wants to show me the stars, but also...this is exactly what I meant."

"I can go back and get Blake," I whisper in her ear. "If you'd rather have him show you the stars."

She wraps a leg up and around my body, then leans in and bites my neck so hard I flinch away. But she darts forward, kissing the place right after, soothing it. "Don't you fucking dare."

Have you ever had sex in the middle of the woods on a clear, cool night with the stars spinning high above your head, making you just as dizzy as the person you're with?

The question I just asked you has me going still, rigid.

It's so easy, talking to you. So easy to ask you things like that. I feel so close to you, so connected, and yet we've never touched. Not really.

I feel my own, hot breath beat back against me as I stand at a pause in front of Luna.

"Where'd you go?" She presses two fingers against my jaw and eases my head to the side, forcing me to look right at her.

"Do you ever?" I start, but stop. I kiss her neck as I take hold of the leg she wrapped around me and drag it higher. "Never mind."

"No," she says. "What were you going to say?"

"It doesn't matter." I suck on the sharp edge of her jaw. Kiss the corner of her mouth. Pull on her lower lip until she lets out a squeak. I press my forehead to hers and breathe in warm bursts of her own oxygen. "I, uh—I have a condom tonight."

She lets out a husky laugh. "Did you have it parachuted in or something?"

"No." I reach into my pocket and pull out the little square packet. "When I went back for the fishing gear that got left behind, I remembered Nick keeps a box in his glove compartment."

"Nick was in the scouts, wasn't he?"

"I don't think so," I say, kissing her softly on the mouth. "He just has compulsions."

The next kiss is not soft. It's rough and slick and needy. As I swirl my tongue down into her mouth, I feel her hands working on my belt.

She pulls away, breathing hard. "I just want to be clear, this is not for research. None of this is for research."

"Okay," I say with an amused chuckle.

"Okay," she pants. Her fingers hover over my zipper, bulging out from my hard-on. "What do you want?"

"Isn't that clear?" I say, shifting my hips so that I'm pressed hard against her hands.

She swallows. "I like to hear you say it."

"You," I say, not hesitating tonight. "I want you."

"All of me?" she asks, voice a whisper.

"Yes, sweetheart. I want all of you."

The zipper of my pants whines as she tugs it all the way down. She keeps her eyes on me as she slides my pants over my hips and the swell of my ass. My breath hitches as she curls her hands around the waistband of my boxers, pausing briefly to hold my gaze before she lets her eyes drop the same moment she frees my cock. Thick. Hard. Trembling for her.

She surprises me by sliding down the length of the tree and pressing a fat-lipped kiss to the base of me, a hand curving around my balls.

Fuck. This *woman*.

IN LOVE WITH YOU

Taking the condom out of my hand she tears the wrapper open. Her eyes flick all the way up the length of my body, catching sight of that borderline crazed look in my eye. Then, she removes the rubber and slides it over me slowly. I don't think she realizes if she keeps up this slow shit, I'll come before I'm even inside her.

I drag a hand over the back of my neck and try and focus on breathing. Try and focus on keeping myself together. I'll admit, I haven't felt this close to tipping over the edge with so little action since right after I was released from prison.

Shit.

Guilt twists in my colon. I made it a rule a long time ago to divulge my past to a woman before things got this far. One night stands? Forget it. But this? Not only have we spent two weeks in close proximity, learning one another in stolen glances and questions asked under the guise of research, but we've shared a tent, a sleeping bag. We've shared more than that, too. *Much more.*

That twist of guilt again. My palms sweat. My fingers buzz.

"Wait," I breathe, taking a step back from her as she starts to take off her boots so it'll be easier to remove other pieces of clothing later on.

"I thought you said...I mean, I thought you were into this?" Her breath is white vapor in the cold, black night. "Men have said I was intimidating, forward, a little too sure of myself, but I figured you of all people wouldn't be put off by that."

Okay. That's a conversation for another time. Who the fuck ever thought it was their place to tell her she was intimidating? Why would she assume I wouldn't be put off by it? I mean, I'm not. She's hella confident, but I can tell when it's genuine and when it's just a ruse. When she's puffed up, peacocking, trying to hide the fact that she's still the awkward little girl who would rather sit in the corner of a room by herself than participate in a game of social charades with people who aren't even close to being on her level intellectually.

That doesn't matter. Not right now. Because she's so far off about why I've slowed things down.

"No, no," I say, trying to keep my voice low and even and caring. Although that last one has always been hard for me to convey when my stomach feels like it's been hurled over a fence. "It's not you."

"It's not you, it's me." She snorts. "Typical. I—"

"Luna," I say. "I'm trying to tell you something. I'm trying to be honest. And it has nothing to do with you. You're perfect."

"Fuck," she says, eyes popping out of her head. Her gaze dips to look at my sheathed erection, still hard with anticipation. "You don't have...issues, do you? It's totally okay if you do. I don't judge, I just want to be able to help if—"

"Just shut up a minute," I bark. I pinch my eyes shut, the sharp tone of my voice still echoing through the trees. Maybe more through my head than the trees, but I can still hear it on repeat. *Too gruff, Ryder.* I take a deep breath and steel myself. Open my eyes. "I feel like we're about to cross a line with each other. I'm not saying that's a bad thing. I just think you need to know something important about my past before you decide whether or not you actually *want* to cross that line with me."

"You couldn't have brought this up five minutes ago?"

"I got a little carried away," I say. "I wasn't expecting you to drag me out here to do...*this*."

"Says the man who had a stolen condom ready to go in his pocket."

IN LOVE WITH YOU

"I was in prison," I blurt out. Not sure how much more my gut can take as it waits for her to be quiet and listen. I think she talks when she's nervous. In fact, I'm sure of it.

"What? When? Why? For how long? Is that why the inscription on that picture of you and your dad mentioned something about the inside?"

But even though she's blasting me with questions, talking faster than a sneaker wave stealing onto the beach, she doesn't seem put off by the idea. Simply...curious. As if I didn't tell her I'd spent time in prison, but instead told her I'd lived in Yucatan for a year or used to work on a fishing boat in Alaska.

"I got out a few years ago for good behavior," I say. "I was inside for eighteen months for assault. And, yes, my mom sent me that picture."

"Assault?" Luna asks. "As in—"

"I almost beat a man to death."

"Why?"

Why? No shock. No tremble in her voice. Unassuming. *Why?*

No woman I've ever told has ever made it to this point. They hear assault and take off. I think they automatically assume I'm possessively jealous or beat on women. Possessively jealous I can understand. But I'd never touch a woman like that. Never.

I shrug one shoulder. "It was a guy Steph was seeing. He was getting pretty rough with her at a bar I happened to be at and I inserted myself. I'll admit, I got a little carried away, but—"

"Good," Luna says with a huff.

"Good?" I let out a humorless laugh. "Luna, I put the guy in the hospital. He had to breathe through a tube for several months. It was not *good*."

"You were protecting Steph," she says, taking a step toward me, toeing off her unlaced boots and shucking them onto the pine needle-covered ground. "That's what I meant by good."

"I'm still not proud of it."

"You can feel however you'd like about it," she says. "But so can I."

"If this changes things between us, I understand," I say.

"Does it change things between us?" she asks, taking a half step toward me. "Meaning, am I horrified to even be standing in your presence?"

I nod.

"Let's take inventory, shall we? Yesterday, you kissed me instead of punching Blake in the face, right?"

I swallow, the taste of her still sharp on my tongue. The craving for more rises up somewhere deep inside of me. But I still can't tell whether or not she's been totally spooked or not. "Yeah."

"And that Timber Razer who made a snide comment about me," she says. Another half step my way. She slides her sweats down to her ankles and kicks them off. Her dark lace panties are a stark contrast against her pale skin, the floral pattern of the lace fully visible in the moonlight. I can feel myself tightening again, growing even harder. "You just poured him a drink and told him to get lost instead of slamming his head into the bar top."

"I did," I breathe. Her hands slide up my abs on the underside of my flannel. I swear I hear her whisper-moan as she traces the deep ridges of my well-defined muscle.

"I might not have known you before you went to prison, Ryder North." She lifts onto her tiptoes to whisper in my ear. Hearing my full name on her lips sends chills through me. "But

I know enough about character arcs to say you've changed. Learned your lesson."

She palms my dick and I groan.

She chuckles. "Did you think you'd scare me off that easily?"

"Wasn't trying to scare you off," I say, bending low to taste her neck. "Just trying to lay everything out in the open before we went any further."

"How chivalrous," she teases. "Do you still want all of me?"

"I think the real question is, do you want all of *me*?"

A subdued, animal-like growl erupts at the back of her throat just before she grips the collar of my flannel in both hands and rips it open, the top three buttons snapping off. Her teeth nibble at my bared collar bone, her lips suck hard against the low swoop of my neck's hollow.

I slide my hands over the globes of her perfect ass, kneading my hands into them once before sliding them down and gripping her thighs. I pick her up off the ground and drop her high on my waist so quickly she gasps against the skin of my left peck. One of my arms slides around to support her full weight so my free hand can reach down and pull her underwear to one side, my knuckles sliding against smooth folds of hot flesh, soaked with her arousal. I must nick that sensitive bundle of nerves at the top of her heat, because she gasps again. Her lips find mine in a frenzy as I back her against the tree.

She reaches down between us, takes my hard length in one of her hands and guides me to her. My tip hovers at her entrance, waiting. I look into her eyes, see the certainty, the hunger, the need, swirling in her irises. Without another moment of hesitation, I swing my hips and drive into her.

Luna feels incredible. Her warmth. Her tightness. The way her inner walls cradle my dick is almost overwhelming. I bury my face in her neck, the sharp scent of the rain-soaked tree at her back dizzyingly strong as it mixes with her natural pheromones. The desire to move is there, but the severe staccato of Luna's breath gives me pause. Like she needs a few more seconds to adjust.

"Ryder?" she asks, her voice small. Her heels dig into the muscles on either side of my lower back, and her hips grind into mine, deepening our connection. "What are you waiting for?"

My movements are slow at first as I listen to the rhythm of her breath, the tiny sounds she makes. I familiarize myself with the topography of her pleasure. I speed up with each movement, and, soon, her hands are clawing at the back of my neck as she tries to hold on. My grip on her is not ideal, but it's firm enough. I can feel the muscles in my arms strain from holding up her weight, but the sensation I feel at the place we're joined overrides everything else, pushes pause on the rest of the world.

She sucks in a shallow breath and whispers, right in my ear, "Can I come?"

Just her asking almost sends me over the edge. But not quite. "Not just yet, sweetheart."

A few more thrusts. A few more gasps. Then, a low-burning warmth blooms to life deep within me, and I know I'm close.

"Now?" she asks, her voice as thin as a leaf shaking in a tumultuous wind. Like she's barely hanging on. Like she's about to fall apart in my grip.

"Almost," I grunt.

A thump as her head flops back against the trunk of the tree. A hiss let out between her clenched teeth. She tugs on my hair as she tries to hold on for one more second.

IN LOVE WITH YOU

"Ryder," she whispers, longing thick in the air between us.

"Be a good girl and come for me now," I say as I reach the point where I feel like I am a car bomb that could go off at any second. My breath is ragged as I drive into her, and I swear just one more push and I'll—"Fuck," I groan as that bomb explodes and a pleasure so intense shoots through me. Luna's inner walls quake around me as we come together.

As we both come down from our high, her full weight sags in my arms. My forehead falls into hers, and, for a while, all we can manage to do is breathe.

Everything is in such sharp focus, and when I look into her eyes, she's looking right back at me. The two of us are tethered together in this one moment, the stars spinning above us, our bodies filled with satisfaction. And I know, the instant I pull out of her slippery heat, that the tether will be cut, the connection lost.

So I hold her close.

For just a little while longer.

Twenty-Nine

Luna

My knuckles are a hair's breadth away from touching the back of Ryder's hand, which rests casually on his knee in the back seat of Nick's Subaru. Mark is babbling about wedding details. Asking us things like what the difference between desert rose and sunset rose might be, who the hell came up with those names, and why the fuck does it matter what his opinion is on it if Gina is just going to veto him anyway.

Normally, I'd be tracking every bit of this conversation. Taking notes internally on Mark's words, his tone, his inflection. I'd be hyper-vigilant about body language, his and everyone else's in the car.

But the only bodies I am aware of are mine and Ryder's.

I feel like a teenager again. Relishing in the tiny touches. The almost-touches. The tension that is threatening to tie me up, strangle me to death unless I give in to my urges. I know he feels the same way, because every time our eyes meet, he looks away, flushing bright pink—desert rose, perhaps? All I want to do is crawl onto his lap, take his face between my palms, and lick him from the joint of his collarbones to the cupid's bow of his lips, tasting every inch of skin in between. My thighs tingle just at the thought.

Of course, being trapped in a car full of people, that would be an impossible fantasy to turn into reality. But I'm about to lose my fucking mind, here.

Dear reader,
Please send help.
Love your favorite romance author,
Luna.

"Mark, man," Ryder says, spreading a hand over my thigh as he leans over me to talk to his best friend. His ear is so close, I could just open my mouth and bite it. I settle for inching forward, letting his long hair tickle the tip of my nose inconspicuously as he talks to Mark. "This weekend was supposed to get you away from wedding stress. Don't spiral before we've even dropped you on your doorstep."

"Spiral, Mark," Blake says, playing devil's advocate from the front seat. "Go on, give us a show. But make it something that'll piss my sister off. Haven't had some decent Gina-Mark drama for a while now. I almost miss it."

Ryder turns into a rigid mess in three seconds flat. Blake, while annoying, yes, seems to agitate Ryder more than anyone else. I know he said they had history, but I wonder what kind?

I don't wonder for too long, though, because the hand he has splayed across my thigh is turning into a vise. Squeezing, squeezing. The veins in Ryder's neck bulge so much I can almost see them jump as his pulse kicks, hard and angry. My hand slithers up his back, a new flannel replacing the one I nearly ripped to shreds last night, and I squeeze the base of his neck firmly. All at once, his hand loosens its grip on me and his body seems to relax a bit more, becoming moldable clay instead of chiseled granite beneath my touch. I watch goosebumps surface on his olive-toned skin. I have to restrain myself from running my lips over them to see what they would feel like.

"We should have left you in the woods," Nick tells Blake, laughing even though everyone can sense he's dead-serious. Nick is probably the kindest, gentlest one out of the group, but I've noticed he, too, has a short fuse when it comes to Blake.

"Last chance," Mark mutters as we round the corner and The Tavern comes into view.

The Sunday afternoon crowd is already starting to arrive. The parking lot is half-full, consisting almost entirely of dirt-encrusted pickup trucks and every flavor of motorcycle you might imagine.

I know exactly what I'm going to do when I say goodbye to Ryder and his friends. I'm going to march straight upstairs to D.J.'s apartment, open my laptop for the first time in a long time, and start the novel that's slowly been taking shape in my head this weekend. Forget finishing my research. Forget waiting to write until I'm back at my place in Oklahoma. The need to tell this story is almost as strong as the need to turn Ryder's neck so I can kiss him open-mouthed right now.

I drop my hand away from Ryder as he sits up, unbuckling his seat belt as Nick's tires bumble over the gravel lot, headed toward the back where Ryder and Blake left their cars.

Blake takes off almost as soon as we get parked, throwing us a head nod as a goodbye. His tires rake up all sorts of dust as he barrels down the road.

IN LOVE WITH YOU

Nick already has my borrowed pack out of the hatch when I round the back bumper. He hands it to me with a sweet-as-pie smile and a gentlemanly kiss on the cheek.

"Thanks for putting up with us for the weekend," he says.

"Nah," I say. "Thanks for putting up with *me* for the weekend."

"You're one of us now," Mark says, slapping my ass playfully, then looking at Ryder with panic in his eyes.

I return Mark's gesture, walloping him a good one, too. "Guess I am."

Ryder smirks before ducking into the hatch to help Nick with the gear. Mark winces and rubs his left butt cheek. "Remind me never to make you angry."

A few minutes later, Nick reverses his car slowly and giving us a small wave. He carefully weaves through the lot and turns onto the main road. Mark ducks into the passenger side of the Camaro as Ryder walks me toward the front door of The Tavern. He snatches my hand halfway there. Pulls me to a stop in front of him.

"You want to head back into the forest?" he asks. "Forget about life for a few more days, weeks, months?"

I laugh and swing our hands back and forth a few times. "I'll see you tomorrow."

"I'd rather see you tonight," he mutters.

"It's Sunday," I say.

He sighs, knowing I'm talking about the *Gilmore Girls* marathon he always has on Sundays with his mom and sister. "Long-standing traditions are bound to be broken sooner or later."

But his face twists almost as soon as the words have slipped out. His eyes turn red as he tries to hold back tears. I don't need to ask him to know what he's thinking, because I've been there. When my mom was dying of cancer there were moments when I'd be away from the house, away from her illness, and I'd forget for a minute. I'd forget she was on her way out the door. And when I'd remember, it always felt like the news of her impending departure was being broken to me all over again.

I kiss the rough skin of Ryder's knuckles. "Tomorrow."

"You can join us, you know." He swallows. "If you'd like."

"I sort of have plans," I say. I swear I see a little bit of hurt in his eyes. Jealousy, too? Does he think I have a date or something? That's cute. I bite my lip. "I have a hot date...with my computer. I'm going to write until my heart is content."

"Oh." A smile breaks free on his face, broad and beaming, before he catches himself. Reigns in his joy until it's nothing but a smirk. "Did the weekend spark inspiration?"

"It did, actually."

He gathers me up in his arms and leans in, hovering just over my lips. "Which parts?"

"You'll have to buy the book if you want to find out," I whisper.

He growls once, then drops a heavy kiss onto my lips. It's one I feel all the way in the tips of my toes. They curl up in my hiking boots. He pulls away with a loud *smack*. "Only if you'll sign my copy."

"And seal it with a kiss," I say.

Another bright smile. This one is not reigned in, just smothered by a second kiss to my lips. His tongue darts into my mouth this time, and I greet it with my own.

The blare of a car horn has me jumping back and Ryder tightening his grip on me. I suppose we know which one of us is fight and which one of us is flight, now. We both turn to find Mark pounding out a familiar tune with Ryder's car horn, shouting, "Let's go."

"Is that Metallica?"

"I'm going to kill him," Ryder grumbles.

"He's probably just excited to get home to Gina," I say.

"Nope." Ryder kisses me hard on the lips before letting me go completely. He takes a few steps away. "He just likes being a pain in the ass."

"At least he's consistent."

"Tomorrow morning," Ryder says. "I'll pick you up."

"We surfing?"

He shakes his head. "I want to take you somewhere."

I bite back a pleased grin. Whether it's for book research or not, I don't care. His words, *I want to take you somewhere* have my heart hammering out a beat that sounds a lot like the one Mark is still playing on the horn. Can you feel it? My heartbeat, I mean.

God, reader, I think I might be in serious trouble here. Remember that help I asked you to send? How's that coming along?

Thirty

Ryder

It's late Sunday afternoon when I finally turn onto my street, the asphalt still darkened by an earlier rain shower and covered in bright yellow maple leaves that have been knocked off their limbs by the wind before they had a chance to drop naturally.

I narrow my eyes at the gray sedan parked behind my sister's car.

My first thought is that Steph invited that douchebag she's been secretly dating over, but then I remember he drives a pickup truck. A nice one I would recognize again in an instant. It must be a friend of Mom's. One who only just heard about her being sick, perhaps? Maybe it's one of Steph's coworkers stopping by for a visit.

I park around the corner, on the edge of the grass, and start to unload my gear from the weekend. My hands go still on the sack that holds my tent when I smell it—rose hips and vanilla. It's as if Luna's scent is forever embedded into the nylon fabric. The aroma makes my heart flutter. Makes my memory ping with images of her beneath me, over me, beside me. Sweat-slicked skin and my name on her lips.

The front door slams against the siding of the house as it opens, and I jolt. Drop the tent. Whirl around to find Steph darting down the steps and across the yard. Her eyes are pink and swollen. She shakes slightly, though I can't decide if it's from the distraught look on her face or the fact that she's only wearing one of Dad's long sleeve shirts and a pair of cuffed blue jeans in this cold weather.

She stops a few feet from me and just stares at my chest, her gaze cloudy and remote. Her lips churn over the top of one another. She wants to speak, but can't. Or doesn't know where to start. This has a slice of panic cutting through me.

"What is it?" I ask.

Steph shoves her thumbnail into her mouth. Gnaws on it. When she was a kid, Mom tried to train her not to chew her nails. Now she only does it when something is really, really wrong.

"Steph," I say when she doesn't speak. "What's going on? Is it that guy from the other night? Did he come back?"

Maybe I should have gone straight inside the house once I saw that mystery car. He could own more than one vehicle. Hell, I don't know, the dude could be married and suddenly his wife has appeared, rocking Steph's world.

My sister shakes her head. Talks with her fingernail between her teeth. "Mom took a turn."

Whatever good mood lingering in me from my weekend in the forest is gone in an instant. "What do you mean she took a turn?"

FAYE DARLING

"Friday night," Steph begins. Lips quivering. Tears welling in the corners of her eyes. She still won't look at me. It's like she's trapped in the memory of whatever happened Friday night. She hasn't even gathered enough strength to finish her sentence, and all I can think is *I wasn't here, I wasn't here, I wasn't here.* Steph sucks in a somewhat steadying breath, though her voice comes out cold and pinched. "Mom had a seizure, so I called her doctor and he—he..."

Fuck.

I grip Steph's shoulders with both hands when she doesn't continue. Those tears of hers keep hovering, keep teetering. It's as if she's willing them not to fall. I give her a gentle shake. "What, Steph? What did the doctor say, what did he do?"

Steph's voice is a skeletal whisper. "He recommended I call Hospice."

I've heard of the organization, but the name alone doesn't have as much of an impact on me as it seems to have on Steph. "What does that mean?"

"It means..." She closes her eyes, twin tear drops streaming down each one of her cheeks. She topples forward and crashes into my chest. I wrap my arms around her, having to fight against her jelly knees to keep her upright. Steph sucks hard on her nose. "We're at the end, Ry."

"How close?" I force myself to ask even though I have no interest in hearing the answer. All I want to do is crawl into your arms right now—however crazy and illogical that might sound after the weekend I had with Luna. It's you I suddenly want, need, crave. I can almost feel your breath as it hits the back of my neck, reminding me you're here, you're right here, and thank fuck because I think without that knowledge, I would entirely fall apart.

IN LOVE WITH YOU

"Maybe a week," Steph whispers.

An invisible hand punches me right in the solar plexus. Steals the air from my lungs. Jumbles my insides.

I was hopeful Mom's health would turn around. Didn't I say this to you just a few days ago? That I had hope?

Now?

Well, now it feels like that trap door has finally opened up beneath my feet. I drop through it. Stomach in throat. Heart a stuttering mess. My skin is cold, ice cold. And numb. So numb I am unable to feel Steph's arms slink around me. Unable to feel much of anything except the desperate need to bolt. To run. To get the fuck away from here.

"Where are you going?" Steph shouts.

I hadn't even realized I was moving. But I've left my sister in the yard and climbed back into the front seat of my Camaro. Revving the engine is my only response to her question. Then, I chuck the car into reverse.

Steph pounds her fists against the hood. Anger overriding her sorrow. "Don't you fucking leave me here alone, Ryder."

But I don't know how to stay. Not right now, with my foot on the gas and the cottage shrinking in the rearview faster than it ever has before.

I speed through town, scowling at every happy little family I spot. In the window booth of the pizza joint. Shifting out the door of the trinket shop. Skipping hand-in-fucking-hand down the sidewalks, the glow of the streetlamps lighting them up like some kind of sickly dream.

Have you ever felt like this before? Like the world was so far away from you that you wouldn't be surprised if you found out you were a time traveler or from an alien planet or trapped in some kind of alternate reality.

FAYE DARLING

I crank the wheel and hit the gas when I reach Mark and Gina's street, but as soon as I spot Blake's car out front, I buzz by their house and head back onto the 101. I plow through town again. Same families, same buildings. I consider ducking into the parking lot of Nick's apartment high-rise—Cove's closest thing to a high-rise, anyway—but I can't seem to ease off the gas in time. Can't seem to bother turning back around, either.

Soon, the downtown strip of Cove becomes nothing but houses that get farther and farther apart, then nothing but trees and twists and turns in the highway as it follows the edge of the roaring Pacific.

To be honest, I'm not even sure where I'm going until I pull into the crowded parking lot outside of The Tavern. I park among a sea of jacked-up pickup trucks and motorcycles. For a moment, I consider kicking over every bike lined up in the gravel just to stir up trouble. I'd rather deal with an entire mob of angry bikers than the shitstorm that is my heart and head right now.

"Fuck," I mutter as I kick the front door open with my boot instead.

It swings wide, and my hands immediately fist at my side.

No one looks at me as I scan the room. Not the leather-bound Timber Razers letting off steam, or the plaid-covered salt bloods trying to escape life for an hour or two, or the middle-aged women with too much makeup on their too plain faces looking to get lost in beer and pathetic conversation.

And it's a good thing no one looks at me, either, because I think one glance in my direction would send a set of knuckles hurdling through their skull.

IN LOVE WITH YOU

D.J. shifts uncomfortably behind the bar when I lean over it, fists tight, eyes boring holes through the grains laid into the wooden counter.

"Didn't think you were working tonight," he says. It comes out like a statement, but I hear the question threaded between his words.

I grind my molars. "Not."

"Pint?"

"Whiskey."

An empty glass clinks down in front of me and the glug of amber liquid follows as D.J. pours me a double. He's barely taken away the bottle when I reach for the drink, knock it back in one swallow, and wave two fingers at him, asking for another. He obliges.

"All good?" D.J. asks as I throw the second drink back just as fast as the first.

"Another," I breathe, fire in my gullet.

D.J. hesitates, and even though I don't look up at him, I can feel his eyes trained on me, scouring every inch of my ugly face for answers I don't even know how to give, let alone want to. He senses this, too. Maybe he senses something more. I don't know. What I *do* know is that the big tattooed motherfucker pours me another glass of whiskey, this time with a little less in it than the two before.

"Go easy," he says under his breath. A warning.

"Mm," I hum, then down the entire glass in one go.

"Fuck's going on?" D.J. asks, then laughs. "You get into a fight with your boyfriend on the drive home from your camping trip or something?"

"Nope," I say, then wave two fingers at him. The whiskey has dulled my edges, but it's somehow not enough. Not nearly enough. I can still feel my stomach stuck in my throat. I'd like to dislodge it if I can.

Distract me, baby.

What am I saying? You're always a distraction, and that clearly isn't doing jack shit to help. Problem is, I know what *will* help. But it'll only help for a few seconds, then it'll hurt a helluva lot.

D.J. sets the bottle down on the low counter on the other side of the bar without pouring me another like I've asked. He spreads his arms out and grips the edge of the bar top, his black dress shirt rolled up to his elbows so the tattoo sleeves on each of his forearms are visible. The inked devil near his left wrist is leering at me with its tongue out. If D.J. wasn't attached to that tat so much, I'd go ahead and wipe that look off its stupid fucking face.

I look beyond the tattoo to the bottle of whiskey sitting on its shelf, my skin buzzing for want of it. I hook my boot heels around the lowest rungs of the stool, stand up, and snatch the hooch. I pour myself a glass, clutching my drink and the bottle close to my chest and leaning out of D.J.'s reach before he can take either from me.

I swallow half of the whiskey before D.J. rips the bottle out of my hands. D.J. might abstain from membership of the biker gang he's a legacy to, but it doesn't mean he's soft. Him jerking the bottle out of my grip reminds me how strong he really is. Like a kickback from a shotgun, I wobble backward. Somehow, I manage to catch myself on the bar before I fall on my ass, but my drink isn't so lucky. A few drops of whiskey spill out of the glass.

IN LOVE WITH YOU

"Fucking made me spill my drink," I grumble, licking a bead of liquor off the sleeve of my green and blue flannel. "Favorite fucking shirt, too."

D.J. sighs. Long, loud, and through a supremely clenched jaw. I watch that devil on his arm warp as he grips the bar tighter.

"What?" I say, more to the tattoo than to D.J.

But it's D.J. who answers.

"Just wondering if I need to call your sister or not."

"Like hell." I raise my glass to my lips and scoff into the drink, the glass fogging briefly before I tilt it, polishing off the last of the whiskey. The glass hits the bar top hard. The force of it rattles through my hand, up my arm, and settles in my nerve endings. My tongue jams into the soft corner of my cheek and I roll my head, everything and everyone going blurry for a second until I see her striding across the room.

Luna.

Hair damp and slicked into a high ponytail. Clean skin poking through a white camisole and jean shorts, a soft denim button down tied around her waist. She's got a notebook and a laptop in her hand, a smirk on her face, her eyes on me. There's a question building behind those eyes, but I don't have the bandwidth or the time to figure it out.

When I took off from the house, my plan was not to show up here. Even as I walked through the doors of The Tavern, it was not my goal to seek her out. But here she is, nevertheless, and I didn't know just how much I needed to see her until I watch her stride across the room.

A bit of my numb heart begins to thaw. Just a little. For the briefest of moments, I feel steady in my body again. Sure.

And then a Timber Razer with greasy hair down to his shoulders has the audacity to slap Luna's ass so hard as she walks past his table that she stumbles sideways. Then, he laughs.

Mistake.

Big. Fucking. Mistake.

My stool shrieks against the floor as I kick it out from under me, already barreling toward the fucker across the room. I hear D.J. say my name in warning, but it sounds distant and garbled because my ears are filled with noises akin to an old electrical transformer popping and humming loudly, about to blow. The rest of my body buzzes in the same fashion. Everything feeling quick and messy and out-of-control, all at once.

"Hey," Luna says as I blow past her. I barely register her fingertips grazing over the back of my clenched fist.

The dead man walking, or sitting I should say, has twisted around in his chair to face two other Timber Razers at the table. He's snickering, reaching for a pint of beer. He's bigger than me, but I doubt he's stronger. I doubt he runs the beach at night when he can't sleep or does sit ups in his room each morning before breakfast because he can't seem to remember that he doesn't have to wait for his cell door to open before he can get food. I doubt he's been in a fight, a *real* fight, in years.

This isn't the movies, baby, so if you're expecting me to say something, get him to turn toward the sound of my voice and watch the shock materialize slowly on his face, that ain't gonna happen. No. If violence ain't your thing, then shut your eyes, my love.

IN LOVE WITH YOU

I step up behind the biker, grab a fistful of his greasy hair, and slam his face into the table, his cheek busting the pint glass on its way down.

The smaller of the two guys at the same table pushes back and stands up in two seamless movements, but a fist straight to his jugular sends him down in only one.

Big man opposite draws a knife.

Oh, I fucking hate knives.

Mark and I used to talk about which we'd rather face, a gun or a knife, and we always, always chose gun. Grab it, kick it—it's only the bullets that make it dangerous. But a fucking knife is fear poised on a hilt. You gotta watch it close unless you wanna get sliced, and—

Fuck me, that whiskey hit harder than I first thought. I swear, eyeing that blade as it salsas around, there are three, not one.

But I am a juggernaut. An unstoppable force fueled by rage and grief, possession and booze—plenty of fucking booze.

I pound my palms into my chest, let my eyes go wide and wild, then scream, voice raw and ear-splitting, right in that knife-wielding motherfucker's face, "Fucking do it."

And he does.

Quick as a snake striking, he slashes the knife across my bicep, and I smile, because, I'm already winding up with the other arm. I counter with a left hook that sends him wobbling, but not dropping. Then, his buddy is up, the fucker who started all of this, and he's got some of that broken glass crushed in his fist. He throws a sliver at me, and I knock it away. But there's the knife again, ripping into my cheek.

"Fuck this," I say, then head butt the knife-wielder. The sound of his nose crunching beneath my skull is like waking up as a kid on Christmas morning to see the tree surrounded by shiny presents.

I'm too caught up in and pleased by my own analogy to notice the fist glissading toward me. It slams into my jaw, sending me sideways. I take a few chairs out as I go, landing on a table hip-first and spilling the beers left abandoned by the folks who must have split the moment that knife appeared.

Grunting, I push onto my feet. My shoulders are hunched over, my head swinging slightly, as I watch the bikers circle me like they're hunters and I'm a grizzly bear. A pissed-off grizzly. Pawing at the ground. Breath huffing in and out through my nose. Eyes dark and zeroed in on the threat.

A shotgun cocks behind me.

The room plunges into silence.

I wait for the barrel of the gun to press against the nape of my neck, but instead I watch as it glides over my shoulder and past my head, taking aim at the Timber Razers.

"You lot, out," D.J. bellows. "Before I call Judah."

I spit a mouthful of blood at their feet as they shuffle toward the door as soon as D.J. drops the name of their ringleader, a man I've only ever heard of.

"You." D.J. taps my shoulder with the barrel of the gun. "Get upstairs and sober the fuck up before I fire your ass on the spot."

"I'd rather you just shoot me," I say, air pumping in and out of my lungs in labored bursts. It's worth a shot, hey?

"Is that what this was?" D.J. lowers the gun and steps up beside me, talking low since about half the room is still watching. "You on some kind of suicide mission?"

"I don't fucking know," I whisper.

Maybe.

IN LOVE WITH YOU

We're at the end. Steph's cracked voice echoes in my head. I shut my eyes and try to blot it out, push it down, bury it with something else.

Luna is a shadow in my peripheral. Watching, searching. Right now, she feels just like you. Here and, at the same time, not. Distant. I want to reach out for her, turn toward her and look into her eyes at the very least. But the shame of what I've said, telling D.J. I'd rather him just shoot me, and the guilt of what I did to those bikers, hits hard. And if I scared her. If I made her fear me in anyway. I don't know if I can handle seeing that reflected back at me.

"Upstairs," D.J. says forcefully. "First aid kit is under the sink in the bathroom. Coffee's in the kitchen. I don't want to see you back down here again tonight. Got it? You can crash on the couch."

"Thanks," I whisper.

D.J. acts like he wants to pat me on the back or drop a hand onto my shoulder. But he doesn't. His massive hand just hovers over me for a few seconds before it falls back down to his side.

When he doesn't say anything else, I sway through the crowd, headed for the stairs that lead to his apartment. I don't turn back until I'm at the pool tables, just steps away from the staircase. Luna stands behind D.J., those amber eyes wide and barely peeking at me from around her cousin's big shoulder. D.J. turns toward her, saying something I can't hear, and she nods.

That's the last thing I see before I disappear up the stairs.

Thirty-One

Luna

So much for writing all night.

I had posted up at the kitchen table after I showered and changed clothes, but the sounds from downstairs seeped up through the floorboards. For twenty minutes I stared at the screen, every glass clinking and voice shouting making me jump. Making me agitated. I thought going down and setting up at the bar, drowning myself in the sounds rather than letting them trickle in and scratch annoyingly, might help.

Then Ryder happened.

I think those three words could sum up the majority of my time on the North Coast. *Then Ryder happened*.

He'd told me about his prison sentence. Told me a bit about why he'd ended up there. It didn't scare me. When your grandfather is a legend among one of the burliest motorcycle clubs in the Pacific Northwest and you spend your childhood vacations in his bar, you learn quickly that nothing is ever black and white. The most gruff, dangerous men were often the kindest to me when I was a girl. And, having spent most of my life observing the lives of others intensely, I always know there's more going on beneath the surface that can be seen.

So, reader, if you're wondering why I'm trailing up the stairs to my cousin's apartment, going after Ryder without a hint of fear in my veins, even after seeing what that man is capable of when he doesn't keep himself in check, it's because I know something happened when he got home. Something bad.

Just a few hours ago he was smiling at me, all mushy-gushy, and now he's here all angry and broken-looking.

My heart pounds hard in my chest at what might have happened at his place. Is it his mom? Is she gone? Is it Steph? Did something happen with her over the weekend? Did something in him just snap when he returned to the harsh world that is his reality?

Pushing open the door at the top of the stairs, the first thing I spot are the drops of Ryder's blood on the scuffed hardwood floors. I set my computer and notebook on the coffee table in the living room and follow the trail of blood into the hallway. A hulking shadow is cast over the width of the floor outside of the only bathroom in D.J.'s two bedroom apartment. The shadow climbs the wall. I watch it jump as Ryder curses through clenched teeth.

Even after the violent show he put on downstairs, he still manages to take my breath away. I lean into the open doorframe of the cramped bathroom and drink him in. His shirt is gone, his hair twisted into a loose knot on the crown of his head. *Fuck me*—look at the muscles stacked above his shoulders, fanned across his back. The sweat clinging to his skin, glistening. The veins in his arms, popping out.

"You're beautiful," I whisper.

He twists toward me, a disbelieving smile on his face. I wince. The cut on his cheek oozes blood, but thankfully looks superficial. The cut on his bicep, however, is deep. Dark, dark red seeps out of the wound and courses down his arm, pooling in the crook of his elbow.

My brows crush together, and I immediately close the distance between us, inspecting the knife wound more closely.

"I think you need stitches," I say.

"No doctors," he says, his voice as loud and harsh as it was when he spoke to those bikers. He must see me flinch, just a little, because when he speaks again it's almost a whisper. "It's just—I can't—they'll find out what happened and—I can't."

"I get it," I say. "They might call the police."

"Yes."

And while about three dozen people caught his little show downstairs, there's an unspoken rule among the patrons of The Tavern. No cops. The Timber Razers wouldn't think of involving the authorities and the locals who come to the rough watering hole know better. Ryder should be safe as long as no bozo gets any bright ideas.

"What about Steph? I bet she can stitch you up quick, being a nurse and all." I jab a thumb over my shoulder. "Want me to drive you home?"

"Fuck no." He turns, giving me his back. I watch the downcast look of his eyes through the mirror. "Sorry. Just. No."

I can almost feel the pain coiling out of him. Not the pain he feels physically, but the strong emotional pain that's sliced him deeper than that biker's knife. I carve a path up his spine with my palm until I reach the smooth gully between his shoulder blades. My fingers spread like ivy over his skin. I want to be able to draw that pain right out of him through my fingertips. But I'll settle for him relaxing, if only a miniscule inch, beneath my touch.

Ryder's lashes fall over the tops of his cheeks as his eyes close.

The question sits on the tip of my tongue, but I'm afraid if I ask what happened, he'll close up on me. He's hurting, yes, but he's here, where I can see him, touch him. That has to be enough for now.

"Sit," I say after a few breaths of silence. I gesture to the closed lid of the toilet beside the sink. "Let's clean you up."

He had managed to find the first aid kit before I got here, but the contents of the kit look like they've been ambushed by a tornado. Either he was already trembling, the way he is now, from the aftershock of that brawl or was too drunk not to make a mess of things. I step up to the counter and begin to organize the kit into what I'll need and what I won't.

Your standard first aid kit does *not* come with a suturing set. However, The Tavern is a place frequented by hot-heads just like Ryder. That's why the kit up here and the one D.J. keeps in his office behind the bar are padded with the extra stuff.

Ryder doesn't say anything as he settles onto the toilet seat. I wash my hands with soap and water, don a pair of surgical gloves, and fill a plastic syringe with tap water to irrigate the wound.

"This might sting," I say, plunging the water into the wound. If it does sting, he doesn't let on. Not even a tic of his jaw muscle. The man isn't trying to act like a badass, he *is* a badass. But, badass or not... "What I do next will *definitely* sting."

I thread the curved suturing needle I've already sterilized and clamp the metal needle driver to the end. I take the tissue forceps, which are nothing more than oversized tweezers, and press them to the top side of the skin on the far end of Ryder's cut.

Still, he's silent. Staring blankly at my blue shower towel hanging over the bar at my back. I take a steadying breath, because I know firsthand what it feels like to be stitched up with not much more than a little whiskey running through your veins. When he doesn't so much as flinch when I plunge the point of the needle into the lower half of his wound, I bite my lower lip, raking over it with my teeth. Worry doesn't even begin to cover it.

"Talk to me, Ry," I say as I twist my hand gently and guide the needle up and out the other side. God, my own arm hurts just remembering what this feels like. Of course, I'd cut myself on a bit of barbed wire at the edge of Uncle Reese's farm back in Oklahoma. This was before my books had really taken off and I didn't have insurance, or the funds to pay for an expensive trip to the emergency room, so Reese had stitched me up himself.

Ryder is holding his breath for some reason. And, I'll be completely honest, it's freaking me the fuck out.

"Breathe," I whisper as I tie off the stitch, not once, not twice, but three times. Just like Reese showed me. I clip the end of the thread with a pair of sterile scissors and move a little ways over on the wound. Then, I drive the needle in on the same plane as the last to try and keep the stitches nice and even.

Ryder hisses at this. Fists both his hands in the shirt tied around my waist. Knuckles digging into hip bone. His touch is hot and real and reassuring. I squint at the wound on his arm as I curve the needle up and out the other side. His grip on me tightens. He hisses again.

"*Now* you feel it," I say.

"Fuck," is his only reply.

"Where'd you go in that head of yours?" I ask as delicately as I can, trying not to sound like I'm forcing his hand. Trying not to sound like I'm trying to pry the truth out of him. "You had me worried for a sec."

His hands fisted around my shirt release, and his palms slide around my hips and down, cupping my ass. "Sorry."

I tie off the third knot on the second set of sutures, guiding it to the top side of the cut like I did the first. Careful not to touch any of the equipment on anything else, I brace my forearms on the top of Ryder's muscular shoulders and lean in until I can taste the whiskey on his breath and smell the blood in his mouth from that sucker punch he took to the face. I dive into the wells of those dark blue eyes of his, a sea of his emotions churning within. I hold his gaze, my lips fluttering over his, until it becomes too hard *not* to kiss him. His lips are hot, scalding me as they collapse beneath my touch, parting so that I can lick into his mouth. Again, I wonder if I can absorb some of that pain I feel strung tight inside of him. Suck it out with my tongue and swallow it down, giving him some of my sure-footedness in return. Although I fear if he does open up to me about what happened back at the cottage, I will need every ounce of my strength to keep from collapsing.

He drags me closer, hands still planted firmly on my ass, until we are chest to chest, my legs trapped between his.

It's crazy how safe I feel right now, yes? I mean, I just watched him lose his shit trying to take on a gang of road-hardened bikers in my cousin's bar. Watched him slam a dude's face into a beer glass and send another man off his feet like he weighed next to nothing. I should be terrified of him, right? If not terrified, then wary at least.

But I'm not. Because, even though something else drove him right to that edge, I'm the thing that tipped him over it. That biker smacked *my* ass. And Ryder didn't think twice about standing up for me. Protecting me like no one else ever has. Like I've never wanted anyone to do before.

Something's different about this man, though, reader. Can you feel it? Can you see it? Is it absolutely insane to say I might actually be falling for him?

"Luna?" He's leaned away from me just enough so he can speak clearly, though I wouldn't call that tremulous voice of his clear.

I open my eyes and don't move an inch. I look at him in a way I hope conveys to him he can continue. He can talk to me. Give me part of his burden.

He sucks in a shallow, quivering breath, closing his eyes. Teardrops wet his lashes, making them even darker than they already are. With a sigh, he sags forward, landing with his face buried in the valley of my breasts. He mumbles something I can't understand.

"What?" I ask, arching away so his mouth is freed from my flesh.

"Mom is—" he starts, but shakes his head. I want to rattle his shoulders. I want to question him until he spits it out. He takes another wavering breath. "Mom isn't doing good at all. She took a turn over the weekend."

My heart is tugged down into my stomach. "Fuck, Ry."

"Steph called hospice," he says, and my blood turns to ice in my veins. "Do you know what that means?"

"Yeah," I say, voice breathy and caught up in the memory of my own mother's final days. The daily check-ins from the nurse. The careful instructions to call them, not emergency services or the police, when she finally passed. *When*. They never said if. Not once. I picked up on that very quickly. "Unfortunately, I know exactly what that means."

Ryder lets out a mangled whimper. Buries himself in my chest, nose driving hard into my sternum, like he can't get close enough. He's holding his breath again. Fists trembling against my back. Knees quaking. He grunts. Inhales through clenched teeth. It's like he's trying to hold it all together. Trying not to...

"You can cry, you know," I whisper. My lips press against the top of his hair, which still smells like campfire smoke and the fresh, clean scent of the forest. "You can let your walls down in front of me. You're safe. You're safe with me."

I lay the suturing equipment onto the counter beside the sink and peel off the blue gloves, wrapping them up inside out before dropping them in the waste basket next to the toilet. I need to touch him. I need him to know that I meant what I said. If I feel safe with him, I want him to feel safe with me.

My fingers thread up through his hair at the base of his skull, kneading the skin and bone that feels too tight. I massage the low curve of his head with one hand, the nape of his neck with the other. The knots that I find—*fuck*. It's like he holds every bit of his tension back here. I locate a particularly tight bundle halfway between the top of his spine and his ear and rub it in circles under my thumb. He releases a vibrating groan into my chest, collapsing into me further.

And with that, his shoulders begin to shake, and the thin camisole I'm wearing grows damp. He sucks hard on his nose before he begins to full-on sob, holding onto me as if I am the only thing keeping him from falling through the floorboards.

I shed a silent tear of my own.

I've spent almost as much time with Ryder's mom as I have with him over the past two weeks. I may not have known who she was before the brain tumor, but I can still see glimpses of that strong, beautiful creature within her. From what I've learned, she's the kind of woman who knows exactly who she is and can love hard because of it. Ryder's behavior after learning the coming days are her last is only proof of that love. Only proof that her loss is going to rock the world of Ryder, Steph, and everyone who ever knew her. Even me.

"I can't breathe," Ryder says through garbled, spit-laden words. He pulls away from me and tries to take in air. He manages a shallow, gasping inhale. Another. They're coming faster and faster, shallower and shallower. His pulse is hammering in his neck.

I put a flat palm to his chest, feeling that jackhammer of a heart pound against me. I look him dead in those tear-stained blue eyes. "Focus on me. Listen to the sound of my voice. Feel the weight of my hand on your body. That's it. Good. Now, try and breathe with me. In. Out. In. Good. Out."

His eyes sharpen with a newfound clarity, and he reaches out to rub his thumb over the top of my cheek, soaking up my tears. "You're crying."

"Of course," I whisper.

He moves to the other side of my face. Rubs his thumb over the opposite cheek. His tears seem to be slowing, his heart returning to a somewhat normal syncopation. Those protective instincts are taking over, distracting him from his own pain. I'm not sure if that's good or bad, but he looks more like himself than he has since I first caught sight of him downstairs tonight, so I decide it's a good thing for now.

"Thank you," he whispers, letting the pad of his thumb trail down the center of my cheek, then veering off to run it over my lips. It catches on the lower one for just a second before he drops his hand to his thigh.

"For what?" I ask.

"For being here."

I'm afraid of the answer I'll get if I ask this question, but I can't stop myself from uttering the words aloud. "Did you come here tonight because of me?"

His eyes glaze over just a little as he stares over the top of my shoulder. "I don't know. Maybe. Subconsciously, I think I needed you. Consciously..."

"You don't have to explain," I say, because I've gotten my answer. And I'm pleased enough with it. I trust a subconscious mind over a conscious one any day. The subconscious is a sponge to the world, and I've found it rarely conceals the truth. Those knee-jerk reactions? Those split-second decisions? Some call it auto-pilot. Others call it instinct. It's all just the part of our brain we're not intelligent enough to always be aware of.

"Hey, Luna?" Ryder asks.

"Yeah?"

His eyes dart down to his half-closed knife wound, the blood still trickling through the open end. "You think you could finish stitching me up?"

I don't know why, but I blush. "Of course."

Thirty-Two

Luna

I WAKE IN STAGES the next morning.

Stage One: I register Ryder's sturdy frame playing big spoon to my little. Arm barred over my waist. Breath hot as it sifts through strands of my dark hair.

Stage Two: The creak of a floorboard sounds in the hall.

Stage Three: My eyes flap open and I peer across my bedroom and through the cracked-open door to find D.J. standing just outside, eyes cutting from Ryder to me, an eyebrow lifting in question.

I roll my eyes at D.J.. Like he wasn't the one who had sent me with the kind of tent I wouldn't be able to use on that camping trip in the first place. The one that eventually forced me to share sleeping quarters with the bear of a man currently at my back. D.J. might as well have been playing matchmaker.

D.J. shifts forward, easing my door open with the tips of his massive square fingers. The old hinges whine, and Ryder hums against my hair, burrowing deeper. He doesn't wake.

Now it's my turn to lift my brows at D.J.

"Those fuckers Ryder fought with last night must have slashed his tires," he whispers.

"Fuck," I say. But it could have been worse. Much worse.

"I already called for a tow truck," D.J. says. "I'm having them take it to a mechanic buddy of mine. He works on classics and owes me a favor."

I get the feeling from the square roll of D.J.'s jaw I don't want to know why his buddy owes him a favor. He wouldn't tell me, though, even if I asked. D.J. is good at keeping secrets. Part of the reason I came here in the first place. Also part of the reason he's so hard to get a read on these days. I guess the older you get, the more secrets you have to keep.

"I'll make sure he gets home today," I say.

"Like you can read my mind."

As if.

I look at the clock on the nightstand. It's not even seven yet. "Making an early run up to Portland, again?"

"Yep," he says, and I already know that's all I'm going to get out of him on the subject.

"Be careful," I warn.

"When I checked the traffic cams earlier, the mountain pass didn't look icy," he says. That's not what I meant by *be careful*, and he knows it. "You gonna be okay today? I know this must be picking at a lot of old scabs."

I shrug one shoulder. Just like Ryder does occasionally. How much time have I been spending with him that I'm copying his mannerisms? Fuck's sake.

"I'll be okay," I say. "I'm in a good place these days."

"Call me if you take a dive."

"Always."

D.J. taps his fingers against the doorframe twice, nods, and shrinks into the shadows of the hallway. A few minutes later, I hear the door to his apartment close. The lock clicks over a second later. Then, all I hear are resounding boot steps on the stairs, the scuff of them out in the parking lot. D.J.'s truck flares up. Tires churn over the gravel. Silence.

Ryder's still out dead to the world. Grief can do that to you—knock you on your ass. I remember how many afternoons I spent during my final years of high school napping instead of doing homework, instead of hanging with my friends. The ones who stuck with me, that is.

I carefully remove Ryder's arm from around my waist and slip out from under the blankets, shivering in nothing but an oversized t-shirt and a pair of satin cheeky panties. All I want to do is open my laptop at the kitchen table and write until my soul is at peace. But my stomach growls and my nerves beg for caffeine and I know as soon as Ryder wakes up and everything hits him from last night he'll need me. So, I make breakfast instead.

The bacon is almost perfectly crisp when I hear footsteps in the hallway, then a groan as Ryder comes around the corner. I use a fork to lift the bacon from the grease and onto a paper towel-covered plate as I take him in from the side of my vision. Shirtless. Olive-green hiking pants sitting low on his hips, unbuttoned, half-zipped. My eyes cling to the thin trail of hair that starts at the base of his navel and skims down, disappearing beneath the waistband of his boxers, which are bunched a little at his waist. My stomach is lifted like a pancake and dropped upside down.

The bacon on the fork teeters. Slides back into the grease. The oil pops. Hits me in the neck. I hiss.

Guess I deserved that for getting distracted.

Ryder rubs the sleep from his eyes as he totters through the living room. I try to focus on extricating the rest of the bacon before it either burns or kills me. It's a hard task to complete once Ryder presses his front to my back, the sticky heat of his body overwhelming me in seconds. He docks his hips against my ass, shamelessly pressing his morning wood into me. He rubs my arms as his chin falls onto my shoulder. He heaves out a sigh, ruffling my hair and sending shivers down my spine.

"G'morning," he says.

With his greeting, it hits me that this is the third morning in a row we've woken up in each other's company. Three is such a small number, but we've managed to find a sense of comfort in each other's presence that suggests three isn't quite as small as it implies.

I rub the hairs on his forearm with my palm. "How are you feeling?"

"Hm," is his only response.

"Start with your arm," I say, clicking off the stove and turning around so I can get a glimpse at the stitches. The wound isn't bleeding and doesn't look infected. It is pink and slightly puckered, though. "How does it feel?"

"All right."

"And your jaw?" With three fingers pressing against his chin I try to ease the fresh bruise into the daylight that's spilling through the bank of windows on the other side of the kitchen.

"Hurts a little."

"Your head?" I ask. "How's that hangover settling in?"

"Bit of a headache," he says. "Need food. Coffee."

I smile at him, tilting onto my tiptoes and claiming those lips of his without a second thought. We've moved into new territory, Ryder and me. I started to feel it after he stopped our lustful game in the forest to share with me the secret I could sense in him the day we met out on the water. I don't know. It's like we stopped hiding from each other. At least, he stopped hiding from me.

Do you understand what I'm saying, reader? Have you seen or felt that shift in us ever since then, too? Are you shaking your head, saying *I told you so*? Or are you backtracking, trying to fit together the pieces to make sense of all of this like I am?

I never do this. I never get involved with my research subjects in this way. I used to tell myself it was because it would make it harder to write about them, if I couldn't separate the real person from the fictional character I would make up after. But now I wonder if I was just protecting myself. Because, even though Ryder's strong arms are wrapped around my waist, tugging me into him. Even though I can *feel* how much he wants me. I still feel like I'm leaving my flank exposed. I still feel hella vulnerable.

And that makes me a little woozy, just admitting it.

"Still hungry?" I ask, breaking away from our kiss.

"Now I'm fucking famished," he says, sliding a calloused hand down the bare skin of my thigh, carving an inward path. He drags his fingertips over my underwear at the base of my legs, and his lips drag into a sly smile when he feels how wet I am for him.

His fingers reach that sweet spot, and just that tiny bit of pressure alone has my body jerking with delight. My left butt cheek hits the knob on the stove, the *click, click, click* of the gas sounding before Ryder tugs me back into his torso with a grunt and a laugh.

"Don't catch on fire, sweetheart," he says, sucking on a pocket of flesh high up on my neck.

"Too late," I grit out as the heel of his hand replaces the fingers on my clit, making me throb deep inside.

I whimper as his hand disappears, and he laughs as he slides his palms down the backs of my thighs, hooks them under my knees, and lifts me off the floor and onto his waist.

"Where's your cousin?" Ryder husks, turning us around.

"Portland."

He grunts, the vibrations of the noise rumbling in his chest and sending hot tingles pulsing between my legs. "Good."

Reader, I can feel you. Senses heightened. Heart thrumming. Maybe something else is thrumming, too, as a desire rumbles in your very core. Or, maybe I'm wrong. Maybe you're holding back. Perhaps you've been told this is wrong, what I'm allowing you to see, what we're making you feel. But it's just me here. And him. I'd like to think you can trust me, trust us. So, let yourself unravel a little bit. Indulge, my friend. Live vicariously.

You know you want to.

Ryder marches across the kitchen, his bare feet slapping against the linoleum. I vaguely hear bird song out the window as the morning air carries their voices loud and clear. Then, Ryder bends at the waist and drops me onto the edge of the kitchen table. His forehead presses against mine. A mischievous smile spreads as smooth and sweet as homemade jam across those cheeks of his, but when I lean toward him, ready to claim those lips with my own, he slides down out of my reach.

"What are you—" I begin, but then his fingers hook around the waistband of my panties, that smile looking a little more mischievous by the second. That's when I catch on. "Oh."

I lift up to help him slide the thin, silky fabric of my underwear over my ass, my toes curling with anticipation. My eyes flick instinctively to the entrance of the kitchen. I am very much aware of the fact that I am naked from the waist down in the middle of my cousin's apartment. I only hope he didn't turn around halfway to the city to come back for something he forgot.

When I tick my gaze back to Ryder, I catch a flash of my underwear as he tucks them into the pocket of his pants. I meet his eyes, which are swimming with so many emotions all at once it makes me a little dizzy. A pang of guilt strikes me, knowing we're chasing our pleasure right here and now while the doom of his reality waits for him twenty minutes up the road. Just as quickly as it struck, though, the guilt is washed away by a flood of lust and need as Ryder ducks low, spreads my legs apart for better access, and tosses my calves over his shoulders.

A buzz of energy precedes his mouth, making me arch back before he even touches me. Scruff of his facial hair. Warmth of his lips. The silky wet slide of his tongue swiping low to high. I wobble on the edge of the table, completely unmoored. One hand planted firmly on the wood behind me, one braced against his shoulder, I try and steady myself.

Sensing my need for an anchor, Ryder's arms lock around my hips, his hands planted firmly over the entire breadth of my back. I arch against his tongue plunging deep into my heat and feel his grip on my back shift with me, keeping me secure.

Sex has never felt like this before. It's always been more like riding a bull. Quick and wild. Hold on for your life. And if you don't? You're on your own to protect yourself from the fallout. But with Ryder it's different. It's like riding bareback on your favorite horse. Raw and real. Full of mutual trust and respect.

He pulls away to look up at me, his mouth glistening with the damp of my arousal. "It's okay to let go, Luna."

I draw in a quick breath. "Thought I was."

"I've got you," he says with a wink and a brush of his thumbs over my ribcage.

"I know," I say.

With a needy growl, his mouth latches onto me again, sucking hard on my clit, before letting the tip of his tongue rove 'round and 'round.

And I feel it then. The tension I've been holding in my body. Stiff joints and clenched muscles. I inhale so deeply I wonder if he can feel it down there. And when I let that breath go, I let every worry and fear and apprehension I didn't know I was claiming go right along with it. My back relaxes into Ryder's hold, letting him support my full weight.

I almost melt into a puddle as his tongue sucks and licks and takes me to a place I didn't know existed. I moan, the sound vibrating up and out of my throat.

"Oh, fuck, that feels so good," I tell him, both of my hands combing through his twisted blonde locks.

He hums his acknowledgement before stamping a trail of slow, sucking kisses from the top of my pubic bone to the soft stretch of skin below my slit. Each press of his lips is a primed detonator. Each drag of his tongue a mini explosion.

FAYE DARLING

I want this moment to drag on and on, but my body has other ideas, and every second Ryder spends buried between my legs, the closer I get to coming completely undone.

He spreads his lips over the entire length of me, the top of his mouth notched against that tight bundle of nerves at the tippy-top of it all. He sucks hard, every bit of me down there feeling him all at once. It's almost too much to handle, my body twitching back in his arms. Then his tongue drags through my dampness again, both lips fit over my clit, and it's game over. His tongue barely brushes me and I'm howling, shaking, rolling through wave after wave of pleasure until I'm a sweaty, panting mess on this kitchen table.

When he finally moves back, he's just as much of a mess as I am. Lips swollen and pink, dripping in my pleasure. Eyes clear, but still a little frenzied.

He presses a gentle kiss to my inner thigh without breaking eye contact.

"Thanks for breakfast," he murmurs, one side of his mouth hitching up.

"Hope everything was to your liking," I say, still out of breath.

"I hope you'll let me help with cleanup."

Before I can respond, before I can even figure out what he means, he ducks back down and strokes his tongue into my heat, sucking and lapping up every single drop of arousal left behind.

This man, reader. I swear. This. Man.

Thirty-Three

Ryder

I RELEASE A SHUDDERING breath in the cab of Luna's pickup truck because of you. I still don't know how this whole thing works, whether you have any choice in the matter or whether it's somehow in my control, but I haven't felt you since I walked away after that fight in The Tavern last night, and I've needed you. Fuck, I've needed you, baby. And I know, Luna's sitting here with me, has been with me ever since she stitched me up in the cramped bathroom at D.J.'s place, but I need her, too.

How the hell is it possible to need two people like this at once? How is it possible to love you and potentially be falling for someone else at the same time?

Nope. Can't think about that right now.

Now that you're here, I can gather my strength. I can do this.

"Just one step at a time," Luna whispers. I know without glancing over my shoulder at her that her eyes are trained on me as I stare at my family's cottage. We've been in her truck so long the cab has gone cold and the windows are beginning to fog over.

"You ever wish you could turn back time?" I ask.

"Every day of my life," she answers automatically.

I swing my gaze her way. Her face is calm, but still unreadable. I think she and I are more similar than we'd like to admit. Hard shells on the outsides with gooey, vulnerable centers we rarely let anyone else see. I caught a taste of that soft side of her this morning, when I feasted between her legs. It was right after I told her she could let go. That she'd be safe with me. It hadn't taken more than a few seconds and she'd relaxed so fully, let me in so deeply, I didn't want to move from that spot. Knees on the linoleum. Arms supporting her from behind. Exploring pieces of her she's worked hard to keep hidden from me.

But now I'm here. You're here. *We're* here. The very place and situation I fled from last night. Now, in the light of a new day, I have to clean up my mess.

The truck door squeals open as I slip out into the bite of the morning air. The rain has just begun. Fat, wet drops that will soon turn into a downpour if the dark clouds shifting in slowly off the ocean have anything to say about it.

I hesitate at the bottom of the porch steps, in front of the door, on the rug just inside the house. Voices in the distance—Steph asking questions to who I can only assume is the owner of the same gray sedan that was here yesterday and most likely the hospice nurse.

Luna presses a hot palm between my shoulder blades when I don't move from the doorway.

IN LOVE WITH YOU

"A fire should be going," I say, my attention swept up by the woodburning stove, cold and flameless. I move toward it, kneel down in front of its heavy door, and open it. I can hear the rain tick down on the ashes inside as a few droplets squeeze through the spout on the roof. I start ripping apart paper grocery sacks, crumpling the pieces up.

A hand on my wrist and a sigh at my back.

"Let me do it," Luna says. Can she sense I'm stalling? Distracting myself? Do you sense this, too?

"But I—" My words fall apart on my tongue.

"Ryder?" Steph's voice floats through the house. Sharp, pounding footsteps. She appears around the corner. Her red, puffy eyes narrow on me, her lips cinch into a tight, angry bundle. She hisses through her teeth as she storms toward me. "Do you know how long I've been waiting for you to come home?"

"Steph, I'm—" I barely make it to my feet before her open fist collides with my chest.

"You fucking left me here, you motherfucking asshole." She hits me again, but her fist and her words have a little less punch behind them this time. "I was alone in this. *Alone.*"

"I know," I say, standing still, not even trying to dodge her next strike. I deserve it. I deserve the full spectrum of Steph's anger.

"You're a selfish fucking prick," she says.

"I know."

"I was worried about you all night."

"I know."

"I could kill you for that." This time, when her hand meets my chest it stays there, fingers twisting up in my flannel. The sob that explodes out of my sister's tiny body is more painful than any wound she could inflict. It scares me more than that knife did last night as it cut through my flesh. She drags herself into my chest, her bones rattling so hard I swear I can hear them jumping around in their joints. I lock my arms around her shoulders. Hold her tight, tight, tight, the way she's liked since she was a terrifying two-year-old barreling headfirst into the world. She told me once that the weight and pressure calms her down, grounds her. Now, she sucks in a noisy breath. "I don't know what I'm going to do without her."

What do I even say to that? Nothing that comes to mind seems satisfactory. Nothing I say is going to change anything anyway. And the truth is, I feel the exact same way.

"This fucking sucks," I mutter, my chin resting on the top of Steph's head.

She scoffs through another sob. "It really fucking sucks."

"Stephanie, sweetie?" A woman's voice, sure and smooth, rises up somewhere at the back of the house. *The nurse.*

Steph sucks hard on her nose, which is pressed into my flannel, so I'm sure she's striped me with a good dose of snot. This poor shirt. It gets sliced. Bloodied. Now, it's covered in gunk. If it wasn't my favorite, if it hadn't been my dad's favorite, I'd burn it. But it could be dragged through mud, backed over by monster trucks, ripped to shreds by a pack of wolves, and still try to salvage the scraps to piece it back together.

"Come with me?" Steph asks, sounding as small and fragile as she did when she was sixteen and Blake had laid a hand on her for the first time.

I nod, then look back at Luna. Her arms are crossed over her chest, her hands gripping her shoulders like she's holding herself, comforting herself. I don't miss the tear fall from the corner of her eye and slip down her cheek. But she gives me a reassuring nod, telling me not to worry, even though I am. Worried this is bringing up painful memories of her own mother's death. Worried this is all too much for her. But I need her here. I need *you* here. Even if I can't say it out loud.

"I'll get the fire going," Luna says as Steph drags me into the kitchen.

"Thank you," I breathe.

Steph lets go of my hand halfway to Mom's room. Shakily, I pad toward the open door. It's not just fear of Mom's fate, of losing her sooner than I'd thought we would, that has me so apprehensive. It's the shame and the guilt from leaving last night, from blowing into The Tavern in such a rage. Just stay by my side, baby. You hear? Stay right where you've been for the past few weeks and I can get through this. Shed a tear for me or don't, I won't judge you either way. I just need to know you're with me.

So, we walk forward, you and I, past the bottom of the stairs that lead up to the loft and into the open doorway of Mom's bedroom.

The overhead light is on, stark and blinding, but Mom doesn't seem to notice. She's asleep in her bed, more pillows than usual propping her up on all sides. Steph is already huddled in the corner with the nurse, talking over schedules and signs to expect and what to do if this happens or that, but I don't really hear them, because I'm drifting toward Mom.

When I left her on Friday afternoon, she looked small. But if that was small, this is fucking microscopic. Her cheeks have caved in, the bones of her skull protruding a few degrees more. Her skin is a pale blue color, except under her eyes where it's dark purple.

FAYE DARLING

I click on Mom's sound soother, the whitewash synthetic ocean waves rolling out of the small speaker. I sit down on the edge of her bed. Brush her cheek with my thumb. Lean in. Kiss the top of her brow.

"Is this your brother?" I hear the nurse ask Steph.

Steph sighs heavily. "Yes. This is Ryder."

"Hello, Ryder, I'm Renée," the nurse says with a professional smile, her alto voice a little bit smoky and somehow very soothing. Probably has to be, doing what she does—nursing those who are at their end, communicating with family members who are already grieving fiercely. Her calm eyes look right at me, and I'm surprised by how steady I feel looking back at them. "I'll stop by twice a day to check up on your mother. Stephanie has my phone number if you need me in between. Don't hesitate to get in touch if anything worries you, anything at all. I'm here for you. All of you."

"I was, uh—" Steph pauses to clear the last of her tears out of her throat. "I was able to take an indefinite time off of work, so I'll be here."

"That's good to hear," Renée tells her. "Your mother will be in very capable hands, then."

Steph says something else, but it doesn't register with me. I'm too wrapped up in Mom. Her dry lips move before she groans. There's a pause before she makes the sound again, but this time it's more of a word than an indiscernible noise—*ma-er*. Hotter? Or water, maybe?

"Are you thirsty?" I ask.

Her eyes quake open and close. "Sss."

Yes.

"I'll get you a drink," I say, popping up straightaway.

IN LOVE WITH YOU

I take a step toward the kitchen, but Steph stops me with a hand to the middle of my chest. Her eyes briefly land on the cut on my face, the bruise on my jaw, but then lock onto my gaze, a pain twisting in her own irises. "She can't have anything to drink."

"What?" I ask, the word hollow.

"She can have some water on a sponge," Renée says, dipping a small, bright blue sponge poised on the end of a plastic stick into a glass of water. She squeezes the excess liquid out against the side of the cup and moves toward Mom. "Just to wet her tongue and lips."

My hand fists at my side, ready to fight for what Mom needs, ready to protect her. "Why can't she have any water?"

"The nurse just said she could," Steph says, her hand still on my chest, as if she can sense I'm about to lose my shit. "Just not like she could before."

"She might choke," Renée says, unphased by the shift in my mood. She leans over Mom and presses the sponge to her lips. Mom opens her mouth and sucks on the damp blue mesh for a moment before she lets it go. "There. That's what you needed, huh, Kendra?"

Mom makes an attempt at a smile, only one side of her mouth getting anywhere. She settles back onto her pillow.

I want to shove that damn sponge up the nurse's ass and then carry Mom down to the beach and get her in the ocean, begging for it to heal her. Cure her. Return her to me the way she used to be.

Does that sound so crazy? To ask the sea to heal my mother?

"This is how it has to be now," Steph says, searching my eyes for understanding. Her jaw clenches. "This is where we're at."

FAYE DARLING

I grit my teeth and nod, her words striking some invisible cord in me. It drags an image to the front of my mind: Steph pounding on the hood of my car as I drove away last night. As I *ran* away. As I left her and Mom all alone.

But I'm here now. And Steph's right. This is where we're at.

I take in a cleansing batch of air. "Just tell me what to do."

Thirty-Four

Ryder

THE NEXT FEW DAYS feel like a sticky dream. One that I will spare you from, because, for the most part, it's the same monotony on repeat. It's the medication administered on a strict timetable, the recurring nightmare of the sponge, the countless soiled bedding changes, the endless sleep Mom seems to have fallen into, but, mostly, it's the hours and hours of Steph and me sitting by Mom's side in silence, at least one of us holding her hand every single second so she knows she's not alone.

Luna is here most of the time, arriving in the mornings with coffee and breakfast from the bakery. Sally and Allen always slip in a 'thinking of you' note for us and an extra bear claw for Steph, because Allen knows they're her favorites.

Monday bleeds into Tuesday which hemorrhages into Wednesday and here we are on Thursday afternoon. I'm sitting on the back deck with Luna while Steph and Mom nap inside.

"Sorry this isn't the kind of research project you had in mind," I tell Luna.

"You know how I feel about that word," she says.

"You don't have to be here."

Luna takes my hand and tugs against me as she gets to her feet. She sits down on my lap, and I fold her into my body. The way I unravel bit by bit with her tucked close is hopefully enough for her to know I'm not pushing her away. I'm simply giving her an out.

She presses her lips into my hair and whispers, "I'm not going anywhere."

Friday passes achingly slow. Saturday is just the same.

On late Sunday afternoon, Steph, Luna, and I are scattered around Mom's room. Steph curled up beside Mom. Luna sitting on the velvet chair in the corner, staring off into space. I watch her idly as I sit on the floor beside Mom's bed. My arm is slung back over my head, my fingers entwined with a few of Mom's. I don't know how long we've all been here like this. Hours, maybe? Ever since last night?

There's a knock on the front door and my ears perk back. Muffled voices on the porch. Another knock. The knob turns, the hinges squeak, and Gina's voice lifts me out of my fog.

"Ryder?" she calls. "Steph?"

I meet Gina in the archway between the living room and kitchen. She's loaded down with glass casserole dishes and a large bowl covered in tin foil. Even carrying all of that she still turns and presses her shoulder into my chest and reaches up so that her chin cups the curve of my neck in a strange kind of hug.

IN LOVE WITH YOU

"Sweetie, you need a shower," she says matter-of-factly. And I'm so taken aback by her starkness, I laugh. It hurts a little. It's been a while. Since I've laughed *and* since I showered. Probably a good thing you can't smell me through these pages.

"Good to see you, too, Gina."

"All right, so my mom worry-cooked you enough food to last a month," Gina says, stepping back and lifting the array of dishes a little higher. "Chicken parm, manicotti, crab linguini, Nonna's homemade garlic knots. I put together a kale salad, because you need greens. And I baked some double chocolate chip cookies. You remember the ones with the sea salt you inhale every time I make them? Of course, Mark ate half of them straight from the oven, so there's not as many as I would have liked. Pound on him if you must, but leave his face alone so my wedding pictures aren't total shit."

At the mention of Mark, I blink past Gina and into the living room. Through the windows, I catch my best friend swaying on the edge of the top porch step, hands stuffed in the pockets of his denim coat. His head is tilted up, like it's his job to watch the rain as it falls from the sky.

"I couldn't get him to come in," Gina says with a sigh. "And he won't say why. Can I put these down? Mom's manicotti is about to burn my fingerprints off here. She pulled it out of the oven right when I showed up."

"Shit," I say, then reach for the food. Gina jerks it away, clucking her tongue and shaking her head. I turn sideways and let her take over the kitchen.

"You hungry now?" she asks, sliding everything onto the counter and moving straight to the oven, turning it to preheat.

FAYE DARLING

"Starved," Luna says from the hall just outside of Mom's room.

I watch Gina carefully, my eyes tight on her profile as Luna's voice registers in her ears. *Play nice*, I try and impress upon my friend. Gina and I might be the same age, but she's always been like an older sister to me, just as protective of me as I am with Steph. She could turn and spit fire at Luna, just to see what she's made of. Just for the hell of it. She's done it before, plenty of times.

Gina turns slowly, giving me her back for a suspenseful beat before I can see her face again. I let out a harbored breath, because—thank fuck—she's wearing a smile. A tight one, yes, but a smile, nevertheless. She gives Luna a quick head-to-toe once-over.

"Good," Gina says eventually. Good as in she's glad someone is hungry? Or good as in she approves of Luna? Then, Gina smirks. "You gonna get your cute little ass in her and help me out or what?"

Luna marches to Gina's side and starts pulling apart the tower of food without hesitation. Gina gives me a look over the top of Luna's head—dark brows raised, eyes pulled wide, lips still pressed into a smirk—like she's impressed. I shrug, trying to come off like I knew all along Gina would approve. I did not. When I imagined them meeting, I pictured a verbal tennis match as terrifying as the finals of the U.S. Open.

Steph skulks out of Mom's room the same time a loud bang sounds outside, followed by the slap of leaves and branches, and Mark's groan.

Gina drags Steph into her arms while she rolls her eyes at me. "Will you go see what the hell my idiot fiancé is breaking?"

"On it," I say.

IN LOVE WITH YOU

A second later, I open the front door to find Mark tangled in the bushes on the other side of the porch. Half of the metal gutter hangs down from the lip of the roof.

"It's not what it looks like," he says, trying to stand. His heel slips in a slick patch of mud and he tumbles back into the wide, rain-soaked leaves of the Rhododendron. He hits the ground with a *thump* and an *oof*.

"It looks like you're trying to demo the cottage," I say.

"Only trying to clean the gutters," he says, attempting to free himself from the bushes again and failing.

"Funny," I say. "I cleaned them out last month. Shouldn't be too bad."

"Well, I saw a—" Mark gestures to the roof. "You know, can't be too thorough this time of year. I figured with—I could at least—ah, shit, man, you gonna give me a hand out of this bush or am I going to become your permanent lawn ornament?"

"You'd make a cute gnome," I say. "Steph can sew you a pointy hat."

"Shut the fuck up," Mark says, nostrils flaring as he tries to cover a laugh.

I can't help but snicker as I lean over the porch railing and give him a forceful hand up. He wipes at the backside of his jeans, which are caked in mud and old, fallen leaves from the neighbor's Alders. He curses under his breath.

"Don't worry, I'll get you a trash bag to sit on for the ride home." I nod to Gina's Mercedes. "Save the Queen's precious interior."

"Look, I'm sorry, man," Mark blurts out.

"It's just a rain gutter."

"Not about that," he says. He tugs on the back of his neck. "I was gonna stop by last week. Turned onto your street several times, but always found a reason to head back home. Then I thought I'd wait for G. I figured having her with me would make it easier to walk through that door. The same way I've walked through it a bazillion times before, but then...I don't know. Just got to thinking how it wouldn't be the same. *She* wouldn't be the same."

"I understand," I say, hands buried deep in my pockets, gaze locked on the ground at my feet. My mom was always good to my friends. Loved on them the way she did Steph and me. The cottage was always a safe place where we could be ourselves, and she was an extension of that safe place. The adult you went to for advice when you needed a bit of wisdom without fear of being judged or punished. And my friends respected that about her. Adored her because of it.

"Ah, shit," Mark says, raising his arms up to his shoulders then letting them slap back down at his sides. "That's a fucking pussy excuse, isn't it?"

He jams the thumb and forefinger on his right hand into his closed eyes, but I still watch a few tears slip past the dam he's created.

"She knows," I tell him.

"What?"

"Mom knows you love her."

"Fuck, man," he says, pulling his hand away, letting me watch him cry. His eyes are rimmed in red and his freckles shimmer beneath the damp sheen of his tears. "How do you do that?"

"Do what?"

"Read my mind."

I shrug one shoulder. "You're not exactly hard to figure out."

"I don't know if I should be offended or not," he says.

IN LOVE WITH YOU

"Not," I say, trying my best to smile at him, to assure him that his open book qualities are what I admire about him. I tap a fingernail against the fallen gutter. "Tell you what. You fix this and then if you want to come inside, you can, but no one's gonna force you. And no one's gonna judge you if you decide not to."

Mark sucks his thin lips into his mouth and nods absent-mindedly. "Thanks, man. Still keep your tools in the shed?"

"Yep."

Mark stumbles out of the bushes and into the yard, then marches around the side of the house, shoulders pivoting sharply as he heads for the shed. The man is never more at ease than when he has a project to occupy himself with. When he's out of sight, I bend around the porch rail to look up at the gutter, wondering where the hell he was standing in the first place to bring himself and the gutter down the way he did. Open book, yes. Brightest human on the planet, not so much.

I take a moment outside, the fresh air in my lungs acting like a salve. Hard to say how long it's been since I stepped out of the house for longer than a minute. My eyes close and I breathe deeply, filling myself up with the sea air blowing gently up the street.

Alone like this, in the quiet, I can feel you fiercely. Almost like I could reach my hand out and find that yours is already sliding into mine. Relax with me, baby. Breathe with me.

Fill your lungs with that sweet, sweet oxygen until there's no room left. Wait a second, then another. Let it out in a slow and steady stream. Is your breath fogging in the air like mine is? Are you outside? Or are you inside? Maybe it's summer where you are, the middle of springtime. That doesn't matter, though.

FAYE DARLING

I take another deep breath in. Sometimes, I forget how good it feels just to breathe.

When Mark's footfalls sound on the pavers that lead to the shed, I duck back into the house, quietly shutting the door behind me.

I pause halfway to the kitchen and press myself against the wall near the fireplace, because Luna and Gina are mid-conversation, talking about me, I'm sure of it.

"Be good to him is what I'm trying to say," Gina tells Luna.

"I will," she replies.

"I mean it." I imagine Gina sticking Luna with one of her meanest glares. Maybe she's got a serving spoon in her hand from dishing up some of the food. Maybe she's using it to accentuate her point, aiming the end at Luna. "Or you'll have me to answer to."

"I don't doubt that." Luna laughs. Silence drops over them, the sound of dishes clattering and utensils scraping rises up. Then, Luna sighs. "You know, I see how amazing he is."

Gina hesitates for a moment. "Not everyone does."

I peek around the corner, just enough to see the sharp set of Luna's mouth and the firmness in her amber eyes as she looks right at Gina. She presses a palm to Gina's shoulder. "But I *do*."

And Luna's gaze lifts up then, catches mine like she knew I was there the whole time and doesn't let go.

Thirty-Five

Luna

TUESDAY NIGHT, I GET back to D.J.'s place late. I could have stayed the night at Ryder's, but I know all of the Norths need some hours to be on their own, to breathe. I know this because it's what I need too.

My feet drag the ground as I wend my way through the packed bar. I bump into several people and I think some guy reaches out to rub my hip, but I don't notice. I just keep walking, needing to get upstairs. My fingers fumble on the key as I turn it in the lock, but, soon, I'm traipsing up the steps, my bed calling to me like a siren in the deep.

D.J. is on the couch when I walk through, glasses on, laptop perched on one knee. His brows cinch tight as soon as he spots me. He jumps to his feet, unbridled panic streaking across his face.

"What's wrong? Why are you crying?" he asks, setting his computer onto the cushion beside him.

FAYE DARLING

I wipe at the tears I hadn't realized were there. I give him a full-body shrug, dropping my tote bag on the ground beside a pile of shoes. How do I tell him everything this past week has finally caught up with me? Has brought back too many memories from my mom's illness? I haven't wanted to be anywhere but nestled in with Ryder, Kendra, and Steph all week, but that doesn't mean it hasn't rubbed old wounds raw.

I try to toe off my shoes, but I trip instead. D.J.'s hands reach out to brace my shoulders and, at his touch, I collapse into him, his hulking form completely enveloping my smaller frame. A sob lets loose from my chest.

"Hey." He palms the braid trailing down my back. "Is she...?"

"No," I garble. "She's still alive, but I—I—"

"You what, Luna?" he asks when I don't finish.

"I'm so tired," I whisper. "It feels..."

"Feels like losing your mom all over again?"

"Yeah."

I half expect him to say, *I told you so*, but I realize quickly that's not my cousin's style.

"Why don't you stay here tomorrow?" he suggests.

"I can't do that," I say, pulling back and twisting an ugly face up at him.

"Why not?"

"Because I *want* to be there," I say.

"Because of him?"

I bite down on my lower lip as another round of tears rake over me. *Yes*, I want to say. *Because of him*. "I—I—I don't want him to think I don't care about him. By staying away, I mean."

"He won't think that," D.J. says.

"He will."

"He'll understand."

"What if he doesn't?"

D.J. exhales a steady stream of air over the top of my head. "I think your best bet is to just be honest with him. If he doesn't understand, then that's his problem to deal with, not yours. But...if I know Ryder like I think I do, it's not going to be an issue."

I nod my head and let him hug me for a few seconds more. D.J. is not a hugger, not in the least, so I'm surprised I even get that much time. Eventually, though, he squeezes my arms twice and sends me off to take a shower, promising to have a cup of hot chocolate with a dash of chili, just the way I like, waiting for me when I get out.

After I've sipped my hot chocolate down to the chalky dregs, I sit at the kitchen table with my phone to my ear, watching the dark silhouettes of the evergreens sway in the wind out the windows as I wait for Ryder to answer.

He picks up on the fourth ring, not saying anything, just breathing into the receiver. It'd be creepy if I weren't doing the same exact thing, or if I didn't find the rhythm of his steady breath soothing on some level.

Minutes unspool between us, never once getting awkward or restless.

I turn the empty cocoa mug around in an aimless circle as I gaze out the window.

"The stars are out tonight," I say quietly.

"I'm watching them from the beach," he says. "Steph wanted time with Mom on her own so she kicked me out."

Silence settles over us again as we gawp at the night sky respectively. I only catch a belt of stars here or a cluster there because of the trees, but I have no doubt Ryder is simply bathing in them on the wide-open beach. I picture him perched high up on the dunes, knees drawn into his chest, neck aching back as he takes in every pinprick of silver in the dark.

My breath studders after another minute, and I hear him suck in a noisy batch of air. He seems to hold it, like he's asking a silent question.

"It's funny," I say, not entirely sure what I'm going to tell him until my mouth starts moving. "People always talk about how heart-splintering grief can be, but they don't tell you how heavy it makes you feel, how exhausted. They also don't say that just the reminders of that loss will scratch everything red and raw again."

"After my dad died, all I wanted to do was sleep," Ryder says softly, his voice barely audible. "I don't think I went to school for almost three weeks. All I did was stay in bed. And then all I wanted to do was hit things."

"They don't tell you how angry grief can make you, either."

"How isolated it'll make you feel unless you're around people who understand it as fiercely as you do." He swallows loudly, and I imagine his throat bowing around the motion, like river water skirting around a rock. "You need rest, don't you, Luna?"

"Yes," I whisper.

"I wondered how long it might take you before you said you needed a break," he says. "You put on a good front sometimes, sweetheart, but I've started to see past it."

I sigh. "After my mom died, everyone always told me how strong I was, because I was able to put on this hard exterior and charge forward. But really..."

My voice cracks. Falls silent. Before I can muster the will to speak again, Ryder's low vibrato pulses through the phone.

IN LOVE WITH YOU

"But really, just beyond that hard exterior you were falling apart, and no one was ever able to see that."

"No." I suck hard on my nose. Wipe up the tears beginning to fall. He's right. No one ever saw. Not my teachers at school, not my friends, not the adults in my life, not even my father. Everyone just sat back and admired how brave I was, when really, all I wanted to do was scream at them to look closer, notice how afraid I was. How fragile.

"You are strong, but not invincible," he says. "You are brave, but not fearless. I admire that rough exterior, but I long for those moments when you let your walls come down."

"Why?" I ask shakily, afraid of his answer.

"Because it lets me know it's safe to let *my* walls come down."

My heart clenches in both anguish and joy. Some people long for someone to love them, worship them, put them on a pedestal. All I've ever wanted was for someone to understand me. Not just the version of myself that's all stoicism and confidence, but the version where I'm that and more. So much more. Fragile and caring and passionate and kind.

And I think Ryder sees both versions. I think, more than anyone else in this world ever has, he sees *me*.

Another tear slips down my cheek and teeters for a moment on the edge of my jaw before it falls onto the sliver of collarbone jutting out of my sleepshirt.

There's more that we could say, but neither of us do. We just sit in silence with one another, listening to one another breathe, our protective walls not just let down, but destroyed completely.

If I listen closely enough behind Ryder's breathing, I can hear the low hum of the ocean. The whisper of the wind in the tall dune grass. The pounding thump of his heart in his chest.

Though, to be honest, reader, that last sound might be my own heart and I confused it with his because I know that right now it beats, just for him.

Thirty-Six

Ryder

I ENVY LUNA.

I envy you.

I envy both of your abilities to take a step back from this when you need to. And I don't blame either of you for it. Skip ahead to the end of all of this if that's what you need. I'll be here, splitting wood behind the shed out back in the dying light on Thursday evening, not because we need more wood to burn inside, but because this is a better alternative than climbing into my car D.J.'s mechanic friend dropped off a few days ago and picking a fight with someone again.

The wound healing on my arm strains as I lift the axe high and bring it down on a chunk of fir, striking it down the middle. The two halves fall away from the chopping block, one dropping near my feet. The other one, unfortunately, skitters beneath the hedge close by.

FAYE DARLING

I set down the old axe and am about to pick up the rogue piece of wood when someone beats me to it.

Nick.

He's dressed like he's just come from a business meeting in the 1920s, peacoat that dusts his ankles and all. He extends the piece of wood to me with his leather gloved hand and adjusts the garment bag in the other one so it flops over his shoulder.

"Thanks," I say, taking the wood and eyeing the bag.

Nick rubs his thick, well-groomed beard with his fingertips and sighs at me.

"What?" I ask, more bite in my voice than I intended. I step away from my friend and reach for another piece of unsplit wood and the axe. Nick has the good sense to let me drive the blade through the wood, the axe head burying deep in the chopping block, before he speaks.

"Worried about you," he says.

"Don't know why," I grumble.

"You missed Mark and Gina's rehearsal tonight," he says.

"That's tomorrow."

"No, it was tonight."

"Rehearsal's on Friday," I say, picking up the newly split pieces of wood and tossing them onto the growing stack near Nick's feet. "Today's Thursday."

"Nah, man, today's Friday."

I don't know why, but his words punch me in the gut. Take all of my air. "Shit, is it?"

"We tried calling you a few times but you didn't answer."

"I've been out here for a while," I say, nodding to the wood pile.

"I can see that."

"Gina pissed?"

IN LOVE WITH YOU

"Surprisingly, no." Nick swings the garment bag off his shoulder and holds it up. "Brought your suit so you could get ready here tomorrow and not have to deal with all the wedding hoopla longer than is necessary."

"Why don't you just give my best man's speech," I say, setting up another length of wood on the block.

"What do you mean? Why would I do that?"

I raise the axe. Let it drop. It snags halfway down on a knot. *Shit*. "I need to be here."

"It might do you some good to get out of the house for a few hours," he says. "I mean, have you even been down to the beach this week? Have you even stepped off of the property?"

"You don't know what it's like." I work the axe free from the place it's lodged. "Watching your mother slowly waste away before your eyes, knowing any second might be the last. If you did, you'd know I can't leave to go to some stupid party."

I raise the axe. Bring it down hard. I can feel the impact through my hands, aching its way up my arms. But the wood splits into two.

"You're right, I don't know what that's like," Nick says. "But it's not just some stupid party. It's the wedding of two of your best friends. Just come for a couple of hours. Stand up there with Mark during the ceremony, stick around for your speech, and then you can fuck off and come back here."

"Again," I say. "You don't know what the fuck this is like."

"Two hours," Nick reiterates, his voice so damn calm that I have the urge to throw a piece of firewood at his head. Simply to piss him off.

"A lot can happen in two hours."

"Yeah," Nick says. "And a lot can't."

FAYE DARLING

I stare at the chopping block, following the cuts in its surface the axe has made and the tiny splinters of wood jammed into them.

"Bring Luna," Nick says when I don't say anything. "You know you're dying to see that woman all dolled up."

I half-scoff, half-laugh. Sometimes, I swear Nick was born in the wrong era. But, out of place in this century or not, he has a point. A point to all of it. Don't you think? I mean, I said I envied you and Luna for being able to step away. Maybe that's just what I need. To take two steps away for a short period of time. Get some perspective. Screw my head on straight. Gather my strength for the final push Mom's nurse keeps saying is coming.

"Two hours," I grit out.

Nick nods his approval. "Stephanie inside?"

"Yeah," I say.

"I'll duck in and say a quick hello to her and Kendra and leave your suit in your sister's care."

"Thanks," I say.

"Anytime." Nick steps forward and grips my bicep firmly in his hand. He looks me dead in the eyes. "I'm always here for you, man. Always."

Thirty-Seven

Ryder

My reflection greets me in the bathroom mirror. Freshly washed blonde hair, half of it pulled up into a knot, the other half hanging down to the tops of my shoulders. A jagged pink line beneath my eye from my brawl at The Tavern. Dark blue eyes, knitted with grief, staring right through me.

I adjust the burnt-orange bowtie Gina picked out for the groomsmen. A different shade in her autumnal color palette for each of us. Apparently, they match the shade of dress the bridesmaid we'll be escorting down the aisle is wearing.

How do I look, baby? Honestly? Do I look tired? Enthused, but forcing it? Like fucking shit? It's okay, you can tell me the truth. I trust you.

I hear Luna's pickup truck rumbling up the street and make my final adjustments.

By the time I got off the phone with Luna last night, she had agreed to be my wedding date as well as my emotional wing woman, ready to drag me into a quiet corner or help me through a panic attack if need be.

When I open the bathroom door and step into the hallway, I pause a beat before pushing straight into Mom's room.

Steph is curled up beside Mom's nearly nonexistent frame, idly running her palm back and forth over the soft fleece blanket covering them both. I'm surprised when not just Steph looks up at me when I walk in but Mom as well.

I kiss Mom on the cheek and pull back to watch her smile up at me. Beam is a better word. Her skin glows with a bit more life than it has in days. The nurse said that was normal. A spike in energy before the last downward spiral. I try not to dwell on that fact.

"Holy shit, you actually look like a real person," Steph says. Mom scowls at her and mumbles something. Steph clears her throat. "I mean, you look really good, Ry."

"Wrr," Mom mumbles.

"What was that?" I ask. It's been harder and harder to understand her the past few days, if she speaks at all.

"I think she said twirl," Steph says, smirking.

"No, she didn't," I say, glaring at my sister.

"Sss," Mom says. *Yes.*

I sigh and let my shoulders sag in their sockets. I suddenly feel twelve-years-old again. First day of junior high. Mom making a fuss over how grown up I looked. Steph saying something sassy over a bowl of off-brand Captain Crunch.

"Go on, twirl for us," Steph says with a sincere laugh. Mom echoes that laugh.

And I suddenly don't care how this looks or how embarrassed I feel, because I've just heard both of them laugh after endless days of solemn silence and weary whispers and, fuck, if this family doesn't need a little bit of entertainment right now.

So, I step into the middle of the room so they can get a look at me from head-to-toe, and then I twirl. Slowly. Arms outstretched. Stupid grin on my face. I twirl, and they laugh. Hell, if I knew this is all it would take to make them laugh, I would've put on this stupid suit and bowtie and spun around like an idiot the second Nick dropped it off last night.

A cat call whistle has me stopping mid-spin, though. It's not Steph or Mom. Luna has let herself into the house and is leaning against the doorway of the bedroom.

My breath leaves my body all at once when I see her. Because holy fucking shit. She looks incredible. She's wearing a tight-fitted silver gown that trails to the floor. Her long black hair falls over one shoulder in dramatic waves, a dozen bejeweled bobby pins keeping the other side tight to her scalp. Cherry-red lipstick. A dusting of blush. A smoky eye for the history books. She looks like some kind of glamorous movie star from the golden age of Hollywood. I can't seem to pull my jaw off the ground.

"Don't stop on my account," she says, looking me up and down. "Give us another twirl, handsome."

"Holy shit, Luna," Steph exclaims. "You look fucking amazing. How did you get your hair to do that?"

"A lot of curling, pinning, and brushing."

"Ohh," Mom says, eyes on Luna. Then, she looks at me. "Ohh."

She says something else, something indiscernible.

"You gotta let me take your guys' picture," Steph says, sitting up.

"Sss," Mom says, like that's what she had been trying to convey, but couldn't.

I chuckle nervously and stare at my feet. "I'll probably break the camera."

"Stop it." Luna sways across the room, her dress picking up different strokes of light as her hips tick from side to side. It's all I can do not to put my hands all over her. "Insecure is not a good look on you. Not when you're sexy as hell in that bowtie."

Mom honks out a laugh and I shoot her a look, my cheeks flushed with embarrassment. It's one thing for a beautiful woman to say you look sexy, but another thing for her to say it in front of your mom and your little sister. Don't you dare laugh. I have a feeling you'd be just fine saying the same thing in front of them, too. You're probably egging Luna on from the other side of the page, aren't you? Maybe you want her to say all the things to me you can't.

I smile at Mom right after my glare sets in, because, fuck, this is a moment I don't want to end either. Feeling somewhat happy again in her presence, despite the top of her dresser being covered in medical supplies, the entire room smelling sour, like death, and the knowledge that she could disappear from this world as fast as a hand clap.

"Put your arm around her," Steph bosses, kneeling on the edge of the bed with her phone's camera trained on Luna and me, her baggy sweatshirt scraping her knees. "Tell her she's beautiful. Act like you like each other."

"You are," I whisper as I slowly slide my hand around Luna's waist.

"I'm what?" she whispers back as I rub at the fabric of her dress with my thumb, curious as to how it feels. Satiny. A bit scratchy from the shine of the silver. Warm from being pressed tightly against her body. Is she thinking about that morning I went down on her in the middle of D.J.'s kitchen like I am?

"Beautiful," I say.

"Smile," Steph says.

One of Luna's hands glides up my back, the other up my abdomen. We both smile across the room at Steph as she counts us down.

"One."

I look at Steph behind the phone, half of her concealed to me.

"Two."

I look at Mom, eyes dull, smile faint and lopsided, already slipping away.

"Three."

I feel Luna lean into me, feel the solidness of her body against mine as she moves closer and closer with each passing day.

"Shit, Ry," Steph says, looking at the phone once she's snapped the photo. "You blinked."

"Yeah," I say hollowly. "I think maybe I did."

Thirty-Eight

Luna

I DON'T KNOW IF it's because it's been a few days since I've seen him or because of the sleek cut of that damn suit he's got on or because weddings really do something to my lady parts, but holy shit, Ryder is stunning. There's just no other way to say it. Blonde waves, tousled and lush. Skin sun-kissed and glowing, even in his grief. Like some kind of salt-dredged god. Like the last delicious morsel of a piece of rich chocolate cake I want to gobble up.

As soon as Ryder carts Gina's maid-of-honor down the aisle and stands beside Mark, arms crossed at the wrists and hanging over the front of his tailored slacks, I can't take my eyes off of him. Even when the rest of the wedding guests stand for the bride, I rise, but my eyes are on him, not Gina. Those shoulders, broad and pushed back. That slack tide quality of his jaw as he watches one of his childhood friends glide down the rose-covered aisle. Then, just when Gina and her father are almost to the front, Ryder's eyes swing up through the crowd and land on me. My cheeks heat furiously. My breath hitches. But, just like that day I caught him listening to Gina's and my conversation in his kitchen, I don't look away. I think the earth could be quaking, the mansion overlooking the sea holding the ceremony could be caving in on itself, and I still wouldn't look away from him.

Minutes pass by, or maybe hours—what is time?—and we're still holding one another's gaze. Then, the officiant goes quiet. An uneasy tension strings throughout the room. Mark clears his throat before he mutters over his shoulder at Ryder. "The rings, man."

Ryder blushes as he finally tears his eyes from me and shakes his head like a cartoon character who's just been punched. "Right. That's *my* cue."

Gina laughs warmly, which sets off a chain reaction among the crowd, easing whatever tension had been building.

I try and watch the rest of the nuptials in earnest. The ring exchange. The kiss. The solid minute and a half of a pop song played by a string quartet while Mark and Gina stand at the front for us to gaze upon them before the officiant announces them as a couple. They dance back up the aisle, and when Ryder and the maid-of-honor follow close behind, my heart hammers in my chest, threatening to leap out and run after him. It almost aches when he disappears through a door that leads out onto the massive deck overlooking the ocean in the distance.

Do you think it would be strange if I followed the last of the bridal party through those doors? Do you think anyone would notice or care? If this were one of my novels, I'd send my leading lady straight through them and have her chase down her man. Have her kiss him until he couldn't see straight. Maybe they'd do some other things in a broom closet. But you and I both know that this is no novel. And I am no leading lady. I'll wait. Patiently. Maybe get a drink in me. Yeah. A drink. That sounds good.

Now, I know I wasn't paying attention, but did you happen to catch where the officiant said the bar was located?

TWENTY MINUTES AFTER THE end of the ceremony, I stride across the wide deck at the back of the mansion, wobbling on whiskey legs after the three shots I took with one of Gina's cousins at the open bar.

Ryder is bent over the railing at the far end, taking in the view of the ocean glistening beyond the tops of the trees that slide slowly toward town from the top of the hill.

I can smell the brine of the sea from here. Can hear the cry of the hungry seagulls as they fight for scraps on the sand. Can feel the hum of the ocean cracking against the shore, again and again. I know Ryder senses all of this and more, his connection with the sea an enviable one. Oklahoma is a sea of wheat fields and red dirt roads. Man-made lakes and low hanging clouds I used to squint at until they looked like mountains in the distance. The Oregon Coast teems with inconceivable beauty.

The sun is setting, painting everything, including Ryder, in a lush copper haze.

One more hour.

That's how long I'd wager he's going to commit to this thing. The vows have been said, the rings exchanged, and now cocktail hour is in full-swing. All that's left is the dinner and the toasts. As soon as he's said his piece, I'm sure we'll climb back into my truck and head back to the cottage.

Doesn't mean we can't have a little fun in the meantime, though.

"I bet they're fucking somewhere right now," I say as I step up beside him. I tilt back a champagne flute and lean my hip into the railing.

"Who? Mark and Gina?"

"Yeah." I smirk, noticing the pink that now stains his cheeks. "Don't you think? Just getting it on in that gorgeous wedding dress somewhere in this big, fancy house?"

An older woman in an expensive-looking tuille tea dress scoffs at me from a few feet away. She tips her nose into the air and shuffles down the deck. The best man blushing at my words, this haughty woman disapproving of me, alcohol blundering through my system in a way that makes me feel helium-light—it's turning out to be exactly my kind of party.

Ryder chuckles, his deep voice dripping out of him like sticky honey I'd like to lick from his lips. "I don't know if that woman agrees."

"Oh, she agrees," I say, turning and nodding to the woman, who is still glaring at us from across the deck. "Otherwise she wouldn't have had such a visceral reaction."

"You think?" He scoots half an inch closer to me, and I breathe in his scent so deeply that my knees shake. He clears his throat. "Did you just smell me?"

"Truth is," I say, lowering my voice to a husky whisper I hope sounds as sexy as I think it does, "weddings make me hella horny."

Ryder's cheeks go from pink to full on red. Maybe I should have been more self-conscious about blurting out what weddings do to me, but those shots of whiskey were strong, and this is *not* the first glass of champagne I've had since. I'm tingling everywhere it counts.

I reach out and let my fingers run a soft trail over the back of Ryder's neck, toying with the soft tendrils of his long hair. Goosebumps rise on his skin, and he shifts even closer to me. His elbow resting gently against my cleavage. His hip getting dangerously close to the very place those tingles are running rampant. I exhale, hot and sticky, just before his head twists toward me, our lips one good flinch away from touching.

We haven't kissed since he ate me out two weeks ago in D.J.'s kitchen. We've been preoccupied. But now, away from that preoccupation, that's all I can think about. My lips on his. His lips on mine. I watch his eyes dart down to watch as my tongue glides over my bottom lip in attempt to draw him in. He swallows. Leans. And—

"Ryder." Nick's smooth voice breaks us apart. We both turn and find Nick standing in the open doorway. He looks out of place in his modern tux. Dapper, sure, but just not as relaxed as he usually appears when he's wearing his vintage ensembles. He smiles and nods at me in greeting, then focuses on Ryder. "They're about to announce the wedding party and Gina wants us all to walk in together."

"Be there in a second," Ryder says, and Nick doesn't hesitate before ducking back inside.

IN LOVE WITH YOU

Ryder snags my half-empty champagne flute and chugs the rest before pressing it back into my palm. My tipsy mouth hangs open, about to protest.

"Sorry," he says. "I'm nervous about my speech. I don't like talking in front of crowds."

"Want a tip?" I ask. After countless readings and discussions in front of crowds three times the size of this one, I feel like I can offer a good one.

"Picture everyone in their underwear?" he asks with a breathy laugh.

"Fuck no," I say. "That'll only distract you."

"All right?"

I rub the back of his neck. "Just pretend I'm the only one in the room."

"Do I still picture you in your underwear?" he asks, the flirty tone of his voice not going unnoticed. Now my cheeks are the ones heating up.

"While that sounds exciting," I say, "you'd better not do that either. We don't need a repeat of the ring debacle. What I mean is, find me in the crowd and pretend you're only talking to me about Mark and Gina. Let everyone else melt away."

"That sounds easy enough," he says. "Thanks."

I bite my lip as he begins to back away. When he's halfway to the door where Nick disappeared earlier, he spins around, giving me his back. My thirsty eyes drop and stare at his ass as he walks, those tingles in me becoming a throbbing ache. Once he's out of sight, I twist around and let the sea breeze wafting up the hillside cool me down. I go to take another drink of champagne, but frown when I find it empty. I close my eyes and try to breathe. Every time I think of Ryder, though, I feel a little woozy.

FAYE DARLING

Alcohol or not, wedding horniness or not, I think I've got it bad for this guy, reader. In fact, I think it might be much worse than that.

Thirty-Nine

Ryder

AFTER A FIVE-COURSE DINNER seated with the wedding party at the head table, I stand up with a glass of beer I talked the young bartender into sneaking into a champagne flute for me to keep up appearances.

Champagne. Maybe you like it, maybe you don't. As soon as I'd downed Luna's glass out on the deck I remembered I did not like it. In fact, I remembered I loathed it. The overexcited bubbles. The aftertaste. Do you know what I mean?

Yes, yes, I know, baby. I'm stalling. I'm nervous.

I find her in the middle of the room—gorgeous Luna. She sits at a table full of Mark's parents' friends, all of them laughing. I tap my knife against the crystal the way they do in the movies. The conversations fizzle out, but before my nerves can do the same, I take a deep breath and speak directly to Luna, those amber eyes locking on mine like some kind of anchor.

FAYE DARLING

"I've known Mark and Gina since we were all kids," I say, swallowing down a few extra nerves bubbling up. I want to take a swig of my beer so badly, but I know that's not how it's done. Luna smiles at me warmly. She's better than alcohol would be at settling my nerves anyway, and I continue. "My mom used to say the three of us were as thick as thieves and just as mischievous. I could spend hours telling you stories about the wild antics we got up to when we were kids, all the trouble and secrets we made. But there's dancing to get to and booze to drink and a good time to be had, so I'll just say this one thing." Now, I break eye contact with Luna and look at the newlyweds beside me. "Mark, Gina, I love the two of you separately for so many reasons, but I love you the most when you're together." A few *awes* rise up from the guests. Gina leans her head on Mark's broad shoulder and smiles up at me. "So, everyone, please raise a glass to the bride and groom. And can I just say—fucking finally!"

The few gasps that are uttered are drowned out by the boisterous laughter that fills the room. Because everyone knows I'm right. This wedding has been a long time coming. I tilt my glass back and take a small sip.

"Thanks, man," Mark says to me once I sit back down.

"I love you, too, Ry," Gina coos, blowing me a kiss.

I force a smile, but now that the speech is over, all I want to do is go home. And as the maid of honor begins a long speech, reading from a sheet of lined notebook paper, Mark senses this. He leans over to me.

"Go if you need to," he whispers. I catch Gina pinch his knee under the table, telling him to shut the hell up.

"Sorry," I whisper, then quietly push back from my place setting.

IN LOVE WITH YOU

I move to the edge of the room and look for Luna again. But she's already slinking along the perimeter toward me, something wrapped up in a yellow cloth napkin held in her hand. I don't question what it is until after we've retrieved my suit jacket from the coat check downstairs.

"You're going to have to drive," she says, wobbling a little as we move up the street, where the asphalt is lined with vehicles. I catch the keys to her truck when she tosses them to me. "I had too much to drink. God, the sky is brilliant right now. Twilight, so fucking magical, don't you think?"

"Uh-huh," I say, but I'm distracted. I have this sudden need to get home. Get home, get home, get home.

But Luna is standing in the middle of the street, staring at the golden haze lingering over the faint pulse of the stars, and her pickup is still half a block away. Uphill to boot. I turn on a heel, grunt, and double back to where she stands. I bend low and fold her over my shoulder, her legs flying up to try and combat the motion. She squeals, then laughs.

"Shit, Ryder. You almost made me drop the cake."

"The what?" I ask as I march up the street, eyes on the prize: Luna's truck.

"I stole us a big fat slice of cake," she says. *So that's what's in the napkin.* "I figured you, me, and Steph could eat it when we got home."

"You cut into their wedding cake?" I ask, half-appalled, half-impressed.

"I went in from behind," she says. "Middle tier. Under the fondant. No one will notice."

"Gina will notice."

"Gina will get over it as soon as she's getting railed in the limo on the way to the airport hotel." Luna starts grinding her hips into my shoulder to get her point across. But instead of picturing Gina and Mark getting it on in the limo, I imagine the scene playing out with Luna and me in their place. Luna in a wedding dress, riding me like a bull. Groan of the leather seats beneath us. The air heavy with the scent of sex.

I swallow down the thought of us and try to focus on the task at hand: getting home.

I force a laugh as I unlock the passenger door. "You're crazy."

"Nope." Luna slaps my ass just before I slide her off of my shoulder and fit her into the cab. "Just horny. I told you—weddings do weird shit to my lady parts."

"Okay, horn dog," I say, setting her down and tugging the seatbelt around her.

I feel her eyes, full of heat and lust, bore into me. I click the belt in place and try to keep my breath even. But my fingertips drag over her lap as I lean away, and my next exhale is more of a strangled groan than anything.

What I wouldn't give to ruck up that pretty little dress of hers right here, right now. Let my fingers play her like a fucking piano.

I shake the idea out of my head. We have somewhere we need to be. *I* have somewhere I need to be.

"Let's get some cake and some coffee in you and see how you feel later," I tell her.

"Like that'll help," she says with the most exaggerated eyeroll I've ever seen. And that's saying something, because Stephanie North, queen of dramatic eyerolls, is my sister.

Luna's arm swings out, her fingers colliding with my belt buckle. She grips it tight and wrenches me forward. My dick kicks against the zipper of my pants. *Traitor.*

IN LOVE WITH YOU

"Later," I tell them both.

I pry Luna's hand off of my belt, and she emits a whimper, her bottom lip jutting out like delicious sin.

Before I give into temptation, before I reach out and bite that lip, I shut her into the cab. Then, I jog around the front of the truck, slide into the driver's seat, and start the engine. Putting the vehicle in gear, I flip a quick U-y and take off down the street.

A thin layer of fog creeps up the hill, turning the dreamy golden twilight into the setting of a Stephen King novel. I grip the steering wheel tightly with both hands, resisting the urge to reach over, put a hand between Luna's legs, and help her in the only way I think she meant when she said coffee and cake wouldn't. But just the thought has guilt swelling in my gut. I should be home. With Mom. With Steph.

Luna reaches into the napkin in her lap and pinches off a rosette of frosting flecked with gold leaf. She presses it against my lips, the sweet aroma of buttercream overwhelming, tantalizing.

"Go on," she coos. "You know you want to."

I exhale forcefully through my nostrils, trying to hold back. Then, I tell myself it's just frosting. Nothing more. It's harmless, really. I fit my lips around Luna's fingers and draw the frosting out of her grip, the tip of my tongue lavishing her skin. She moans so loudly that it sends shockwaves from my mouth down to the juncture of my thighs, causing my dick to hum in rhythm with my heart from all the blood rushing to it.

My mouth has frozen around Luna's finger. I can taste salt on her skin as well as sugar from the buttercream. And I can't help it, I can't hold myself back any longer. I give in to desire and glide my slick mouth back down her finger, all the way to its base. I suck hard on the appendage as I keep my eyes steady on the road snaking out before me. As slow as I can allow myself to go, I pull away, lapping up every last bit of disintegrated frosting from her body.

A rumbling mewl at the tippy-top of her throat. Amber eyes drifting back in their sockets. Straight white teeth thrash against her full bottom lip. She's practically shaking when the pickup rolls up to the intersection of Highway 101.

"Pull over," she pants.

I shake my head, then look both ways. Headlights barreling toward us from both directions. My feet tremor on the pedals. "I can't."

"Just for a minute."

"Sorry, sweetheart," I breathe.

She swallows audibly. "Please."

Fuck, this woman is impossible. Distracting. Hot as hell. What should I do? Should I pull over? Do you want me to? Are you just as hot as she is right now? I can feel the rise of your pulse—a faint murmur, but still noticeable.

Maybe I *should* pull over. Park the pickup in a strong shadow and give Luna what she wants, give myself what *I* want. Burst the bubble. Find some release.

But I also want to go home. I feel like I need to be there. To check on Mom. I've only been gone for a few hours, but it feels like days. The last time I was away from her for that long was Mark's bachelor weekend. Images of my return flip through my head. Steph breaking the news to me of Mom's downward spiral. Me getting punch-drunk at The Tavern, picking that fight. Panic settles into my veins, tunneling my vision, making me nauseous.

Fuck. What if Mom's gone already?

IN LOVE WITH YOU

No, Steph would have called.

My chest aches, and I press the heel of my hand against the spot to try and soothe the pain. Maybe I need a distraction. A way to get out of my head for a bit and, if not calm my racing thoughts, at least escape them for a few minutes.

"I'm not going to pull over," I say as I turn onto the highway behind a log truck. "But hike that sexy little dress up and scoot over here, sweetheart."

"Fuck yes," Luna whispers, placing the slice of stolen wedding cake carefully on the dashboard before doing exactly what I've told her to do. Dress tugged up to her hips. Her side pressed against mine. She moves her legs and straddles the tall gearshift.

"No," I say, guiding the leg closest to me back to the other side of the shift. I still need to be able to drive. I still need to be able to get back home. "Both legs stay over there. Now, twist a little so your back is against my shoulder."

"Like this?" she asks as she settles into position.

"Just like that." I peck a kiss to the top of her head. "Good girl."

The string of buildings that make up the downtown section of West Cove blur in and out of the street lights as we buzz past. I shift into a higher gear as soon the speed limit jumps up, the heart of the town slipping away as fast as it came.

"Spread your legs for me, sweetheart," I say, nudging one of her knees until they both flop apart. One high-heeled foot on the floor, the other jammed into the passenger door. *Damn*. If this woman isn't sex personified. I am *literally* about to bust the zipper on these pants I'm so hard for her.

"Is this okay?" she asks. Her breaths come out hard and fast, and I haven't even touched her yet. *Fuck*.

"Perfect," I say.

"Call me a good girl again," she says.

I quirk a brow, a smirk materializing on my face. "Do you like that?"

"Yes."

"How much do you like it?" I whisper just before I hook my arm around her waist and drop my fingertips low, hovering just inches over her clit. I want her to feel the heat spooling off of me. I want her to feel the buzz of anticipation. But I don't want her to feel my touch. Not yet.

I catch a glimpse of her reflected back at me in the rearview. Pretty face lit up by the lights on the old dashboard. Her lower lip is clutched in her teeth again. Her cheeks are as red as her lipstick, looking like she's just finished running a marathon on the driest section of sand on the beach.

She still hasn't responded to me yet.

"Did you hear me, sweetheart?" I ask. Still hovering. Still taunting.

"Mm?"

"I asked, how much do you like it when I call you a good girl?"

I tap the pad of my middle finger once against her clit and pull away, draw my arm back from around her waist. This has her squirming, panting.

"I like it," she says. "I like it so much."

I chuckle low against the curve of her ear. Snake my arm back around her waist. I drop my voice to a whisper. "Then I'm afraid you're gonna have to work for it."

"Fuck," she breathes, her back sagging against me at the same time her hips buck, the lace of her panties scraping up against my fingertips.

"Off," I husk, snapping the waistband of her underwear so hard she hisses. "Unless you want me to rip them."

I'm not serious about ripping her panties off of her, but either she doesn't understand or doesn't care, because the next thing I know she says, "Do that."

"What?" I ask, my voice breaking slightly.

"Do it," she says steadily. "Rip. Them. Off."

I groan, low and long, knocking the back of my skull against the headrest. I'm no longer straining against my zipper, I'm throbbing. Like I could nut at any moment.

We're still a couple of miles from the turn off for my neighborhood, so I jam my knee into the steering wheel to hold it straight. Both of my hands dip down Luna's hips. Wrapping my fingers around both legs of her panties at the same time, I clench my fists and tug hard.

Rip!

The fabric gives without putting up too much of a fight, and when I drag the ruined lace into view, Luna gasps. She reaches out for the panties, but I jerk them just out of her reach and slide them into my pocket. I have another pair of her stolen underwear. The ones I slid cautiously from her body right before I ate her out on D.J.'s kitchen table. But this pair is better. They will remind me just how devastatingly I ruined her tonight.

I grip the wheel again with my left hand while my right hand slides back down between Luna's legs.

"Fuck, sweetheart," I say when my fingers are met with nothing but the slick of her arousal. "You are absolutely dripping."

How long has she been this wet?

FAYE DARLING

"I've always wanted to do this," she says, reaching an arm back and stroking my neck with her palm. I've always held my tension in my neck, and the soft pressure of her touch alone has me melting into her. I have to fight hard to keep my eyes from fluttering closed.

"What have you always wanted to do?" I ask. "Massage a man into oblivion?"

"No." Her fingers thread up into my hair, winding around the roots. She tugs roughly, and I grunt. "Have sex in a moving car."

"For book research?" I ask, my blood cooling slightly at the idea that I might be getting worked up over her alone, but she might be getting worked up over what I can lend to her writing.

Her eyes find mine in the rearview mirror, her face as serious as it was the day she plowed into me on that wave. She shakes her head. "Ryder, there are some things I do for research and some things I do just for me."

"And this?"

"What do you think?"

It's not exactly a clear answer, but—splayed wide across the bench seat, fingers twisted through my hair—she's too fucking tempting. I dip two fingers into her heat, curving them slightly as I dock my thumb to her clit. She arches back, my name on her lips.

"Do you like that?" I ask.

"Yes," she says as I pump my fingers in and out, in and out. She hisses. Strengthens her grip on my hair. "Oh, fuck, I love that."

I continue to thrust into her with my fingers, rolling my thumb in slow circles over her clit. She rocks her hips up to match my rhythm, taking my fingers deeper each time. When

IN LOVE WITH YOU

I cut a glance to her, my eyes travel up her body, from the tension in her knees to the movement between her thighs to her nipples, hard and alert beneath the thin silver fabric of her dress.

It's then that I realize she has no bra on. And it's a good thing I didn't have this knowledge before, because it's dragging a low groan out of the depths of my throat that would be embarrassing in any other situation but this one.

When I look back to the road, I can't help myself. I grip the lowest curve of the steering with one knuckle and try my best to palm the tent in my pants, needing some kind of relief from this torture she's putting me through.

"You're such a good fucking girl," I breathe as I work us both over at the same time.

"Say it again," she says, her voice high and airy.

"You're a good girl," I say, not even thinking about dangling my praise in front of her like a treat this time. My head feels like it's about to explode.

My thumb jerks over her clit in rough, tight circles as the fingers buried inside her walls continue to curve back and up, brushing over a spot that has one leg twitching, the other locking at the knee as she pushes firmly against the door.

She shifts back, her elbow bumping into my wrist, bent at an awkward angle as I try to steer the truck and manage my needs at the same time. A harsh breath. A swivel of her head. Her eyes catch my little side act and a smirk drags across her cheeks.

"Fuck, that's hot," she says.

"Mm," is all I can manage. I'm not the best multi-tasker, and between me, her, and the truck, I'm about tapped out.

FAYE DARLING

Luna rolls onto all fours, forcing me to drag my hand away from her. She keeps a hold of my wrist as she takes the two fingers I had plunged inside her heat into her mouth and licks her own arousal from my skin. Before I can even begin to list the ways in which that's sexy, she's got her mouth on mine and her tongue inside. I can taste the sex on her. I can taste *her* on her, and, yeah, I'd say that definitely trumps anything I had on my list. She rakes her teeth over my lower lip as she pulls away, giving me a clear view of the road again. We're only a few blocks away from our turn.

"You know," she says as she works my belt loose. Her dress is still rucked up around her hips, the smooth curve of her ass so tempting from where I'm sitting. I slide my free hand around it, kneading into the softness of her. It doesn't seem to stall her. She just unbuttons my pants, slides down my zipper, and keeps talking. "I didn't want to tell you this when we fucked in the woods a couple of weeks ago, because I didn't want it to go to your head, but you have a big dick, Ryder. Not just big, buddy. We're talking gargantuan. See?"

She tugs on my boxers and my 'gargantuan' dick springs free, practically waving at her in greeting and leaking pre-cum. I laugh. Watch as she stares down at me for a moment, admiring the view. I think that's what she's doing. I hope it is. Otherwise, what? *Ah.*

I run my palm back toward her hip and around. I nudge a knuckle against her worked-up clit. Maybe I just want her to stop taking mental notes of my dick to use in her book later. Maybe she moved before I could help her finish, and I don't want to leave her unsatisfied.

"Oh," she gasps when my nudge becomes a tight circle.

IN LOVE WITH YOU

"You like this?" I whisper, sticking just the tip of my pinkie inside her slit.

"Mm-hmm," she says, dipping low and licking my cock from stem to stern, her tongue circling along the head. "Do you like *this?*"

She takes me into her mouth while her hands massage the base of my shaft. My vision blurs for a second, and I blaze past the road where I was supposed to turn. I curse under my breath and she laughs, her voice humming against me. My vision blurs again as she takes me deeper into her mouth. Maybe I close my eyes for a second. Maybe I full-on black out. But the next thing I know, a bright light catches my attention, and I jerk the wheel to keep us from driving headlong into another car.

"You're going to kill us," I say. "*I'm* going to kill us."

And I can't get home if I'm dead on the side of the road. There's also a very good chance, if I take D.J.'s cousin out along with me, he'll find a way to bring me back to life just so he can make me dead again. He's considerate and understanding, but I know there's a terrifying beast he keeps locked away. A beast I'd rather not meet.

Shivers race through me, my skin going cold, then hot. Heart thundering, I pull us off of the highway and park alongside the train tracks. It's dark here. Not a streetlamp or a porchlight to cast a shadow. The wind racks against the truck, and the ocean rumbles in the background. There's not another soul in sight.

I press two fingers against Luna's chin and her gaze slowly swoops up to meet mine. She looks so fucking beautiful with my dick in her mouth.

Even so, I'd rather have that dick somewhere else.

FAYE DARLING

"Are you a good girl?" I ask her, a devilish quality to my voice.

"Mm." She whimpers and nods, eyes nearly bugging out of her head.

I crook my finger at her. "Then slide that sweet pussy onto this gargantuan cock and ride me until I can't see straight, *good girl*."

And quick, I think to myself and only to myself. And you.

Fuck. You.

Baby, I—I—there's no excuse for it. Like I said, I'm not the best multi-tasker, and I nearly forgot you were here. What are you thinking? How are you feeling? Am I breaking your heart or am I turning you on? I hope it's the latter.

I really fucking hope it's the latter.

Because Luna's unearthing a condom from some undisclosed location and is sliding it onto me before she drags her dress higher and straddles me and I can't think clearly. All I am is flesh and feeling and desire. And I want her. I want all of her.

Right fucking now.

She hovers over the top of me, the tip of my cock barely notched at the start of her heat. I grunt loudly—the only way I'm going to keep from losing my mind at this point—and she takes the hint and begins to lower herself down. I hold onto her waist, my fingertips touching on either side of her ribcage. The woman is an hourglass if I've ever seen one. Voluptuous breasts, curvy hips, and a cinched-tight waist in between.

Her fingers lace around the back of my neck, using me as a brace as she sits herself all the way down, every inch of me buried inside her.

I twitch my hips against her and, as I pull away I push up on her waist, lifting her whole body an inch or so off of mine before I drop back down, both of us gasping as we slap together. Rinse and repeat, over and over until we're moving at jackhammer speed. Then, Luna lets out a shriek and I feel the walls of her pussy clench around my cock as she slams through an orgasm. She drops her forehead onto the top of my shoulder as I lift her one last time, before I come hard and fast, rocking my hips slowly against Luna.

"You did it, sweetheart," I say in a husky whisper.

"Did what?" she breathes against my neck.

"Rode me until I couldn't see straight."

"Am I a good girl?"

"You're the best."

Forty

Ryder

"Why do you both look so...unkempt?" Steph asks, eyeing us over a bite of the stolen wedding cake balanced on her fork.

Despite my worrying, Mom's status hadn't changed since I left for the wedding. Unless you count the fact that Steph says she's been fast asleep ever since I kissed her goodbye. Now, Steph, Luna, and I are huddled around the kitchen table, wedding cake placed on a plate between us. It's disappearing quickly.

A sly grin stretches across Luna's face as she reaches for another bite of cake.

Steph wrinkles her nose. "You know what, never mind."

There's a tension in Steph's voice that goes beyond general disgust at whatever she thinks Luna and I got up to tonight. I want to ask if it's just because of Mom or if that boyfriend of hers who showed up in the middle of the night a few weeks ago has anything to do with it. But I haven't heard the rumble of his truck engine. Haven't seen any more cuts or bruises appear on my sister's face.

So, I let it go and take another bite of cake, my fork clashing with Luna's as we both vie for a piece with one of the icing rosettes.

"Get your own bite," Luna snaps, the tines of her fork pushing hard against mine.

"No way, the rosettes are the best," I counter.

"Be a gentleman, will ya?" she asks.

"Ryder?" Steph scoffs. "A gentleman?"

"It's your fault for introducing me to those rosettes in the first place," I say, smirking at Luna and ignoring Steph's mocking. "Be a lady and let me have it."

"Down with the patriarchy," Luna says, digging the tines of her fork in deep.

"Here, here," monotones Steph.

"Split it?" I suggest.

"I grew up an only child," Luna says. "I don't share well."

"I'll make it worth your while, sweetheart."

"Oh for the love of all that is holy," Steph grumbles. She stabs the majority of the rosette with her own fork. Pops it in her mouth before Luna and I can even move. "There. Problem solved."

I glare at Steph. It's mostly in jest, but then I see it. A tear trembling in the corner of her eye. Her neck is heathered with pink splotches and her breaths are coming in shallow bursts. One of her thumbnails digs in hard to the string on her hoodie. She's trying to hold it together. Trying not to fall apart in front of us.

FAYE DARLING

My gaze knits with concern as I reach out to cover her hand with my own. But she jerks back before pushing away from the table, her abandoned fork clattering violently in her wake.

"I'm fine," she snips before I've even had a chance to ask.

Steph marches into Mom's room and shuts the door as quietly as her emotional state will allow her to. Not that Mom is coherent enough to be disturbed. The latch clicks hard into place, and the air whooshes out of the room.

"Is she okay?" Luna asks.

"I don't know," I whisper-growl. I set my fork down on the table, suddenly not interested in eating fucking wedding cake right now.

"Should we check on her?"

I shake my head. "Best to give her some space."

Luna nods. She's sitting not a foot away from me, but she feels far away all of the sudden. Eyes glazed over. Muscles a little more rigid than they had been a minute ago. She pokes at the cake with her fork. Turns a big piece of it into nothing but crumbs. I want to ask her where her head is. What's she thinking about? Is it her mom? Is she remembering how that all went down? Is she wanting to run back to The Tavern again and escape all the pain being here is dredging up in her?

"If this is too much..." I begin, but trail off. Selfishly, I don't want to be the one to suggest she heads back to D.J.'s apartment.

"I don't want to leave," she whispers.

"But if it's hurting you."

"It's going to hurt either way," she says, looking me right in the eye. "I want to be here. With you. *For* you."

"For me?"

IN LOVE WITH YOU

She slides a hand into mine, her spindly fingers cupping mine firmly. Her lower lip quivers right before her mouth opens, but whatever words she wants to say are caught somewhere in her throat.

They stay caught, too, because the only answer to my question is her lips pressing against my knuckles. When she pulls her mouth away she fans my palm across the top of her chest and covers it with her own. Her heart is beating hummingbird-fast, but when I look into her eyes, all I see is ten shades of calm. It's an earnest serenity. Nothing like the hard look in her eyes when her guard is up. That look, that heartbeat—the clash of them, really. I think she's trying to tell me what she's feeling without words. I think she's trying to say that in the face of her fear she also feels safe.

"I understand," I say.

"Good."

She lowers my hand from her chest and lets it fall into her lap as she cups it in hers again. Instinctively, my fingers curl through hers, trying to multiply the places where we are joined. She's soft and she's warm and she's mine. That last thought steadies me a bit.

"Will you stay the night?" I ask, my voice a passing whisper.

She nods.

It's not even nine o'clock, but I know Steph's been sleeping in Mom's bed with her every night, and I don't want to drive her out of the room, away from the comfort she clearly needs right now. Don't get me wrong, I want to be by Mom's side, but she's not just *my* mother. And I'd do anything for Steph, even if it means not sitting up with Mom through the night.

Being home after a full afternoon and evening, I feel myself letting down. I feel exhaustion settling into my bones.

But I can't make myself move.

Luna and I sit at the table in silence, the minutes ticking by as we listen to the creaks and groans of the cottage, the wind and the buzzing ocean half a mile away. I can hear Steph and Mom breathing as they sleep.

The next time I glance at the clock it's five minutes to eleven.

My back is starting to ache, my skin crawling with the need to get out of this damn suit.

I look at Luna. Her eyes are half-closed, her body slumped partially against the wall. Only my pinkie is clutched in her grip. I brush her sweat-soaked hair back and out of her face, and she jerks upright, eyes bright and glowing for a brief moment before they rattle shut again. Open once more. Shut.

I chuckle, quiet and low. "Tired, sweetheart?"

"Nope," she whispers, her eyes remaining shut. "Wide awake."

"Let's go to bed," I say, brushing the tip of my pinkie over the side of her hand several times. "I don't want to assume anything. Even after all our fun on the drive home. So, it's your choice. Steph's empty bed at the front of the house or my bed upstairs, with me."

"I don't think I can be alone," Luna says, sliding her palm all the way into mine.

I pull her onto her feet. She stumbles forward and presses herself into my chest.

"Can you walk?"

"Carry me?" she mutters.

I scoop her up into my arms, and she automatically curls into me, one set of her fingers gripping the collar of my dress shirt. I can feel her hot breath on my neck. It's like being close to a roaring fire, warming and intoxicating all at once.

The stairs are narrow and steep, but I've learned to master them in the dark. I don't flick on the lights when I reach the loft, either, but my eyes quickly adjust to the dim light.

"Do you want to sleep in your nice dress?" I ask Luna as I lay her down on top of my comforter. She shakes her head. "Something comfy then?"

This time, I get a nod.

I quickly change out of my tux, sliding on a pair of joggers and a crew neck sweatshirt with a hole in the collar from the time Mark cast his fishing pole and hooked me by mistake. For Luna I find an old, soft t-shirt from a metal concert I went to a few months before I landed in prison and the smallest pair of sweats that I own. I hover over her, keeping my head bowed so I don't scrape it on the severe slant of the low ceiling. My breath stutters out of me as I gaze down at her.

Even though I literally ripped this woman's underwear off of her body earlier this evening, even though, not five hours ago, my dick was buried deep inside her pretty pussy, I still feel the need to ask. "Can I undress you?"

"Mm-hmm," she says, raising her arms up over her head.

I kneel down and hook my thumbs under the hem of her silver dress, letting the pads of my fingers graze up her calf, her knee, her thighs. I linger on her hips, recruiting more fingers to pull the rest of the dress up and over her head. I lay her clothes over the railing of the loft before I turn and allow myself to fully look at her. Even in these dark shadows, she's magnificent. Soft, supple lines curving and curving. She has no bra on, and it's a good thing I didn't know this earlier or her dress might have been the second piece of clothing I ripped from her body tonight.

My eyes trail over the milky drips of her breasts, catching in the hypnotic swirl of her perked-up nipples before dropping down to run along the flat cut of her upper abdomen, following its length as it rolls smoothly over the slight bulge of her lower belly, which is poised over the dark patch of hair tickling that gorgeous little pussy.

I'm drinking in those sexy thighs of hers when her voice causes me to pause.

"Ryder," she whispers, not lifting her head, not opening her eyes.

I swallow audibly. "Yeah?"

"I'm cold."

I chuckle. "Well, that's a first."

Kneeling again, I ease her head through the t-shirt, then pull her arms gently through the sleeves. I sit her up, leaning her forward against my chest, and roll the shirt the rest of the way down before ducking low to slide her feet into the legs of the sweats. I pull them up to her knees, then stop. I can't stave off the temptation.

I drag my lips up the inside of one of her thighs, plant a firm kiss to the top of her pubic bone, then trail my lips down the other thigh.

When I cut a glance to her face, to see what she thinks about those sensual kisses, I find her eyes are practically closed, her body swaying. I half-chuckle, half-sigh. She's still fighting sleep. Hell, she might *be* asleep. I ease her head onto my shoulder before I finish dressing her, guiding the sweat pants the rest of the way up her body. They're long on her, the fabric bunched around her calves.

IN LOVE WITH YOU

"You're cute in my clothes," I tell her.

"Mm," she hums against my shoulder, her arms wrapping loosely around my waist. She flattens her lips against my neck, lingering there.

"Actually, you're beautiful," I whisper.

"Mm," she hums again, not able to understand what I'm saying, too far gone.

A tremor in my chest. A shot of adrenaline zipping through me. I barely have time to think before I decide to speak. To test something out on my tongue while she still isn't completely coherent.

"I love you," I whisper.

"Mm."

I sigh as I draw back the covers and help her into my sheets. Then, I slip in beside her, resting my head onto the middle of my pillow and pulling her close. Automatically, her head finds a place in the center of my chest. Her small fists knead into my sweatshirt for a moment, almost like a cat, before she goes still. Nothing but heartbeat. Nothing but breath. And before I can even really start to think about the fact that this feels so *right*, the world fades to black and I fall into a hard, deep sleep.

Forty-One

Luna

"Are you making bacon?" Steph and Ryder ask at the same time, his tone enthused, hers disgusted.

I crinkle my nose and turn, sweeping past Ryder to look at Steph, who looks a peaky shade of yellow. "Is that all ri—"

Before I can even finish my sentence, Steph gags. Bolts for the bathroom. She slams the door shut, but the thin walls in this old cottage don't do much to block out the sound of her retching. I look warily at Ryder as he comes fully down the stairs.

"Does she not like bacon or what's the deal?" I ask, twisting back to flip the crisping pieces over.

"Steph loves bacon," Ryder says. In the reflection of the microwave above the stove, I catch him scowling at the bathroom door. He lifts one toned shoulder in a shrug. "More for us, I guess."

IN LOVE WITH YOU

I don't want to be the one to bring it up, because the last thing this cottage needs is one more worry to discuss, but, being an astute observer, I've noticed the slight weight gain in Steph's face since I met her almost a month ago. The fact that she only ever wears massive sweatshirts. And I'm not entirely sure it's not just her personality, but her mood seems to swing. A lot. Now, a food she apparently loves is making her sick? In the morning? You draw conclusions, the way I'm sure you already are, dear reader, but I know what my theory on it all is.

My eyes tick back up to the microwave's reflection again and find Ryder ogling me, his gaze drifting from my messy bun to my bare feet. I'm still wearing his clothes, the drawstring on his sweats cinched tight to keep them from dropping off of my hips. His eyes linger low on my body. He chuckles.

"What?" I ask, placing the bacon slices onto a paper towel-covered plate beside the stove. I made pancakes, too, but they've been warming in the oven for almost an hour. My phone buzzing downstairs had roused me from sleep. It was just Vera, my agent, demanding pages again. I sent her a quick text—*soon*—and tried to lose myself in something. Making pancakes from scratch was a good distraction. Until I made as many as I could and had nothing to do but sit with my own spiraling thoughts about my writing career. I figured the smell of bacon would rouse the late-sleeping North siblings. And I was right.

"Just never realized how short you were until you put my sweatpants on," Ryder says, closing the distance between us. He presses his chest to my back and wraps his arms around my shoulders.

"I'm not short," I say, peering down to glimpse the elephant-leg-wrinkles stacked up from my ankles to my knees. "I'm 5'8". You're just freakishly tall."

"I'm only 6'4"."

"*Only 6'4*"," I mock.

"D.J. is way taller than me."

"Yeah, well." I click off the stove and move the greasy pan to the back burner. "He's part werewolf."

"And werewolves are tall?"

"Everyone knows that," I say, grabbing an oven mitt and sticking him with a wicked gaze through the reflection of the microwave before I bend over to open the oven.

I only manage to open it a crack before my ass makes contact with Ryder's morning wood. My breath hitches, and he shuffles back a few steps, probably thinking I need better access to the oven. Access without so much friction holding me back.

But honestly, reader? I'm digging the friction.

There's nothing like realizing the sexy-as-sin surfer/bartender you're falling for has a hard-on for you. Talk about a fucking confidence blast.

I drag the oven open all the way, stepping back and pretending to adjust my angle to the oven for better pancake extraction. Really, I just want to roll over Ryder's bulge again. And I swear in the two seconds since I felt it before it's gotten bigger. Harder. My insides are jellified, just like that. I can't tell if it's the heat of the oven or the heat of this entire encounter that's making me sweat.

"You like that, sweetheart?" Ryder asks in a husky whisper. He plants his fingertips to the points of my hips and eases me back, grinding into my ass slowly.

IN LOVE WITH YOU

"Y-yes." Tingles spring to life between my legs and I have to keep my lower lip clutched between my teeth to keep from letting out a rowdy moan.

But then the toilet flushes, Steph groans, and the bathroom faucet flicks on right after. She'll be coming through that door any second now. And if the smell of bacon made her vomit, I wonder what the sight of her brother grinding his boner into a woman's ass in the middle of the kitchen will do to her already weak stomach?

Ryder must think the same thing, because he releases my hips and takes a half step back. Then, he slaps my ass so hard I have to reach out and grip the counter to keep from flying into the oven on the verge of orgasm. I close my eyes and let the mix of pleasure and pain skitter through me.

The bathroom door opens a second later, and Ryder sidesteps into the laundry room directly to the right. As I attempt to take the pancakes out of the oven with jelly arms, I watch him adjust himself so that he's sister-appropriate.

"You okay?" I ask Steph, turning to look back at her. She stands on this side of the bathroom door with her hand clutched to her stomach, her fingers carefully twisted around the fabric of her oversized hoodie and not her stomach itself.

"Fine," Steph says.

"Do you have a stomach bug?" Ryder asks her, stepping back into the kitchen. Not even a hint of a boner in sight. It probably has more to do with the fact that the tough exterior of his is building again in the presence of his little sister.

Steph shakes her head.

"I'm just thinking about Mom," he adds, nodding to the cracked bedroom door where Kendra's audible wheezing can be heard. "The last thing she needs—"

FAYE DARLING

Steph looks at him with molten iron gurgling in her eyes and her fists clenched tightly at her sides. "I don't have a fucking stomach bug."

Steph looks like she could murder her brother if he says one more thing, and I can't see Ryder letting her get away with that kind of behavior, so I peel back the foil the pancakes have been stashed in and announce in my best 1950's housewife voice, "Breakfast is ready."

We settle into what have become, over the past few weeks, our usual spots around the table. Steph and I on the ends, Ryder in the middle. This breakfast is a subdued event. Nothing but sounds. Clatter of utensils. Noisy sips of coffee. Kendra's unusually loud breathing, ever present in the background.

I eye Ryder in between bites of food. He can't stop watching Steph. Looks at her in that serious, protective brother way. That way that makes me think he might be trying to telepathically weasel secrets out her. The way Steph scowls at her pancakes without looking up tells me she knows what he's trying to do. By the time I've finished the food on my plate, I'm almost holding my breath in anticipation for one of them to snap.

After six pancakes and just as many slices of bacon, Ryder throws down his fork, pushes back from his chair, and stands, looming over the table. But his eyes are no longer fixed on Steph. No. They're locked on the dark opening of his mother's bedroom, where her breathing has become more and more pronounced, more and more irregular as breakfast has gone on.

"I can't stand to hear her breathe like that anymore." His brows knit together as he looks back to Steph. "What's wrong with her?"

"Nothing's wrong," Steph mutters, chewing and chewing and chewing the bite of pancake in her mouth until I'm certain it's nothing but cakey mush. "Well, everything's wrong, but as far as her illness is concerned—" Steph pauses to swallow—"this is a normal step in the process."

"What process?" he asks.

"Don't be an idiot," Steph whispers, wiping the corners of her mouth with a paper towel and tossing it onto her half-finished plate.

"I'm not a fucking idiot, Steph."

I reach out and curl my hand around his, rubbing my thumb across the back of his palm. He's been making me nervous standing up like that. Hovering. So, I tug on his arm until he's sitting back in his chair. When I speak, I try to keep my tone even and calm, even though what I have to say makes my heart feel like it's about to crack in two.

"Steph means her irregular breathing is a normal step in the dying process," I say.

Steph's eyes are trained on the salt and pepper shakers in the middle of the table. I notice for the first time how bloodshot her eyes are, how absolutely exhausted she looks. In a flat, almost haunted tone she mutters, "The death rattle. That's what they call it."

"That's a shit name," Ryder snaps. "Who came up with it?"

"Who cares," Steph says.

"They should be hanged," he says.

"It's just a name," I whisper, squeezing his hand.

His lower lip quivers before he drags it into his mouth and sucks in a sharp breath. "It's still a shit one."

"You're right. It's a shit name. In fact, it's all shit, Ryder." Steph slides out from her chair and wobbles toward Kendra's bedroom, tears streaking down her face. She turns back when she reaches the doorway. "All of this—shit."

With that, Steph disappears.

The moment she does, Ryder squirms in his seat. I can feel the need rising up in him. The need to bolt. The last time he ran off, he'd needed my cousin's shotgun to keep him from getting worse than a few stitches. I doubt he'll be so lucky this time around. I keep a tight hold on his hand. Like that will be enough to stop a man his size from leaving if he really wants to. But I have to try, don't I, reader? Wouldn't you?

"Was it?" he asks. It's only the start of a question, really, but his voice cracks on a sob halfway through asking, and he goes quiet.

"Was it, what?" I ask cautiously.

"Your mom," he whispers, like it's the only level he can speak at now without the words crumbling to bits. "Was it like this? At the end?"

I wish I could say it wasn't. I wish I could say my mother drifted off peacefully, noiselessly. I wish I could say I didn't hear that death rattle in the shadows of my memory for years. But I would be lying. And for what? Lying won't help anyone.

"Yes," I say.

Ryder squirms again, then jolts forward.

But it's not to flee the cottage.

He crashes into me, the whole weight of his big body slumping into my arms. His sob breaks on my neck, and I can feel his hot, salty tears slipping down my skin. My arms wrap around his shoulders, my thumbs kneading into the tight, clenched muscle there.

When I close my eyes, I'm no longer in the cottage. I'm sixteen and back in my childhood bedroom in Oklahoma, listening to my mother's rattling wheeze carry down the hall from the living room. My god-fearing preacher father had been praying for close to twenty-four hours straight over her sick body, but it wasn't doing a damn thing. I'd stayed close when he'd first begun to ask mercilessly for healing, but, after a few hours of listening to both of them carry on, I just couldn't take it any longer. I had run to my room, burying my sobs into my pillow. I'd left the door open, but no one came after me.

Not Dad.

Not any of our family or friends who were cycling in and out of our house.

No one.

I hold Ryder closer to me now, my own tears beginning to fall. He won't be alone in his pain. He won't be like me—a buoy, unanchored. No matter how much it hurts, no matter how many tragic memories this unearths in me, I won't leave him. I decide I'm going to stick around this time. Until the end.

Forty-Two

Ryder

RAIN TAPS OUT A rhythmic beat on the window pane Monday evening. The light is fading from the world, making the lamp and candlelight in Mom's room a little bit brighter. I've got her favorite album playing on the turntable she's had since she was a kid, and I'm laying flush against her side, my long body covered in the blanket at the very top of her stack. My toes stick out at the end. There's a chill on them, but I haven't wanted to move to put on a pair of socks.

Luna insisted Steph drive with her to Bun on the Run just for a change of scenery, a chance to breathe. They've been gone for almost an hour. Should be back any minute.

"My first memory of you is in the sea," I tell Mom. When the nurse stopped by early this afternoon, she said there was a good chance Mom wouldn't wake up again. She also said there'd been studies done proving she'd still be able to hear us if we talked to her. So, I've been doing just that. Telling her everything I want to say before I don't have the chance to. It was something I never got with Dad—to tell him all the things I needed to—and I promised myself I wouldn't let that be something I regretted with Mom.

I've got a hold of her hand. I give it the lightest of squeezes before I continue.

"I don't know how old I was. Two, maybe three," I say. "We were bobbing in the breakers somewhere along the coast. I remember salt on my tongue and your long hair catching fire in the sun. You held me close to your chest when a wave would come, but you'd let me float out from your extended arms in between sets, giving me a bit of freedom, teaching me not to be afraid of something that held more power than every man on earth combined."

I nuzzle into Mom's hair and breathe her in. She smells different. Once upon a dream she smelled of ocean brine and sage and my father's cologne she sneak onto her skin. Now, she smells of salt, but the kind from a sick sweat, and the clinical soap the nurse has been sponging her down with.

That rattle in her lungs is softer than it was yesterday morning, but her breaths are growing farther and farther apart, which almost scares me more. I sigh heavily against her, and don't even try to stop the tear that falls from my eye. It runs sideways down my cheek and pools in the curve of my nostril.

"You were always so quiet," I tell Mom, my voice a raw whisper now. "But there was a strength inside you. An easy kind of strength. Not the kind some of us have to force or struggle daily to keep control over. You were like the ocean. You *are* like the ocean. Beautiful, powerful, affecting everything you touch so deeply.

FAYE DARLING

"And I know it's time for your tide to go out, for you to leave this shore and journey to another, but don't think for a second that I will stop loving you, because I won't. I won't stopping missing you, either. Not in this life or the next. You're the best, Mom. You've always been the best and you always will be the best. I love you."

I squeeze Mom's hand again.

Maybe it's a trick of the senses, but I swear—I swear—she squeezes back.

Forty-Three

Ryder

Luna's body is hot, pressed against mine. I kick off my half of the covers, careful not to let the cold of the loft get to her. I've been awake since midnight, almost two hours now. A lot has been on my mind. Mom, Steph, Luna, you.

You.

You're still like a shadow at my back. I can feel you, but every time I turn around, I can't see you, because you're not really here. It would be easy to say you've been nothing more to me than a vivid figment of imagination, but I don't think that's the truth. I've had many fantasies before and they've never felt like this. Never felt like you. I loved you. I really did.

But then the last couple of days happened and…I don't know. Something has shifted.

This is the third night in a row Luna's slept in my bed and, while I'll admit I've wanted to cross that line with her—fuck her senseless, if only to escape the heavy emotions I've felt—I haven't. And neither has she. We've simply existed in one another's presence. I've never been able to do that so easily with anyone before...even you.

And that's made me do a lot of thinking. About us. You and me.

I sigh and run my fingers through my hair, raking it back. Luna hums against my chest as she shifts, burrowing into my side a little deeper, still lost in sleep.

The thing is, you've both been here through every single moment of this journey with me, and I am grateful for it. But when I take a step back and really examine what I have with each of you...

Maybe it's just the middle-of-the-night crazies talking, my mind having nothing to do but whir out of control. I don't know.

If you could show up on my doorstep in the flesh tomorrow and prove to me that you're real, that you exist in my world, then this might be different.

But I've wished that countless times and look where we're at.

It hurts me to say this—fuck, if you could only know how much it hurts—but, as it is, I just don't see how we can work moving forward. And I know I'm still not sure how Luna feels about me yet. But I can't put you on hold while I figure that out. I'm not that kind of guy. I'm just not.

So, I think you know what I'm going to say next. Don't you? Haven't you seen this coming for a while? Maybe you've even been waiting for this conversation. Maybe you've been wishing it would come sooner.

I think a part of me will always love you. But I love her, too. Just a little bit more. Because of that, I have to let you go.

Forty-Four

Luna

I STARE OUT THE windows of D.J.'s kitchen Wednesday afternoon, tracking the raindrops as they skitter down the pane, blurring the evergreens in the distance.

Ryder's mom passed away early, early this morning. We'd all been there in her room, Ryder, Steph, and me. Even the nurse was there when it happened, which made it all a little bit more manageable. One less person to call.

I stuck around for a few hours. Long enough to give Steph a big, tight squeeze. Long enough to hold Ryder against me while he cried and cried.

To tell you the truth, reader, I hadn't wanted to leave. But I also hadn't wanted to force either of them to ask me to. Making funeral arrangements is hard enough. I knew it would be easier if Ryder and Steph could do it on their own without a third person making it complicated.

But I told them I would be back. When they were ready.

FAYE DARLING

I've been sitting at the kitchen table ever since D.J. cooked me grilled cheese and homemade tomato soup for lunch a few hours ago. He'd been on his way out the door, headed down to his office, but changed his mind as soon as he saw me teary-eyed and wobbly. He hovered like a vigilant crow while I ate and has been working on his laptop in the living room ever since I cleaned my plate.

I should write. I've hardly gotten anything down but a bare bones chapter and a rough, rough outline since I arrived in Oregon.

My phone vibrates with an incoming call, and I answer without looking at who is on the other end of the line, because I assume it's Ryder. Or, at least, I hope it is. I've been dreaming about curling up into his chest for the past forty-five minutes.

"Hello?" I ask, my voice froggy from all the intermittent crying I've done today.

D.J.'s fingers slow on the keyboard in the next room. I can picture him pushing his glasses up his nose, leaning in.

"Luna, darling, it's me." Vera, my agent. I inwardly groan. "Where are we at in this mysterious surf romance of yours?"

"It's not all about surfing," I grumble.

"That's our hook, I've decided," she says, so perky I want to stab my soup spoon through my eyeball. "Please tell me you have more than just a vague idea and research notes."

"About that," I say.

A tight sigh on her end of the phone. I imagine her standing in front of the wide windows of her corner office. Hand on one hip. Eyes glaring out at Manhattan. If I listen close enough, I think I can hear the blare of a taxi's horn, the whir and bang of a construction project near her office. But the wind outside D.J.'s kitchen windows buzzes against the wooden tavern walls, and the rain plops hard on the glass, gobbling up any other sound.

"We need this project to gain some traction or we're going to lose our contract," she tells me. Like I don't already know these things. Like my responsibilities to my career aren't constantly itching at the back of my skull.

"I've had a lot on my mind lately, Vera," I say, trying to keep my voice even when all I want to do is scream. "The project makes up a small fraction of the shit stewing in my brain."

"Make it a larger fraction." Another sigh. "We cannot lose this contract."

"You mean, *I* can't lose the contract."

"The day you signed with me, Vera and Luna became *we*."

"Then why don't you write it?" I snap.

D.J. pokes his head around the corner, questioning me beneath those hooded browed eyes of his. I shake my head at him in a *not now* fashion, and he slinks back into the living room.

"I'm going to take a guess and say you're having a bad day," Vera says. "I'm going to write this entire conversation off as out of the ordinary. Then, I'm going to wait one week to hear that you have three drool-worthy chapters for me and that you're only a few weeks away from a rough draft you're excited about."

"I'm not going to force the story," I say. "That's not how I work. You know this."

"It doesn't have to be perfect," she says. "Your writing always takes its best shape around draft three anyway. I just need something to placate our publisher. Understand?"

"Three chapters," I say. "One week. Got it."

"Wonderful," Vera chirps. "Now, I'm meeting some colleagues for drinks in an hour, so I've got to run. I look forward to your email."

"Sure," I say, and the line goes dead.

I groan. Let my forehead drop with a loud *smack* on the table.

"All good?" D.J. asks from the next room.

"Fuck my life," I groan.

"You should have told her what happened."

"It's none of her business."

"No, but it might have bought you some time."

"Don't you have some bikers to help get drunk?" I ask.

"Three chapters, is it?"

I roll my eyes, head still planted on the table. "Yes."

"Surely you've scribbled enough notes to piece together three chapters," he says.

"I don't feel like it, Deej."

"Okay, then," D.J. says. "Sit there. Stare out the window for the rest of the day. I'm going to butt out of it."

"Great."

"Grand."

But I groan, rising from the table. What am I if not a master compartmentalizer?

I march through the living room and into my bedroom, snagging my laptop and little red notebook. I glare at D.J.'s smug smile as I return to the kitchen. I open my laptop, stare at the cursor blinking in the middle of a blank document, and stare and stare and stare some more.

Forty-Five

Ryder

WE SCATTER MOM'S ASHES on a Thursday, a little over a week after she died. It's just Steph and me, bobbing on our surfboards in a calm evening swell the way Mom had wanted.

The sky is clear, save several wisps of clouds strung near the horizon, where the sun is sinking just beyond the jut of the cliffs. The water is a mirror image of the sky. Violet and pink and indigo and a hint of electric blue—Mom's favorites. Neither of us say this out loud, but I know we're both thinking that she's here with us, watching us from every crest of the silky waves moving toward shore.

I clutch the open urn in my hand and lock eyes with Steph briefly. When she nods, I turn Mom's ashes out into the bulge of the sea, sending her body to meet her spirit once again.

We float out there for some time, the chill just starting to penetrate the thick neoprene of our wetsuits.

FAYE DARLING

"It's just us now," I say softly when the murk of Mom's ashes has been washed away, folded into the salt of the sea.

"But it's not," Steph says.

She won't look at me. Her eyes are fixed on the dark blue line on the horizon, where the sea nudges the sky. I can see it, swirling in her eyes, though. The secret she's been keeping is beginning to surface.

"What do you mean?" I ask.

Steph nods her head back to shore. I follow her gaze to where Luna's dark form is curled against the trunk of one of the massive fir trees on the overlook. She asked Steph if she could come and sit on shore before she even asked me. I'd like to think she knew I'd say yes, no matter what. We've been together almost constantly throughout the week since Mom's passing, doing what we do best—simply existing in one another's company. Even though I've had plenty of time to tell her how I feel, I haven't had the guts to say the words out loud yet.

"I'm not sure if she even thinks of me like that," I say to Steph. I turn away from Luna and look back at the vast expanse of the sea.

"You're an idiot if you think she doesn't," Steph says. "She's an idiot if she turns you down. But that's not only what I meant when I said there's more than just the two of us now. There's something else I need to tell you."

"Oh?"

Her hand comes up to touch the slight bulge of her belly protruding through the form-fit of her wetsuit. "I'm pregnant."

I try to keep my blood pressure in check, because that is not what I was expecting her to say. At least, I don't think it's what I was expecting her to say. Now that the cat's out of the bag, there had been signs. The bacon incident being one. The baggy clothing.

"How?" I ask, meaning *how did I miss this?*

She rolls her eyes. "You mean *who? Idiot.*"

"Yeah," I say, trying to cover. "Who? When?"

"I'm about fifteen weeks along," she says. "Due in May. Close to Mom's birthday."

"Did she know?" I ask.

"Yes," Steph says, her voice shaking a little. "I mean, I told her that is. God only knows if she could actually hear me, actually understand."

My surfboard lifts as a new set approaches. "You never told me who."

"Yeah, I was hoping we could breeze over that part," she grumbles.

I narrow my gaze on the horizon. "Who?"

"You know that guy who stopped by in the truck? The guy I stopped you from murdering?"

"Not him." My hands fist at my sides. "Tell me it's not him."

"It's not," Steph says. "I thought it was until a friend at the hospital ran some tests. Helped me out with exact dates. Turns out I was already pregnant when I met him."

"Good," I say.

"You might not think so in a second."

"What?" I twist toward my sister. She's staring at the nose of Mom's old surfboard, chewing on her lip. "Stephanie Louise, who is the father?"

Her voice is barely audible. "Nick."

"Nick?" I ask. "Nick who?"

"You know," she says. "*Nick* Nick. Your Nick."

"My Nick? Nick Forester?"

"We sort of bumped into each other at a bar in Seaside one night back in the summer," Steph says. "He was escaping some family drama and my friend had ditched me to hook up with a guy she'd just met. He sent me a drink and we got to talking and then—"

"Okay," I say, cutting her off. "I don't need to hear the details about how one of my best friends knocked up my baby sister. Fuck's sake. Does he know? Has he been keeping this from me too? Is that why he keeps asking about you?"

"He asks about me?" Steph wrinkles her face. I can't tell if she's pleased about Nick checking up on her well-being or not. I always thought he was just being friendly. Maybe not.

"Yeah," I say.

"No."

"No what?"

"No, he doesn't know about the baby."

"Are you going to tell him?"

Steph shrugs. "I didn't find out it was his until a few weeks ago."

"Are you completely sure it's his?"

"Hey, there was overlap, but I'm not that kind of girl," Steph barks.

"Never said you were."

"It's his." She takes a deep breath and lets it out in fragmented bursts. "I'm positive."

"Well," I say, trying not to lose my shit. My first instinct is to punch the dude. But it's Nick. He's so steady and even. Has been one of my best friends since I was fourteen. I don't think I could hurt him like that. And he wouldn't even know why. I push past the fact that he and Steph, well...you know. Maybe Nick is the kind of guy Steph needs in her life. Maybe this is a good thing. So, I quickly swap out protective older brother for wise older brother. "If it were me—"

"Here we go," Steph says. "Some unsolicited brotherly advice."

"If it were me," I say, talking over her. "I would want to know."

"I don't need Nick to be around or anything."

"I know, Miss Independent," I say. "But Nick is a really good guy, one of my best friends, and whether you need him in your life or not, that niece or nephew of mine might. Maybe not today, but someday."

"Yeah," Steph says quietly, chewing on her lips.

"I can't be that kid's only male influence," I say, then laugh. "Hell, could you imagine?"

"Oh god," Steph says, and we both laugh.

The sun dips behind a thin line of clouds, casting bands of gold across all those paint strokes of color in the water. Our laughter fades at the same time, both of us taking in the brilliance of the sea.

"Mom would have been so happy for you," I say. "And proud. Dad, too."

"Are you?"

"What?"

"Are you happy for me?" Steph asks.

I reach out and take my sister's hand in mine, my palm engulfing hers completely. "The happiest. So long as you name the child after me."

Steph throws my hand back at me and scoffs. A half-smile pulls on the corners of her lips. "You're an idiot."

"So you've told me," I say. "Many times."

"Well," she says. "It's the truth."

Forty-Six

Ryder

I FIND MYSELF STARING at the ceiling later on Thursday night, trying to find sleep. My bed is empty tonight. After we scattered Mom's ashes and spent a few hours sitting on the beach closer to home, watching the stars wink in and out of the passing clouds, Luna told me she needed to go back to The Tavern and try to get some writing done. I don't know much about her job, but I'd say being a writer is a lot like being a contractor. If you don't get your work done, you don't get paid. So, I let her go. I didn't want to. But I did.

I can almost feel sleep scratching at the back of my eyelids as I stare at the ceiling. But then there's a knock on the front door, and I'm suddenly wide awake.

Steph went back to her house tonight, saying if she didn't go now she might never, but she has a key to the cottage, so I know it's not her.

Another knock as I'm pulling on a t-shirt in the kitchen.

IN LOVE WITH YOU

Another as I'm passing the woodburning stove in the living room.

The streetlamp across the road puts the top of Luna's head in silhouette, but I'd recognize that sleek inkwell of black hair anywhere. It's almost blue in certain lights, the way it is now as she stands on the welcome mat.

"I'm leaving," she blurts out as soon as I open the door, not looking up at me.

I swallow. Hard. "What?"

"Tomorrow, I'm leaving."

I rub my eyes as if I'm trying to rub the sleep out of them, but then I remember I haven't slept yet.

"Why didn't you say this earlier?" I ask. "Why are you here so late?"

"Can I come in?" She shifts from foot to foot. She's got a coat pulled over an oversized t-shirt that hits her mid-thigh, and that's it. No pants. No shoes. It's like she ran out of D.J.'s apartment in a frenzy.

"Always underprepared for the weather," I mumble, turning sideways to let her in.

"I told you I'm on a tight deadline with my novel?" Her voice tilts up like it's a question, but I know better. It's a statement. More to come. "A deadline that has passed. Like, yesterday, actually."

"Okay?"

"I can't write here," she says. "I've tried every room in D.J.'s apartment. Downstairs at the bar. I even went to the bakery in town to try and string a few sentences together. Nothing. I'm not just blocked, I'm beyond blocked. Writing is not like being a plumber where if you run into a snag, you switch tools or call in another expert hand to rescue you. And no plumber could fix my problem. Not with a plunger or an ogre or a brand-new set of copper pipes. No, sir. This blockage isn't just bad morning breath, it's carnivorous monster breath screaming down my throat."

"Luna." I squinch my eyes shut, trying to keep up with her runaway freight train of an explanation. There are too many metaphors to sift through. "Quit talking about plumbers and bad breath and just tell it to me straight."

She sucks in a noisy breath and continues. "The only place I've ever truly been able to write a first draft is at my uncle's hunting cabin in Oklahoma. It sounds so stupid and I so, so don't want to leave, but…"

"You need to."

She holds onto her bottom lip with her teeth as she nods, still not looking at me. "I'm sorry."

"But do you have to leave tomorrow?" I ask. "It's all so sudden."

"I already bought my plane ticket and D.J. is taking me to the airport in a few hours."

"Fuck," I say. Really, I want to ask if I can come along, but I can't find a way to form the words.

"I knew if I didn't buy my ticket when I had the nerve, then I wouldn't buy it at all," she says. "And then everything I've worked toward in my writing career would be gone…if it isn't already."

I swallow again. Close my eyes as I ask, "Do you think you'll come back?"

"I don't know," she says coldly. Too coldly. Not at all like the Luna I've come to know. Like she's already shutting me out. Why? Have I been too blinded by my love for her to realize I've gotten caught up in yet another fantasy? She looks at me with an apathetic expression that chills me right down to the marrow of my bones. "Once I finish research for a book, I rarely return."

"Was that all this was to you?" I ask, taking a step away from her, my voice plummeting off a cliff, making it impossible to disguise my hurt. "Was that all I ever was? Research? And my mom and my sister and what happened? All this time, were we only fodder for your writing?"

Luna's face twists in anguish. She reaches out for me in the dark, but I take another step back so she can't touch me. I'm not sure what I'll do if she does.

"I told you, it wasn't like that."

"When? When did you tell me?" My voice is loud again, reverberating off the thin walls of the empty cottage.

"On the way back from the wedding," she says, not matching the brashness of my tone, but yielding to it, almost. She wrings her hands together as if...as if she's nervous. She pauses to swallow, and that's when I see it. The truth behind the thick walls she's built around herself again. Maybe I'm a fool, but just the sight of it has the tension easing in me bit by bit. "When you made love to me in the truck, I said some things I did for research and some things I did just for me. You, Ryder, became that something just for me. Your body, your heart—mine."

I can't help it. I laugh. Just once. A nervous, sneaky laugh.

Her face pinches together. Eyes narrowing, eyebrows colliding. She sets her lips in a hard line. But her voice is anything but hard, anything but pinched. It's soft and trembling. It's nothing but a delicate breeze wafting off of the sea. "W-what's so funny about that?"

FAYE DARLING

"That's what you thought I was doing that night in the truck?" I ask. "You thought I was making love to you?"

She hugs her arms tightly around her chest. Stares at a spot just over my right shoulder. "Were you not?"

"No," I say. This time, I don't laugh. None of it was funny to begin with. The laugh had been more of a byproduct of my immense relief than anything. I take a step toward her, closing the distance between us. With my fingertips, I nudge her chin upward so she has nowhere to look but directly into my eyes. "But I'm about to."

I trap her lips in a greedy kiss as my palms run down the outside of her bare thighs until they reach her knees. I grip the backs of her legs with sure hands and pop her little body up onto my hips with a swift jolt that makes her gasp. I start walking through the house, toward the loft.

Since we're the only ones in the cottage tonight, I take my time. If I can't find the words to tell her how much she means to me, maybe I can show her. The two of us have always been better at that anyway. And maybe, just maybe, I can change her mind about leaving.

I set her down on one of the steps halfway up the staircase. I fist my hands and plant them on the carpet on either side of her hips, leaning in. I kiss her slow and deep, memorizing every taste, every smell, every sensation. Just in case.

Just in case she's one more person I'm forced to say goodbye to.

Her hands slide up into my hair, clenching around the roots. I grunt. Lean closer to her. I suck on her lower lip as her legs wrap high around my waist. She grinds her hips into mine, demanding more.

I pick her up again, finishing the climb to the loft, flicking on every single light as I go.

"What are you doing?" she gasps, squinting against the brightness.

"I want to look at you," I say. "Not in a dark tent or the cramped cab of a truck or in the dim light of this loft. I want to see you, sweetheart. Every. Last. Beautiful. Bit."

She laughs, that sugary, confident laugh I've only ever heard her use with me, and I reward her with a kiss to the soft spot just below her ear. My lips trail down her neck as I push her coat off of her shoulders one arm at a time. And no one said a puffer jacket could be sexy. *Please*.

I toss the coat over the back of the loft railing and when I turn back I recognize a familiar black t-shirt dropped over her body. The one I leant her when she slept over after Mark and Gina's wedding. My dick twitches at the sight of it.

"Did you steal my shirt?" I ask, my voice gravelly.

"Borrowed," she answers.

"Keep it," I husk. "It looks better on you."

"Really?" she asks, ducking down to pull the shirt up and over her head. "I was thinking it looked better *off* of me."

A low growl vibrates through my chest as I take her in. She stands before me wearing nothing but a lace bodysuit stained a deep shade of maroon. Wide gaps in the lacey pattern. Her pebbled nipples peeking through. She bites her lip and smirks before she bends a knee and flicks her hips to one side, turning her body into a curvy S-shape.

"Fuuuck," I whisper. Clearly, she came prepared for this. That means I'm going to need to do a lot more convincing than I thought to get her to stick around.

"Too much?" she asks, curving her hips to flip that S in the opposite direction. "Goodbye sex sounded a little too nice."

"Does it have to be goodbye?" I ask.

But I don't give her time to answer. I press my mouth against hers with an urgency that hadn't been there earlier.

For a time, we're all roaming hands and tongues down throats and heavy panting, but I manage to slow us down. A kiss to her collarbone, letting my lips linger as I pull away. With the tip of my tongue, I trace a line up to the joint of her shoulder, where I plant another kiss, the lace of her lingerie between us. I take the strap of her bodysuit between my teeth and watch her from the corner of my eye as I tug it down her arm, her breast popping free. I kiss the edges of her nipple, then suck on it in a way that sends her hands to my hair again and a moan tumbling out of her lips.

Her fingers plunge beneath the waistband of my sweatpants. Thumbs hooking around the fabric and dragging my pants as low as her arms can manage—just below the base of my throbbing erection.

"Tell me what you want, sweetheart," I whisper in her ear.

We sway in a slow circle, just inches from my unmade bed.

She surprises me by sinking her teeth into the top of my left peck, just enough to hurt, more than enough to set my dick on fire.

"Fuck, Luna," I hiss. "Tell me what you want."

Her hand curves around my cock, pulling it out of my pants completely. She massages gently, but my body has other plans. My hips thrust forward, fucking into her hand once before I regain control. My pulse is still thrumming through my dick, though, and the need to chase my pleasure is a wild animal held back by nothing but a frayed rope.

IN LOVE WITH YOU

"That's a loaded question," she says.

"And yet you're holding the gun," I say, glancing down at her hand still wrapped around me. "Literally."

She laughs, letting go and wrapping her hands around my neck instead. I release a subdued whimper in the wake of her absence. Then, she jerks me toward her and we fall back onto my bed.

I manage to catch myself with my hands planted on either side of her shoulders so I don't crush her beneath my full weight.

"What do I want?" she asks.

"Yes."

"I want my agent to stop breathing down my neck," she begins. "I want to be able to write wherever, whenever. I want to surf with you in the mornings and share a bed with you in the nights. I want one more day with my mother and for you to have one more day with yours. I want my dad to accept me for who I am, not who he wishes I was. I want D.J. to find happiness and for Steph to find someone who will love her completely. I want so many things, Ryder."

"But now," I say, the sneaky tear that started to form when Luna mentioned our mothers finally sliding down my cheek. "What do you want right now?"

She lifts up and kisses the teardrop off of my face, holding herself up, so close that the air I'm breathing is hers and the air she's breathing is mine.

"Right now, what I want is you." She nips at my ear lobe before she lowers her voice to a whisper. "You and that gargantuan cock, of course."

A low laugh tumbles out of me, and I kiss the tip of her nose before I stand up, stepping out of my pants completely and reaching into the top drawer of my nightstand for a condom. I open the wrapper and roll it on before returning to her.

With a feather-light touch, I slide the soaked fabric at the base of her bodysuit to one side and press my tip against her hot, wet opening, pausing for a moment as I find her eyes. As soon as she looks at me, I thrust myself into her completely, and a shuddering moan passes her lips. The sound she makes sends tingles from the top of my head to the juncture of my thighs. I start to move, those tingles increasing with each grunt she heaves against my ear.

This bed is old. I've had it for years, and I bought it secondhand to begin with. It creaks with each forward drive and gasps each time I slide away, rivaling the noises Luna makes.

It takes me a moment of searching, of moving one way as opposed to another to find the place Luna seems to respond to the most. I'm positioned at a slight angle, holding one of her thighs off the mattress.

I don't want her to go. I don't want her to leave this bed, let alone the state. Maybe it's because I'm thinking of that, maybe it's because she feels so fucking good, but my thrusts become more powerful as I plunge deep inside her body. As if I am trying to bury myself inside of her. Lose myself entirely in her folds.

"Oh, god," she cries out, scratching her nails down my back. "Don't stop. Don't fucking stop."

"I wouldn't dream of it, sweetheart," I say.

I'm nearing that edge, that point of no return. A heat is swirling low in my belly and the need to release is strong. I inhale sharply, willing myself to wait for her. And, just when I think I can't hold onto control for a second longer, Luna gasps.

"Ryder, I'm coming."

IN LOVE WITH YOU

I feel her clenching around me as the rocket that's been preparing to launch takes off, the entire world spinning for a few glorious seconds—like an hours-long drug trip compressed into a single moment—and then, the spinning stops, the world is as clear as a crystal champagne flute, and I collapse on top of Luna, the two of us still joined.

My lips find her neck as I slide out of her, kissing her as I lay down beside her, one of my arms draped across her lace-covered torso.

"Mm," I hum against her skin, so satisfied I can't even form words.

She laughs. "My sentiments exactly."

And for a second, I think I've done it. I think I've convinced her. Shown her that this kind of sex could be hers all night, every night, just like she said she wanted.

"Stay," I whisper, hoping she hears everything I'm not saying.

"Okay," she says.

I pop out of the bed long enough to clean myself up and flick off the lights. When I return, Luna snuggles into my side, her breathing easy and hypnotic. We lay there for what feels like hours, but is probably only minutes. Then, my eyes flutter as sleep drags me down. And I let it, falling quickly, deeply, with Luna by my side.

Forty-Seven

Luna

Mt. Hood hovers below, the soft hues of dawn light cast over its snow-covered peak as the plane climbs and climbs.

Am I an idiot, reader? For leaving Ryder not long after he fell asleep?

I didn't shower. Didn't change out of my lace bodysuit. I just put some comfortable clothes over the top of my lingerie, packed myself into the cab of D.J.'s truck, and headed for Portland, my suitcase shifting around in the bed as we tracked the dark and curling highway through the pass of the coastal range to get me to the airport in time for my flight.

Maybe I should have asked Ryder what I'd really wanted to. Asked him to come with me. But he'd looked almost angry when I'd told him I was leaving, a little bit hurt. Then everything happened so quickly and I said so many other things, but somehow, because I'm me, I didn't say what I really wanted.

I love you, come with me.

Is that so damn hard to verbalize? I write characters who say that at least once in every one of my novels. So, why am I afraid to say it?

I love you, come with me.

What's the worst that could've happened? He would've said no?

"I love you, come with me," I whisper as Mt. Hood shifts out of view.

"Sorry, did you say something?" the woman sitting in the seat beside me asks.

"No," I say, still staring out the window. "Just talking to myself."

I feel her shift a little to the side, but I don't really care. Let her believe she's sitting beside some lunatic who talks to herself and smells of sweat and sex and regret.

I love you, come with me.

"Anything to drink?" the flight attendant asks, his voice breaking through my inner dialogue.

"Jack and Coke, double," I say. He gives me a judgy look. "I know it's not even seven in the morning, but I don't really care. That's what I want."

He scoffs. Scribbles down my order on a pad of paper and looks apologetically at the woman beside me.

I love you, come with me.

Oh, I'm an idiot, aren't I? Actually, reader, don't answer that. I can already feel your anger boiling up, reaching me from beyond.

Forty-Eight

Ryder

THE BED IS COLD beside me when I wake in the morning.

"Fuck," I say, sitting up.

Luna's coat and my old t-shirt are gone.

"Fuck," I say again, louder this time.

I look at the clock on my nightstand—7:33am—and jump to my feet, I throw on the same sweats from last night and race for the door. She said her flight was leaving in the morning, but she didn't say when. Maybe she hasn't left yet.

But as I'm speeding toward The Tavern, the new tires D.J.'s buddy just put on feel like they're creating too much friction, slowing me down, causing my hope to dwindle.

The windshield wipers are going full-blast, making it hard to see, but I can still make out illuminated taillights near the dumpsters when I pull in. They haven't left yet. My hope returns as I skid to a stop beside D.J.'s big black truck and jump out of the Camaro.

IN LOVE WITH YOU

"Wait," I shout, waving.

The downpour soaks me instantly and I shiver in nothing but a t-shirt and sweats as I watch D.J. crank his window open. His dark eyes are stitched with concern, but I ignore the look, staring past him to the passenger seat. The *empty* passenger seat.

"Is she still inside?" I ask over the noise of the rain pounding against the square hood of his truck.

"Who? Luna?" D.J. asks. "Nah, man, you missed her."

"What?"

"I dropped her off at the airport at five o'clock this morning," D.J. says. "I'm just getting back."

"No," I say, more to myself than to anyone else. It feels like D.J. has just punched me in the gut. I stumble back, as if I've been bowled over by the pain.

"I thought she said goodbye?"

I lean forward, bracing my hands on my knees. Bile rises in my throat. I can feel the dilapidated walls surrounding my world threatening to crumble for good. As if losing both of my parents hadn't weakened them beyond repair.

"Has her flight left yet?" I ask.

D.J. steps out of the pickup truck, the rain bouncing off his black leather jacket. "Yeah, man. She's long gone by now."

"Fuck," I say.

"Come inside," D.J. says, clapping me hard on the back. "I'll pour you a drink."

FAYE DARLING

THE TAVERN IS DIFFERENT early in the morning. Peaceful, almost.

Peaceful if I didn't feel like my world was spinning off its axis.

D.J. must have learned not to pour me whiskey when I wasn't in the mood to handle myself because I sip on the beer he gives me instead and watch the droplets of condensation slide down the sides of the glass while I try and listen to his words.

"She's never been good at relationships," D.J. says. "Because she's never been good at staying in one place. She told me once she's never found a place she hasn't wanted to leave five minutes after arriving. I think it's how she found writing. It was always her way to escape when she physically couldn't. Do you know what I mean?"

I think of you, for some reason. Maybe because I can still feel you nearby, still not willing to go yet, I suppose?

"Yeah, I get needing to have an escape," I say.

"I think she's just waiting for a sign," D.J. says. He takes the beer I've barely touched and slides it away from me. I quirk a brow at him. "A sign that she doesn't have to escape anymore. That it's good and safe to live in her own reality finally."

"Are you going all Yoda on me right now?"

D.J. takes an old receipt stabbed to the little stake near the register behind him and turns it over. He scribbles something down with a pen on the blank side. He folds the receipt in half and turns back to me, holding the paper between his middle and index fingers.

"I think you might need that same sign, brother," D.J. says.

"Is that the sign?" I nod to the receipt.

IN LOVE WITH YOU

"No," he says, sliding the paper across the countertop. "This is just going to help you both find that sign."

"Okay?" I ask, picking up the receipt and cocking my head to one side, trying to decipher the mix of numbers and lines. "What is this?"

"Coordinates," he says. "The hunting shack has no physical address, but it's just outside a forgotten township called Driftwood, near the city of Enid."

"In Oklahoma?"

"That's right."

My heart is thrumming in my chest, my hands trembling a little as I look at the numbers and lines in a new light. "What if she—"

"If you don't get your ass off that stool right now, you never will," D.J. says, a bite to his tone. "Who gives a fuck if she's in love with you or not. You're in love with her, right?"

I nod.

"Right?" D.J. asks again, loudly, obviously needing a verbal confirmation to that question.

My eyes snap up to meet his. I nod again. "Right."

"Then you have to try," he says. "Otherwise, you'll spend the rest of your life regretting sitting idly by and watching her slip through your fingers."

A jolt of adrenaline rocks through me. I slide off of the stool, my boots hitting the floor with a slight squish from all the rainwater clinging to my socks.

"If I go, will you keep an eye on Steph?" I ask D.J. as I move toward the door.

"You know I will," D.J. says, the hint of a smile forming on his face.

FAYE DARLING

Guilt twists through my stomach at the thought of leaving my little sister right now. After Mom, after what Steph told me yesterday on the water.

But I know D.J.'s right. If I don't chase after Luna, I'll regret it. Even if she rejects me the moment I show up on her doorstep, at least I'll know I tried everything.

"Thanks, man," I tell D.J., a hand on the door that leads to the parking lot. I lift the receipt. "Thanks for everything."

"Get the fuck out of here," he says, full-on grinning now.

And I do.

I stop off at the cottage, throw some clothes into a duffel, and drive across town to Steph's place.

"You're driving to Oklahoma?" she asks, propping one hand on her hip, the other on the frame of her door. She looks flushed, sweaty. A little bit like she might run for the toilet to puke at any second. "Right now?"

"Yes," I say.

"When will you be back?"

I shrug. "Don't know yet."

"Can't you just call her on the phone or something?" Steph asks. "Do you really have to drive halfway across the country just to say you miss her?"

"It's a little more than missing her."

"Okay?"

"Steph, I love her," I say, then swallow down the lump in my throat.

"Holy fucking shit," she says, like she can't believe it. And why would she? I've never been this in love with anyone ever. The closest I came was with you. "I've never heard you say that before."

"Well, it's true."

IN LOVE WITH YOU

"I know," she says, squeezing my hand once and not letting go.

"You'll be okay if I leave, though, right?" My eyes drop down to her stomach, concealed by an oversized purple hoodie. She rolls her eyes when she catches me staring at her baby bump.

"Yes, I'll be fine," she hisses. Pulls her hand back. Slaps me across the arm.

"Ouch," I say with a laugh. "You gonna tell him while I'm gone?"

"Thinking about it," she says.

"Well, let me know when you do so I don't spill the beans." I glance back at my car parked on the curb in front of her house. She slaps me again, and I whip my head around. "What was that one for?"

"To get you off my porch," she says. "Now, go."

I wrap Steph in a tight, tight hug, making sure to keep the pressure on her shoulders and nowhere near her stomach. She hugs me back ten times harder.

"You sure you'll—" I start, but Steph cuts me off.

"I'm fine," she says. "Really."

I drop a kiss onto my sister's cheek and pull away, a stupid, wide grin on my face when I think about what I'm about to do. I start backing toward my car. "I'll call you every day."

"Please don't," Steph groans.

"Every hour on the hour, then," I say as I open the driver's side door to the Camaro.

"I'll turn my phone off."

"You wouldn't."

"Try me."

FAYE DARLING

Whatever remnants of a smile are left on my face dissipate at that. "Seriously, though, don't do that. I need to know you're safe."

"Whatever." Steph rolls her eyes. "I'll keep it on."

"Thank you," I say. "Bye, I love you."

"Love you, too, you big idiot."

With that final endearment, I'm gone. Snow chains in the trunk, along with a spare tire. Dad's old cassette tapes spinning through the speakers. I blaze through Portland by late morning, Pendleton by the time the sun is setting, and crawl through Boise, Idaho, close to midnight. I pull over near Salt Lake City to snag a few hours of sleep and a hot meal at a diner decked to the nines with Christmas decorations even though Thanksgiving is still a week away.

I wake with the sun to a view of the Rockies and hit the road again, using my chains in one of the snowy mountain passes near Wyoming. I skirt around Denver, watch the flatlands of Kansas pass by in the dark, and creep across the Oklahoma state line around one in the morning. By then, the road is a blur again and, even though I want to see Luna, I also don't want to scare the shit out of her or stumble upon the wrong hunting cabin in the middle of the night and get a shotgun pulled on me. So, I pull into a motel in Enid and sleep until my alarm goes off the next morning at seven.

The cabin isn't too hard to find using D.J.'s coordinates. Luna was right, though. This is most definitely the middle of nowhere.

Barren fields, a few scraggly stalks of corn left behind here and there. Even fewer trees, their bark a washed-out gray, their limbs stripped of leaves. This is nothing like the lushness of the Pacific Northwest. There's no green to speak of, no rich browns. No hills or mountains. No fir trees climbing so high you lose track of their tops if you stand underneath them.

I haven't thought of you hardly at all during my entire trip east, but somehow I find myself wondering if you live in a place like this. Are you from the Midwest? From farther east? Do you even live in America?

And there's a pang in my heart, a kind of sorrow-filled guilt.

I loved you, I really did, and I still appreciate the company, knowing I'm not alone, but can't you see that I don't just love this woman that I'm going to find? I would go to the ends of the earth—quite literally—to get her back.

Thank you for being a part of my life, no matter how short that part might have been. Thank you for listening, for distracting, for letting me love you. I needed you more than you'll ever know, and although I know there is no future for us, I don't think I'll ever quite be able to forget you.

But I have to let you go completely now. I have to say my final goodbye. And soon, you'll have to do the same.

Can't you understand that?

I slam on my brakes, my GPS pinging for me to turn down an almost nonexistent road that tumbles along the edge of an empty field and leads to a cluster of trees in the far distance. I drive as far as the road allows, then, I walk.

The wind feels different here. I notice that the moment I start through the woods. It's thick and unforgiving and has absolutely no trace of the sea. All I smell is dirt and dead, rotting leaves.

Through a break in the trees, I spy it: the hunting cabin.

It's about half the size of my family's cottage and the wood is weather-beaten and without paint. A single window looks out from the front, curtains pulled back to let in the light. Luna's boots sit haphazardly on the small porch beside an old rocking chair, a flannel blanket draped over one of the arms. A laptop sits alone on the chair, which I realize is still rocking slightly, and I don't think it's because of the wind.

I step onto the porch the same moment the front door opens. Luna walks out of the house, a cup of steaming coffee clutched in both of her hands. She's wearing nothing but my old t-shirt and a pair of mismatched wool socks that trail up to her knees.

She blinks up at me in silence, perhaps wondering if I'm real or imagined.

"Sorry to—" I say at the same time she asks, "How did you find this place?"

We both laugh nervously, looking down at the slats of the porch floor. I clear my throat when I'm ready to speak again.

"D.J. told me where you'd be," I say. "I tried to stop you, the day you left for the airport."

She bites back a smile. "You did?"

"Of course," I say. "You never even said goodbye."

"Is that why you're here?" she asks. "To say goodbye?"

"Hell no," I say automatically, and she doesn't hold back her smile this time. It's as wide as the distance between here and the Oregon Coast and as breathtaking as the sun sinking down into the sea. "I don't ever want to say goodbye to you. And I don't care if that means I have to follow you from place to place to satisfy your need to roam, because I love you, and I don't want to spend another second without you."

Luna tosses her mug of coffee off the porch and throws her arms around my neck, kissing me so forcefully, I nearly tumble backward into the dirt. I find my balance, and when I do, I pick Luna up off her feet and hold her against my chest, our lips still locked.

"I love you, too," she says when we break apart. She laughs that sweet little laugh. "You know, in case the kiss didn't make that clear."

"I think you could be clearer," I say, jesting.

She cups my face in her hands and kisses me until my knees feel like they're about to buckle beneath me. She laughs against my mouth. "How was that?"

"Better," I say.

"Before we roam the earth together," she says as I carry her through the open door of the tiny cabin, "can I ask a favor?"

I kiss the hollow of her neck. "Anything."

"You never did show me how to split wood, you know," she says. "Do you think we have time for a little more book research? I've got a scene that I want to write..."

I locate the bed in the corner of the room, a twin mattress covered by an old quilt with an intricate pattern. I head toward it.

"Sweetheart, we've got all the time in the world," I say right before I flop onto the mattress with Luna in my arms, both of us bouncing against the old, giving springs. Luna's squeal morphs into a laugh. I don't think I'll ever get tired of that laugh. I nibble on her neck until she laughs again, then I lean back so I can look into her eyes. "But first, I want to do a little research of my own."

Now, this, my dear friend, is when you finally let me go.

The "With You" Series Continues!

Please Enjoy a Sneak Peek of Steph & Nick's Story, IN THIS WITH YOU, Available for Pre-Order Today

One: August

Nick

IT'S ALWAYS BEEN YOU.

Stephanie North, my best friend's little sister.

It all started out so innocently. When you were twelve and I was fourteen. Your grumpiness and witty digs and sarcasm used to make me laugh at a time when I needed to laugh most. Then we got older, *you* got older, and amusement and comfort became infatuation and, eventually, love.

Now that I'm thirty, I'm starting to wonder if this is actually love or if it's slid into something darker, something more akin to obsession.

Maybe if I'd ever been able to act on my feelings, it would be different. If I'd been allowed to kiss you, touch you, fuck you. Maybe I would have gotten it all out of my system.

But you've always been off-limits in my mind.

And for good reason, too.

FAYE DARLING

I once watched your brother beat a man almost to death protecting you, and I decided a long time ago I never wanted to be on the other side of his fists.

Your brother isn't the only reason I've never acted on my feelings, but it's the only reason I'm willing to give you now, as you laugh at the opposite end of this crowded bar, your hand on some other dude's bicep, your smile peeled wide just for him.

Can I tell you a secret?

I don't really care for your smile. I've always preferred your frown. The way your forehead scrunches up like an accordion. The way the whites of your eyes disappear, leaving nothing but stormy blue in their wake. The way your lower lip rolls away from the upper one, making me want to kiss you so badly it hurts. Just a little.

The ice in my whiskey glass rattles as I knock back the last swallow. It's the fifth one I've had since I sat down on this stool long before you sauntered in. Because, no, I did not follow you here. My dysfunctional family drove me to this bar in Seaside, an hour up the coast from West Cove, the tiny town on the North Oregon Coast you and I both call home.

That's where I'd rather be—home.

But this bar was closer to my parents' house, which is just a few miles north of here. When I rolled through town in my Subaru, the idea of drowning myself in whiskey sounded pretty damn good. And seeing you in that strapless purple dress, the gothic rose inked over your left shoulder blade winking at me from across the room while the rest of you remains oblivious to my presence, sounds even better.

I watch your hand glide from the dude's bicep down to his hand as you prop both of your elbows behind you on the bar and arch against it, your small, but utterly delicious, chest lunging out toward him. You bite your bottom lip and shake your head ever so slightly, the curtain of your dark auburn hair shivering delectably.

Heat washes over me from head to toe in a sick kind of baptism. My dick twitches in my tweed trousers, and I let slip an audible groan.

Ugh. It's like I'm fucking thirteen-years-old again and unable to control myself.

"All right?" asks the bartender. I've been trying to place her accent all night. At first, I thought Scottish, but her voice has more of a lilt to it than a low punch. Irish, I've decided, but which dialect is yet to be determined. My grandmother grew up in Roscommon, Ireland, and this woman sounds nothing like her or any of my other Irish relations. Not that it matters.

I subtly adjust myself as I slide my empty whiskey glass across the bar top. "Can I get another, please?"

"Depends," she says.

"On what?"

She waggles her eyebrows at me. "The test you're about to take."

As she leans over the bar, the cleavage on display through the deep v of her t-shirt inches toward me. Her curly, black ponytail falls over one shoulder, and her bright green eyes sear holes through mine. She's an attractive woman, there's no denying it. Smooth features and a hot body. She seems like she could be a good time.

But she's not you.

They're never you.

FAYE DARLING

My semi wilts in my pants the longer this woman stares at me. That should tell you something right there about the power you hold over me.

I swallow. "Well?"

"Not in terrible shape, I suppose," she says with a beaming smile I'm sure gets her just as far as that accent of hers does in the States. "I reckon you could handle another."

"Good," I say, my stupid face returning her smile. It's automatic, my niceness. My need to keep everyone at peace. It's why my family twists and gnaws at my insides so much. They're never happy when they're at peace. Quite the opposite, really. They thrive in the chaos. It's why I moved out of my parent's house and in with my grandma right before high school. That and other things. Things your brother, my best friend, my confidant, doesn't even know about.

I allow myself to glance your way once more and am surprised to see you hunched over the bar, scowling into your nearly-empty drink. And it occurs to me now that you're all alone.

What happened to Mr. Beef Head?

"Do me a favor?" I ask the bartender as she pours a couple of fingers of whiskey into my glass. "Send a Dirty Shirley to the woman in the purple dress over there. But don't let her know who it's from." The bartender quirks a brow at me. It reads more as concerned than curious so I add, "She's my friend's little sister. I don't want to bother her, but she looks like she could use a win right now."

"I don't think she's the only one who could use a win." The bartender's hooded gaze drops over me again, and her mouth cranks up in an alluring smirk.

IN LOVE WITH YOU

I give her another smile, this time forcing it to be tight, tight, tight so she doesn't get the wrong idea. If you weren't here right now, I'd probably have already asked her to meet me after her shift. Bury myself balls deep in her Celtic pussy and fuck you off my mind. But I can't bring myself to pick up some chick with you standing over there like a withering little daisy. So sad. So dejected. So scowly.

"I'll be fine," I tell the bartender.

She nods and drifts off to make your cocktail.

I know if I keep staring at you I'll be on my feet in no time, weaving through the crowd to join you on your side of the bar. And if I do that, I'll start talking to you. Leaning in because of the noise. Catching whiffs of your perfume. The bartender might have thought I was sober enough to have another drink, but I'm definitely drunk enough not to think about the consequences of what I might do if I get too close to you tonight.

Who knows, between leaning in and catching whiffs, I'll probably brush your hair off your shoulders and end up dragging my lips up the length of your long neck.

Once I do that, once I get a feel for your skin on mine, we'll both be in serious trouble.

Don't believe me? Just ask my dick, which is already returning to half-mast simply at the thought of being close to you.

"Fuck me," I murmur into my tilted whiskey glass right before I take a huge swig.

When I set the glass down, I stare at the backs of my hands so I'll stop staring at you. The only tattoos on my body cover me from the tips of my fingers to the hilts of my wrists. They tell a story. *My* story.

FAYE DARLING

A clover at the lowest joint of my left thumb to remind me how lucky I felt when my grandmother helped me get out from under my father's roof. An ocean wave curling over the width of my right wrist to represent the peace I always find in the cold of the North Pacific.

There are countless other tattoos—too many to list—but do you want to know my favorite one?

The massive gothic rose spread over the back of my left hand.

It didn't used to be my favorite. I had only wanted a way to keep in mind that there can be beauty in pain. Blooms and thorns. Then, one day, you complimented the rose, asked who the artist was, and drove with your friends to the tattoo parlor in Portland that afternoon. I was still at your house, hanging with your brother, when you came home. You'd strode through the door, shrugged your sweater down on one shoulder and revealed a fresh tatty that matched mine. I think my heart about burst out of my chest when I saw the ink. I tried not to read into it too much. Tried to tell myself you hadn't meant it as some big gesture of love. Nevertheless, the rose we shared became my favorite that day.

"Did my fucking brother send you to look after me?"

Your voice is like machine gun fire ripping through me. And I like the pain of it. I like it way too fucking much.

With a heavy hand you drop your cocktail onto the bar beside me, drops of vodka, grenadine, and soda splashing out of the glass. I guess while I was distracting myself, you got my present. O*bviously* it wasn't as hush-hush as I would have liked. I glance up, catch the not-so-subtle wink the bartender shoots me—like she's content playing matchmaker now when not five minutes ago she was trying to seduce me with cleavage—and then swing my gaze to you.

Do you know that when you get angry, red splotches creep into your deep, olive-toned skin and climb from your chest up to your cheeks? It always makes me smile. Even now.

"Why are you smiling?" you ask with a grunt. "This isn't a fucking joke, Nick."

"Oh, Stephanie," I say, long and drawn out, because I just love the way your full name tastes on my tongue. "It's *not* a joke. Not in the least."

"What the hell does that mean?" You seal your arms over your chest and scowl at me, which only makes my rogue little friend perk up again, straining against the zipper of my tweed suit pants.

Maybe it's the whiskey. Maybe it's the fact that your anger has always been a turn-on. Maybe it's that I'm simply tired of hiding from you. Whatever it is, it has me reaching out and pinching your elbow lightly between my fingers. You're not exactly a giant, Stephanie, so even though you're standing and I'm sitting, our eyes are level. I stare into you like it's my fucking job, and let me tell you, I have a *strong* work-ethic.

"Your brother didn't send me to keep an eye on you," I say. "Ryder doesn't even know I'm here. Most people would call our meeting a good old fashioned coincidence, but me? I don't believe in coincidences."

"Are you saying you followed me here?"

"I could argue that *you* followed *me* here," I say with a cluck of my tongue and shake of my head. Your brows crinkle as you frown, but all I do is grin back at you and keep talking. "I got here long before you waltzed through that door, babydoll."

"Oh." Your anger starts to fizzle out, and I have to admit, I'm more than a little disappointed. But then you reach for the cocktail you slammed down a minute ago and hold it up to me. I let go of your elbow, pick up my whiskey, and clink it against the lip of your glass. We both take a sip. You mumble this next bit. Like you're embarrassed or something. It's cute. "How'd you remember Dirty Shirleys are my favorite?"

Because I remember everything about you, Stephanie North.

"I took a stab."

"Impressive stab."

"I'm a pretty impressive guy, if you hadn't noticed," I say with a big ass grin.

You roll your eyes big and bold. Sarcasm drips off of your tongue. "Okay, Nick. Sure. You're really fucking impressive."

I laugh. Take another sip of my whiskey to stop myself from kissing you. I sigh against the burn of the liquor.

"What happened to your friend?"

"My friend?" you ask.

"The beef head you were getting cozy with a minute ago."

"Oh, *him*." You scoff. "Yeah, he is *not* my friend."

"Is that so?"

You've never been good at picking guys, Stephanie. I don't think you'd argue with me about that. Your first boyfriend, Blake, was a douche bag of epic proportions, and I'd still like to kick his balls back up inside his body for all the shit he put you through. Then it was a series of men who treated you like dirt. Each time you came home with a new bruise, your brother would go out hunting for blood, and my heart would break a little bit each time.

IN LOVE WITH YOU

But the way you tell me that dude whose arm you were caressing is not your friend makes me hopeful that you've turned a bit of a corner. Have been able to sort out the right ones from the wrong ones finally.

"I only came out tonight to get some shit off of my mind, if you know what I mean," you say, not making eye contact with me.

I'm not entirely sure what you mean, actually. If you mean fucking something off your mind then, yes, I know precisely what you mean. Anything else and I'm lost.

"Maybe you could elaborate," I say.

"My friend Misty came out with me tonight," you say with a sigh that makes your whole body heave. "She planned to do the usual wing-woman shit. But what a *shit* wing-woman she turned out to be. Making out with some tourist I'd been flirting with while I went to the bathroom in the first bar we went to. Being hell-bent on screwing this guy whose friend, the beef head, wasn't on the market. Even though it took him until Misty and his buddy left and I asked him if he wanted to get out of here, too, to tell me he was engaged. Fuck's sake, why am I telling you all of this? I've only ever been your best friend's annoying little sister, I'm sure. You don't want to hear this shit."

"I've seen you as many things, Stephanie, but never as my friend's annoying sister," I tell you, boldly dropping my palm onto your bony hip. And at this point I just can't fucking help it—I lean in. My lips sifting through your hair to get to your ear. My semi-hard pressing slightly into your leg as I bring my knees to rest on either side of your tiny body. Your breath hitches the moment you realize what's touching you. But you don't jolt away. You don't push me back. "I can help, you know."

"Help?" you ask, your smoky voice plunging low before rocking up.

"You know," I say, breathing in deeply, the scent of sandalwood and something floral filling my nose. My teeth scrape lightly over your earlobe as I nuzzle my face closer to you. "I can help you get the shit out of your head."

"Really?" your tone is all playful and sexy and fuck me, you just leaned into my erection slightly, eliciting a groan I can't rein in. You laugh at this. You laugh at me. But then you surprise me when you ask seriously, "What exactly did you have in mind?"

Acknowledgments

I would like to thank you, the reader, first and foremost. I am beyond grateful that you took a chance on this book. Here's hoping you enjoyed reading it as much as I enjoyed writing it, but if you didn't, that's okay, too, because I don't like every book I read and don't expect all of my readers to like my books, either. So, whether you loved this novel, hated it, or fell somewhere in between, I'd appreciate it if you'd leave a review on Amazon.

The next thank you goes out to my ex-stepsister (wherever you are, I hope you're doing well) for planting the seed of this book idea in my head over ten years ago while we read and journaled and gabbed with our heads jammed under the Christmas tree. It took me a while to start writing the "What if the main character falls in love with the reader" book, but I told you I would get it done, so here it is. Thanks, lady. :)

A big thank you to old college roomie who let me gush about this crazy, spicy book during a long walk on the beach.

Your encouragement of my writing has always meant the world to me.

Thanks to my pops for supporting me in my writing dreams. If for some reason you are actually reading this, then it means you've read this book, and therefore I am invoking Fight Club rules. But thanks for reading it anyway.

Mama, this next thank you is for you. It's been almost thirteen years since you've been gone, but there's not a day that goes by that I don't think about and miss and love you. Thank you for helping me have one of the best childhoods, where I could disappear into the little worlds of my own invention with comfort and ease. <3

About Author

Faye Darling is the pen name of a writer who rather likes the idea of being anonymous. She has an MFA in Creative Writing, has written over a dozen novels in the last decade, and has a growing catalogue of short stories published in various online journals. When she isn't writing, she's usually strolling along the beach near her house on the Oregon Coast or reading in the bathtub. Find Faye on Instagram for updates on her upcoming novels: @fayedarlingauthor

Printed in Great Britain
by Amazon